Allegiant

By SARA MACK

Allegiant (Book 2 in The Guardian Trilogy)

Cover art by Breena Slayton & S.M. Koz
Edited by Abbie Gale Lemmon

Dedicated to
A. J.
Thank you for remaining allegiant to me.
I love you.

Table of Contents

Prologue ~ James

The connection between us is indescribable. Limitless. It is as if an invisible elastic band stretches between us, and I'm powerless to ignore its pull. The band holds a soft electric hum that sits in the back of my mind, reminding me of its presence and my duty. Reminding me of her. Reminding me of what I've lost.

There are moments when I feel gentle tugs on the band. Instinctively, I know which are more important than others. Only once, since becoming her Guardian, have I felt an overwhelmingly strong pull, but I could sense she wasn't in danger and focused all of my energy on resisting the urge to go to her. She asked me to stay away, and I trust her. I still need time. Time to convince my mind and my heart that I can no longer love her.

I curse Garrett under my breath. Where did he go? His guidance is needed now, more so than ever. My feelings for her have yet to diminish. How much more time do I have before The Allegiant step in? Before they realize my poor Guardianship and take my memories and love for her by force? They have the power to eliminate her from my life, for eternity.

I feel a gentle tug on the band again and close my eyes tightly. I have to stop loving her. I have no other choice.

Chapter 1 - Emma

There is only so much time you can spend alone before you start to go mad. Now, I understand why they put prisoners in solitary confinement. Solitude gives you plenty of time to dwell on things. The past. The present. The future. What you've done; what you didn't do. What you would change if you could. My list of regrets grows daily. This afternoon I've added the following:

I should have kept myself surrounded by my family and pushed back my move to school.

I should have controlled my shocked reaction to my new neighbor telling me his name is Garrett, because he hasn't talked to me since.

And, I should have apologized to Dane before I left, regardless of his hatred towards me.

I close my eyes to erase the memory of Dane's anger. It's useless. His expression haunts me. I try harder and his face morphs, changing into James. I feel the familiar squeeze around my heart whenever I think of them, and tears start to well behind my eyes.

I miss James more than I can comprehend. Before his death we were inseparable. After his accident, he chose to become a Guardian instead of passing on, in order to stay in my life. He would visit me and stay throughout the night. His mentor, Garrett, eventually pulled him away to be trained, so that one day he could be assigned a Ward of his own. James' absence led me to lean on a friend more than I should have. Dane took my mind off the sadness of losing James, stood up for me when I couldn't stand up for myself, and played a huge part in saving me from someone from my past. I was in denial about his feelings for me, and I was allowing him to get too close. James could see this, and it didn't make him happy.

When it came to me, Garrett knew how tortured James was by his limitations. He could see how my relationship with Dane was affecting James and determined the possibility of my releasing James when I die was fading. When my own Guardian was released from their duty, Garrett decided it would be best for James if he were assigned to me. As his Ward, I would be connected to him forever. But, unfortunately, there are rules, and Guardians are forbidden to love their Wards. It clouds their judgment too much, interferes with their purpose. So while James will be bound to me for my lifetime, he is no longer allowed to love me.

It's been a month since I've seen him, and my mind reels, wondering what he's going through. James said he would be punished, his memories of us erased, if he could not learn to control his feelings. I told him to stay away, for as long as it takes to stop loving me, but our separation is haunting. Not a minute goes by that I don't think about him. Or last summer. Or my mistakes.

I shake my head to clear it. I need a distraction. I roll over and pick up my phone to call my best friend Shel. I have to be careful, space out my calls to her, and monitor what I say. She would be the first person to recognize that I wasn't doing well on my own, being as she knows me better than anyone else. What I wouldn't give for her to drop everything and come stay with me like she did this past summer, after James died. But she's at school too, in Ann Arbor, and she's dating Matt now. I'm sure he is there visiting her every chance he gets.

Shel picks up on the third ring. "Hey!"

"Hey. What are you doing?"

"Watching Matt rub my feet."

Speak of the devil. "Oh, okay. I'll let you go."

"No, you don't have to."

"Shel, I'm not going to talk to you while Matt rubs your feet. It's weird. Just call me later."

She laughs. "Will do. Oh, wait a sec." I hear her adjust the phone as she talks to Matt, their voices slightly muffled. She returns to me. "Good news! Matt's able to come with me to visit you for your birthday."

I'm grateful that she can't see me rolling my eyes. Not that I don't want visitors; I do. But I was looking forward to having a girls-only birthday celebration. You know, a gallon of ice cream and a movie or two. The last thing I want to watch is Matt and Shel make goo-goo eyes at each other. "That's *great*," I say, trying to put some genuine enthusiasm into my response. It still sounds forced.

"Emmmmma...." she draws out my name, sensing my irritation.

"Call me back when you're free," I say, ignoring her whine and hanging up. I roll on to my back and stare at the ceiling. Now what? I play with my phone, scrolling through the pictures I have saved. Most are of James before his accident. A few are of Shel. And then there's the last one. I stare at the picture of Dane that I snapped after we finished playing mini golf a few weeks ago, when he volunteered to help heal my heart. Little did I know that, merely days later, I would be hurting his.

I sigh and toss my phone aside. Things really suck right now.

On August 30th, the buzzer from the front door sounds in my apartment. I rush to answer. "Hello?"

"Happy birthday to you! Happy birthday to you! Happy birthday dear Emma! Happy birthday to you!"

Only Shel would sing into an intercom. "I'll be right there," I laugh.

I leave my apartment and head down the short hallway to the main entrance of my building. It's actually an old house that's been converted into four apartments for students at Western Michigan University. James and I had planned to live here together during our last year of school, but, well, you know.

I throw open the door, anxious to see my friends. "Hi!"

Shel steps forward and tosses her arms around me. "Happy birthday!"

"We've already established that," I say into her shoulder. "Where's Matt?"

"He's coming. He's getting your gift out of the car."

A moment later, I see Matt turn the corner of the sidewalk carrying a large box. It's perfectly square and colorfully wrapped. "Hey Emma!"

"Hey," I smile as he approaches us. I hold the door open for him as Shel and I enter the hallway. They follow me to my apartment.

"This is cute," Shel says, glancing around my place as we enter. "Very nice. Better than my digs, that's for sure."

"I can't complain," I say as I close the door behind Matt. Looking at the box in his hands I ask, "Why did you guys bring me a present? You didn't need to do that."

"It's your birthday," Matt says. "Presents are mandatory." He walks over and sets the box down on my small coffee table. "You should probably open it sooner rather than later."

"What's the rush?" I ask, just as the box moves on its own. I eye the two of them suspiciously. "What's in there?"

"See for yourself," Shel says with a self-satisfied grin.

I approach the box cautiously. "It isn't going to jump out at me, is it?"

Matt smiles. "Maybe. Maybe not."

I shoot him a questioning look. "Let me re-phrase. It's not going to bite me, is it?"

He shrugs.

I see the lid is wrapped separately from the rest of the box as I tentatively place my hands on either side. The box moves again as I grab the lid and jump back, much to Shel and Matt's amusement. As soon as the cover is off, two little ears appear at the top of the box followed by two tiny white paws. A fuzzy gray head peeks over the edge, and my heart dissolves instantly. It's a kitten. I let out an "awwww" as I step forward to scoop him out of the box. "Where'd you find him?"

"Her," Matt corrects me. "She was the last of a litter brought into my dad's clinic about a week ago." He smiles and reaches out to scratch behind her ears. "She's three months old and very friendly. I made sure all of her shots were up to date."

"We thought you could use a friend out here," Shel says as she steps forward, offering me the plastic bag I noticed her carrying. "Here are some supplies for the little booger."

I laugh. "Little booger?"

"She's been tromping all over my stuff for the last few days. I've been babysitting until we came out here."

I snuggle my new little friend. She's so soft and has big copper-colored eyes. "Thanks you guys. She's awesome."

Shel smiles at me. "You're welcome."

"You can have pets here, right?" Matt asks.

I nod as the kitten squirms against my arms. I crouch down to set her on the floor and watch her as she starts to explore the living area.

"Let's get this stuff set up before she has an accident," Shel nods toward the bag. We head to the kitchen, and I pull out two small bowls that can be used for food and water.

"So, what's the plan for tonight?" Matt asks, plopping down on the loveseat. He nearly sinks to the floor. "Whoa! What's up with this couch?" he laughs.

I look over my shoulder. "Oh, sorry. It's old. It's been hanging out in my parent's basement." I fill one bowl with water and place it on the floor next to the wall while Shel fills the other with cat food. "For now, it does what I need it to do."

Matt readjusts himself to sit on the edge.

"Where do you want the litter box?" Shel asks.

"Probably the bathroom? So it's out of sight?"

Shel nods and heads down my tiny hallway. She pauses at my bedroom and then finds the bathroom on the right. I look into the bag and find the last of the kitten's supplies, two little red mouse-shaped toys. I walk into the living room and toss them on to the floor. The kitten comes running. Kneeling down, I grab one by the tail and dangle it in front of her as she bats at it. Her playfulness makes me smile. The realization hits me, yet again, that I have amazing people in my life. The kitten is just what I needed. I look up at Matt. "Thank you. Like, sincerely. You don't know how much I've needed something to take my mind off things."

He smiles. "Shel thought you might be a little stressed out."

I nod as I hold the toy just out of the kittens reach. She jumps to grab it and snares it in her claws, making me laugh. "She would know."

"So," Shel says, reappearing behind me. "What's for dinner?"

"There's a great Thai place close to here," I suggest. "We could go there."

"Do they have carryout?" she asks.

I look at her confused. "Yeah, but I figured you guys wouldn't want to stay here all night."

"Where's the menu?" She turns toward the kitchen.

"On the fridge."

She walks over, grabs it, and then picks up her phone. "You don't mind going to grab dinner, do you hun?" she asks Matt.

"Nope," he answers.

I think Matt would do anything Shel asked of him – walk over hot coals, jump off a bridge, eat glass. You name it. Of course he doesn't mind. Shel starts to peruse the menu. "Good. Emma and I need some girl time."

"If we needed 'girl time' why did you drag him here with you? I feel bad."

I glance at the door Matt just left through. It's been about twenty minutes since we placed our order.

"I needed his help with the cat," Shel says as she sets her glass on the coffee table. "And, believe it or not, he wanted to see you."

"Does he do everything you ask of him?"

She considers my question and then nods. "Just about."

"How do I get one of those?" I muse wistfully.

Shel snorts. "You *had* one of those, remember?"

I look at her with wide eyes. Did I say that out loud? She turns her body to face me on the couch and crosses her legs. She tosses her long brown hair over her shoulder, revealing bright red highlights underneath, and trains her chocolate brown eyes on my green ones. She cocks an eyebrow. "You haven't been honest with me."

I scrunch up my nose. "About what?"

"You know."

"Um, no. I don't know."

"Dane."

I groan. After James was assigned as my Guardian, the depression I felt after his accident threatened to return. I didn't want my friends and family to worry about me. I tried to maintain a sense of normalcy and ended up alienating one of the best people that has ever come into my life. Dane will never forgive me after what happened between us, as well he shouldn't. "I told you everything. It's my birthday. Do we have to discuss this?"

"Yes, because I'm here and I can see your face. You can't lie to me in person."

This is true. It's much easier for me to lie over the phone. "What do you think I'm lying about?"

Shel crosses her arms to match her legs and narrows her eyes at me. "Matt told me something about the fight you had with Dane. A major detail that you neglected to mention to me."

I stare at her confused.

"It's a *major* detail," she presses.

I rack my brain. I thought I told her everything about the fight. About how Dane wanted to know if I could ever love him. How he said he would wait for me until I was over James. About how I told him no, because it would be unfair to make him wait indefinitely. About how he stormed off after Matt interrupted our argument.

"I'm going to ask you a question," Shel says. "And I want the truth."

I look at her, perplexed.

"Did you almost sleep with Dane?"

Oh shit. I can feel the blood drain from my face, yet it feels hot at the same time. I can tell from her expression that she knows it's true.

"Why didn't you tell me?" she asks, her eyes wide.

"Because it was a mistake," I whisper. Did Matt and Dane really have this conversation about me? I know they're good friends, but come on! I start to feel my face flush deeper at the realization that Matt knows about this too.

Shel throws her arms in the air. "Do you realize how bad I fought with Matt over this? I told him Dane had to be lying because you would have told me. What the hell Emma?" She pouts.

I can't look at her. "I...it shouldn't...."

"Did he pressure you?" she asks, suddenly concerned.

My head snaps up. "No! It wasn't like that." I push myself off the couch and head toward the kitchen. My mouth feels dry all of a sudden.

"Well, then. When?"

"After dinner at Louie's; when he left and I was mad." I open the cabinet and grab a glass. I fill it under the sink faucet and take a big gulp.

"No wonder," Shel murmurs.

I turn around to face her and lean against the sink to stare into the living room. "No wonder what?"

"I couldn't understand how one fight could make you two so angry with each other."

Unfolding her legs, she pats the cushion next to her. I walk toward her slowly, side stepping my new buddy who's chasing her tail. I take a seat, and Shel wraps her arm around my shoulders.

"I wish you would have told me sooner. We could have talked about it. You've got to stop keeping all this stuff in."

I nod as I stare at my glass.

"And I'm sorry I lit into you when I found out about the fight. That was wrong of me."

I give her a small smile. "No apology needed. I deserved it."

She grimaces. "I don't know about that."

I set my glass on the table next to Shel's. "Do you think Dane will ever speak to me again?"

She gives me a sympathetic look.

"How bad is it?" I ask.

"I haven't talked to him."

"But Matt has?"

She sighs. "I asked him if he would talk to Dane, to see if things could be worked out. I knew you were feeling bad and thought maybe, after some time, you could at least be friends again."

"And?" I cringe.

"Matt's unsure if that can happen. He said Dane's got a lot going on right now and any contact from you would probably be a bad idea. He said he needs time to sort things out."

I frown, but nod in understanding. What did I expect?

"It's only been two weeks," Shel reassures me. "Things will get better. There's nothing that a little time can't heal."

I'm not so sure about that. She wasn't there; she didn't see the look on Dane's face. It was as if I had reached into his chest and pulled out his beating heart with my bare hands.

We hear a knock on the door, and Shel jumps up to open it. I turn to see Matt walk backward through the doorway carrying two bags of take out, both balanced in his arms and tucked under his chin. "Some guy let me in at the front door," he says as he turns to us. He walks over, puts the bags down on the counter, and smiles. "Who's hungry?"

I give him a weary glance and slowly rise to get some plates. He looks suspiciously at me and then at Shel. "Oh, I took the liberty of picking up one of these," he adds, opening the second

17

plastic bag dramatically. It's a small chocolate cake. It doesn't bring the reaction he was hoping for, and he looks at me confused.

"Thanks," I say and stop to give him a one-armed hug. I hang on a little longer than necessary and he notices. His eyes dart to Shel accusingly.

"Aw, hell. You told her we knew, didn't you?"

Chapter 2

The next morning, I wake to find Shel still asleep next to me. I stare at the ceiling recalling how odd, yet great, this birthday was. I'm so thankful for my friends.

Shel and Matt decided to stay the night; despite Matt's annoyance with my crappy 24-inch tube TV and lack of surround sound. I reminded him at least I had cable, and James had been the one with all the hi-tech toys, not me. His teasing stopped after that. There was no further mention of Dane, thankfully, and the three of us spent the evening eating cake, watching the Tigers, and reminiscing. We've been friends since we were ten, and that includes James. Matt once told me he and Shel felt like James was still a part of their lives by spending time with me. I love that.

Around midnight, Matt fell asleep on my less-than-ideal loveseat, so Shel and I crammed ourselves into my full-size bed with the kitten. We spent another hour trying to come up with a name for her. By the time I drifted off, we were leaning toward Little Booger.

Speaking of, where is she? I raise my head to look around my bedroom and can't find her. I pull back the blanket and swing my legs off the side of the bed, silently hoping she hasn't fallen in the toilet. I take a few steps across the hall to the bathroom and turn on the light. Nope. No cat swimming here. I turn and head into the living room and stop short. There, on the couch, is perhaps the most adorable thing I've ever seen.

Matt remains asleep on his back, his body weight causing my loveseat's sad springs to sag low. He's a big guy, and his long legs overflow one end. His head is wedged at an odd angle between the corner of the armrest and the back of the couch; I can barely make out his blonde hair. He looks incredibly uncomfortable. But there, in the center of his chest, lies Little Booger. She's curled up asleep, in a contented little ball, soothed by the rise and fall of Matt's breathing. I can hear her loud purr as his two huge hands surround her in a protective little nest. I have to take a picture.

I sprint back into my bedroom and grab my phone off the nightstand. I creep into the living room and get as close as I dare so as not to wake them. I take the picture and then look at it, smiling at my memento. Yep, this was a pretty awesome birthday.

A day later, my parents paid me a visit to celebrate. They were infatuated with Little Booger, almost as if she were a grandchild. At first I thought it was strange, but then I remembered they treat my brother's dog, Jake, the same way. They weren't too impressed with my choice of name for her though, so I think I'll shorten it to LB. And, of course, they brought me birthday gifts. The first bag held two new outfits, while the second contained a box of Bisquick. My dad explained it was his contribution, so I could learn to make pancakes. I laughed when I opened it. No one can make pancakes like my dad.

I spent the majority of Labor Day weekend with my parents, since they decided to make an extended trip of my birthday and stay at a local hotel. They wouldn't admit it, but I think the main reason for their mini-vacation was to make sure I was safe on my own so far away from home. I know they are worried about me. James was by my side for two years at WMU, not to mention I was attacked this past summer by a former classmate. I understand their concern. This is new territory for me – and for them.

As I finish reminiscing, I get ready to attend my first class of my senior year. I'm ecstatic. I finally have something to do with my time, other than dwell on the past. I hope my schedule of Analytical Foundations, Communication in Business, Intro to Ethics, and Business Statistics will give me a lot of homework. I stop and make a face at myself in the mirror.

Really Emma? Get a life.

I comb my hair and pull it into a ponytail, noticing it looks more auburn than brown these days. I quickly apply a pale green eye shadow over the light skin of my eyelids, throw on some clear lip gloss, and turn off the bathroom light. My morning routine is not very intricate.

As I head out the door, I bend down and kiss LB. "Be good," I remind her as she watches me go. I have a feeling she'll be getting into my hair ties again. "I'll be home in a few hours." I shut and lock the door behind me, then try the knob for good measure.

"Hey there."

I look over and see my neighbor, Garrett, leaving his place as well. We haven't spoken since I first moved in; since the day he told me his name and I acted all shocked and flustered. I've never met another Garrett in my life; the odds of my neighbor having the same name as James' Guardian mentor had to be a thousand to one.

Garrett looks overdressed, even though I have no idea where he is headed. He's wearing pressed khaki's and a blue button-down shirt, which make his odd turquoise eyes really stand out. He looks like he just came from the barber; his brown hair is cut neatly on the sides but still wavy on the top. His skin also looks more tan than I remember. "Hey," I give him a small smile.

"Headed to class?" he asks.

"Yep."

"Which one?"

"Intro to Ethics," I say as I walk toward him and the front door. "You?"

He smiles. "The same. Who've you got?"

I reach into my bag and pull out my schedule. I didn't memorize my instructor's names. "Johnson."

"Well, that's a coincidence. So do I."

My mind unwillingly flashes to Patrick, the lab partner that decided he liked me a bit too much and signed up for all the same classes as me. The same person that James changed schools to protect me from. The exact same person that attacked me over the summer. I push the image away. This is a coincidence. Not all people are psychos. Just to make sure, I ask Garrett what other classes he has this semester.

"American Military History, Entrepreneurship, and Small Business Management."

I breathe easier. He opens the front door and stands aside. "After you."

"Thanks."

We head to campus together. On a nice day like today it's about a ten minute walk, but when winter hits I'll be driving for sure. "So, where are you from?" I ask.

"Hope Mills, North Carolina."

"Oh." I was expecting him to say a city in Michigan. "I've never heard of it."

"It's a small town."

"What made you choose Western?"

"I heard it's an excellent school for business majors."

We reach the street corner and pause for the light to change. "My major is Management. Have you had Pittinger for Organizational Behavior yet?"

Garrett shakes his head. "Nope, I just transferred. This is my first semester here."

"Well, avoid her," I give him words of advice. "Like the plague."

He laughs as the light changes, and we cross the street.

"So," he asks me, "did you get a cat or do you have some sort of mewling alarm clock?"

I shoot him an apologetic look. "You can hear her? I'm sorry. She's just a kitten."

"Only in the morning," he says, "before I've had my coffee. I thought I was hearing things without the caffeine."

"No, that would be LB." I shake my head. "She's quite demanding when she's hungry."

"LB?" he asks.

"Little Booger." I look at him sheepishly. "It's the best name Shel and I could come up with. Obviously she's living up to the title."

He chuckles. "Is Shel your friend with the red in her hair?"

His question makes me pause. How would he have seen Shel?

"And Matt's her boyfriend?"

I stop on the sidewalk. "How...how do you know my friends?"

He stops a few steps ahead of me. "I don't. They were over last week, right? I ran into the guy carrying some bags and let him in. He introduced himself." He walks back toward me. The expression on my face must alarm him because he says, "I didn't mean to startle you. Again."

I blink and resume walking. "Sorry." I feel like an idiot.

He falls into step beside me, and we make it to the next corner. We wait for the signal to change and then cross the street in silence. Halfway up the block, he clears his throat. "I didn't mean to make you uncomfortable."

"You didn't." I give him a reassuring look and, wanting to shift the focus off me, ask, "Do you go home to visit often?"

Garrett's jaw tenses. "I don't think I'll be going home anytime soon. I left for a reason. No one knows where I am."

That sounds serious. "Are you in the witness protection program?" I half-heartedly joke.

One side of his mouth quirks up. "No."

I don't know why, but I feel sorry for Garrett. It must be rough without having any friends or family to talk to. "Well, if you need anything, I'm right next door."

He flashes me a smile.

We make it to the edge of campus and start to cross over to the main building. Out of the corner of my eye, I think I see James. Surprised, I inhale sharply and turn to my left, my heart skipping a beat. My eyes search the bench where I thought he was seated and find it empty. I frown as disappointment washes over me.

"Everything all right?" Garrett asks.

I nod and continue to walk, giving him a lame smile. Suddenly, to my right, I see James again, casually leaning against a light post. I catch myself smiling and take a step to rush and greet him. He appears to ignore me, and I stop in my tracks. I blink, and he vanishes.

"Are you sure?" Garrett asks.

I'm starting to wonder. My gaze shifts to the left. James is there, walking in my direction, although he doesn't appear to notice me. I close my eyes, then open them to look forward. Sure enough, I see him again, but now he is standing several feet away beneath a maple tree, oblivious to my presence. If he were truly here, he would at least make eye contact or speak. My breathing becomes erratic as I realize I'm seeing things.

Garrett steps into my line of vision. "You look pale. Did you eat this morning?"

I nod. I had a banana and a granola bar.

All of a sudden, blood starts to pound behind my ears, and I'm having a hard time hearing and focusing. Garrett's face blurs before my eyes. I don't understand what's happening. Is this some sort of post-traumatic stress breakdown?

I feel Garrett grab ahold of my elbow. "I think you need to sit down." He leads me over to a nearby planter box where I gratefully take a seat. I hold my head in my hands in an attempt to make the pulsating stop. It only grows worse and more painful.

"What's wrong?" he worriedly asks. His voice sounds muffled to me.

"I think I'm getting a headache," I say as I lean forward to rest my elbows on my knees. James' face appears in front of me, even as I stare at the ground. When his image is the only thing that will stay in focus, I close my eyes. My first time back on campus without him is messing with my head.

"Do you have a fever?"

It sounds like Garrett has moved to crouch in front of me. I feel his hand rest against my forehead to check my temperature. It's freezing cold. Maybe I do have a fever.

"Okay, now you're shaking," he observes as he removes his hand.

I sit up and attempt to open my eyes. Things are hazy, my ears feel hot, and with every beat of my heart my temples pulse in pain.

"Does it hurt?" he asks as he sits on his heels in front of me.

I nod.

"Do you trust me?"

I narrow my eyes in confusion. Do I trust him? I barely know him. But the longer he stares at me with those odd turquoise eyes the calmer I feel. "Do you wear contacts?" I ask absentmindedly.

"That's not what I asked," he says.

Right. Trust. "I guess I trust you."

He nods decisively and stands. He looks around, as if making sure no one is watching, and then places his hands on either side of my head, just above my ears.

"What are you...?"

"Quiet," he tells me.

He closes his eyes as he applies gentle pressure to my head. When he does this, it feels like all the pain and fuzziness gathers at the top, like he's pushing it there. A moment later, frigid air blasts through my body, traveling from the top of my head down through my toes, taking my pain with it. It happens so fast I don't have time to react.

Garrett opens his eyes and releases my head. "How do you feel?"

I look at him in awe. I feel good. Actually, I feel better than good. I feel amazing. I feel energized, like I could run a marathon. My blood sings in my veins.

"How did you...what was that?" I ask him, shocked. "The pain is gone."

He glances at his watch, like what he did was no big deal. "We have to get moving or we're going to be late."

I stand, and we head toward the main building. I feel like skipping; I have so much energy. I try to contain myself. "How did you do that?" I whisper.

He holds the door open for me. "It's called reiki."

"Reiki? I've never heard of anything like it."

When we find our classroom, Garrett takes a seat next to me. I fish my textbook out of my bag, set it on the desk, and then look over at him. "Thank you. I don't know how I would have made it through this class without your help."

He nods and then opens his book, pretending to be interested in the first few pages. I get the feeling that he doesn't want to discuss it anymore, so I drop the subject.

Eventually, Ms. Johnson arrives to begin class. I have to force myself to concentrate on what she's telling us. I make a mental note to research reiki when I get home. I'm finding it hard to focus, but in a good way. My body still feels like it's humming.

Intro to Ethics is my only class on Tuesdays. Afterward, I stop and get a significantly more substantial lunch compared to what I ate for breakfast. I also stop by the library to reserve two of the recommended reading books assigned by Ms. Johnson. Better to be safe than sorry. I get caught up in the fiction books for a while, and before I know it, it's almost four o'clock. By now, LB may have very well torn up the place.

I make my way back across campus toward my apartment. The feeling from the reiki has subsided to an almost non-existence, and I'm starting to feel a little tired. I make it off campus and to the first cross street without any reoccurrence of my James-induced trauma fit. I silently pray that it will never happen again.

As I approach my place, I see a large industrial van parked in the street. Two men are busy at the back, setting up a ramp for a delivery. As I get closer, I notice the truck appears to be full of furniture. The front door to my building is propped open, so I maneuver around them with a smile and head inside.

"Excuse me?"

I turn around.

"Are you Emma Donohue?"

I hesitate as I make eye contact with the burly delivery man. "Yes."

"We have a delivery for you." He grabs a clipboard off the back of the truck and walks toward the door. "I need you to sign here and here." He marks each spot with an X.

I take the clipboard from him, confused. I read the invoice. It's for a couch and a television. An expensive couch and television. And it's marked PAID IN FULL. "I didn't order these things." I hand the clipboard back to him. "There must be some mistake."

The man looks over the billing. "Hmm. Let me see."

Just then my cell beeps, letting me know I have a voicemail. Funny, I didn't hear it ring. While the delivery men try to figure out the mistake, I pull my phone from my bag. There's a missed call from my parents, probably my mom. I touch the screen to clear the alert, and notice I have a missed text as well. My phone must not get a signal in the library. Since Jim Bob and Darryl haven't figured out the problem yet, I decide to read the text.

Someone told me you needed a few things. They should be delivered today. Happy belated birthday.

It's from Dane.

Chapter 3

Awestruck, I stare at my phone. Are you kidding me? There's no way I can accept his gift. It's way too much, and besides, my saggy loveseat and tube TV work just fine.

I look up, and the two delivery men are still mulling over the supposed error. "I'm sorry," I interrupt them. "I guess the items really are for me." I hold out my phone, indicating the message. "But I won't be accepting the delivery."

One of the men looks at the invoice and then back at me. "Sorry, but whoever purchased these items paid a surcharge for a confirmed delivery," he says. "We're obligated to leave the merchandise."

I frown in frustration. Of course Dane would realize I wouldn't want to accept such an extravagant gift. The delivery man hands the clipboard to me again, and under duress I sign by the X's. "I'll go open my door."

He nods and turns to help his coworker finish setting up the ramp. I head to my apartment and make my way inside. LB comes running the minute she hears my entrance.

"Hey there, fuzz ball," I say affectionately as I scoop her up with one hand. I kiss her head and snuggle her to my chest. "I'm going to have to keep you in the bedroom for a minute. Apparently you just got a new scratching post." I walk into the bedroom, set her on the bed, and throw my bag on the floor. "I'll be right back," I say as I close the door behind me.

Voices carry into my apartment, and when I stick my head out the door, I see Garrett attempting to help guide the delivery men down the hallway. I step out of the way as Garrett enters my place first.

"How'd you get involved in this?" I ask him.

He smiles. "I heard a bunch of voices, so I thought I'd check it out."

The men work to round the doorway into my place, and I glance back at my old loveseat and then at Garrett. "Will you help me shove that out of the way?"

"Sure."

We push the loveseat over, against the back wall, so the new couch can fit into the room. It looks huge compared to what I had. The men put it into place and then remove the protective plastic. It's a soft taupe color, overstuffed, with three seats instead of two. When the delivery men leave my apartment to bring the TV, I walk over and touch the fabric. I should have known. It's not fabric. It's leather.

"Nice," Garrett says, moving to stand next to me. "Birthday present?"

I shoot him a puzzled look.

He shrugs. "I heard you talking in the hallway with your friends."

Before I can ask him if his apartment walls are made of paper, one of the delivery men reappears with the television. Judging from the box, it's a 37" LED flat-screen. We move out of his way as he carries it over to my pitiful entertainment stand, sets it down on the floor, and goes to work opening the box.

"What are you going to do with your old stuff?" Garrett asks me.

I can't help but notice the interest in his voice. "Would you like it?" I ask. I know my parents don't want either item back. As a matter of fact, I think my mother would like to torch the loveseat personally.

"Actually, I would," Garrett says. "I moved kind of quickly, and I don't have a lot of stuff."

"Then it's yours." I walk over to stand behind the armrest of the loveseat. "You pull, and I'll push?"

He nods and grabs hold of the opposite end. It takes us a little maneuvering, but we manage to get it into the hallway and down to his apartment. He opens his door and then pulls on the armrest, walking backward. I push on my end until I'm completely over the threshold. I stand up straight, take in his place, and gasp.

There is absolutely *nothing* in here. Okay, there's a wood dining chair. And books. Lots of books, stacked on top of each other against the wall in the living area. I eye Garrett. "You weren't kidding, were you?"

He shakes his head.

"Do you have a bed at least?"

"I have a mattress."

His apartment is laid out in the mirror image of mine. I look into the kitchen, and the only thing I see on the counter is an old stainless steel coffee pot. It looks like it's from 1952. "Is there anything else you need?" I ask, concerned.

"I have all the necessities," he says. "Roof over my head, running water, clothes on my back. What more could I want? Well, besides a couch and a TV," he smiles.

I frown. Not only does he not have any family or friends, he possesses next to nothing. "Let me go get the TV for you," I say and start to leave.

"I'll get it." He jumps around me. "It's probably heavy."

"I'm not that big of a wuss," I protest, but he leaves out the door anyway. I look around his apartment again and curiosity gets the better of me. I creep down the short hallway to peek into his room. I see a mattress on the floor, covered by a thin blanket. His clothes are neatly folded and stacked against the walls like the books, separated into piles by shirts and pants. I turn, and my eye catches the bathroom. It contains only a towel and a toothbrush. He doesn't even have a shower curtain.

31

I return to stand by the loveseat, so he won't know I've been snooping. I make my mind up immediately. Garrett will be receiving a few things courtesy of me.

He rounds the corner moments later, his arms full of my little tube TV. "The delivery guys have something to ask you."

I nod. "You want me to help you place this thing?" I glance at the couch.

"Nope, I've got it. Thank you."

"No problem." I start to leave. "Remember, if you need anything, I'm right next door."

He smiles as he sets the television on the floor. "I remember."

I give him a small wave goodbye and head back to my apartment.

"Do you plan on hooking this up to anything other than the DVD player and the cable box?" the delivery man asks. He has the TV set up on my stand. Even with it projecting nothing but static, it looks like a movie screen compared to my old set.

"No. That's all I've got."

"Then," he tightens something in the back and a crystal-clear picture appears, "we're finished here."

The other delivery man collects the box and plastic from the television as they both head out the door. "Enjoy your new things."

"Thanks." I shut the door behind them and then promptly move to let LB out of the bedroom. "Sorry," I apologize to her. "Come check out this new stuff with me." I pick her up and walk over to the couch. Tentatively, I sit down on the middle cushion and then lean back. Darn it if it isn't incredibly soft and comfortable. I look down at LB and her claws. Kitten claws and leather aren't a good combination. "I take back what I said LB. You cannot use this as a scratching post."

A few hours later, after I've covered the couch with two winter blankets to protect it from LB, eaten the leftover Chinese takeout, and read the first two chapters for Intro to Ethics, I sit in the living room holding my cell phone in my hands. I know I should thank Dane for his generosity, but I'm nervous. Matt said I shouldn't contact him. But he contacted me first. I sigh and suck it up. I type *Thank you* and hit send.

My phone chimes with a text almost immediately. *You're welcome. You like?*

I smile. *Yes. But you shouldn't have done it.*

Why? Matt needs a decent place to sleep when he stays.

He plans on staying more often, does he? *It's too expensive* I send.

No worries.

I pause, thinking of what to say next. A simple good night would probably be best. Minutes pass. I can't possibly ask him what I truly want to know, which is "Can you ever forgive me?"

He texts again. *I'm sorry.*

I've missed our sarcastic banter. *For sending me a couch? You're forgiven.*

That's not what I meant.

I swallow nervously. *I should be the one apologizing.*

No. What happened was because of me. I started it.

True, but I'm not letting him take all the blame. *I should have stopped it sooner.*

Fifteen minutes pass. I start to think I won't hear from him again and set my phone down. It chimes against the table. *Friends?*

Why do I feel like this is a loaded question? On one hand, I feel relieved. But as the relief sinks in, my heart starts to ache a little. I still love James, but I also care about Dane more than I should. Would it be the best idea to remain friends with him? Will this hurt both of us in the long run? Depending on my response, I could open a door or end everything right now.

Friends I confirm and hit send. I should really stop asking myself questions I already know the answers to.

Out of a deep sleep, I jolt awake. I glance at the clock; it's after midnight. I look down to see LB curled by my side. I try to change position without disturbing her, but it doesn't work. She gets up and stretches, then turns around and lies back down. I shift to my side, hug my pillow, and close my eyes. Suddenly, the dream I was having returns to me.

I was with Garrett. We were in a really bright place, almost like we were standing in a ray of light. The ground looked soft, but it wasn't. I know this because, as we walked together, I felt no spring under my feet. Wherever we were felt really warm, like a summer day, but not hot and sticky. He was explaining something to me and gesturing with his hands, but I don't recall the conversation. As we walked, we passed other people, and I got distracted. The other people would nod and smile at me. I couldn't help but notice they all had the same color eyes as Garrett; that odd turquoise blue color. I remember looking at him, confused, and asking for an explanation. We stopped walking, and he asked if I trusted him. I told him yes. He placed his hands on my head and...

I woke up.

That's it. The reiki. I didn't get a chance to investigate that.

I try to go back to sleep for over an hour. LB gets mad at my changing positions and decides to leave me, curling up on the floor by the air vent instead. When two a.m. hits, I give up. I crawl out of bed, grab my laptop, crawl back into bed, and start researching reiki.

I find plenty of information on the topic, and the description sounds similar to what Garrett did, but it doesn't exactly fit. What he did seemed supernatural. I try searching for similar things, typing in "relieving headaches by touch" and "moving pain through the body." I read article after article, and many are in regard to homeopathic medicine. I even search for first-hand accounts of something similar. Nothing matches.

I finally grow tired, and my eyes start to hurt from reading the computer screen in the dark. I turn off my laptop and set in on the floor. So much for that research. I'll just have to ask Garrett more questions about his "reiki" when I see him again. I scoot down under my covers and close my eyes. I'm relieved my first class doesn't start until eleven tomorrow morning.

My thoughts turn to Dane and what happened today. Things started out pretty terrible with my James episode, but the day ended on a high note. I'm grateful for the things I have. I inadvertently think of Garrett, who has nothing. I feel really bad for him. I start to make a mental list of things I could get for him. A shower curtain. A comforter or at least a heavier blanket. Sheets. Maybe towels. I shake my head into my pillow. How could he have none of these things? He looks to be my age. What would have made him leave his home so suddenly?

My eyes snap open. Maybe he does have weird powers, hence the reiki excuse, and he was cast out. Shunned. He said he came from a small town. Maybe his powers were revealed, and they wanted to experiment on him medically, so he ran away. Or maybe he's a psychic. That would explain how he knew I just had a birthday, and that Matt was Shel's boyfriend. I'm not sure I buy his defense of "I overheard you talking." Or maybe he's ill. He does feel extremely cold; maybe he has some rare disease and is seeking alternative medicines. That would explain all the books. When he felt my forehead this morning, his hand was freezing. I've never felt anyone that cold except for James.

"James," I whisper in disbelief and sit upright. Was my first instinct correct? Could my neighbor Garrett and James' Garrett be one and the same? No, not possible. Garrett is human, not a Guardian. His hands don't pass through objects; he can physically move heavy things. He drinks coffee. He goes to college. And if Garrett were hanging around me, wouldn't James have shown up with some sort of an explanation?

I lie back down, mulling things over. Garrett seems nice enough. I wonder what his real story is. I don't feel an inkling of danger when I'm around him. James would let me know to be cautious because that's what Guardians do. Maybe all Garrett needs is someone to talk to, and I have plenty of time on my hands. I'm curious. I can't help it.

It looks like the universe just handed me a hobby.

Chapter 4

My instructors aren't playing this semester. Business Stats and Analytical Foundations were brutal yesterday, and it was only the first session of each. Communications in Business looks to be my easiest class, with Intro to Ethics somewhere in between. I chalk my struggle with them up to the fact that I'm still tired from spending all of Tuesday night contemplating Garrett. I hope to ask him to lunch today after Ethics, in an effort to get some of my questions answered. I immediately spot him when I enter the classroom and take a seat beside him.

"Good morning," he says.

"Good morning. How's my couch treating you?"

"Great. Thank you again."

"You're welcome." As I dig through my bag I ask, "Do you want to get some lunch after class?"

He raises an eyebrow like he's surprised I suggested it. "I have Management until two. Is a late lunch okay?"

I nod. "Where do you want to go?"

"I'll cook," he says. I must look confused, because he follows with, "I do own a pan or two."

Touché. "Should I bring the plates then?"

He smiles. "No. But you might want to bring a table."

We laugh as Ms. Johnson appears at the front of room. She sets a stack of papers on her desk and brings us all to attention. Today's lecture will be on the riveting topic of Aristotle's defection from the teachings of Plato.

Garrett told me to show up any time after three. I finished an assignment for Stats, and now I'm wasting time by playing with LB on my bed. I have a mental list of questions compiled for him. I hope I can be subtle. His life is his business. Why should he share it with me?

My phone chimes, and I reach for it on the nightstand, still trailing a piece of yarn for LB to catch. There's a text from Shel.

How are you enjoying your birthday presents?

I see my extravagant gifts have come up in conversation. I drop the yarn and decide to be facetious. *I'm playing with LB right now. Enjoying it very much.*

Haha. I know about Dane.

Duh.

Why didn't you tell me?

Classes are rough.

I'll say.

I look at the clock. It's ten after three. *Having a late lunch with a friend. Call you later.*

Anyone I know?

My neighbor, Garrett.

I set the phone down and give LB a good rubbing with both hands. "See you in a little bit," I tell her. I pick up my cell and my keys, and head toward the front door. My phone goes off again.

????

I roll my eyes at Shel. I know what she's thinking. I quickly type *It's not like that* and hit send. I look at my phone and decide I don't need to bring it with me. I set it on the couch and head out. When I approach Garrett's door, I can smell whatever it is he's cooking and my stomach growls. It smells delicious. I knock and hear him shout, "Its open!"

When I enter the apartment I find him in the kitchen, bent over a large pot on the stove, stirring. "I thought you said you owned a pan?"

He looks over his shoulder at me and smirks. "I own a pot, too."

"What are we having? It smells amazing."

"Fennel soup," he says. "Ever had it?"

I shake my head no. Garrett moves to open the oven door and check what's baking there. I feel like he's doing too much. "Can I help with anything? I'm the one who invited you to lunch."

He closes the oven door. "It's not a big deal. Besides, I owe you for the couch and the television." He resumes stirring the soup. "There are two bowls around here somewhere. Can you find them?"

I nod and move inside the kitchen, opening the first cabinet I see. It's empty. I try the next. It's empty as well. I step around him to the next cabinet. Ah ha. There they are. Two white bowls. I grab them and set them to the right of the stove, because the left side appears to be covered in flour.

"We have a couple minutes left on the biscuits," he says and turns the stove burner down to simmer.

"Biscuits?"

"From scratch. Southern style."

I'm majorly impressed. My best dish is a grilled cheese and tomato sandwich. "Do you cook like this often?"

He shrugs. "I make all of my food. I wasn't able to cook where I was staying before."

I lean against the counter. "Where did you learn?"

"A little from my granny back home. But most of it I picked up from the army." He gives me a wry smile. "I was a field cook."

"Army? How old are you?"

He opens the oven door, bends down to check the biscuits again, and sighs. "Older than you think."

I look at him and determine that he couldn't be any older than 25. How long does it take for someone to serve their term and get discharged from the army?

"These look about done," he says and opens the oven door completely. He reaches for the hot cake pan without an oven mitt, grabbing it with his bare hand.

"Don't!"

He looks at me confused as he pulls it from of the oven. He sets it on the stove. "Don't what?"

I look at him incredulously and grab his hand. It feels frozen as I turn it over. He's not burned at all. "How did you not burn yourself?"

He snatches his hand out of my grasp. "Ah..." He avoids my eyes and picks up the spoon to start stirring the soup again. He stares at the pot. "I used to grab hot things all time while I was out in the field. My nerves are shot."

I frown at him. He expects me to believe that? I mean, it is believable, but it doesn't explain how there is no mark on his skin.

He turns off the burner. "Let's eat." He picks up the pot by both handles and carefully pours the soup into each bowl, not spilling a drop. If I had tried this, I would have been wearing the soup for sure.

"What is fennel?" I ask.

"It's a vegetable. It looks like a feathery plant above the ground, but we're eating the bulb." He sets the pot back on the stove.

All right. I'll take his word for it.

He pulls a biscuit from of the pan. "I usually crumble these over the top," he says. "Would you like yours separate?"

I pick up a soup bowl and hold it out to him. "Crumble away."

He mashes the biscuit over my bowl and then does the same to his. "This way." He starts to walk out of the kitchen. "You'll have to sit on your old couch to eat."

I follow him. "That's okay. I've missed her."

He looks back at me. "Really? With that Cadillac sitting in your front room?"

Front room? He sounds like my grandmother. I laugh. "I was kidding."

I make my way to sit down. He must have hit up a garage sale in the last day or two, because a small table stands in front of the couch. I take a seat, and Garrett sits on the floor.

"Oh." He stands back up. "I guess we need spoons." He leaves the room and reappears moments later with two spoons.

Hunger takes over, and I taste the soup. I was expecting a vegetable flavor, like potato, but it's surprisingly sweet. "This is really good," I compliment him.

He nods.

I want him to feel comfortable around me, so he will open up about himself. I already found out a couple tidbits in the short time I've been here: he served in the army, and he can touch hot things without being burned. I'm starting to suspect he may be a military prototype, like Captain America.

Trying to appear casual, I lift my spoon and lick the back of it. "I was researching reiki the other night. It's funny; nothing I could find came close to what you did the other day."

He smiles. "I knew there was a reason you asked me to lunch."

"Well, you did blast a trauma-induced headache from my body."

"Trauma-induced?"

Whoops. I don't want him to think I'm nuts. I resume eating.

Minutes pass in silence, and Garrett finishes his soup first. He sets the bowl on the table and looks at me expectantly. "Well?"

"Well what?"

"Do you want to talk about your trauma?"

I give him a resigned look. "Not really. I want to talk about your reiki."

He tilts his head and regards me for a moment. "I'll tell you if you tell me."

I set my bowl on the table. I'm dying to know what's up with him, so I concede. "I lost someone recently. My boyfriend. He...he died."

This doesn't seem to faze him. "Life can be difficult when you lose someone you love," he says. "It really hit you hard the other day, didn't it?"

My shoulders sag. "Yes."

"You know," he says matter-of-factly and shifts his weight on the floor, "the connection between the human world and the

41

spiritual world is very strong. I'm sure your boyfriend watches over you today."

He's doesn't know how right he is. He sounds like some sort of medicine man. "What are you? Some sort of shaman?"

His eyes light up and he chuckles. "I can't believe you guessed that. The answer is yes. Kind of."

"Kind of?"

"We'll just say I'm a shaman. It's easier."

I look at him suspiciously. "You're not going to tell me about the reiki, are you?"

"I just told you what I was," he says. "What more do you need to know?"

It turns out Garrett is very good at avoiding the topic of himself. As the late afternoon turned into evening, he managed to turn every question I asked of him back on to me. Eventually, he tried to distract me by teaching me to play poker. I was asking him some questions about the army, and he went off on a tangent about what they used to do to pass the time in the field between missions. I told him I was a horrible liar, so poker probably wouldn't be the best game for me. He insisted that learning it would improve my lying abilities and pulled a tattered deck of cards from his bedroom. We snacked on the remaining biscuits for dinner and, by eight o'clock, I was still confusing a straight with a straight flush. That's when we decided to call it a night with the promise of future lessons.

After pulling on my pajamas, I plop down on my couch to think about today. I still have a million unanswered questions. When I sit, I land on my phone. "Ow," I say to LB, who has jumped up to be scratched. I pull the phone from beneath my tush and see that I have missed text messages. I tap the first alert.

How was lunch? It's from Shel.

Next message. *Are you still out?*

Next message. *Text me when you're done. I'm curious.*

There's a shocker.

I reply to Shel. *Hey. I'm home.*

I absentmindedly pet LB as I wait for her to respond back. I think about Garrett. How can I find out how he became a shaman? LB bumps my hand with her head, and I drop the phone.

"LB!" I pick the phone up off the floor.

After a few minutes, when Shel doesn't respond, I text her again. *Lunch was fun. Garrett gave me a poker lesson. I'm not very good.*

My phone vibrates. *Poker? You should stick to Crazy 8's.*

I smile. *Don't I know it.*

So who's this Garrett?

Good question. *He's my neighbor. And a classmate. And a mystery.*

Oooo. Sounds sexy.

I laugh. He may be cute, but he's not sexy. *Um, I don't think so.*

Take a picture and let me judge.

Sarcastically, I respond *I'll get right on that.*

What? You don't think I can judge another man's sexiness?

I roll my eyes. *I'm sure you can.*

So why won't you send me a picture?

Why does she want to see Garrett so bad? *Because he's not hot. And how would I explain taking his picture?*

Tell him it's for research.

I sigh. *I'm not taking his picture.*

I think you're hiding something.

What? *I am not!*

Then why won't you let me see him?

What is the point of this? *Because.*

I'm just curious. What color hair does he have?

Brown.

Eyes?

Turquoise.

You're lying.

Am not.

He sounds dreamy.

This is ridiculous. *Are you high? I'm telling Matt!*
Why would Matt care if I'm high?
Lord, help me. *Garrett is a friend. That's all.*
Be careful. We all know what you do with your male friends.
Is she referring to Dane? *Rude much?*
It was supposed to be funny.
It's not. It should never have happened.
I bet you think about it though.
I decide to confess. *I do.* It's the truth. I can confide in Shel.
How often do you think about it?
Why does she want to know this? *A lot.*
Like every night?
No! But a lot.
My phone goes silent for a minute. What is up with her tonight? I contemplate actually calling her.
My phone vibrates again. *So do you think I'm hot?*
What in the world? She's acting all kinds of crazy. I shake my head and decide to play along. *Yes. Very.*
Really? I think you're hot too.
Okay. This has gone far enough. *Are you psychotic Shel? I was kidding. Why would I think you're hot???*
Shel? This is Dane.
Oh my God. *Are you kidding me?*
Nope.
I scroll back through our conversation and blood rushes to my face. The screen must have jumped to a thread with Dane when LB knocked the phone on the floor! Holy embarrassment! I just confessed I think about us a lot.
Hello?
I panic. *I have to go.*
Of course you do. He knows I'm running away from the conversation.
I send him one last message. *I'll talk to you later. Good night.* I flop down on my side and close my eyes.
My phone vibrates in my hand, and I peek at it.
For what it's worth, I think about it a lot too.

44

Chapter 5

I spend the next week alone, thinking about Dane, contemplating Garrett, and missing James. On top of homework, I tried to get in touch with Shel a few times, but she started volunteering at a local hospital and her hours are all over the place. When I'm asleep, she's awake. When I'm awake, she's sleeping. Her aspirations are much higher than mine. She wants to be a doctor.

I did manage to talk to her once, briefly, after the Dane text debacle. She thought it was hilarious and a step in the right direction. Me, not so much. I know she hopes that, one day, Dane and I will permanently make it past the friend's stage. It's no secret how much she likes him. I wish I could tell her about James being my Guardian and how difficult it is for me to know that he is tied to my every move; how he can see what I'm doing. I still feel sick when I think about him watching my momentary indiscretion with Dane this past summer. Regardless of his limitations in loving me, my heart suspects that is the real reason James has stayed away for so long. I don't doubt that he feels like I cheated on him. I feel that way, too. Lately, though, the logical side of my brain speaks up, and asks me if I plan to stop living all together. I've got a good sixty years or so left, I hope. That's a long time to be alone, to get over my guilt, and spare James his feelings. Would he really begrudge me any future relationship with Dane? With anyone?

James once asked me if I could resign myself to a lifetime of solitude, to be known only as the crazy old cat lady. At the time I thought I could, because he would be able to visit me. Now, after spending these last few weeks virtually alone, a lifetime of solitude sounds about as appealing as swallowing nails. How much am I willing to sacrifice to assuage my guilt? James is my Guardian. He can no longer love me no matter how much I love him. I can no longer release him from his Guardianship when I die because I am his Ward. Am I willing to sacrifice happiness in this lifetime and eternity as well?

I look at LB and sigh. It looks like I may have my answer. I've already started my crazy old cat lady collection of felines. Maybe I should get a rocking chair and start learning to knit too.

"Thanks for your help."

"No, thank you," I say as I stand. I watch Garrett pile his textbook on top of his notes. "This class is going to kill me."

He laughs. "Well, Johnson is going to kill me."

By the end of the second week of classes, it was apparent that I would need some outside Stats help. I mentioned looking for a tutor, and Garrett told me that he had no problem with Stats at his previous school. He was, on the other hand, having a hard time following Ms. Johnson's train of thought in Ethics. He received a C on his first essay while I received an A. We agreed to trade tutorial services on Fridays, since neither of us have anything better to do. Plus, I thought it would be a convenient opportunity to learn more about him. Unfortunately, today's session left little room for other topics.

Garrett heads toward my apartment door. "Same time next week?"

"Absolutely."

He opens the door to leave as I bend down to grab LB before she sprints outside. "Have any plans this weekend?" he asks me.

I stand and shake my head. "I'm not much of a socialite."

He smiles. "Me either." He walks outside. "Have a nice weekend."

"Thanks. You too." I shut the door and lift LB up to look her in the eyes. "It's just us kid. Whatever shall we do?"

I eye my scattered notes and textbook and decide to clean them up. As I stack everything neatly, I see that Garrett left a few papers. He'll probably need those. I pick them up and head toward the door and stop. Wait! There are a lot of things he needs...

I spend the afternoon shopping. Working at Bay Woods this past summer built up my savings, and I've barely dented it since I've been away from home. I pick up some essentials for Garrett: for the bathroom, a shower curtain and a set of towels. For the kitchen, an oven mitt and a set of four plates with matching glassware. I also manage to find a plain, navy blue comforter on clearance for half off and a bundle of plastic hangers for a dollar. As I carry my purchases to my car, I find myself smiling. Not only does it feel great to help out a friend, but I actually feel like I accomplished something worthwhile with my time. Now, all I have to do is get him to accept my gifts.

As I drive home, I sing along with the radio. It's been a long time since I've felt this good. I pull into the parking area for my building, grab the two large plastic bags out of my trunk, and hum my way to the front door. When I get there, I stop at my mailbox and head inside.

"Oh no, you don't," I admonish LB when I open my apartment door. I block her exit with one of the bags. "Stop trying to sneak out!" Ever since she managed to get into the hallway the other day, this has become one of her favorite games. Every time the door opens she tries to escape. I press my back against the door to shut it while blocking her with the bag and my feet. "Do I have to ground you?" I ask her. I set the bags against the wall and head to the kitchen, tossing the mail and my keys on the counter.

I open the fridge, find a bottle of water, and take a drink. LB comes in and rubs herself against my leg, as if to apologize for her antics. I crouch down to pet her. "You're forgiven you little stinker." She rubs herself against my hand and the bottle, and purrs while I scratch behind her ears. "Do you want to come with me to give Garrett his gifts?" I ask her. "Will that make you happy?" She lets out a tiny meow, and I laugh. "Are you talking back to me now?" She doesn't answer; she just stares at me with her big copper eyes. I pick her up, kiss her, and set her back down again.

Standing, I decide to sort through my meager mail. There's a bill from the cable company and a postcard advertising discounted Laundromat services. I frown as I pick up the third item. It's a plain white envelope with my name printed neatly on the outside. There's no return address. I tear it open and pull out a folded newspaper article. It's from my hometown paper.

Local Student Returns from Abroad

Says Environmental Conservation Has Never Been More Important

Not many people will ever experience what Teagan Meyer has. Teagan, a 2006 graduate of Lake Fenton High School, has returned home after spending nearly a year and a half overseas researching the Amazon Jungle.

Upon graduating from Wayne State University with a degree in Environmental Science, Ms. Meyer competed for a spot on a ten-man conservation team created to conduct research and evaluate the state of the world's most famous rainforest. Of being selected out of the more than 9,000 applicants, Ms. Meyer says the feeling was "indescribable" and "a dream come true."

Sponsored by educational grant dollars and headed by the World Wildlife Federation, the conservation team migrated through the countries of Brazil, Peru, and Bolivia recording the impact of deforestation in the area. "The rainforest and fresh water systems of the Amazon are incredibly fragile," says Meyer. "The countries that contain the Amazon are rapidly expanding. Without properly planning the creation of roads and dams, not only are animal species threatened but the livelihood of farmers and fishermen. That's on top of the catastrophic effect that deforestation has on the global climate." Ms. Meyer hopes to bring her experience and knowledge to local groups and schools in the area, in order to affect change. "Every generation needs to know how important the rainforest is on a global scale," she says. "We can all make a difference."

While she says she wouldn't trade her time in South America for the world, Ms. Meyer admits that she enjoys being back home and the amenities she left behind. She tells us she plans to spend some down time with her family and fiancé before launching an awareness program based on her travels. "It will be nice to finally get the wedding plans under way," she says. Teagan is the daughter of Luke and Susan Meyer, prominent community members and owners of Legionnaire, a local advertising company. Teagan is engaged to Dane Walker, son of Charles and Lily Walker, owners of the Bay Woods Golf Course.

I must read the last sentence of the article five or six times before my shaking hands make it impossible to continue. The clipping flutters from my fingers, and I melt to the kitchen floor, stunned. My emotions betray me as the news of Dane's engagement brings out feelings I've been trying so hard to repress. We can never be more than friends. Ever. My brain screams, *"But isn't that what you wanted?"* The tears that trail down my face answer that question.

LB comes to find me, rubbing against my knee. She knows I'm upset. I pick her up and hold her to my chest in an attempt to keep my heart in one piece. It's doesn't work. I can still feel it break.

It doesn't take long for my sadness to turn into anger. Setting LB down, I wipe the tears from my cheeks. I pick myself up and walk into the living room, toward the couch. I rip off the blankets that I had protectively wrapped around it and throw them on the floor. My eyes find LB. "Have at it."

I walk into the bathroom and stare at myself in the mirror. My eyes are puffy, and my face is covered in red splotches. I try to process what I've just learned thanks to – thanks to whom? Who sent the article? Obviously not Matt or Shel; they would have told me something this huge in person. Was it Dane? Is this his way of letting me know? He couldn't man up and tell me face to face, or at least over the phone? What a coward! Of all the low, selfish, and inconsiderate things to do! I thought he cared about me. At least he acted like he did. Wasn't he just flirting with me over text messages?

I turn on the faucet and watch the water run down the drain. Not only is Dane engaged to the smart, probably beautiful, world-saving Teagan, the company he works for is owned by his fiancées parents! Why did he even pretend to care about me if he was in love with someone else? Here I am beating myself up over what happened between us when he had a living, breathing girlfriend all along. We almost slept together! Oh God. I close my eyes. Now I can add "other woman" to my list of faults. My reputation grows closer to what Mrs. Davis, James' mother, thinks of me. She called me a whore once. Maybe she was on to something. Tears threaten again, and as I stare at myself in the mirror, I make a pact with my reflection. I'm not going to bury myself in a grave of self-loathing over this. I had no idea he was engaged.

After I splash some water on my face, I walk back out to the living room and see LB has curled up to sleep on the blankets instead of clawing the couch to pieces. I eye Dane's gifts and scowl. I don't want them anymore, but I know someone who might. Walking over to the television, I quickly disconnect the cable wires and AV cords. I attempt to pick up the TV and find that it's light, but awkward to hold. I set it back down and head to Garrett's apartment, knocking loudly on his door.

"Yes?" he asks when he appears in the doorway.

"I need my old stuff back."

He looks wounded. "Oh. Well...all right." He turns to look at my old loveseat and television, which is turned on. "It'll just take a second to disconnect..."

"I want you to take my new stuff," I add hastily. "In trade." I don't want him to think I've suddenly turned into a raging witch.

His eyes widen in surprise. "You don't want the Cadillac?"

I cross my arms. "Not anymore."

He takes a minute to assess me and notices I've been crying. "Are you okay?"

"Perfect," I say a bit too harshly. "Come on."

He follows me to my place, and we walk over to the television. "You take one end, and I'll take the other."

He grabs one side. "Are you sure you don't want this?"

I look him in the eye. "Absolutely."

We carry the flat screen over to his apartment and set it on the floor. Garrett collects my old tube television and starts to carry it out the door, but stops. "You're sure?" he asks me again.

"Yes!"

I follow him back down the hallway and then reach around him to open my door. We walk across the room again, and LB looks up at us annoyed. We're interrupting her nap.

Garrett works to reconnect the cables. "So, what happened?"

I shake my head. "I wouldn't want to bore you with the details."

"Try me."

Just then we hear a knock. I look at Garrett confused, and he shrugs. I move to open the door and find Samantha and Todd, our neighbors from upstairs, standing in the hallway.

"Hi!" Samantha grins at me, all perky and blonde and made-up.

"Hey," I try to smile at them. I pray that my red splotches have disappeared by now.

"We haven't seen you in awhile," she says and looks past me. She notices Garrett. "Oh good, we can invite him too," she tells Todd.

"What's up?" I ask.

"We wanted to know if everyone wanted to hang out," Todd says. "We all live together, but we hardly know each other.

Jessica's in." Jessica is our other neighbor upstairs. "How about you guys?"

I look at the two of them. I remember when I first moved in and met them. I thought then that they appeared to be the typical sorority-fraternity type; you know, homecoming royalty, social butterflies. It seems I was right. I glance back at Garrett with my eyebrows raised, silently asking *yes or no?*

"I think that's a great idea," Garrett says enthusiastically, surprising me. He walks over to us. "What did you guys have in mind?"

"We're heading to Wayside," Samantha says. She looks me up and down. "Meet you there in, say, an hour?"

If she's expecting me to get more dressed up than this, she's sadly mistaken. I eye what she's wearing, and she's all dolled up in a small-little-white-tank-top and skintight jeans. I've been to Wayside on several occasions; it's a big place with several bars, a large dance floor, and a huge game room. I can blend in easily without needing to dress cute, especially on a Friday night. I look at Garrett and shrug.

"We'll meet you there," he says with a smile.

"Great," Todd says. "We'll hang around the entrance until you guys show up."

"Bye!" Samantha wiggles her fingers at us over her shoulder as they leave.

I close the door and look at Garrett.

"What?" he asks.

"I thought you weren't a socialite?"

"Can you blame me for wanting to get out once and awhile?"

"No." Actually, I'd like to get out once in awhile. I need to get out, especially after my recent discovery. "Meet you at your place in fifteen?"

He smiles. "Sure thing."

Less than an hour later, Garrett and I arrive at Wayside. I ended up changing clothes before we left after all, but my outfit is a far cry from Samantha's painted on one. I made sure the remnants of my tears were gone, threw on some lip gloss, pulled a comb through my hair, kissed LB, and out the door I went.

The bar is packed. At first, we have a hard time locating Samantha and Todd. We finally find them standing by the bar, not the entrance, with Jessica. She waves excitedly at us, and I can't help but notice how cute she looks, all five feet of her, with her brown hair meticulously curled. I instantly feel a pang of regret for not taking a longer time with my appearance. Both girls appear to be looking for a night out on the town. I just wanted to leave my apartment.

"Hi guys!" Samantha greets us. She turns toward the bar, grabs something, and turns back toward us. She's holding a shot glass in each hand. "For you." She hands one to Garrett and then one to me. I notice Jessica and Todd are already holding theirs.

"To new neighbors!" Todd says and raises his glass.

Ah. Barbie and Ken like to party. I should have guessed.

"To new neighbors!" We clink our glasses and throw back the shots. I try to keep my composure as the liquor burns its way down my throat. What was that? Samantha, Todd, and Jessica slam their glasses down on the bar. I look at Garrett and make a face at my glass.

"Whiskey," he answers my question.

Ouch. My throat burns. "Remind me not to do that again," I whisper, and he laughs.

Jessica spies an empty table between the dance floor and the bar. "I'm going to claim that before someone else does," she says and heads over.

I follow her. The table has a good view of the dance floor, and I sit on the end, so I can people watch without having to look over heads. Garrett sits between Jessica and I; Samantha and Todd take seats across from us.

"So," Todd says, simultaneously snapping his fingers at a passing waitress, "how's everyone enjoying our humble abode?"

"My apartment is great," Jessica pipes up from beside Garrett, "aside from the paper thin walls." She eyes Samantha and Todd pointedly. "Really? Three a.m.? *Every* Saturday?"

I'm surprised by Jessica's boldness. She's such a little thing. I look at Todd and Samantha for their reaction, expecting them to be embarrassed. Instead, it's just the opposite. They show no signs of remorse.

Todd smirks. "I'll buy you some ear plugs for Christmas."

I look at Garrett, my eyebrows raised, and he looks at me with the same expression. What is up with these two? I'm immediately grateful I live on the bottom floor.

The waitress stops by our table. "What'll it be?"

Todd defers to me first. "Nothing. Wait, water, please," I order.

Everyone but Garrett looks at me with a puzzled expression. Todd moves on to Garrett, who orders a beer, Jessica gets a Fuzzy Navel, Samantha orders a Cosmopolitan, and Todd gets a Jack and Coke.

"You don't drink?" Samantha asks me, like it's a tragedy.

"Not very often," I shrug.

She turns her attention to Garrett. "I can't help but notice your eyes," she says in a flirty tone. "Where do you get your color contacts? I get mine online."

I study her eyes. Obviously they are not naturally blue. My gaze falls to her chest. I'm starting to doubt that's real as well.

Garrett smiles. "I don't wear contacts."

"*Really?*" Samantha looks impressed. "You must have some amazing genes. Does that color run in your family?"

Garrett shakes his head. "Nope. I'm the lucky one."

"I bet your kids will have that color," Jessica says, joining the conversation. I notice the dreamy expression on her face as she looks at Garrett. Does she have a thing for him?

Todd snaps his fingers loudly and points at me. "That's where I know you from!"

I look at him confused. "I'm sorry?"

"I knew you looked familiar," he says. He looks at his girlfriend. "Didn't I tell you she looked familiar?"

Samantha nods empathically.

"Your James Davis' girlfriend, aren't you? The guy who died winter semester."

I'm shocked to hear James' name. I've never met Todd before I moved in a few weeks ago. I slowly nod.

"I knew it!" He slaps the table like he just won a bet. "I was at that bonfire thing this summer for his birthday."

"Did you know James?" I ask. I can't imagine James being friends with someone like Todd. He's too arrogant.

"Not personally. I crashed the party with some buddies of mine that knew him."

Well, we can add rude next to arrogant on Todd's list of character traits.

"You crashed a party for someone who died that you didn't even know?" Jessica asks skeptically. "That's kind of low, don't you think?"

I shoot her a grateful look for saying aloud what I was thinking. She gives me a smile.

"It was no biggie," he shrugs.

Samantha leans forward, her fake-blue eyes wide. "Is it true that he was trying to outrun the cops when he crashed?"

My face twists in irritation. "No. He fell asleep."

"Well, I heard that he was either high or drunk or both. He had to be to hit that tree as hard as he did."

"That's insane," I say, agitated. "Where did you hear that?"

She shrugs. "Word gets around. I also heard that he got in a big fight with his girlfriend...I mean, you, that night."

My heart starts to pound, and I snap, "That's none of your business."

Samantha leans back and holds her hands up in front of her likely fake breasts. "Whoa. Okay."

My mouth settles into a thin line. I don't want to make enemies of my neighbors, but these two are something else.

Noticing the tension, Garrett interrupts, trying to change the topic. "So, what do you think about the football team this year?"

"Oh, hey!" Todd grabs the arm of someone walking by our table. He seems unfazed by the fact that he's just been called out as extremely rude, and his girlfriend and I almost came to blows.

"Hi Todd!" a female voice squeaks. He stands up to give this person a hug. She walks around him and hugs Samantha. "Hey, you!"

When she faces the rest of us, I recognize her immediately. My chest constricts, and my expression hardens. It's Rebecca. The same girl who, at the birthday bonfire, accidently told me about the time she spent with James – my James – the night he died. Now I understand who Todd crashed the party with. This does not improve my opinion of him one bit.

"Who are your friends?" Rebecca asks slowly, focused on me.

"These are our neighbors," Samantha says, oblivious to Rebecca's change in demeanor. "Jessica, Garrett, and Emma." She points at each of us.

Rebecca gives us all a tiny smile, but she's still focused on me. "Nice to meet you." Her hands wrap around the arms of a sweatshirt she has tied around her waist, and her action pulls my attention away from her face. Judging by the way her fingers clutch the material, it can only be one thing. James' hoodie, the one he gave her the night he died. Does she never take it off? My eyes widen, and I inhale sharply. Garrett notices, giving me a questioning look.

Our waitress appears with our drink order, distracting everyone. Rebecca makes a hasty departure, saying goodbye to Samantha and Todd, as the glasses are passed around. The waitress hands me my water, but I stop her by asking, "Could you bring me something stronger?" This day has gone from bad to worse, and a little numbness sounds appealing.

"Sure. What would you like?"

I consider her question for a second. "A Long Island Iced Tea."

The waitress nods. "I'll be right back."

Todd overhears my order and nods approvingly. "Now that's what I'm talking about!"

I've never been this drunk in my life. The daiquiris at Matt's on the Fourth of July were nothing compared to this. That was giggle drunk. This feels a little more serious.

I downed my first Long Island quickly and, with the whiskey shot from earlier, I was pleasantly buzzed and having a much easier time of putting up with Todd and Samantha. It also helped that they left the table to grope each other on the dance floor. To my right, however, I did have to listen to Jessica coming on to Garrett for most of the night. She wasn't being overly obnoxious though. She's actually a very sweet girl. I ordered another drink for something to do, and I was half way through it when things started to get fuzzy. I'm such a lightweight.

"Everything okay?" Garrett moves toward me as Jessica leaves to use the restroom.

"Umm hmm." I blink slowly. "I think she likes you."

He smiles at me. "What's not to like?"

I laugh hard enough to snort, which makes me laugh harder.

"It looks like I'm driving us home," he says and finishes the last of his beer. When the waitress comes back to ask if he wants another, he tells her no.

"So," he says, "you don't handle stress well."

I pretend to be shocked and press my hand against my chest. "Whatever do you mean?"

"Just the thought or the mention of James pushes you over the edge."

"Pffftttt." I playfully push him away from me. "What was your first clue? My nervous breakdown or," I pick up my glass, "my random drunkenness?" I take a drink.

"Both."

I wink at him. "Well, I'll tell you what. If James could love me the way I love him I wouldn't be in this state of which you behold me now."

He smirks. "That makes absolutely no sense."

"It does!" I say adamantly.

Garrett reaches for my nearly empty glass and takes it away from me. "I think you've had enough of this." He places it far out of my reach on the table.

I cross my arms and pout dramatically, which makes him laugh.

"Are you going to tell me what happened today?" he asks.

My face lights up. "Yes!" My voice is a bit too loud, and I reach for his arm. Holding on to it with both hands, I shake it. "I went shopping and I bought you all kinds of good stuff and I was singing."

He looks at me, puzzled. "You were singing about buying me stuff?"

"No silly!" I shake my head. It feels wobbly on my neck and my vision blurs. I reach out and grab his shoulder to anchor myself. "It *made* me sing."

Garrett pries my fingers from his shoulder with his frigid hand. "You're stronger than you look."

I lean in to him conspiratorially. "Not on the inside," I whisper and then look around. "Don't tell anybody. It's a secret."

He deposits my hand back into my lap. My body feels like it's swaying, like I'm on a boat in the water. I set my elbow on the table and then rest my head against my hand. "Why are you so cold all the time?" I ask. "Are you sick?"

"No, I'm not sick." He looks me in the eyes. "I'm healing."

"From what?" I ask, overly serious.

"From a lifetime of servitude."

I roll my eyes in an exaggerated way. "Now who's not mandating sense?"

"Still you," he chuckles.

I turn and look at the dance floor. I see Jessica talking with Samantha while Todd has his face practically buried in his girlfriend's chest. *Gross.* "Do you think they're happy?" I ask Garrett.

"Who?"

I gesture toward the dance floor. "The Samanthas and Todds of this world."

He looks past me and grimaces. "I think they're made for each other, that's for sure."

I sigh and rest my head on my hand again. "Do you think you can fall in love with more than one person at the same time?"

Garrett looks surprised. "I don't know. I've never done it."

My eyes grow wide, and I sit up straight. "Me either!" I say emphatically. "I'm still in love with James! You believe that, don't you?"

He eyes me, puzzled. "Sure. Whatever you say."

"But Dane, he's engaged. Engaged!" I grab Garrett's arm again and whisper, "Do know what that means?"

"It means he's getting married?"

"Yes! To some woman named *Teagan,*" I twist her name in my mouth.

"I take it you don't want him to get married?"

I let go of his arm and move to rest my head against the table. I try to put it down gently, but it makes a thud and pain shoots across my forehead. "No, I don't!" I whine. "And ow!"

"Do you love Dane too?" Garrett asks me.

I stare at the table. "Yes. No. I don't know."

"It would be okay to fall in love with someone else," he says softly.

"No, it wouldn't!" I pull my head off the table too fast and when I look at Garrett he has three faces. "James is my Guardian! He can *see* me!"

Garrett looks around quickly, as if making sure no one else heard my outburst. "We need to get you home," he suddenly decides and grabs my elbow to help me stand. "Where are your keys?"

I pull my keys out of my pocket and hand them to him. The room starts to spin and my stomach begins to twist. "Should we tell the others we're going?" I ask, holding on to the chair for support.

Garrett looks over my head. "I don't think we'll be missed."

We head to the parking lot, and I concentrate on trying not to stumble. Now that I'm standing and moving, I realize I'm more drunk than I thought. My world is spinning; I want to get home as fast as possible. I walk as quickly as I dare in the direction of my car, not paying attention to my surroundings. A blaring horn and blinding headlights stop me dead in my tracks.

Garrett grabs me by my shoulders and yanks me out of the way as a car passes inches from us. "Emma! God! You were almost hit!"

I look at him stupidly as I try to regain my balance. "Sorry," I mutter.

Garrett helps me to my car and places me inside. I close my eyes and rest my head against the passenger side window the entire way home. Thankfully it's a short distance because my stomach is very unhappy.

When we get to the apartments, Garrett escorts me to my place. He helps me inside and starts to deposit me on the couch. The downward motion makes my insides churn.

"No!" I choke out. "Bathroom!"

He helps me to the bathroom where I dive to my knees in front of the toilet. I'm too sick to be embarrassed as he holds my hair while I retch. When my stomach stops convulsing, I lean over and rest my head against the cool porcelain of the bathtub.

"I'll get you a glass of water," he says and leaves the room.

The longer I lie there with my eyes closed, the more the room feels like it's standing still again. What a horrible day this has been. First Dane, then Rebecca. I almost get run over, and then I get sick in front of Garrett. I think about crawling into my bedroom on my hands and knees, so I can hide under the blankets on my bed.

That's when I hear the voices. It takes me a minute to focus, but I swear I can hear two people talking. I open my eyes and tentatively sit forward. I push myself to stand using the toilet for balance, and hear someone angrily say, "Where have you been?" I make it to the bathroom doorway and peer around the corner.

"Where have I been? Where were you tonight? She managed to get herself stupid drunk and was almost hit by a car!"

"I've been trying to do what you told me to," James seethes.

"I didn't tell you to get her killed!" Garrett fires back.

I blink my eyes. James is in my living room.

And he's arguing with my neighbor.

Chapter 6

James takes a step forward. "I felt the pull," he snaps.

"And you just ignored it?" Garrett asks, shocked.

"No! It disappeared as quickly as it came!" He moves toward Garrett with his fists clenched. "Can you explain that to me? Can you explain why that keeps happening?" The two of them are nose to nose as James sneers, "Can you explain why nothing works the way you said it would?"

Garrett doesn't flinch under James' icy stare. He crosses his arms. "I thought I'd trained you better than this."

"Better than what?" James steps away, frustrated. "From what I've been told, you barely trained me at all!"

"Who have you been talking to?" Garrett asks, narrowing his eyes.

James gives him a cold smile. "Wouldn't you like to know."

I'm mesmerized, clinging to the bathroom doorjamb for support. My neighbor Garrett was James' Guardian all along. *All along.*

Garrett nods at James approvingly. "Your confidence has grown."

"Don't try to flatter me," James spits. "I'm not under your guidance anymore. I don't need your approval. Not after what you've done."

Garrett tilts his head. "And just what have I done?"

James' eyes flash. "You disappeared. You assigned me and then you disappeared."

"You were ready."

"You know I wasn't!" James growls. "You left Emma's fate in the hands of a Guardian who can't protect her!" He face hovers inches from Garrett's. "And for that I will *never* forgive you."

Seconds pass and Garrett stares at James accusingly. "You still love her."

James sets his jaw. "I never stopped."

My breath catches. These months apart have been for nothing?

"You have to get your feelings under control," Garrett says.

"You think I don't know that?" James asks. "That lesson I did learn."

LB appears at my feet, meowing softly, as if asking what's going on. I bend down carefully to pick her up before her mewling distracts them, but when I stand, I'm too late. Both James and Garrett have directed their attention toward me.

"Hi," I say quietly. I feel embarrassed for eavesdropping. I make eye contact with James, and his face instantly softens, his eyes flooding with relief.

Garrett glances between the two of us and sighs. He walks out of the living room and into the kitchen as I decide to leave the bathroom doorway. I hear the clink of glass and the sink faucet turn on as I walk toward James. I stop a few steps away from him, clutching LB. My pulse accelerates at the sight of him, his sandy brown hair falling haphazardly over his forehead, his clear blue eyes swimming in mine. His skin still carries a slight pallor, and he's wearing the same jeans and polo shirt that he always does. Despite looking the same, he also looks different. He appears more solid to me, and I can't help but notice that his shirt fits him more tightly across his chest.

"Who's this?" James asks softly, his eyes flicking to LB and then back to me.

"You don't know?" I ask, confused.

He looks hurt and shakes his head. "I've stayed away."

Garrett returns to the living room, pulling my attention away from James. I turn toward him, and he holds out the glass of water he promised me. Allowing LB to jump from my arms, I reach for it, giving him a small smile of thanks.

Just as I wrap my fingers around the glass, it's knocked forcefully from my hand. I jump back in surprise as water flies everywhere, and the glass bounces off the carpet. I look at James, shocked by what he's done, and he wears a murderous expression. He lunges at Garrett, grabs his shirt in his fists, and drags him across the room, slamming his back against the wall next to my television. The sound makes me cringe.

"Why can she see you? How does she know you?" James demands through clenched teeth.

I've never seen James act so violent. It scares me. I take a step back, my heart pounding. The only other time I've seen him fight was with Patrick, and even then he didn't initiate it. His reaction was in self-defense.

Instead of looking scared, Garrett looks impressed. "I see your skills have improved as well."

"Talk!" James shouts.

"We're neighbors," Garrett says calmly. He looks unaffected by the body slam; his arms hang loosely by his sides.

"What are you trying to pull?" James growls.

"Nothing."

He pulls Garrett off the wall and then slams him back against it, making me flinch.

"Calm down." Garrett looks like a parent trying to wait out a two-year-old's temper tantrum.

James stares my neighbor in the eyes and then releases him, pushing off his chest roughly. He turns to me. "How do you know him?"

"He moved in when I did," I whisper.

He turns back to Garrett. "This is where you've vanished to? To college? To her?"

Garrett steps away from the wall. "I came here to keep tabs on you."

"Why?" James demands. "Why not stay in the Intermediate?"

"I had to leave," Garrett says, taking a step toward James. "Because of that I had to be near Emma. I knew if she was doing well, then you would be fulfilling your duty."

"And if she wasn't?" James snaps.

"Then I could step in if necessary."

I remember my lack of self-preservation in the parking lot as we left the bar. "Like tonight," I say, without thinking.

They both turn to me, reminded that I'm still in the room. Pain is written all over James' face. He should have been the one to help guide my actions tonight, not Garrett.

"This is why," Garrett says. "This is why you have to get your emotions under control. You're too angry; you're trying too hard to let her go. You've all but abandoned her in your effort to stop loving her." He crosses his arms. "You've stayed away when you need to be present."

"You knew this would be difficult for me," James says, gritting his teeth. "I'm dealing with it the best way I know how." He turns to face his mentor. "With no help from you."

Garrett gives James a stern look. "I trained you to the best of my ability. I'm sorry I couldn't tell you I had to leave. If you had been fulfilling your duty to Emma, you would have known where to find me."

James' eyes flash at the accusation of his poor guidance, and he clenches his hands into fists. "And now that I've found you? Now what?"

His expression and his reaction frighten me, and I envision him punching Garrett...or worse. I take another step back and Garrett notices.

"We'll have to work together," Garrett says, his eyes leaving me and focusing on James. "To protect us both." He pauses, giving James a hard stare, then sidesteps him and heads for the door.

"Where are you going?" James asks in disbelief. "Don't walk away from me! What do you mean to protect us both?"

Garrett ignores him and continues toward the door. James lunges at him again, making me jump. He grabs the back of his shirt and forces him to turn around. I retreat further into the living room, away from them, as anxiety continues to creep up my spine.

Garrett looks at James and utters one word. "Concentrate."

It takes a moment, but the angry expression on James' face slowly changes into one of deep concern. His eyes flash to mine, and he releases Garrett. "I'm sorry," he apologizes to me.

I look between the two of them. "For what?"

"I'll let him explain it you," Garrett says. He moves to open the door and steps outside. His eyes lock on James. "I'll talk to you after you've calmed down." He gives me a sympathetic look and closes the door behind him.

James and I stand in silence as my heartbeat returns to its normal rhythm. His entire body relaxes, and he no longer appears upset or angry. He looks like my James. The one I love.

"I'm sorry I scared you," he says, his voice full of regret.

"It's okay."

He shakes his head. "It's not."

Despite all that's happened, my heart aches. The only thing I want to do is wrap myself around him. To tell him I love him and how much I've missed him. To keep him from leaving. "Can you stay?"

He's inches from me in two strides. "There's no place I'd rather be."

The changes in James are amazing. Before he left, he was just starting to move light objects, like my hair. But when he lies down beside me tonight and wraps his arms around my waist, he physically pulls me back against his chest. I had assumed he was able to manipulate Garrett during their argument because they were both Guardians, but he can now move me. He stills feels cold, but his arms are somehow heavier. I try to lace my fingers through his without concentrating and end up with my hand in a fist. Although I still move through his body, the air that is him feels thicker, like I'm moving through water. There is no resistance to his form, yet I can feel more than just his temperature. I relax into him, glancing down in order to lace my fingers through his again, cupping my hand around the new feeling that is his skin.

"What are you thinking?" he murmurs against my hair.

"That I may have died and gone to heaven."

I can feel him tense up behind me, which is new as well. "That's not funny."

I look at him over my shoulder. "It wasn't meant to be."

He regards me seriously for a moment then his face relaxes a bit. I release his hands and shift myself to wrap my arms around his waist. "You don't know how much I've missed you."

He holds me tighter.

"What made you visit?" I ask.

"I sensed danger around you," he says. "Then it instantly disappeared. I needed to see that you were safe."

"I'm glad you came."

He leans his cheek against the top of my head. "Garrett's right. I've been doing a terrible job."

"You haven't," I raise my face to look at him. "I'm still in one piece."

James stares at me and confesses. "I can feel you. I know things have been hard. Every time you feel a strong emotion, I feel the pull."

I frown. I've been upset a lot lately, but I've been happy too. Like on my birthday and this past afternoon.

"I don't need to manifest in order to guide you. But I am supposed to look in on you and see what's needed. I haven't even been doing that," he sighs.

"Why?" I search his face. "When I told you to stay away, I meant physically."

He presses his forehead to mine. "I'm trying to get over you. I told myself I would only check in or intervene if you were in danger. I thought it was the best way."

"And how's that working out?" I ask wryly.

He raises his head and gives me a crooked smile. "I think you know the answer to that."

My heart melts upon seeing that smile, and I have the overwhelming urge to kiss him. He can tell, and his smile fades into seriousness again. "It probably wouldn't be a good idea."

I lean forward. "Does it really matter?"

"Yes," he says, but the word sounds stuck in his throat.

The emotions surrounding his return overcome me, and I don't care about any Guardian rules. The electricity running through me is tangible. He's here. *He's really here.* I press myself closer, my lips centimeters from his. "Are you going to stop me?" I whisper.

"No."

I practically attack him. His arms tighten around me as we kiss; his lips just as eager as mine. Kissing him is easier with his new form; I don't have to concentrate nearly as much. I feel his hold shift as he grasps my waist with one hand and runs the other up into my hair. I wrap my fingers around what I think is his neck, to pull him closer to me. I open my eyes for a brief second to see that I've managed to grab his shoulder instead. After a few breathless minutes, his mouth leaves mine, and I silently pray that it will reappear somewhere else on my skin. It doesn't.

I open my eyes. "What's wrong?"

"This isn't helping."

"So?"

"Emma," he groans and releases me, rolling on to his back.

"What?" I lean over him.

"Nothing has changed." He looks at me. "The rules haven't changed."

"I can't help it," I confess. "I love you."

He looks at me, defeated, and a soft expression takes over his features. "And I still love you."

I move to kiss him again, but he stops me by gently pressing his hand against my shoulder. "We shouldn't."

I know what he says is true, but it hurts to hear. In all the time we've been together, he has never stopped me from kissing him. My bruised ego speaks for me. "Why? If Garrett is here with us now, who's going to tell?"

He stares at me for a moment, his bright blue eyes clouding over to a stormy gray. He releases my shoulder, shifts his gaze, and trails his fingers lightly down my arm. My pulse accelerates.

"That's not helping," I say quietly.

His stormy eyes refocus on mine. He reaches around my neck with his free hand, pulls me toward him, and kisses me softly. His lips leave mine to find the corner of my mouth, my jaw, my throat, and then my collarbone. He moves forward to wrap a cold hand around my arm as he presses me on to my back, leaving a trail of gentle, urgent kisses along the opposite side of my neck. His hand brushes down my side and wraps around my waist as our lips meet again. He presses the length of his body against mine, and my insides nearly combust. I've missed him so much.

Suddenly, he disappears. "Damn it!" I hear him curse.

I look over to see him lying beside me, the heels of his palms pressed against his brow. "Even if Garrett didn't say anything," he says, "sooner or later The Allegiant would find out."

"The Allegiant?" I ask, trying to breathe normally.

He sets his hands on his stomach and stares at the ceiling. "They watch over the Guardians. They maintain order and balance. They make sure we're fulfilling our duty." He turns to me. "They will find out."

I turn on my side to face him. "Maybe we could talk to Garrett and see how much time we have." I know I'm grasping at straws, but I want to keep him and what we have as long as I can.

He gives me a skeptical stare. "Aren't you freaked out yet?"

"About what?"

"Garrett is my mentor. A Guardian. You're okay with that?"

"I didn't realize he was a Guardian. I thought he was human."

"What made you think he was human?"

I sit up. "Why would your Garrett be my neighbor? He has Ethics with me; he tutors me in Stats. He cooks. He eats and sleeps. He wanted my old couch."

James looks more confused now than ever. "How much time have you spent with him?"

"Quite a bit," I admit. "He's my only friend here."

James sits up to face me. "Emma," he says seriously, "Guardians don't eat or sleep."

"I know that."

"You're sure you saw him do those things?"

"Well, I haven't seen him sleep, but he has a bed. A mattress. And he made us lunch and ate it right in front of me. He had a few beers at the bar tonight, too."

James looks frustrated as he contemplates what I've said. It makes me worry. I shouldn't have brought up Garrett. His mood makes me want to march next door immediately and demand answers. Come to think of it, I should be pretty pissed at Garrett for assigning me to James, then disappearing on him and lying to me.

Just then, LB jumps up on the bed deciding to grace us with her presence. "Where have you been?" I ask her as she steps on my leg. I grab her and present her to James. "This is LB. Little Booger," I clarify. "LB, James."

James finally relaxes and smiles, reaching out to pet LB. "Where'd you find her?" he asks.

"She was a birthday present from Matt and Shel. They figured I was lonely."

James' smile vanishes and his face twists. "I'm so sorry," he says.

"What for?"

"For missing your birthday. For leaving you. For screwing everything up."

I set LB down and reach for his hand. "It's not your fault."

"Everything is my fault."

I shake my head and scoot closer to him. "Don't be sorry. Or sad. Or angry. I hate to see you like that. You scared me tonight."

"I've been mad at myself. And Garrett. Finding him here was a shock and I...I just lost it."

I pull him to lie down next to me, to snuggle in for the night, and LB makes her way in between us, curling into a ball. "I'm glad you've calmed down, and I'm glad you're here."

"So am I."

"Promise me you won't leave."

James kisses my forehead. "Like I said, there's no place I'd rather be."

"I love you."

"Until the end of forever."

I smile. "I hope The Allegiant aren't paying attention."

He tucks a piece of hair behind my ear. "We'd know by now if they were."

I raise my eyebrows. "So, can we, you know..."

James pretends to look shocked. "What's gotten into you? In front of LB?"

"I think she's asleep."

He smiles, but gives me a resigned sigh. "As much as I want to, I think it would be best if we didn't."

I grimace. "Fine. When did you turn into such a rule follower?"

"Since I've been threatened with Erasure. The idea of having my memory erased doesn't appeal to me."

Yeah, that sounds just as horrible as it did the first time I'd heard about it.

"You need to get some sleep," he tells me.

"That's not going to be easy."

"Do you want me to sing you a lullaby?"

"Please no!" I laugh. James' singing voice is terrible.

"Twinkle, twinkle, little star..." he warbles.

"Stop!"

"How I wonder what you are. Up above the world so high..."

"Arrggh!" I plug my ears.

"Like a diamond in the sky..."

Even LB looks up annoyed.

"Twinkle, twinkle, little star..."

"I'm sleeping!" I smash my eyes together. "See!"

He laughs then kisses my nose like a parent would. "That's better."

He holds me tighter and eventually I drift off, content in his arms, where I never thought I would be again.

Chapter 7

I awake to the delicious smell of cinnamon, and my stomach growls. I roll over, reaching beside me in the process, and find myself alone. Frowning, I open my eyes and look around the room. The sun is shining around the blinds on my window, and the clock reads 10:58. Apparently, all the activities from last night wore me out. Rubbing the sleep from my eyes, I swing my legs to the side and leave my bed. I find James in the kitchen, standing over the toaster, with LB sitting at his feet.

"Good morning," he says. He catches the time on the oven and smiles. "I mean, good afternoon."

"You're making toast?" I ask.

The bread pops up. "I'm making breakfast." He removes the slices from the toaster and grabs a knife. He opens the butter dish. "Cinnamon raisin okay with you?"

"Well," I move to lean against the counter beside him, "since I bought the bread, I would say it's perfect. What brought this on?"

"You said Garrett cooks." He runs the knife over the toast. "I thought I'd give it a try."

I laugh. "I don't know if toasting bread counts as cooking."

James looks at me and raises an eyebrow. "Do you want the toast or not?"

My stomach growls loudly, reminding me that everything that was inside of it ended up in the toilet last night. "Yes, of course I want it." I stand on my toes and kiss his cheek. "Thank you."

He hands me the plate and moves to the refrigerator. He opens the door and pulls out a carton of orange juice. I watch him, mesmerized, as he grabs a glass from the cabinet and fills it. "For you." He holds it out to me.

I take it from him tentatively. He puts the carton back and shuts the fridge door. I haven't moved.

"What?" he asks.

I blink. "It's like...it's almost like you're not a Guardian."

A sad expression flashes across his face, then the corner of his mouth quirks up. "Maybe with some culinary practice I could be your butler."

"Ooooh, I like that," I smile. "It would be nice to come home to a clean apartment and a hot meal every day."

He laughs and reaches around me to collect the bread and the butter dish, putting things back where they belong. I step out of his way, carrying my breakfast into the living room and setting it on the coffee table. I sit down and pull off a piece of toast. "So, what's on the agenda for today?" I call into the kitchen and pop the bread into my mouth.

A moment later he appears in the doorway. "Are congratulations in order?" he asks, holding the newspaper article and the envelope I received in the mail.

The bread suddenly feels dry in my mouth, and I choke it down. "Apparently so." I turn my attention to the orange juice. I forgot I left the article about Teagan on the counter.

"When did this happen?" he asks.

I swallow my drink and nod toward his hands. "It sounds like a year and a half ago. I don't know."

James frowns. "You don't know?"

I pull off another piece of toast and try to look unaffected. "I just found out about the happy couple yesterday."

"From the mail?"

"Yep."

James looks irritated and starts to walk toward me. "How are you?"

"I'm fine."

He reaches me and sits down on the couch I now hate. "Don't lie to me."

I don't want to talk about Dane with James. I'm nervous about how much he knows. Before he left, he knew we were friends and suspected Dane wanted more. I was adamant that he didn't. I was wrong.

"I'm not lying." I shove a piece of toast in my mouth. "I'm really fine."

He gives me an exasperated look. "You forget I can feel your emotions, and you're still a terrible liar." He stares at me intently. "Yesterday was a very hard day for you."

I look down, embarrassed. If he felt my emotions yesterday, what did he feel when I was with Dane before I left for school? I try to eliminate him from our conversation. "I also ran into Rebecca at Wayside last night." James is familiar with the bar; we used to go there often.

He crumples the article and the envelope in his hand, his jaw tensing. "I'm sorry she upset you."

I shrug and go back to picking at my toast. James stands and begins to pace. He stops. "He really didn't tell you he was engaged?" he asks in disbelief. "After all the time you two spent together?"

I look at him annoyed. "No, he didn't. Can we drop this?"

"No." I can tell he's getting worked up. "I know you care about him."

I freeze, alarmed by what he just said. He knows I care about Dane? "H–how do you know that?" Do I even want the answer?

My reaction causes him to pause. He tilts his head. "You're nervous. Did something happen?"

This is it, I think and start to sweat. My mind flashes back to when I found out about Rebecca, when I learned about her and James. I remember how hurt I was that it had happened, but even more so that he had kept it from me. I can't be like that; I have to be honest. My face searches his, and I know I look guilty. I open my mouth to confess.

"Don't," he cuts me off before I can utter a word. He closes his eyes and clenches his hands into fists, as if trying to keep his emotions in check.

I imagine the conclusion he's jumped to. "It's not what you think," I say hurriedly, as I stand and walk toward him. *But it kind of is*, my subconscious pipes up.

He opens his eyes. "I don't want to know," he says, even though his jaw is still tense. "It shouldn't matter to me anymore."

I look at him, pleading. "But I want to tell..."

"Emma, stop." He stares at me, his eyes intense. "I don't care about the details."

I know he's lying.

"What matters is that he hurt you and that is unacceptable." He starts to pace again.

I'm at a loss for words. I want to make him feel better. I want him to know that whatever was between Dane and me was brief and obviously over.

James walks past me. "I could kill him," he mutters under his breath.

I'm worried that angry James is going to make a return appearance, and I try to diffuse the situation. "It's not that serious."

He stops pacing and looks at me. "Everything that involves you is serious. It's my duty."

I realize his reaction has more to do with jealousy than his duty. "It's really okay," I protest, even though I'd like to say a few choice words to Dane myself.

"No one should ever hurt you," he says defiantly. "You don't deserve it."

I walk toward him. "Let's not talk about this anymore. I want to forget about everything involving Dane."

"You deserve an explanation," he says. "You can't let him get away with this. Stand up for yourself."

I give him an exasperated look.

"I mean it. If you don't do something about it, I will."

"Like what?" I try to make light of the situation. "Haunt him?"

"Amongst other things."

I don't think I want to know what the others things might be; I want to drop the subject. "I'm done talking about this." I walk backward to the couch, sit down, and pick up my breakfast again. "Where were we? Oh yes," I pause. "What are we doing today?"

He looks at me pointedly. "Don't let him get away with it."

I roll my eyes. "I know. I got it."

"Do you really?"

"Yes!"

He eyes me warily. "You know I'll know."

"Yes Dad, I know you'll know." Why won't he let this go? "So, about today?"

He sighs and studies my face. I chew on my now-hardened cinnamon raisin toast. He finally relaxes a bit. "I think we should pay a visit to your neighbor."

"I agree," I say and finish up my orange juice. "Just let me shower and we can leave."

About twenty minutes later I emerge from the shower, wrapped in a towel, to find James playing with LB on my bed. I stand in the doorway for a few seconds, taking in the sight of them playing together. He drags a piece of yarn back and forth for her to catch. The scene makes me sentimental. It looks so normal, and I get caught up in it. This is exactly how things should have been for us, would have been for us, if it wasn't for that horrible night. Tears unexpectedly jump behind my eyes. What I wouldn't give to go back in time and change our future.

James turns to me in a flash. "What's wrong?"

I blink quickly, trying to hide my tears. I walk into the room and past him. "Nothing." I open a dresser drawer and search for something to wear.

He's behind me in an instant, setting his hands on my shoulders. "Tell me," he says softly.

I continue to search through my shirts and a tear escapes. "You and LB...it just hit me, that's all."

He stands behind me, patiently waiting for me to elaborate. I select a shirt and move to the next drawer. I pull out a pair of jeans and then move on to find some underwear. I try to brush the tear away indiscreetly with the back of my hand, but its hard holding on to my clothes and the towel, and I miss. He turns me around by my shoulders, looks into my eyes, and runs his thumb across my cheek. His sweet gesture makes my eyes well up even more.

"Tell me," he says again, concerned.

I hesitate. I don't want to bring up unpleasant things. "I got caught up in the moment, watching you with LB. It reminded me of our plans before...how you should be here..."

Without a word, he pulls me against his chest, wrapping his arms around me. He tucks my head beneath his chin and remains quiet while tears fall silently down my face. What can he say? There are no words that can change our reality. I need to pull it together. That he is here at all is a miracle, and I don't want to make it seem like it's not enough. I stand up straight and step out of his arms. "I'm good," I say, wiping my face. I drop my clothes in the process.

"You're not." He bends down to collect my things and then stands. "My being here is too hard for you."

"You're wrong," I say adamantly.

"I should go. It would be easier for the both of us."

I look at him, crushed. "You want to leave?"

"Of course not."

"Then don't." I take my clothes from his hands and turn to place them on top of the dresser. I let the towel fall to my feet, and pull on my underwear. I put on my jeans next, and then reach for my shirt.

"That's not helping," James says quietly from behind me.

I freeze. I wasn't thinking; I'm so used to being alone. I glance over my shoulder, and he's no longer there. "I told you not to leave!" I say loudly as I throw the rest of my clothes on.

"I didn't!" I hear him yell from the living room.

I walk into the bathroom to grab my hairbrush and then go to find him. James is sitting on the couch, playing with the remote. "This TV sucks," he says, punching buttons.

"Okay, Matt," I say and sit cross-legged beside him, pulling the brush through my hair.

He gives me a funny look.

"Matt told me the same thing when he was here," I clarify.

James nods. "You should really think about getting a new one, especially if I'm going to be hanging around more."

I laugh sarcastically. Would Garrett consider another trade?

"What?"

I shake my head. "It's nothing." I comb the tangles out of my hair, and remove a tie from the handle of the brush. "Ready to go?"

"Yeah," he sighs and turns off the television. We stand and head to the door. On our way, he stops abruptly in front of me, and I walk right through his body.

"What...?"

Suddenly, he grabs my upper arms and pulls me to him, his mouth coming down hard on mine. His kiss is demanding and just when I begin to relax in his hold, he stops. I look at him, bewildered.

"You need to keep your clothes on," is all he says. He releases my arms and walks around me to open the door. He ushers me outside before LB can run out.

"It's my apartment, you know." I try to be annoyed, but inside I'm beaming. I still have the same effect on him that he has on me.

He shoots me an agitated stare and says nothing.

I lead him to Garrett's door and tentatively knock. As we wait in the hall, I mull things over. Their situation really has nothing to do with me. "Should I be here?" I ask.

James steps forward and knocks harder. "Yes. Garrett involved you. You deserve to know what's going on as much as I do."

I have to admit I am curious. We wait, and James knocks again. When the door remains unanswered, he says, "Wait here."

"Where are you going?"

"We tried the polite way, now it's time to be rude." He steps forward and disappears through Garrett's door.

I'm left alone in the hallway, staring stupidly at where James just stood. I don't think I'll ever get used to what he can do.

Minutes later, he reappears. "He's not home."

I roll my eyes. "I could have told you that." We head back to my place. "So, did you learn anything from your B & E?"

He laughs. "There was no B. Only E."

"Very funny. I'm serious."

James walks through my apartment door and opens it for me from the inside.

"Show off."

He smirks. "No, I didn't learn much. Except..." He looks across the room longingly.

I close the door behind me. "Except what?"

"He has an amazing TV."

James and I spend the rest of the day wrapped around each other on the couch. I get caught up in a *Pretty Woman* movie marathon, and James periodically disappears to see if Garrett has returned. I tried to talk him into making me lunch in order to improve his cooking skills, but that was a no go. As evening fell, I tried to coerce him into making me dinner as well.

"Actually, I should get back," he sighs and untangles himself from me. I try to hold on but grab only air.

"You're leaving?" I ask, worriedly.

"I need to be seen. I don't want to raise any suspicion." He stands over me as I sit up.

"What about Garrett?"

He frowns. "If you see him, tell him I'm looking for him."

"When will you be back?"

He leans over me and kisses my forehead. "Soon."

I wrap my hand around his neck to keep his eyes level with mine. "You promise?"

He flashes that familiar James smile that makes my heart beat faster. "I promise."

I hear my cell chime from the bedroom, telling me I have a text message. "Somebody is looking for you," he says and stands.

"It's probably my mom. Or Shel," I say, standing as well.

James takes a step back and starts to evaporate.

"Can I still tell you I love you?" I ask as he fades.

"Only with your clothes on," he teases.

I look down at myself in an exaggerated way. I'm fully clothed. "I love you."

He has completely disappeared, but I still hear his voice. "Until the end of forever."

My cell chimes again, and I go to see who needs me. When I pick the phone off my nightstand, my stomach drops to my toes.

Hey Grace.

It's Dane. I earned that nickname after a rather grace-less fall in front of him. What could he possibly want? The last thing I want to do is respond; I need more time to plan what to say. But James' voice rings in my ears from this morning – *"Don't let him get away with it."* Let's get this over with.

What do you want? I send. I hope my rude tone is implied.

Just to say hi. How have you been?

How have I been? Well, let's be honest. *Pissed. Sad. Intoxicated. You?*

What's wrong?

I let out a short, harsh laugh. *You tell me.*

How would I know what's wrong??

I'm not in the mood for games. *Really? Ask your fiancée.*

It takes less than a minute for my cell to ring. Dane is calling, and I refuse to answer. I prefer to handle this over text; I don't want him to hear my voice. I'm terrible at lying, and I'm terrible at fighting. I want to come across as angry, not emotional. He calls three more times, and I send each call to voicemail.

He texts again. *Answer the phone.*

No.

Please.

I don't want to talk to you.

Let me explain.

Explain what? That he's a liar? *No need. I understand perfectly.*

You don't understand anything at all.

It's pointless to argue; he lied and we're through. *Lose my number.*

The phone goes silent. The longer it stays that way, the more pressure builds inside my chest. I set the phone down and curl on my side on the bed, pressing my face against the pillow. My heart hurts again, and I'm unsure if it's due to sadness or anger. I fight back tears as I silently wonder how long it will take James to realize my pain and return to me.

Almost instantly, I hear a knock on the door and bolt upright. Who could that be? James wouldn't knock. When I open the door, I'm surprised to see Garrett standing there.

"What's up?" I try to ask normally. A suspicious lump has formed in my throat.

"Is James here?" he asks, looking anxiously around the room.

"No, not right now. He's been looking for you all day though."

Garrett steps inside. "You need to call him. It's urgent."

"Call him how?"

"There's no need," James says from behind me, making me jump. "I'm right here."

Chapter 8

"We need to talk," Garrett says and walks around me.

James crosses his arms. "I agree."

The two of them stare at each other, as if at an impasse, and nothing of consequence has even been said. I close the door. "Don't let me get in your way." I blink to get rid of any lingering tears and start to make my way to the bedroom.

James reaches out and stops me. "Everything okay?"

I nod and give him half a smile. "I didn't let Dane get away with it."

His jaw tenses. "He's hurt you again?"

I glance at Garrett, and his attention is directed to me as well. "Everything's fine." I look back at James. "I'll leave you two alone." I start to head out of the room.

"Wait," James says. "I think you should stay."

Garrett speaks up. "I'm not sure that would be wise."

James turns to him. "Why? You're the one who involved her. She deserves an explanation just as much as I do."

Garrett shoots James an exasperated look. "Now is not the time to be complicated."

"We're a package deal." James takes my hand. "You know that."

Garrett looks frustrated as I nervously shift my gaze from him to James and back again. I don't want to hang around if things are going to get nasty.

Apparently my neighbor concedes because he heads to the couch. We follow. He sits at one end, and I take a seat at the other, folding my legs beneath me. James remains standing. Garrett leans back, looks around for a moment, and assesses the furniture. "The Cadillac is comfortable," he smirks at me. "Are you still willing to give it up?"

I grimace. "Definitely."

Perturbed and confused, James asks, "We're discussing how the couch feels?"

Garrett turns to him. "Sorry. It's been awhile since I've *felt* anything."

James raises his eyebrows in surprise.

"Listen," Garrett leans forward, setting his elbows on his knees and clasping his hands in front of him, "we have a problem."

"We?" James crosses his arms again.

"Apparently, my absence hasn't gone unnoticed."

James scoffs. "That sounds like your problem, not mine."

"Did you tell anyone I was gone? Ask about me after I left?"

"My demeanor hasn't exactly been conducive to making friends."

"So you've talked to no one?"

"I've tried to keep to myself," James pauses. "But no, there is one person I've been speaking to."

"Who?"

"Thomas."

Garrett narrows his eyes at James. "What does he look like?"

James shrugs. "He's an older guy with glasses."

And with that, another person takes form in my living room. It startles me, and I spring off the couch and to James' side in two steps. He wraps his arm protectively around my shoulders.

The man appears midway between Garrett and James. He's an older gentleman, with light brown hair and a moustache that is starting to gray. He's wears thin-framed eyeglasses and a white shirt, covered by a tan sport coat with matching slacks.

"Hey kid," the man smiles at James in a fatherly way.

"Thomas?" James blinks, surprised.

Garrett turns to Thomas and stands. "You've been speaking with him? I asked you to keep an eye on him, that's all!"

"The boy was miserable," Thomas defends himself. "I couldn't let him suffer. Besides, you said yourself that you didn't have enough time with him before you left."

"You've been training him?"

Thomas hesitates. "Not exactly. Just filling in some blanks."

"What about your duty? What about Arnold?"

"My Ward is fine," Thomas says and puts his hands in his pockets. "He's been moved to a nursing home. He can't get into too much trouble there." He smiles at James and me.

"Why are you here?" James asks. "Can someone start making some sense?"

Thomas takes a step forward. "Garrett asked one of us to accompany him tonight, just in case you lost your temper again. Two against one might keep you a little calmer." He shifts his focus and gives me warm smile. "You must be the lovely Emma."

My gaze leaves Thomas and shoots to James. He gives me a reassuring look and then turns his attention to the two other Guardians in the room. I do the same. "Um...nice to meet you?" I cautiously say. Is there a protocol I should be following here?

"Likewise," Thomas says and nods.

Garrett rubs his fingers against his forehead as if he can physically clear his mind. "If you're the only one he's talked to, then what did Joss and Meg overhear at Assembly? Maybe they're wrong."

Thomas turns to Garrett. "Joss wouldn't lie."

Garrett sighs, frowning. "I know she wouldn't." He looks defeated. "We need to meet. All of us."

All of us? I think. Are more people going to materialize in my apartment? I'm starting to reconsider the whole need-to-know thing on my part.

"Do you think that's a good idea?" Thomas asks. "If we're all away at the same time..."

"I don't think we have a choice." Garrett puts his hands on his hips and shifts his weight.

"Hold on," James interrupts, removing his arm from my shoulders and walking toward the two Guardians. "Meet who? About what?"

James is out of the loop, and it's starting to piss him off. I think now would be the best time for me to exit this little gathering. If a fight is about to break out, I'd rather not be present.

Thomas and Garrett start to speak over one another.

"The rest of..."

"James, I think..."

"Ah, hello?" I give a small wave, so I'm noticed. The conversation ceases and everyone turns to face me. "I'm sorry for interrupting but being as how I'm the only human in the room, I should probably go." I take a few tentative steps. "I'll just head out for a few hours and you guys can –"

"I'm human too."

I freeze in place, staring at Garrett.

He gives me a tiny smile. "Well, half human, anyway."

My focus immediately shifts to James, and he looks completely blindsided, as if he's been slapped in the face. Thomas takes a measured step and stands between the two of them. "Just in case," he nods to me. "They can't hurt each other, but they can sure scare the hell out of you."

"How?" James asks quietly, disbelieving.

Garrett steps to the side. "The method was stumbled upon, and I'm the guinea pig."

James looks away from Garrett and to me, as if looking for confirmation that I'm hearing this too. I stare back at him, wide-eyed. A million questions pass between us.

Thomas relaxes and steps out of the way.

"There is a group of us that no longer wish to be Guardians," Garrett explains. "The opportunity to be released has passed us all." His expression twists. "None of our true loves chose us. After years of serving The Allegiant, we've finally found another way out."

"How?" James asks again, this time with more determination. "What's the method? Count me in!"

"Whoa," Thomas says, stepping back in front of James. "It's not that simple."

"Right now, we need to concentrate on keeping this a secret," Garrett continues. "We need you to lay low and keep your eyes and ears open. The Allegiant won't come around asking questions without good cause. Do your best by Emma and don't call attention to yourself. Without a reason to question my teaching, they shouldn't need to talk to you – or me. They cannot find out that I've left the Intermediate or where I've gone. We need to find out what was overheard and where it came from. If The Allegiant get even a hint of what we're up to, it's the end for all of us."

James steps back. "Fine." He gives them both a hard look. "But I want in. All the way. Who else knows about this?"

The three of them have obviously forgotten that I'm in the room.

Thomas turns to Garrett. "We'll have to introduce him, one by one, to the others. Unless you decide to hold a meeting."

Garrett frowns in thought. "Let me think about it some more. Are you meeting Joss tonight?"

"As soon as I get back."

"Find out if she can get more specifics from Meg."

"Will do."

Just then I hear my phone ring from the other room. It distracts only me. The Guardians – and Garrett – are deep in conversation. I don't want to interrupt them again by moving, so I ignore it, praying that whoever is trying to get ahold of me leaves a message.

"I could take him to meet Joss with me now," I hear Thomas suggest.

Garrett appears to consider it. "I'm due a visit as well, from Jack."

"Does it matter who I meet first?" James asks.

My phone rings again, and I silently curse it. James looks at me and nods over his shoulder. "Maybe you should get that?"

I give the group an apologetic smile and dart around them as I head out of the room. I grab my phone off the bed and see that Shel is calling. I sit down and answer her in order to avoid any further interruptions.

"Hello?"

"Oh! I'm so glad you answered!" Shel's voice wavers.

Her panicked tone sends my already heightened nerves into overdrive. "What's wrong? What is it?"

"It's Matt," her voice breaks.

Matt? My pulse starts to accelerate. Has something happened to him? "Is he all right?"

"Yes," she says through tears. "It's...we had a fight."

Relief floods my body. I want to say "Is that all?" but I catch myself. I think this may be their first fight ever. "Aw, Shel. What about?"

"Dane." She spits his name out like it's poison.

Dane? My expression twists. "Why were you fighting about him?"

"Because he knew, Emma! Matt knew he was engaged!"

A sick feeling starts to curl around my stomach.

Shel sniffs. "Dane called Matt and accused him of telling you. When did you find out?"

"Yesterday," I say quietly.

"I overheard Matt arguing on the phone and demanded to know what was going on. He told me and then we got into it about you. How could he do that to you Emma? How could he keep this huge secret? You're our best friend!"

I'm at a loss for words. Why would Matt keep this from me? He knew Dane and I were getting close. I hear Shel sniff again, and I'm reminded of how upset she is. "I'm sorry that you guys fought because of me."

"It's not your fault! It's theirs!"

I hear what I think is a car horn in the background. "Where are you?"

"Driving. I'm on my way to you."

"You are?"

"Yes. I stormed out. Is that okay? I don't want to go home; Matt will look for me there. I don't want to talk to him right now."

I know the feeling. "Of course you can come here. How far away are you?"

"About an hour."

"Okay. Hang up and get here safe."

"'Kay. See you in a little bit."

I end the call and stare at my phone. Matt knew about Dane all along? Feelings of betrayal start to swirl in my chest. Thanks for the heads up, jackass.

"What's going on?" James appears in my doorway, startling me.

"Shel's on her way. She got into a fight with Matt." I neglect to tell him about Matt's secrecy. I don't need another person for him to be mad at.

"Oh good," James says absentmindedly, glancing back into the living room.

I frown at him. "It's good they got in a fight?"

"What?" He focuses back on me. "Oh, no. It's good that Shel is coming here. Thomas is going to take me to meet Joss."

"Now?"

"Yes." He steps forward and plants a kiss on my forehead. When he leans back, he looks at me intently. There's an excitement in his eyes that I haven't seen in a very long time. "You heard what I heard right?"

I nod.

"Do you know what this could mean?" he whispers enthusiastically.

I can't help but smile at his boyish grin. "The thought did cross my mind."

He leans forward again and catches my mouth with his, kissing me hard. When we stop, I tease him. "I thought we weren't supposed to do that?"

He responds by kissing me again.

"You're going to get caught," I reprimand him.

Someone clears his throat behind us. "He is caught."

James turns around and I jump off the bed. Thomas is standing in the doorway. The way he looks at us makes me blush.

"You're still her Guardian, you know," he chastises James. He tries to maintain his stern expression, but his eyes crinkle as he breaks into a smile. "No wonder Garrett asked me to keep an eye on you."

James laughs nervously. "Can you blame me?"

Thomas shakes his head. "Not in the least. Come on. We have to go."

James turns to me. "I'll see you soon. Stay out of trouble."

"Me? Get into trouble? Never." I smile.

"I don't know." James tilts his head, doubtful. "Shel is on her way."

It's so nice to see James happy for once. "Don't worry. I'll be on my best behavior. Scout's honor." I hold up my hand.

He smiles and leans in to kiss me again.

"Ahem," Thomas subtly clears his throat from the doorway.

James stops. He reaches out, takes my hand, and squeezes it, smiling at me. I mouth "I love you." He winks at me and then drops my hand.

"Ready?" Thomas asks.

"Ready," James confirms and takes a step back.

"It was nice to meet you Emma," Thomas says to me.

"You too. Come by any time."

The two of them fade from my vision, James a little more slowly than Thomas, and I'm left with LB to wait for Shel. She's been napping on my bed this whole time. It's funny how a place that was so full moments ago can now feel so empty. That is, assuming Garrett has gone. I walk out into the living room, and it is indeed empty. He must have left while I was on the phone.

My stomach growls, and I realize I haven't had any dinner. I check the clock and it's almost eight. Shel should be here around nine. I head to the kitchen to make myself something to eat. This is going to be a long night.

Chapter 9

When I greet Shel at the door, the evidence of her emotional state is worse than I imagined. I thought the drive would have calmed her some, but her eyes are rimmed in red, her mascara has run down her cheeks, and her nose looks raw from wiping.

"Hey," she says quietly and takes a deep breath.

I instantly open my arms to her and she steps into them for a hug. "This sucks," she says against my shoulder.

"Yeah." It's all I can think to say.

We make our way to my apartment, and LB greets us at the door. "She's getting so big," Shel says as she crouches down to pet her. "What are you feeding her? Super food?"

"Nah, just the regular stuff. Maybe I give her too many treats? She's spoiled."

"As she should be," Shel says and shrugs out of her jacket. "All us women deserve to be spoiled." She stands and lays the jacket over the back of the couch, setting her purse on the floor. "Is this the...?"

"Birthday present?" I finish for her, making a face. "Yes."

She runs her hand across the leather and looks impressed. "It's nice." She glances at the television. "I thought..."

I roll my eyes and sit down. "After I found out about Dane's...um...situation, I didn't want his gifts anymore. I gave the TV to my neighbor."

Shel joins me on the couch. "That Garrett guy?"

I nod. "He barely owns anything. He has my old loveseat too, which I'm planning to trade for this hunk of junk as soon as I can."

LB jumps into my lap to be scratched and, as she makes herself comfortable, Shel asks, "So, how *did* you find out about Dane?"

"I received a newspaper article in the mail all about the lovely Ms. Teagan Meyer," I say sarcastically. It's easy to let my true emotions show around Shel. If anyone will understand how I feel, it's her. "The end of which prominently discussed her upcoming nuptials."

Shel's mouth falls open. "Who sent it?"

I shrug. "I don't know. There was no return address."

"Can I read it?"

"Sure." I pick up LB, move her to Shel's lap, and then pause. James crumpled the article earlier today in his fit of frustration. Maybe it's still near the top of the garbage can. "Let me get it out of the trash." I head over to the kitchen, peer into the basket, and pluck out the article-ball. I bring it back to Shel and hand it to her. "Sorry. I got a little upset."

"Understandable," she says and takes the wadded up piece of paper.

I sit down opposite her, and LB makes her way back to my lap. I scratch behind her ears and concentrate on listening to her purr as Shel unfolds the ball and reads the news story. When she finishes, she crumples it back up and tosses it across the room. "Well, that's just shitty," she says. "Why are men such morons?"

I laugh. "Good question. Maybe we should be asking ourselves why we fall for them in the first place."

Shel smiles, but then her amusement fades. "How can I trust Matt after this? How can you?"

I shake my head. "I have to believe he has a good reason for keeping Dane's secret. If not, I will gladly be your accomplice in his murder." I pause. "Did he try to explain himself? What happened?"

Shel rearranges her body on the couch to get comfortable. "We were hanging out at my place when he got the call from Dane. I take it he found out you knew?"

"He sent me a text tonight and asked how I was, so I told him. I said I was pissed, he asked why, and I told him to ask his fiancée."

This makes Shel smile. "Oooo, nice."

"He tried to call me, but I wouldn't answer." LB stretches out her front legs and kneads her paws against my thigh. "He texted me again, and I promptly told him to lose my number. I haven't heard from him since."

"Well, he must have called Matt right after." She tosses her hair over her shoulder. "They started to argue, which is weird for them, and when Matt jumped off the couch and started pacing, I knew something big was up. He kept saying, "It wasn't me, it wasn't me." So, naturally, when he hung up the phone I asked him what was going on." She grimaces. "When he told me, I lit into him about keeping this from you. He knows what you've been through! The last thing you need is more heartache. At least if he had told me the truth I could have steered you away from Dane instead of pushing you two together! I'm so mad at him!"

I can't help it and laughter escapes me. I slap my hand over my mouth.

"What's so funny?" Shel asks. "I'm upset here!"

"You," I say with a smile. "You just admitted to setting me up with Dane."

She rolls her eyes at me. "Please. You knew that all along."

"True, but you rarely admit to anything." In the beginning, Shel found creative ways to get Dane and I in the same place at the same time, all the while denying her "involvement." But, as time went on, she didn't need to intervene anymore, and that was my own fault. I'm responsible for my own feelings and my own actions.

"What is it?" Shel asks.

"What? Nothing."

"You just went from laughter to sadness in, like, a second."

I sigh. "I do wish that Matt would have said *something*, even if he didn't admit the whole truth. Maybe he could have just said 'he's not relationship material' or something like that, instead of going along with your plans. But even so, Dane's the one who's ultimately to blame here. At least he is in my eyes."

Shel scoots over to sit closer to me and LB. "You don't blame me then?"

I frown at her. "No! Why would you think that?"

"Because I was rooting for Dane and Matt's involved! I swear to you I didn't know about Dane's engagement. If I had, you sure as hell would have known too."

I give her a reassuring look. "I know that. It never crossed my mind that either of you knew. I promise."

Relief visibly floods through my best friend and her shoulders relax. "Thank God," she says. "I was beating myself up the whole way here."

"Is that why you're so upset?" I make a face. "Don't be! Calm down."

She laughs. "At first all of my anger was directed at Matt, but as I drove my thoughts started to turn to my part in this. Let's just say it didn't help things. I feel so bad, Em."

"Well, don't. I've been through worse. Besides, it's not like Dane and I were a couple anyway. We were friends that should've stayed friends. Now we'll just be...nothing."

I hear the familiar chirp of Shel's phone, and we both glance in the direction of her purse. "I bet I know who that is," I smile.

She groans and gets up off the couch. She searches through her bag and finds her phone, dismisses the call, and tosses it back in.

"What are doing?" I ask. "Wasn't that Matt?"

"Yep."

"Aren't you going to talk to him?"

"Nope."

"Come on," I say and unfold my legs. They're starting to go to sleep. This disturbs LB and she looks at me, annoyed. "You should at least let him know where you are."

Then I hear my phone ring. We look at each other and laugh. "Don't answer it," she says.

I stand. "Let me at least see who it is." I jog into the bedroom. "It's Matt!" I holler to Shel.

"Don't answer it!" she yells back.

I do as I'm told; although, I don't feel good about it. I walk into the living room. "How long are you going to be mad at him?" I ask.

"That depends. How long are you going to be mad at him?"

"Shel." I give her a condescending look. "Don't fight with Matt over me. Call your boyfriend and make up."

She shakes her head defiantly. "No. He needs to learn that if he messes with you, he messes with me. We're all supposed to be best friends; we're all supposed to have each other's backs. We don't keep secrets that hurt one another."

I cross my arms and give her a stern look. "I will not be responsible for the two of you fighting or worse. Call him."

"Not right now."

"Shel..."

"He needs to stew about things for awhile. Men have to be trained, Em. He needs to learn a lesson."

I look at her skeptically. "What is he, a dog?"

She laughs.

I give up rationalizing and bend over to pick up the crumpled Teagan article to deposit back in the trash. "I take it you're spending the night then?" I ask as I head toward the kitchen.

"Would that be okay?"

I toss the ball into the garbage can. "Of course." When I return to the living room, I find Shel sorting through my meager collection of DVDs. "Movie night?" I ask.

She nods enthusiastically. "Let's camp out on the floor and watch movies like we used to when we were kids. We can gorge ourselves on popcorn and other junk. Sound good?"

"Sounds awesome." I move to gather my purse and smile. "Go wipe that mascara off your face and let's get some snacks."

Shel and I returned from the store with three bags of junk food, plus a new movie to watch. I don't know why we felt we had to purchase *The Lucky One*, because it's a love story and that's the last thing we need right now. But Shel heard it was good, and I hadn't seen it either, so we got it. We also bought a large assortment of sweet and salty snacks – chips, popcorn, pretzels, red licorice, gummy bears, and, of course, chocolate. You can't go wrong with Twix, M&M's, and Butterfingers. We moved my small coffee table out of the way and pulled my blankets and pillows off the bed to set up our "camp" on the floor in front of the television. After we changed into pajamas and set out our snacks picnic style, I pressed play on the DVD, and we proceeded to get lost in the relationship of Beth and Logan. Around two in the morning, with the movie over and our stomachs stuffed, we called it a night.

"Thanks for letting me stay," Shel says to me in the darkness.

"You're always welcome here. Don't ever question it."

She yawns. "Next time you need to come out to my place."

"Will do," I say sleepily.

I drift off, but after an hour or so, I wake up needing the bathroom. It must be from all the Coke I drank. I pull myself off the floor and lazily shuffle to the bathroom, cursing my bodily functions. I'm so tired. I wonder what it would be like to not have to do this anymore. The next time I see James I'll have to ask him if he misses going to the bathroom.

When I sit down, the toilet seat is freezing and the feeling wakes me up a bit. As I sit there, my mind wanders to Matt and Shel. I wish they wouldn't fight over me. It's stupid, really. If anyone should be fighting, it's me and Matt. Or me and Dane. Wait. We are fighting. Back to me and Matt. Did I mention I was tired?

As I leave the bathroom, I have a thought. Maybe I can help fix this. I tiptoe to my purse and pull out my phone. Shel made me turn it off after we got back from the store as to avoid any more calls from Matt. I sneak back into my bedroom and turn it on. I have three voicemail messages.

"Emma? It's Matt. I know you're upset. Please call me."

"Me again. Do you know where Shel is? I'm worried. Call me."

"Obviously you're beyond angry. I'm sorry. Please tell me that Shel is with you. She won't answer her phone. Okay. Bye."

I send him a quick text, which was my plan all along. He's probably asleep, but he'll see it in the morning.

Shel is here.

At least he'll know where she is and stop worrying. I set my phone down and head back out to the living room to go to sleep.

As soon as my head hits the pillow, my phone chimes, telling me I have a message.

"Shoot!" I whisper to myself. The last thing I need is for my phone to wake up Shel. It will go off a least four times if I don't check it. I get up as fast as I can without waking her, taking huge steps like an idiot to get to my bedroom quickly. I snatch the phone from my nightstand. It's Matt.

Thank God. I'm on my way.

What?! No! Shel will kill me! *What are you doing awake?! You can't drive here in the middle of the night!*

I'm up worrying anyway.

What do I say? That she doesn't want to see to him? *You CANNOT come here.*

Dane is with me. He wants to see you.

Oh, hell no! *Don't you DARE bring him here!*

Be reasonable.

You be reasonable! It's late and I'm tired. I don't want to argue right now. All I was trying to do was ease Matt's worry; which I now realize was a mistake. And what is Dane doing with him at this hour? What are they, attached at the hip?

How mad is she?

Very.

How mad are you?

Extremely.

I wait and there is no response. I imagine the two of them getting in the car for the long drive out here. A ball of nerves forms in my belly and sits there like a rock, or maybe it's all the junk I ate coagulating in one spot. Probably a combination of both. Man, I really screwed this up. I switch the phone to vibrate, in case it goes off again before daylight. I stand to go back to our campsite. How am I going to sleep now?

Buzz. *I'll see you in a few.*

I could cry. *NO.*

Don't worry. I'm alone.

I barely manage to sleep the rest of the night in anticipation of Matt's arrival. If he left when he said he did, he should be here soon. I look over at Shel, who is sleeping peacefully, and imagine her wrath when she finds out. I contemplate waking her, so we can make a run for it. Instead, I decide to get up and get dressed.

When I'm decent, I leave the apartment to wait by the front door for Matt. I don't want him pressing the intercom and waking Shel. I lean against the sidelight, peering through the window, so I can see him when he arrives. I pick at my cuticles to pass the time and silently wonder if James will visit today. He was so excited yesterday and, the more I think about it, so am I. If Garrett is partially human, what could that mean for us? Who knew that was even possible?

My light is temporarily blocked by a passing shadow, and I turn to open the door quickly. Matt jumps as my action startles him and he freezes, his finger hovering over the intercom button. I give him a stern look, step outside, and close the door behind me.

He relaxes. "Em, I..."

"Wait." I stop him before he can say anymore. I cross my arms and take a step forward, looking up and down the sidewalk to make sure he came alone.

Matt sighs. "He's not here."

I turn to face him, raise my eyebrows, and snap, "At least you listened to one thing I said."

He runs his hand through his hair. "I just want to make things right. This is killing me."

I take a moment to really look at him, and he does look worn. His usually styled hair falls flat against his head, his eyes are red from lack of sleep, and his clothes are wrinkled and unkempt. Geez, it hasn't even been 24 hours.

"Matt, I only contacted you so you wouldn't worry. Not to make you come out here."

"Shel can't avoid me if I'm here and neither can you," he says and puts his hands on his hips. "I feel terrible, and I deserve a chance to explain, to apologize. Is she awake?"

"She's sound asleep and has no idea you're here. Do you know how much trouble I'm going to be in when she finds out?"

"I won't tell," he says, trying to look innocent. "We can pretend like I took a chance that she was here and just showed up."

"Fine." I pull my keys from my pocket and unlock the front door. I step inside and warn him, "This may not be pretty. Are you prepared?"

He grimaces. "As much as I'll ever be."

"Give me a minute and then press the intercom," I tell him. "It'll probably wake her and she'll be none the wiser."

"Got it. And thanks."

I give him a sarcastic smile and close the door. I head to my apartment and enter as quietly as possible. I creep over to Shel, and she's still asleep on the floor. I barely take two steps away from her when the intercom buzzes, making me jump. Impatient much?

Shel stirs, but doesn't open her eyes. I pick up LB, who has left the cozy comfort of Shel's side, and head to let Matt in, leaving my apartment door open. When we return, Shel is sitting up and rubbing her eyes. She takes one look at us, blinks to focus, and then opens her mouth. "What the hell?"

"It's not Emma's fault," Matt rushes to defend me. "I figured you would be here."

Shel throws off the blanket and gets to her feet. "What part of my *not* answering your calls didn't you understand?"

"I needed to see you. I was worried." He looks genuinely concerned, as if he thought Shel might have fled the country.

"I'm a big girl. I'm fine. Now leave."

"Shel..." he pleads.

"I'm serious!" she shouts.

I hate to see them fight, especially when it's over something to do with me. I speak up. "Guys, stop! I'm the one who should be mad, not you."

They turn around.

"This is between Dane and me." I put LB down and give Matt a hard look. "Although, it would've been nice to have had some warning."

Matt grimaces. "Dane is my friend –"

"So is Emma!" Shel snaps.

Matt closes his eyes then opens them slowly. He takes a deep breath. "When he told me he was starting to have feelings for you, I told him he had to tell you. Demanded it, actually." He glances at Shel then back to me. "He assured me that he was going to break things off with Teags; he said he didn't love her anymore. Said maybe he never did."

"Teags?" I ask. My mind flashes back to the day of my fight with Dane, when I was packing up to move to Western. When he told Matt, *I'm headed to the airport. Teags will be here in a few hours.*

"We've been calling her that since high school," Matt says. "Em, the girl has been gone forever. I was surprised to hear that she was finally coming home. Then you and Dane stopped speaking to each other, and I thought bringing it up now wouldn't do any good. It's really not my place if you two aren't together."

I stare at him in silence, digesting what he has said.

"How did you find out anyway?" he asks.

Shel and I make eye contact and I nod, giving her the go ahead to explain. "She got a newspaper article in the mail, a spotlight piece on Teagan about her trip. The end of it talked about the engagement."

Matt looks at me, confused. "Who sent you that?"

"I have no idea."

Matt takes a few steps toward me. "Em, Dane is wrecked over this. He feels horrible that you didn't hear about it from him personally. You should really talk to him."

"Ah, not gonna happen," I say adamantly. "He basically cheated on her with me. Besides, he'll be fine. His woman is home to take care of him now."

Matt lets out a sharp laugh.

"What? Is there trouble in paradise?"

"Teagan isn't exactly the maternal, caring type."

"What are you trying to say?" Shel asks.

"That she's a raging bitch," Matt says matter-of-factly. "She always has been. I've never liked her."

I can't help but smile as images from the show *Bridezillas* flash through my mind. "Well, I guess that will make for an interesting wedding."

Matt shakes his head. "Who says there's going to be a wedding?"

Chapter 10

By early evening, I'm sitting cross-legged on my bed, finishing an assignment for Communications in Business. On the floor, LB plays with the discarded edges of my notebook paper as I brainstorm ways to differentiate between the advantages and disadvantages of non-verbal communication. It's not a riveting topic.

This afternoon, Matt and Shel left on better terms. Shel was still a little salty, but I'm not sure if her mood was an act or not. She may still be doing that whole "Matt needs to be trained" thing. Matt repeatedly apologized over breakfast, after we decided to go out to eat instead of consuming the leftovers of our junk food picnic. There was a lot of eye rolling on Shel's part, especially when Matt refused to elaborate on his statement regarding Dane's possible wedding. He said it wasn't his place to discuss Dane's business and that it would be best if I called Dane to let him explain what's going on. I know what he's doing; he's trying to bait me into speaking to him again. Well, I'm not going to fall for it. I have too many conflicting feelings when it comes to Dane; now is as good a time as any to cut off any and all contact. I'll stay off that emotional rollercoaster, thank you very much.

Suddenly, I hear this horrid gurgling noise coming from beside my bed. I throw myself over to the edge to witness LB throwing up on the floor.

"LB!" I exclaim with worry as I sit there, stunned. She finishes retching, backs up a few steps, and starts to clean herself as if nothing happened. I bend over the bed further to examine her vomit pile and it appears she decided to eat the paper remnants instead of just play with them.

"Really?" I scold her, annoyed.

She stops washing to look at me innocently.

"I thought you were sick," I grumble as I slide off the bed to find something to clean up the mess. I return with a damp dish rag and some paper towel from the kitchen and set to taking care of the grossness. LB apologetically rubs against me.

"No more paper for you," I tell her and pick up the last bits from the floor, the ones she didn't eat. "Let's stick to pet store toys from here on out."

After I discard everything, I decide to turn on some music while I finish my homework. I plug my phone into the dock in my room and shuffle my way through my favorite playlist. I select Maroon 5's "Payphone" and hum along, attempting to complete my dull assignment.

Halfway through the song I hear laughter. Female laughter. I pause to listen, but don't hear it again. I shake it off and continue writing; it was probably in the song and I never noticed it before. A minute later, I hear it again. What the heck? I lean over and turn down the music, listening for the mysterious laughter sound. I wonder if Samantha and Todd are being overly loud upstairs.

Movement in my peripheral vision catches my attention, and I turn to see James taking form on the opposite side of the room. I start to get up off the bed to greet him, but then stop as I realize he is with other people. People I've never met before.

"Hi," he smiles broadly and walks around my bed to be closer to me. His guests follow. "I wanted to introduce you to some friends."

I rearrange my face to offer a smile at the two women James has brought with him. One woman is petite, with straight, shoulder-length, fiery red hair, and a dash of freckles. Her eyes are an odd shade of brown, almost caramel, and she wears a soft yellow peasant blouse and embroidered bell-bottom jeans. She can't be much older than sixteen. The other woman is tall, almost as tall as James' 5'11 inch frame, with striking blue eyes that remind me of the Mediterranean. Her dark brown hair falls in shiny waves to her lower back, and she wears a cream colored sundress that falls just above the knee, the style showing off her toned arms and legs. The color complements her sun-kissed skin tone, and I notice she's wearing cowboy boots as well.

"This is Jenna," James nods to his left indicating the red-haired girl. "And this is Meg," he nods and smiles to the woman standing at his right.

Jenna twists her fingers together nervously as Meg confidently steps forward and extends her hand. "It's a pleasure to meet you," she says with a slight southern twang.

I tentatively take her hand to shake it, standing as I do. She feels just as cold as James, but the consistency of her hand somehow feels more solid. "It's nice to meet you too," I say quietly, somewhat stunned that I am meeting yet another Guardian. Meg releases my hand and steps back, flipping her long hair over one shoulder and revealing a perfect white smile. Geez, could she get any prettier? I suddenly feel self-conscious in my sweatpants and old Muse t-shirt.

Meg glances at Jenna and nods toward me. "Um, hi," the girl says shyly.

I give her a genuine smile, hoping to make her feel more comfortable.

"These two were on their way to check in with Garrett," James says. "I was headed to see you, so we came together."

"Oh," I say, for a lack of anything better.

"He was pretty anxious to get here," Meg says with a laugh. "We won't keep you." She steps around James and nudges Jenna's arm. She looks back to flash us another amazing smile. "See y'all."

I say "okay" lamely, and James gives them a small wave as they turn together and walk through my bedroom wall. I'm sure I look dumbfounded. When I feel his cool arms wrap around my waist, I snap to attention.

"What is it?" James asks.

"I'm never going to get used to that."

He leans in to me. "Walking through walls is no big deal."

"Not that," I say and then correct myself. "Well, yes that, but what I meant was other people appearing in my personal space." I give him a stern look. "If you're going to bring company by could you at least warn me? I look like crap."

He grins. "You never look like crap."

I look down at my comfy ensemble and then back at him. "All of you look really nice," I say, pouting. "Meg is gorgeous and Jenna is super cute. Thomas is all business-like. What happens when you die? Does everyone get some sort of after-life makeover?"

James laughs. "We're stuck with what we're buried in, Em. Of course we'd have on nice clothes."

I give James a once-over, raising my eyebrows. "Your mother allowed you to be buried in a polo and jeans?" I have a hard time believing this. His mother is so....uppity.

"Actually," he smiles, "she wanted me in a suit. My dad wanted me in my hockey jersey. They compromised and went with what you see here."

I gape at him. I knew he checked in with his parents from time to time, but I didn't know it had started so soon after the accident. His casket was closed; I never saw...I swallow. I despise thinking of that day. The day of my meltdown, the day it hit me that James was gone forever.

"Hey," he says softly, concerned.

Our bond must give away my emotions, so I shake them away. I step back and tip my head, assessing his outfit in further detail. "Well, I'm glad your mother didn't get her way," I say appreciation. "You've never been a suit kind of guy. Besides, all those layers would have covered up this." I reach out with one hand and touch his chest, running my fingers over his much more prominent pectorals. "Have you been working out?" I ask, engrossed.

He inhales sharply. "No."

My eyes follow my fingertips as I trail them slowly down his side. "Then what's going on?"

"It's a side effect."

My fingers travel across his now defined abdominal muscles and up the opposite side of his body. "Of what?"

"My strength as a Guardian."

My hand lands back where it started and I meet his blue eyes. "How strong will you get?"

His hands land on my hips and he pulls me to him. "Apparently not strong enough."

His mouth meets mine and moves against me insistently, frigidly. I expect him to stop abruptly, like the last time we kissed this way, but he doesn't. I can't stop my pulse from racing. He puts pressure on my hips and turns me, pressing me back. My leg hits the bed, and I tense up so I won't fall. He feels my reaction and moves his hands to my waist to steady me, his mouth disappearing from mine. It reappears beneath my ear and leisurely travels down my throat while his hands slide from my waist around to my backside. All of my nerves jump to attention.

"I thought you said this wasn't a good idea," I breathe.

"It's not," he says against my neck.

He leans into me and pushes me back, forcing me to reach out and brace myself against the bed. I try to do this gracefully, but I end up falling right on top of my textbook and notes. The binding of the book slams against my back. "Ow!"

James releases me suddenly. "What happened?"

I roll onto my front. "I landed on my book." I start to laugh, then whine, "That hurt." Only I would do something this idiotic.

"Where'd you land on it?" he asks.

I reach around and point to the middle of my back. "Right there, on my spine."

He lifts my shirt and reaches beneath it, pressing his cool hand against my skin. "Right here?"

"Yes." I swallow. "What are you doing?"

"No need for an ice pack with me around." I can hear the smile in his voice.

I try to look over my shoulder, eyebrows raised. "Are you sure that's your only motive?"

He laughs and then sighs. "I miss you."

"I'm right here."

"No. I mean I *miss* you," he says, emphasizing his utterance of miss, so I pick up on his innuendo.

I move through his hand and roll over on to my back, propping myself on my elbows. I look at him quizzically.

He gives me half a smile. "Do you have a question?"

I sit up. "You're getting stronger."

He nods.

"You feel different than you did before, and Meg's hand felt even more solid than yours." I tip my head. "What else is changing? How far could you have taken this?" I gesture between us.

James gives me a resigned sigh. "Unfortunately, not far enough." He gathers my books from the bed, sets them on the floor, and sits down beside me. "You know we can't...I can't..."

"You've said that before." I twist my body and lean over to kiss his cheek. "So why are you acting like this?"

"Old habits die hard, I guess." He gives me a guilty smile.

I rub my hand reassuringly against his back. "You're going to get into trouble," I remind him and then move to the head of my bed, so we can lie down together. I curl myself into him and change the subject. "Will you feel more solid eventually, like Meg?"

"The way Meg feels is the most 'solid' I'll get," James says. "We reach our full form in about six months, but Meg's been a Guardian for nearly forty years."

I look at him, impressed. "She ages well," I joke. "Is there a beach in the Intermediate?"

His brow furrows. "What do you mean?"

"Meg has a nice tan. She must lay out."

James stifles a laugh. "No, there's no sunbathing in the Intermediate. There are beaches, though, when The Allegiant feel like recreating them."

"Huh?" I ask, perplexed.

"The Allegiant decide what each day will look like," James explains. "Yesterday, the landscape was Paris at night, complete with a faux Eiffel Tower, bistro chairs, and gas street lamps. The day before that was a random spring meadow, dotted with lilacs and tulips. I sat beneath a weeping willow tree."

"Really?"

He nods. "I've walked along the edge of a recreated Grand Canyon and wandered through mossy forests. Why? What did you think it looked like?"

I shrug. "Bright, with fluffy white clouds."

He smiles. "No; there's no fluffy white clouds."

LB decides to join us, jumping up on to the bed at our feet. We watch her as she lazily makes her way between us. She finds a comfortable spot and curls against my belly. James scratches behind her ears and she purrs loudly.

"So, how's Shel?" he asks, moving his hand to scratch under her chin.

"Better," I say. "Matt showed up and they talked. She still seemed a bit testy when they left, but knowing Shel she'll get over it soon enough."

"What were they fighting about?"

I groan. "Dane."

James stops petting LB. "Huh?"

I figure it's okay to tell James about Matt's secrecy since it doesn't upset me that much anymore. "Matt knew Dane was engaged and he didn't bother to share the information. Shel was upset because she thought he should have told me."

James' face twists. "Yeah. I agree."

"He was under the impression that Dane was breaking it off."

"Did he break it off?"

"Who knows?" I say and shift my weight. "It doesn't matter."

James gives me a knowing look, and I decide not to talk about Dane anymore. "Tell me what happened last night," I ask. "Did you meet that Joss person?"

He nods. "I think you would like her. She's older, like Thomas. Her real name is Joslyn, but everyone calls her Joss."

"And?" I press.

"Thomas asked what she heard from Meg, but then took the opportunity to introduce me to her as well and get the information from the source."

"Wait." I'm confused. "How is it that you don't already know these people?"

James smiles. "Everyone has a Guardian remember? The Intermediate has just as many Guardians as there are people on the planet."

"Sounds crowded."

"Not any more so than here." He moves to prop himself on his elbow and his eyes light up. "This group of us, we have to stay scattered. Talk discreetly and meet in different locations. A large group continually disappearing together would be noticed."

"And that would be bad, right?"

James gets more animated as he speaks. "If The Allegiant find out what Garrett's done and discover who's protecting him, they have ways of making us talk. They will want to know where he is and will try to stop him before he's completely Reborn. We'll all be punished."

I prop myself up to meet his eyes. "So what do you have to do?"

"Keep Garrett hidden. Quell any rumors and keep him updated, in case he needs to relocate. The more time goes on, the more it will be noticed that Garrett is missing. Guardians just don't up and disappear forever."

"Keep him hidden for how long?" I ask.

"About six months."

"Huh," I say, as my mind turns over what he has shared. "Six months to become a full Guardian and six months to undo it." I meet his eyes and whisper, "Do you know how it's done?"

James frowns and shakes his head. "Garrett won't share the method. No one knows except him and his brother. He doesn't want us revealing anything in case we're questioned."

"Garrett has a brother?" I ask, surprised.

James nods. "I haven't met him yet, but I will soon."

"Wow." I lie back down. "This is just...it's just crazy."

James leans over me and he regards me with a smirk.

"What?" I ask. "You're really enjoying this covert operation, aren't you?"

"Damn right." He breaks into a grin.

"Of course you are," I grimace. "Don't get caught. It worries me."

He moves closer. "I wouldn't think of it," he says and kisses my forehead. When he leans back he's smiling like a little kid who just got away with stealing a cookie before dinner.

"Why are you so happy? You haven't been this relaxed since you came back."

"Because," he leans in to me again, "if Garrett succeeds, I plan on being human again, too."

When Garrett didn't show up for Ethics on either Tuesday or Thursday, I was concerned. When he didn't show up for our tutoring session on Friday, I was annoyed. Just because I know what's going on doesn't mean I still don't need help with my Stats homework. It would have been comforting to see him in our regular setting. I haven't had a chance to speak with him one on one since last week and, for some reason, it bothers me. Maybe I'm just worried that if I don't see him something terrible has happened; James can only check in with me so often. I do want Garrett to succeed and for purely selfish reasons. There is a way for James to come back to me – really come back to me. We need this to work for us.

It's Saturday afternoon and the fall weather has officially arrived. I know I have a soft, comfy cardigan somewhere and, as I rifle through my closet, I come across the household items I purchased for Garrett. I'd forgotten about the bags because I moved them out of the way when Shel was here, to make room for our campsite picnic. I smile to myself. I just found an excuse to stop by my neighbor's apartment, to make sure everything is okay, without appearing nosy.

After finding my sweater, I knock on Garrett's door with the bags in my hands. I hope he's home. I haven't seen James in a couple of days and knowing everything is moving along as planned would be a comfort right now.

The door cracks open and turquoise eyes appear. "Yes?" Garrett realizes it's me and opens the door wider. "Oh, hi Emma."

I raise my eyebrows. "You forgot our tutoring session yesterday."

He presses the palm of his hand against his forehead. "I completely forgot. I'm so sorry." He steps back and fully opens the door. I walk inside, and he shuts the door behind me. "Did you bring your book? I have time to go over some things now if you want."

"No." I hold up the bags. "I just came by to give you this." *And make sure you're still around,* I think.

"What is it?"

I set the bags down by my feet. "The things I bought for you before the bar incident."

Garrett smiles. "I remember. The stuff that made you sing."

My face flushes in embarrassment. "Right. Remind me never again to drink anything with tequila in it." I open the first bag. "Okay. So I got you a comforter for your bed, a shower curtain, and some hangers." I open the second bag. "And some dishes, some bathroom towels, and this." I pull out the oven mitt and laugh. "You'll need this eventually. You can't grab hot pans with your bare hands forever."

He steps forward and takes the oven mitt from me. "Thanks," he says and fondly looks at the mitt. "When you're a Guardian for 68 years you tend to forget a lot of human things."

I try not to look surprised. "Sixty-eight years?"

"And 45 days," he adds.

I frown. "You hated it that much?"

He gives me half a smile. "I didn't use to." He backs up a few steps and rests against the arm of my old loveseat. "But when certain things pass you by, things you were counting on..." he hesitates. "Let's just say it's easy to become disenchanted. Being bound for eternity starts to feel a little...claustrophobic."

I think I understand. Garrett's love chose not to release him. "Who was she?" I quietly ask.

Garrett pauses for a moment and then looks down, turning the oven mitt over in his hands. "She was my everything," he says softly. "I didn't think twice when I was offered the Choice."

"The choice to become a Guardian?"

Garrett looks up and nods. "There was no way I could refuse the chance to stay in her life. Especially when I left the way I did."

My face fills with sympathy. "What was her name?"

"Amelia," he says, a small smile flickering across his lips.

"She sounds beautiful."

Garrett breaks out into a grin, and his turquoise eyes seem to glow brighter. "Oh, she was," he says and adjusts his weight on the arm rest as if physically energized by the memory of her. "And she knew it too." He gestures for me to take a seat, and I do. I want to hear this story.

"How'd you meet?" I ask.

"On the street," he laughs, remembering. "She was actually seeing my brother at the time, but I hadn't met her yet. I was in town running some errands for my grandmother, walking down the sidewalk, and out of nowhere comes this feisty brunette." He shakes his head. "She was headed right for me with this murderous expression. I had no idea who she was."

I imagine Garrett standing in a sea of people on a sidewalk and the crowd parting as Amelia strides toward him. I can see him glancing behind himself, perplexed, wondering who she's headed for. The idea makes me smile.

"She marched right up to my chest, pointed her tiny little finger in my face, and ripped right into me in front of everyone. She started accusing me of standing her up to go out with some other girl named Linda." Garrett shrugs. "I didn't even know a Linda!"

I laugh.

"Turns out she'd mistaken me for my brother, thought I was Jack," he chuckles. "He did have quite a reputation with the girls."

"She thought you were your brother? You two were...?"

"Twins," Garrett says, finishing my sentence. "It caused us, well, me, quite a few problems in my time among the living."

I smile. "Then what happened?"

"She came to her senses and decided I was the better of the two brothers," he jokes. "We were together for almost two years. Lived and breathed one another." He pauses. "Then Pearl Harbor was bombed, and Jack and I enlisted."

My face falls. "I'm sure she wasn't too pleased with that."

"She wasn't," he says and stands, tossing the oven mitt onto the coffee table. "We fought about it. But it was the thing to do; patriotism was running wild and I was seventeen. The next thing I knew I was at Fort Bragg and then deployed."

My chest begins to ache as I stare at him. I'm certain I know how this story ends.

"Before I left, I'd promised to marry her," Garrett sighs. "But I didn't have enough money for a ring..." he trails off, and his expression suddenly hardens. "It wouldn't have mattered. Omaha Beach ended any real future for us."

Tears jump behind my eyes as I imagine how horrible that must that have been. "What about your brother?"

Garrett gives me a distant look. "He died fighting right alongside me. We didn't even make it halfway up the beach." Suddenly, he smirks. "Over-achiever."

I don't know if he's talking to himself or to me.

"He just had to be first, thought he could take out the Germans single-handedly."

I force a smile. "And you had to be by his side, right?"

He focuses on my face. "Yeah, like an idiot, following my older brother."

"Older?"

"By three whole minutes," he smiles.

I return his smile, but it quickly fades. "I'm so sorry."

"Don't be." He returns to sit on the couch. "I have a chance at another future now."

I nod and try to blink away the few tears that sit in my eyes. "Do you think you'll always love her? Amelia?"

"I know I will," he says matter-of-factly. "She'll always be a part of me. I watched over her until she passed. I witnessed her successes and her failures, her loves and her losses. Even at nearly eighty years old she still held my heart." He sighs. "But she didn't choose me. And now it's time to live for myself."

I can sympathize with how he must feel, spending years waiting for your soul mate to join you only to be rejected in the end. Suddenly, understanding hits me like a ton of bricks. "That's why, isn't it?"

"I'm sorry?"

"That's why you assigned me. To James. You didn't want what happened to you to happen to him."

Garrett eyes me warily. "In part, yes."

Irritation starts to bubble in my chest. "I....You..." I try to sort out my thoughts. "Amelia didn't choose you."

"Thanks for the reminder," Garrett scoffs. He gives me a knowing look. "Just like you wouldn't have chosen James."

My mouth falls open. "You don't know that."

He tilts his head. "Don't I?"

"You have no idea what my choice would have been!" I stand and look down at him. "I'm not Amelia."

He stands to face me. "You forget that I've known you just as long as James has. I was there when you came into his life, and I was there when he left yours." He pauses. "I know about Dane."

All of a sudden my face feels hot. Is there anyone on this planet who doesn't know about my personal life? "Dane is irrelevant," I say in frustration. "I'm talking about James and me. You've made things extremely hard on him; on us. He's been beating himself up trying to stop loving me."

Garrett annoys me by crossing his arms and leaning into my personal space, as if he is a teacher about to scold a student who thinks she knows it all. "And have you ever considered that you are the one to free him of that?"

I shoot him a befuddled look.

"All a Guardian wants – needs – is for their Ward to be happy and safe. For their Ward to lead a life well-lived. Find it in yourself to move on, show him you can find happiness. The less emotional you are the easier his job will be."

I shake my head. "I can't move on from James."

"Can't you? Think about it," he says. "Moving on will allow him to perform his duty *and* allow you to have a full life."

"You just want him to stop loving me, so he won't draw attention to himself and your absence. I love him. I always will."

Garrett sighs. "And I'll always love Amelia. Emma," he shifts his tone and tenderly reaches out toward me, "seriously think about this. Don't you want James to be happy too?"

"Of course I want that."

"Look, if I were Amelia's Guardian, I could have been as close to her as possible for the rest of her life. I could have been her best friend. Instead, I ended up as a boyfriend killed in a war, no longer needed, and pining away for her for eighty years. Trust me," he says softly, "what I did was the best for both of you."

"I...it's..." I scowl. "I don't see it that way."

Garrett nods. "I think you will as time goes on."

I take a deep breath. I think it would be best if I left. I didn't come here to listen to how great it is that James is my Guardian and how much better it would be if I abandon him. Besides, what's the point if James can be human again? I start to walk around Garrett.

He reaches out and brushes my arm. "Hey. Don't go. I didn't mean to upset you."

"No, it's okay. It's just...a lot to take in." I make it to the door.

"Please don't be angry," Garrett says, following me.

I need to get out of here. "I have some other things I have to do." I nod toward the bags on the floor. "I hope you like your stuff."

He looks back at his care packages and then meets my eyes. "Thank you for thinking of me."

I try to smile and head out the door. "See you in Ethics?" I ask.

"I'll be sure to make it this week."

I nod and walk to my apartment without looking back.

Chapter 11

"Are you sure you're okay?"

A chill rocks my body from my head to my toes. I'm freezing, yet sweaty, and covered by a winter blanket. James stares at me, worried, from the other end of the couch. "It's probably a 24 hour thing," I say and pull the blanket tighter around my neck. I must look like a turtle with just my head exposed.

"Do you want me to get you something to eat?"

Oh no. Food is the last thing I want right now. I shake my head, then look at him apologetically. "I'm sorry I ruined our day together." James' visits have been sporadic, and I was looking forward to spending some time with him.

"Don't worry about that." He frowns. "Maybe you should see a doctor."

I roll my eyes. "No, I've only felt sick since this morning." Leave it to me to get some sort of flu at the beginning of October, before the really cold weather and typical flu season hits.

James gets up and crouches in front of me, resting his hand against my forehead. It feels arctic. "Whoa. Even I can feel how hot you are."

I take the opportunity to be sarcastic. "I thought you already knew how hot I was?"

He smirks. "Oh, I do. You look especially sexy wrapped in this cocoon." He looks back at my half empty glass of water. "You probably need something like Gatorade. Do you want me to see if Garrett has any?"

"Yeah, you probably should." I haven't had anything but water since I woke up this morning. I have absolutely no desire to eat or drink anything. I'm due for some more Motrin and washing it down with something other than water is probably a necessity by now.

"Okay. I'll be right back." James fades from view, not even bothering to walk out or through the door. I lie on the couch and wait, shivering, while trying to pick up in the middle of an episode of *My Fair Wedding with David Tutera*. I can't concentrate and end up just staring at the TV. I hate being sick. My eyelids start to feel heavy.

Out of nowhere I hear James' voice. "He doesn't have any."

My eyes snap open.

"But I sent him to the store for some." He walks in front of me and sits on the edge of the couch again.

"You didn't have to do that," I say.

"He said it's not a problem."

I roll on to my back from my side and stretch. I toss the blanket off and start to get up for some more pills.

"What are you doing?" James asks.

"Getting some more medicine." I slowly pull my legs over the side of the couch.

"Let me get it," he says and jumps up, taking my water glass with him. I gratefully lay back down. LB finds me and hops up, stepping on to my shoulder to put her little nose in my face. "Hey LB." She rubs her head against my chin. "I love you, too," I tell her.

James returns from the bathroom. "Here." He holds out two pills.

I prop myself into a sitting position, which makes LB jump off the couch, and take the Motrin. He hands me the glass of water, and I swallow and smile. "I like it when you take care of me."

He sits on the edge of the coffee table. "I'm your Guardian. That's my job."

His response bothers me, and I make a face. "I meant by choice not by force."

He regards me for a moment and his expression softens. "I'll always take care of you, no matter what." He takes the glass from my hands. "Maybe you should sleep some more."

I groan. I've been sleeping most of the day. I know I need it, but I'd rather stay awake while he's here. Regardless, I scoot to lie down, and he tucks the blanket around my neck again. He kisses my forehead quickly and then sits at the other end of the couch. I make it to another commercial during *My Fair Wedding* and feel myself drifting off.

"Can I change the channel?" he whispers.

I nod into the pillow, which I moved from my bed to the couch this morning, and press myself against the cushions. Not that I would tell anyone, but I'm secretly grateful I haven't yet been able to exchange Dane's birthday present for my old loveseat. It's definitely more comfortable, and it gives me another place to lie down instead of being trapped in my bed.

I'm just on the edge of sleep when I hear another voice. At first I think it's the television, until I hear James respond, "She's not feeling well."

"Aww, poor thing. I don't miss getting sick."

I pry my eyes open and squint. Meg is standing in front of James all tall, toned, and tan. She looks one hundred times healthier than me and she's been dead for years. "Hey," I croak and start to sit up.

"Oh hun, don't get up on account of me," Meg says, sounding like a southern belle. She gestures for me to lie back down. "You look positively miserable."

I ignore her and adjust my back against the pillow. "What's going on?" I ask cautiously. If Meg is visiting, something must have happened.

James gives me a reassuring glance. "I forgot I was supposed to meet with someone today. No big deal." He turns his attention to Meg. "Tell Jack I'll get with him later."

"Not an option," a man says, appearing on the other side of the room.

My mouth falls open in surprise as I take in Garrett's brother. He is absolutely identical to Garrett; the only difference is that he has brown eyes instead of turquoise. He's dressed in army fatigues, and the last name Abernathy is printed across the left side of his chest.

James stands to face him. "There's nothing to discuss."

"Doesn't matter." Jack crosses his arms and approaches the two Guardians. "We have a schedule. We stick to it." He speaks in a clipped tone, obviously irate.

I notice Meg roll her eyes.

James sighs and tosses the television remote on the coffee table. "Fine. I officially have nothing to report to you. Satisfied?"

Jack's brown eyes flit to me and then back to James. His expression hardens making me think I shouldn't be here, even if this is my apartment.

"This is where you spend your time?" he asks, seemingly irritated.

James gives him a sideways glance. "You know I'm Emma's Guardian."

Jack scowls. "That doesn't give you free license. You know the rules."

Obviously, Jack does not approve of James spending time with me. Or is he alluding to the fact that he still loves me? My hands start to feel clammy.

James stands taller. "I don't answer to you."

Jack takes another step and clenches his teeth. "I don't want this mission compromised."

"And just how is it being compromised?"

Jack's eyes dart to me again. He stares at me with contempt as he clenches his jaw. Inwardly, I cringe. What have I ever done to this man?

"Look at *me*," James says roughly, feeling my anxiety.

Jack focuses on James. "Keep it in check, Davis," he threatens. He takes a step back and then fades as quickly as he appeared.

Meg lets out a low whistle as James turns to me. "Well, that was fun."

"Not really," I say as I adjust my features to look less worried. "I take it he doesn't like me?"

"More like he doesn't like love," Meg says with a hint of a smile.

"Jack's wound pretty tight," James says and then glances at Meg. "Maybe tighter than usual?"

Meg's golden brown shoulders rise and fall with a shrug.

"You," James says as he walks toward me, reaching out to feel my forehead again, "are still really hot."

Meg giggles.

I can't help myself, and I shoot her an annoyed look. Is she laughing at the irony in that statement? I normally don't look this terrible. Wait. The last time she saw me I was in sweats and a t-shirt. I sigh.

"Lie down and let the medicine work," James says.

"Yes, sir," I say sardonically. "You know, I'd be asleep by now if your friends would stop dropping by." Whoops. That came out a little harsher than I intended.

James pauses, puzzled by my uncharacteristically bitter tone.

"I'm sorry," I say quickly and give them both a remorseful glance with my haggard green eyes. "I'm just tired and I feel gross and Jack was angry..."

"It's all right, hun," Meg says and steps beside James, so they're both hovering over me. "I'd be ornery too, if I were you." She flashes her perfect, dazzling smile.

Man, she's irritating me today. It must be the flu. I shift myself to lie down as James tucks the blanket around me again. "I'm sorry," I mouth. He smiles.

When he stands, Meg turns to him. "So, when will you be back?" she asks.

"Depends. I want to make sure Emma is feeling better before I go."

Meg glances from James to me. "Do you mind if I stay? My Ward's been pretty easy going and I haven't watched TV in *years*." She looks excited, like she's just been told fairies exist.

"Um..." I really want to tell her no.

"We'll be really quiet," she nods innocently, "and I'll get you whatever you need."

What I need is time with James, I think. But then, what are we really going to do anyway? I'll be sleeping while he watches me. How exciting for him. "Sure," I concede. "Whatever you want."

"Thank you!" she says enthusiastically, her southern accent growing thicker in her excitement. She turns to pick up the television remote and hands it to James. "Show me how this works," she drawls.

James laughs. "When were you born again?"

"1950. Now show me how it works."

Meg and James move opposite me, to stand directly in front of the television. James launches into his remote tutorial. "Now this particular set is old, but..."

I close my eyes and try to block them out. It would be amazing if I could fall asleep instantaneously. I consider moving to my bedroom, but then decide against it. This is my place, damn it, and if I want to be sick on my couch I will.

Eventually, I fade into a restless sleep. I'm brought back to consciousness a few times, by a word or a laugh, the loud sound followed by shushing. When the volume returns to a whisper, I fall back to sleep only to be woken again. By the fifth time, I'm over it. It's maddening.

"Guys!" My eyes snap open and I prop myself up. I find James seated at the opposite end of the couch with Meg leaning against the arm rest, her hand casually resting against his arm. My eyes narrow and I wish I had the energy to get up and knock it away. "I. Can't. Sleep." I enunciate each word.

Meg pulls her hand back and stands. "She's right." She looks at James with remorse. "We're not being very polite."

"You think?" I snap.

She looks at me. "I'm sorry, Emma."

"I'm sorry, too," James says, his eyes registering my feelings. He's knows I'm upset.

I've really had enough of both of them, which I hate to say because I treasure all of my time with James. But seriously? "Why don't you two just go," I say and pound my pillow, fluffing it. "Check on me later. Garrett should be back any time with the Gatorade." I flop back down.

James gets up and stands over me. "You really want me to go?"

"Yes. Please." I close my eyes in reaction to what I've said and then open them again. "You know what I mean. I'm just getting more and more irritated the worse I feel. Please, just go for now. Check on me tomorrow; I'm sure I'll feel better by morning."

James hesitates. "You're sure?"

"No," Meg steps in. "I'll go. You stay."

"Ugh!" I pick up the pillow and put it over my head to block them out. Why don't we stand around and argue about it? That will solve everything!

"I'll see y'all later," I hear Meg say, her voice muffled by the pillowcase. I wait a moment and then pull my head out from under the fabric. James is looking at me, pained. I sigh. "What?"

"You haven't been this angry in a while."

"I feel like crap."

He kneels down, so his eyes are level with mine. "I know. I'll stay."

Really, I just want to sleep. I look at him sincerely. "No. Go do something productive with your time. I'll be fine. You'll know if I need you, right?"

He nods and then gives in. "I guess I should be seen, seeing as how Jack was all bent out of shape."

I pick my head up and lean forward, giving him a soft kiss on the forehead. "That's a good Guardian."

He smirks.

I lay my head down. "Promise me I'll see you tomorrow," I say as I close my eyes.

"I promise," he says and gives me a quick kiss goodbye.

Incessant ringing wakes me. When I open my eyes, I know I've been asleep for a while because it is pitch black in my apartment; no light shines through the windows. My cell is lit up on the table, going off like crazy. I lazily scoot to the edge of the couch and reach for it, squinting when I read the screen. It's after nine o'clock and Shel is calling.

"Hello?" I answer, my voice rough.

"Em?"

"Yeah."

"What's wrong with your voice?"

I rub my eye with the heel of my hand. "I caught some sort of flu bug. I feel like road kill."

"Aw. I'm sorry; I won't keep you. I just wanted to let you know that Dane's birthday is this Saturday, the sixth, and he's invited Matt and me to a party."

Fantastic, I think sarcastically. What do I care?

"You're invited too, but I didn't think you would come and neither did Dane, really. I wanted to let you know in case..."

Her rambling becomes incoherent to me. Hell would have to freeze over before I would go to Dane's birthday party. Has he lost his mind?

"Em?"

"Hmm?"

"Will you be mad?"

"Mad about what?"

"I just asked you if you would be mad if I went and you didn't say anything."

I let out an exasperated sigh. "No, Shel. I don't care if you go to Dane's party."

She sounds relieved. "Okay. I really don't want to go but Matt's going, and I have no other choice if I want to see him this weekend."

Yeah, yeah, I think to myself.

"Plus," Shel's voice gets quiet, "I can do a little recon."

As much as I hate to admit it, I am curious about little Ms. Teagan Meyer. "You have fun with that," I say. I didn't tell her to find out anything...but I didn't tell her not to either.

"I'll let you go, so you can relax," Shel says sympathetically. "I hope you feel better soon."

"Me, too. Talk to you later."

"'Kay. Bye."

I end the call and toss the phone aside. Yawning and stretching, I look around in the darkness. I eye the door and wonder where Garrett is with the Gatorade. I pull myself off the couch and shuffle my way to use the restroom. What a waste of a day.

Once in the bathroom, I decide to take a shower because my skin feels sticky. Maybe I can wash away this sickness. I stand under the warm water, allowing it to beat against my neck, shoulders, and back. It feels comforting. When my skin is sufficiently pruny, I get out and change into a fresh t-shirt and sleep shorts, deciding to spend the rest of the night in my bed. The sheets feel cool against my warm skin, and I snuggle into them, allowing my mind to fade and drift. You would think there would be no more sleep to be had, but I slip into unconsciousness again. This time is different though, as my mind weaves a dream out of the day's events.

"You look beautiful."

The skin of my exposed neck tingles as I hear Dane's voice behind me. I turn and feel something brush against me, low on my legs, and look down to see I'm wearing a floor-length coral gown. Its strapless, with an empire waist, and it's covered with a flowered lace overlay. Delicate rose appliqués of the same coral color are scattered over the bodice and throughout the full skirt. I place my hands on my hips and swing from side to side for a moment. The soft chiffon moves with me, back and forth, mimicking the motion of a bell. I've never worn anything so elegant.

I lift my eyes to find Dane walking toward me. He wears a black tuxedo vest over a white dress shirt, which is tucked meticulously into a pair of black pants. The collar of his shirt and the next few buttons are undone, and he carries a black necktie in one hand and his tuxedo jacket in the other. "Can you help me with this?" he asks, grinning.

I smile as he approaches me, and I reach out toward him. When he's within arm's length, I set my hands against his shirt and scrutinize the small clear buttons. No wonder he's having a hard time. I fasten the first, the second, and the third, making my way up his chest. When I reach his collar, the shirt is tight around his neck, and I have to wrestle with it a bit. I press my body against his as I concentrate on pushing the button through the fabric without choking him. He sets his hands on my waist to steady me, still clutching the tie and his jacket, and my heart begins to pound. Even with the added items between us, I still feel like he's touching my bare skin.

When I get the button fastened and lean back, he releases me and hooks one finger over his collar, trying to stretch and loosen it. He hands me the tie, and I loop it around his neck, tying it into a Windsor knot. "Thank you for doing this," he says as I diligently work.

I smile into his chest. I don't know when I learned to tie a necktie, but I appear to be very good at it. I tighten the knot under his collar and then smooth the tie, tucking it into his vest. I step back to admire my work and to admire...well, him. His dark brown hair is perfectly styled to look carefree, his jawline hints of a five o'clock shadow, and his hazel eyes soften as they gaze at me.

He swings the jacket around his shoulders and shrugs it on, fastening the one button at the waist. The jacket fits him perfectly, like it was made specifically for him, cut to accentuate his broad shoulders and narrow waist. He turns to his right to check his attire in a floor-length mirror and make any necessary adjustments. "Teagan doesn't have many friends," he says to my reflection. "It means so much to us that you agreed to be a bridesmaid."

Over his shoulder, I catch my surprised reaction in the mirror and quickly adjust my features. I look down to avoid his eyes and find there is a boutonniere in my hand. A single coral rose and off-white calla lily are wound with ribbon. "Do you mind?" he says, appearing in front of me.

I look up and force a tiny smile, pulling the stickpin from the boutonniere and placing the flowers against his lapel. I work the pin through the fabric and the ribbon, securing it in place. I continue to look at the flowers as I step away from him, afraid to meet his eyes because tears linger behind mine.

"Em," he says my name gently, stepping forward. He places his fingers beneath my chin to lift my gaze; his fingers are hot against my skin. He searches my face and then moves his hand to touch a tendril of hair that has fallen from my messy chignon. He starts to lean in to me and I close my eyes, expecting a kiss. Instead he whispers in my ear, "You had your chance."

I quickly turn away, so he won't see the tears that fall down my face. I keep my eyes closed for few brief seconds and when I open them, I find myself standing in a large church, at the altar, in line with two other girls dressed identical to me. Looking out over the congregation, I see the pews are packed shoulder to shoulder with guests. My hands clench from nervousness, and I feel a sharp pinch against my ring finger. I pull my hand away and look down, realizing I've cut myself on a thorn from one of the roses in my bouquet.

The minister's voice booms, redirecting my attention. "I now pronounce you husband and wife. You may kiss the bride!"

My eyes fall on Dane as he and his new wife turn to face one another. I take in the sight of her back; she is overflowing in tulle, the train of her dress spilling down the steps of the altar to the floor. The same rose appliqués that are on my dress dot hers, only in white, and her shiny brown hair is artfully swept around a sparkling tiara that sits on the crown of her head. Dane leans forward and kisses her romantically, swinging her to the side and dipping her low. The entire church erupts in thunderous applause.

"Don't you just want to cry?" I hear Shel ask from beside me. I snap my head to the left, shocked to see her standing next to me in the same coral gown. She wears a beaming smile and tears of happiness roll down her cheeks.

I turn my attention to the bride and groom just in time to see Dane release her from their kiss. She rights herself, and I can see her shoulders shaking with laughter. She twists her body to grab her flowers from the first bridesmaid in line and catches my eye. I inhale sharply when I see her face. It's not Teagan. It's Meg.

My knees crumple beneath me, and I catch myself on the altar step, crushing my bouquet in the process. The wedding guests continue their rousing applause as Meg grasps Dane's hand and leads him down the stairs. They pause as a photographer jumps into the aisle to take their picture. When he moves out of the way, Meg glances over her shoulder and meets my wide-eyed stare. She is several feet away from me, but I still hear her loud and clear. "Oh hun," she says with a sickly sweet smile, "don't get up on account of me."

The guests continue to applaud the happy couple and it roars in my ears. As they descend the aisle, I hold my head in my hands. I can sense the people leaving the church to follow the newlyweds. Slowly the clapping dies down until one lone person is left, their applause bouncing off the hollow church walls. I raise my head to find James, alone in the front pew, bringing his hands together methodically as if clapping with sarcasm. He stares at me with disdain and it breaks my heart.

My eyes fly open and I spring up, breathing heavily. I look around my bedroom, trying to focus, and hear a frantic banging at the front door. Startled by the noise and my dream, I untangle myself from the sheets and scramble out of bed as fast as I can. When I head through the living room, I flip the light switch, and then throw open the door. I catch Garrett mid-knock, and he almost loses his balance.

"Emma! Good grief! I was so worried."

The light hurts my eyes and I blink rapidly. I glance at his arms and he's carrying two large bottles of red Gatorade. I step away from the door, so he can come inside.

"I stopped by twice tonight," he says, walking forward. "If you didn't answer this time I was calling an ambulance."

I give him a tired smile. "I was sleeping."

He takes the initiative and walks through my apartment and into the kitchen. I follow as he places the plastic bottles inside the refrigerator door. "You know, I had no idea what Gatorade even was," he says. He shuts the fridge. "From the looks of the label it can't be any better than my chicken noodle soup." He pauses. "How are you feeling?"

I shrug and remain mute. I have no words for today.

"Have you been crying?" he asks, moving toward me.

I feel my cheeks. They're tacky. "I had a bad dream," I say quietly.

"Come here," he says and moves past me, grabbing my hand as he does. I follow along lamely, too drained to care.

He leads me to my bedroom and then stands aside, gesturing toward the bed. I crawl in and pull the sheet over my body, pressing my head against the pillow. He leans over me. "Do you trust me?"

I nod. Of course I do.

He places his hands on my head again, like he did before on the first day of classes. "I know this isn't reiki," I mumble.

"Really?" he smirks at me. "Close your eyes."

I do as I'm told. A very tiny, very brief wave of cool air flows through my body from my head to my toes, relaxing me instantly.

"Go to sleep," Garrett says. "Dream no more."

Chapter 12

"Well, when *are* you coming home to visit?"

I stir my chicken noodle soup around the bowl with my spoon. I should head home for a weekend soon. I miss my family. "I'm not sure. When do you want me?"

"Before Thanksgiving," my mother says, her voice dripping with sarcasm. "Wait." I hear papers being shuffled in the background. "The community center is having their Halloween party for the kids in two weeks. I've been roped into helping again this year."

I roll my eyes. My mother is never roped into anything. She just can't say no.

"We need volunteers; it's a Wizard of Oz theme. What do you say?"

Hanging out with a bunch of cute little kids and my mom? I think I can swing that. "Sure. Put me down."

"Great! Now who do you want to be?"

"What do you mean?"

"Who do you want to be? All the volunteers are dressing up. Pick a character."

"I have to dress up?" I make a face. I don't own anything Wizard of Ozish. "What are my choices? Who are you going to be?"

My mom laughs. "Auntie Em."

Aw. That's fitting, although I kind of think I should be Em since I'm, well, Em.

"You don't have to decide now," my mom says. "Actually, let me get with Sophia and look at the sign-up sheet. I'll let you know what's left. A local theater group is supplying the costumes."

"That's cool," I say and take a sip off my spoon. The soup is starting to get cold. "Hey, can I call you back later? My dinner is getting cold."

"Of course," she says. "I'm glad to hear you're feeling better and eating."

I smile into the phone. My mom always wants to make sure I'm eating. "I'm almost one hundred percent."

It's been four days since the onset of the craptastic flu. By the second day, I caved and called my mom whining about my sickness. She directed me to bed, the use of cold compresses, flat Coke to settle my stomach, and the consumption of clear fluids and Jell-O. I recruited Garrett's help by asking him to pick up some items from the store. He did so and more. He made me a pot of his homemade chicken noodle soup, and he's been camped on my couch since Thursday night to make sure I'm okay. It's now Saturday, and he still sits in my living room, flipping the channels between baseball games.

"I'll talk to you soon. Love you," my mom says.

"Love you, too," I say and hang up. I carefully lift the soup bowl and carry it into the living room from the kitchen, setting it down on the coffee table.

"Was that your mom?" Garrett asks.

I nod as I sit cross-legged on the floor so I'm level with the table. "Yes. I have to pick a character from the Wizard of Oz to dress up as for a Halloween party. Who should I be?"

He tilts his head and smiles. "I was fifteen when that movie came out and so in love with Judy Garland."

I laugh then try to look serious. "I'm shocked. What would Amelia say?"

He grins. "How's that saying go? What you don't know can't hurt you?"

I smile as I chew. The soup is really good. "You know, you should open a restaurant when you're human. I know I've only tried the two soups, but I can't imagine anything you make would be bad."

"Thanks," he says and leans forward, propping his elbows on his knees. "I've actually considered it." He looks at the television for a few moments and then back at me. "I'm going to have to get a job eventually, right?"

"Aren't we all?" I say and swallow another spoonful. Suddenly, I remember that I need to pay Garrett for the things he's picked up for me. "How much money do I owe you?" I gesture with my spoon toward the soup.

"For what?"

"For the soup and all the other supplies."

He brushes me off. "You don't owe me anything."

"Yes, I do," I say adamantly. "That's not fair."

He eyes me. "You were in no condition to be running to the store. Consider it a favor."

I shake my head and get to my feet. "Let me pay you."

"It's really okay," he says. "It wasn't that much."

I pause for a moment and try to calculate in my head everything he's purchased. If you add in the ingredients for the soup it has to be at least forty dollars. I turn and walk into the kitchen to grab my wallet out of my purse.

"I know what you're doing," he half-yells to me. "I won't take your money!"

"Yes you will!" I half-yell back to him. I reach for my wallet and as I open it up, my cell chimes against the counter. I look at it.

Wish you were here.

It's from Shel. There's a picture attached, and I touch it to make it bigger. I'm greeted with smiles from both her and Matt as they pose together at Dane's party, dressed for a night out and seated at what looks like a restaurant table. Shel leans against Matt's arm and beams. They look so cute. I text back *You guys look nice* then slide my phone into my back pocket. I take two twenty dollar bills out of my wallet and head back to the living room.

"Take this." I hand the money to Garrett.

He ignores me.

"I'm serious!"

He changes the channel with the remote.

"I'll feel bad if you don't take it," I say.

He looks at me annoyed. He plucks the money from my fingers and tosses it on the table instead of putting it in his pocket.

I cross my arms. "I didn't mean literally."

"Has anybody ever told you that you're stubborn?" he asks.

My mind flashes to both James and Dane, making me sigh. "Yes."

My cell sounds again, from my jeans pocket, and I pull it out. There's another picture from Shel with the caption *Operation recon in full effect.* I tap the image and the picture grows larger, revealing a distant and crooked photo of Dane and a woman who must be Teagan. They stand side by side, just in front of a door surrounded by people. The lighting is dim, and it's not a very clear shot. I squint to make out her features.

"What's so interesting?" Garrett asks.

"Nothing, really." I close the picture and hope Shel can get a better shot. I pause. Do I really care? Unfortunately, yes. Yes I do.

I turn my attention back to the money exchange and threaten Garrett, pointing at the cash. "I'm going to find a way to make you take that."

He gives me a condescending look that says, "I'd like to see you try." I give up for now and take a seat to finish my dinner. I curl my legs to the side and set my elbow on the table. "If you're so rich, maybe I should start charging you rent." I raise my eyebrows. "You have been here for two days straight."

He smirks and then stands. "I guess I'll be going then." He takes a step toward the door.

"No!" I sit up. "I was kidding. Sit back down; I'm not fully well yet." I really have enjoyed his company. The days go by so much faster when you have someone else to talk to besides the cat. James did come back the day after I got sick, like he promised, but he only stayed for a few hours.

Garrett takes a seat, pretending to be inconvenienced, then turns to me with kind eyes. "It does get pretty lonely, doesn't it?"

I nod. Sometimes I forget that he's all alone too, on top of becoming mortal. "Is it hard?" I ask. "Becoming human?"

He pauses, thinking. "Not physically, no. I think mentally, wrapping your mind around the things you're giving up and the things you have to relearn, is the hardest part."

My cell goes off, and I pull it from my pocket. "Sorry," I apologize. I see Shel has sent another picture and the message reads *And I love him why?* The picture is of Matt, who has decided to put drink stirs up his nose. I laugh and then show Garrett the picture. "This is why you chose to become human again, isn't it?"

He chuckles. "For sure."

I take another look at Matt and shake my head, then lower the phone. "So why did you decide to do it?" I ask, intrigued.

"That's simple," he says. "For a chance to live the life that was taken from me."

I frown. "But will it be the same without...her?"

"There's more to being human than being in love," he says without hesitation. "But no, it won't be the same. She can never be replaced." He pauses. "Maybe I will find love again. Get married and have a family. Or maybe I won't. But that's the point. I have a second chance. I can make this life whatever I want it to be."

His ruminations make me smile.

"Do you want to know what I've missed the most?" he asks.

"What?"

"The taste of food." He grins. "Physically touching and actually feeling. Sleeping again. There's something to be said for the satisfied feeling of a full stomach and good night's rest."

I agree. "Those are good things. I think I would add taking hot showers to the list, too."

"Yes!" His eyes light up. "And changing clothes! Although, I'm not too fond of doing laundry." He makes a face. "I'm not very good at it. First I had to figure out the washing machine and which soap to use, and now I'm wearing pink underwear due to someone's misplaced red sock."

The image of Garrett in pale pink tightie whities nearly makes me lose the soup in my mouth through my nose. It hurts trying to contain my laughter, and I grab my sides.

Garrett pretends to be offended. "It's not *that* funny."

My cell interrupts us again, and I manage to swallow, blinking away the tears from my hysterics. I look at the screen and another picture from Shel is waiting. I open it and immediately crash from my laughter high. It's a clearer image of Teagan. How do I know it's her? Because I've seen her before. She's the same girl in the framed photo that I saw on Dane's side table, the one I saw after the incident with Mrs. Davis last summer. The same picture of him with his arm draped around a beautiful girl, a girl I thought could be a sister. I don't know how Shel took such a close photo unnoticed, but I can clearly see Teagan's long raven black hair, dark almond shaped eyes, gorgeous lashes, and full, pouty lips. She could be a model. She appears exactly as she did in the photo of her I've already seen. I guess back then Dane wasn't trying to hide anything from me. But what did he expect me to do? Ask him about the girl in the picture? I remember him giving me permission to snoop around his apartment when he left. I mentally kick myself for not taking him up on that offer.

"Tell me again what's so great about being human?" I ask Garrett quietly.

He looks at me concerned, and I show him the picture. "Dane's fiancée," I say.

He gives me a sympathetic look. "You were curious?" he asks in an effort to understand.

"I tried not to be." I close the picture and tuck my phone under my leg. "Avoiding all things Dane is easier said than done. Especially when your best friends are his friends too."

"It sounds like he may be a part of your life whether you like it or not," Garrett says wisely.

I never thought about it that way. Being friends with Matt and Shel will inevitably have me running into Dane from time to time. I won't be able to avoid him forever.

"You know," he says, "maybe Dane was meant to be in your life. Did you ever consider that?"

I roll my eyes sarcastically. *Riiiiight.* The phone chimes under my leg. "Geez!" I complain. "I'm just going to turn it off." I don't want to see any more pictures of Teagan.

I pull the phone out and, yes, there again is another image from Shel. I can tell it's not Teagan though, and reluctantly I touch the screen. A picture of Dane enlarges before me, and it's a close-up. He must be sitting down because his forearm rests against a table, and the frame is filled with his face and torso. He looks directly into the camera, wearing an apologetic expression, and he holds a small white napkin over his forearm so it's clearly in view of Shel, but not anyone else. There, in black and white, is a message just for me:

I miss you.

Chapter 13

Putting a cat in a pet carrier should not be this hard! You would think I was trying to murder her.

"C'mon LB!" I wrestle with her as she twists her body in my hands. "Do you really want to stay here alone?"

I'm attempting to leave Kalamazoo for home. Tomorrow is the Halloween party I promised to help with, and I get to dress up as a citizen of the Emerald City. I'm a little worried about it because I remember the movie costumes being a bit bizarre, but at least I didn't get stuck with Toto. All the other popular choices were taken.

LB lands a good scratch on my forearm, and I let her go. "Dang it!" She runs to hide under the bed as blood starts to slowly seep from two of the three claw marks. I groan in frustration and pull myself off the floor to find a Band Aid. I'm starting to think she will be okay here by herself for a few days.

While I apply some antiseptic to my wound, I hear three distinct thumps on the wall that separates my apartment from Garrett's. We've been communicating this way since last week, when he decided to move back to his place after I survived the flu and he dropped a stack of books against the wall. The sound was so loud I thought he was being attacked and went running over there. Turns out he was just being clumsy, but we discovered a cool way to say hi every now and again. I peel the paper from a Band Aid and press it to my skin as I walk into the kitchen. I give the wall three good thumps back which are meant to say "Hi. I'm still here." I look around the kitchen and grab two breakfast bars I left on the counter to take with me for snacks for the road. I knew I was forgetting something.

I head to my room and place the bars in my backpack, then zip it up. I have some clothes left at home, and I don't need to bring much with me other than a few toiletries and my homework – and LB. She's still hiding underneath the bed. I bend down, pull back the bed skirt, and let my eyes roam the darkness until I see hers. "Come out of there, you," I say. "Don't you want to go see Grandma and Grandpa?" Lord, if anyone heard me they would think I was insane. LB thinks I'm crazy too, because she hisses at me. She has never done that before. What a stinker!

I sit back on my heels. I need to get going, and I don't feel like forcing her out of there and making her even angrier. I look to my left and think of Garrett on the other side of the wall. I bet he would agree to feed her while I'm gone. "Looks like you might get your way LB," I say as I stand. I walk out of my apartment and over to Garrett's, grabbing his door handle and letting myself in. This is another thing we've started since having the conversation about feeling lonely. We leave our doors unlocked during the day, so we can come and go between each other's places. Of course we let one another know we're home by the thumps. It's just easier.

"Hey," I say as I enter the apartment, looking around the door. "I was wondering if..." I stop short. Garrett, Thomas, and another woman are standing in the living area. "I'm sorry," I immediately apologize. "I'll come back later."

"No, it's okay," Garrett says. He looks between me and the other Guardians. "You already know Thomas and this is Joslyn," he introduces us.

Thomas smiles his fatherly smile and raises his hand to wave. When he does, he also raises Joslyn's hand because he holds hers firmly in his. She laughs and pulls her hand away, giving me her own small wave. "Happy to meet you, Emma," she says. "You can call me Joss."

Does everyone know who I am? I feel like there must be a poster of me somewhere in the Intermediate. "Hi." I nod, embarrassed for interrupting. I look at Garrett. "I didn't know you having a meeting, so I'll just..."

"Oh, stay," Joss says and walks forward, holding her hand out to me. Her black hair is peppered with gray, and she wears it in a bun on the top of her head. She's about my height, and has on black slacks, heels, and a bright royal blue blouse with a cowl neck. Her complexion is peaches and cream which, paired with the blouse, make her gray eyes sparkle. "Let's talk while the boys conduct business."

She grasps my hand, and I allow her to lead me to my old loveseat. Thomas and Garrett resume their discussion and Joss looks at me warmly. What could she possibly want to talk to me about? I really need to get on the road.

"So," she says, patting my hand, "what are you up to today?"

I give her a confused stare. "Um...I'm going home for the weekend?" My statement sounds more like a question than a fact.

She smiles. "Do you have big plans?"

"Nooo." I look over my shoulder to send Garrett a questioning glance. He just smiles at me and continues speaking with Thomas. I turn back to Joss. "I'm helping my mom with some volunteer work."

"That's nice." She sounds genuinely excited. "What will you be doing?"

"Helping out at a Halloween party for little kids."

"Oh!" She releases my hand and places hers against her chest. "That sounds darling! I miss doing things like that."

Okay, I get it now. She misses being human. I relax and give her a smile.

"Actually, it's my grandkids that I miss," she says. "Helping them get all dressed up for Halloween."

"How many grandchildren do you have?"

"Eleven." She beams. "And one on the way."

I can't help myself and an "awww" escapes. I can't wait for my brother and Kate to get married and start having kids.

"I miss them," she sighs. "The feel of their little hugs, my refrigerator covered in artwork. I used to spoil them rotten."

"I bet."

"That's actually what drew the two of us together," Thomas pipes up, leaning over the back of the loveseat and into our conversation. "The discussions about our grandkids." He looks at Joss like a love-struck teenager, and I get the feeling if she could blush, she would.

Wait. "Are you two dating?" The question is out before I can think twice.

Joss laughs. "You could call it that," she says. "Who knew you could find the love of your life after you're no longer living?"

What? The idea never crossed my mind that Guardians could fall in love with each other.

Thomas leans forward and plants a kiss on Joss' temple. She smiles at him and then shoos him away. I'm sure I look stupefied.

She leans in to me conspiratorially. "Fat lot of good I did marrying all those husbands. No wonder none of them would release me."

I blink and rearrange my face. "How many husbands did you have?"

She shakes her head and chuckles. "Five."

"Five?"

"And none of them compared to me," Thomas boasts.

"Would you go away?" Joss teases. "We're trying to have a nice talk."

I smile at Thomas. The two of them are so cute. He listens to his woman and retreats a few steps.

"So," Joss says, "what about you and Garrett? Will you be having children?"

Whoa! Where did that question come from? "Ah, no." I blush and look at Garrett, my expression panicked.

"Joss," Garrett steps in quickly. "Emma is with James, remember?"

Joss looks between Garrett and I, puzzled. "I thought James was her Guardian?"

"He is," Garrett says. He smiles at me apologetically.

"But I thought he and..."

"Emma," Garrett interrupts her. "Did you need something?"

"Yes," I say and stand. This is the perfect opportunity to get out of this awkwardness. "LB is giving me a hard time about the carrier; I can't get her into it." I flash my forearm. "Could you feed her for me until I get back on Sunday? I don't feel like wrestling with her anymore."

"Sure. The food is...?"

"Under the kitchen cabinet. I'll feed her today; you'll just have to do it tomorrow and Sunday."

"Got it."

I start to make my way toward the door. "I'll bring my key over to you in a few minutes." I turn to say goodbye to Thomas and Joss. "I really have to get going; it's a three hour drive back home. It was nice talking with you."

"You too." Joss gives me a genuine smile. "We'll have to do it again sometime." She eyes the boys. "With just us girls."

I laugh. "Sure."

"Drive safe," Thomas says as I reach the door.

"Thanks, I will." I open the door and step outside. "I'll be back in a sec with my key," I tell Garrett.

"Sounds good."

I close the door behind me and walk to my apartment, shaking my head. That was one of the weirdest conversations I've had in awhile. Finding out Guardians can fall in love? The idea of Garrett and me together? I almost laugh out loud. He's a nice guy and all but...

I open my door and LB comes running. "Oh, now you come out," I chastise her. I bend down and pet her roughly along the sides of her body. "Don't worry. You're staying here."

Well, Auntie Em looks great. I look ridiculous.

When I arrived home on Friday, my mom hit me with the news. Someone named Mildred had to back out of the Halloween party because apparently her dog, Fluffnstuff, was ill. I couldn't stop laughing from the name. Fluffnstuff? Seriously? My dad proceeded to make a lame joke about the dog being sick because it ate some fluff...and stuff, which pushed my giggle fit to new heights. But the really funny part was that I was now bestowed the honor of dressing up as the Wicked Witch of the West. When my mother first produced the costume from my old closet, it wasn't too bad. Just a basic black dress with a black witch's hat and a broomstick. It was the green face paint, wiry wig, and prosthetic wart that made me cringe.

"You have to wear it," my mom said. "What's a Wizard of Oz party without the Wicked Witch?"

And now I stand here, behind one end of a snack table, watching all the little kids line up as far away from me as possible. I scare them and rightfully so.

I look around the community center teaming with people. They really go all out for this event. There's a DJ, several trick-or-treating stations, a bounce house, face painting, multiple games, and four refreshment tables. During a lull in the snack activity, I ask my mom to take a picture of me with my phone to send to Shel. She's going to crack up.

"This is priceless!" my mom laughs when she looks at the picture. "Send it to me, too."

I shake my head and set to messaging when I hear someone ask, "Would you like a picture of the both of you?"

My head snaps up, and I meet the eyes of the Scarecrow. Except it's not just the Scarecrow. It's Dane.

"Sure, that would be nice." My mom smiles and steps to my side, putting her arm around my waist to pose.

If my face wasn't covered with green makeup I'm positive it would be flaming red. My heart feels like it wants to beat out of my chest. What is he doing here? He holds out his hand for my phone, and I tentatively place it in his palm. His gives me a tiny smile and holds the phone up to take the picture, centering us on the screen.

"Ready?" he asks.

"Yep," my mom says, hugging my waist. I do my best to force a smile and hear the audible click as he presses the shutter.

My mother steps away from me. "Dane? Is that you?"

"Unfortunately." He lets out an embarrassed laugh. "How are you Mrs. Donohue?"

"Great!" she says. Dane is one of my mother's favorite people, seeing as how he helped take out Patrick when he attacked me last summer. She turns to me. "Did you know he was going to be volunteering tonight?"

I shake my head. My mom isn't aware that Dane and I aren't speaking.

She turns back to him. "I didn't see your name on the sign-up sheet."

"That's because I'm filling in for Teag —" He stops and his eyes dart to me. "For a friend's dad."

I avoid his stare. A little boy dressed as Batman comes to the table thirsty. I busy myself ladling him some punch.

"There you are!" a bubbly voice says. I look up to find Dorothy, aka Teagan, approach us all decked out in a blue gingham dress, ruby red slippers, and pigtails. My stomach drops. It figures she would be dressed as Dorothy and I her nemesis. "Connor, I told you to stay with the group," she says sweetly to the little boy. "Go stand over there to play the game," she directs him to a nearby beanbag toss. She stands up straight, leans in to Dane, and smiles at my mother and me. "Who are your friends?" she asks.

Dane clears his throat. "This is Mrs. Donohue and..."

I don't know what comes over me, but I have the overwhelming urge to introduce myself to Teagan. Maybe I just want to see Dane squirm, to make him pay for lying to me. "I'm Emmmma," I say as sickly sweet as I possibly can. What's that saying? Kill them with kindness? "You're Teagan, right? It's so nice to *finally* meet you! You look great." I nod, indicating her costume.

Teagan narrows her eyes at me infinitesimally. She keeps her smile plastered on her face, but I can see her body tense. "Thank you!" she says, her response equally as fake as mine. "How do you know Dane again?"

"Hasn't he mentioned me?" I ask, wide-eyed. "We spent a lot of time together over the summer."

She tilts her head reflexively and her smile wavers.

"Working at the golf course," I lean forward and clarify.

"Oh, that's right!" She looks up at Dane. "This is Matt's friend; the one you sent the furniture to."

She knows about that?

"The one you said couldn't afford to get herself anything new." She fakes sympathy for me with an exaggerated pout.

Did she just call me poor?

Dane speaks up. "No. I never said –"

"You must be mistaken," I cut him off, feeling the need to set her straight. "The furniture was a birthday gift."

Teagan forces an obnoxious laugh. "How silly of me! I must have forgotten." She smiles, but her eyes shoot daggers. "Now I remember you. Your picture on the Bay Woods website doesn't do you justice." Her look is smug as her eyes roam my body. "You look *so* much prettier in person."

Really?! She wants to call me poor *and* ugly? It's time to bring out the big guns. I maintain my sugary tone. "And you look just like your picture in Dane's apartment." I look directly at him. "You remember, right? I saw it the night you took me to your place?"

I can feel Teagan's eyes boring into me, and Dane looks slightly pale. I must have a death wish, because I add, "You know. The night you tried to kiss me for the first time?"

My eyes skip to Teagan, and she finally loses the smile. Her jaw flexes, and she moves her right hand to her left, noticeably playing with her engagement ring. Hmmm. I've found a way to get under her skin. "I don't remember it being there after that, though," I continue, feigning confusion. "But then again, we didn't spend much time in the living room."

I can feel both Dane and my mother staring at me in shock. Teagan's snobbery has unleashed something inside of me that I can't control and, little do they know, there is so much more that I could reveal.

"Emma," my mom politely interrupts our tense conversation. "We really should get back to..."

"Yes," Teagan releases me from her death stare. "We should be getting back to the kids." She flashes my mom a smile and obnoxiously loops her arm through Dane's. "It was nice to meet you, Mrs. Donohue," she says, intentionally neglecting to tell me the same.

My mother nods although I can tell she's not impressed. I glance at Dane before he's led away, and he looks amused, almost like he approves – like he's just seen the most entertaining thing ever. It irritates the hell out of me.

"That was quite the performance," my mom says after they've gone. "I didn't know you could be so dramatic. Care to let me in on what's going on?"

I sigh, finally relaxing my shoulders. "Dane and I...we're not friends anymore."

"Apparently."

"We got close..."

"Hence the kissing?" She raises her eyebrows at me.

I blush under my green skin. "Turns out he was engaged the whole time. I just found out."

"Engaged? To that sassy thing?" My mom blanches. She steps over to me and raises her hand. "Give me five."

I slap her hand. "For what?"

"The way you handled that..." she drifts off and wraps her arm around my shoulder. "That's my girl."

After the party ends I head to the restroom to change out of my costume, removing my wig and my wart, but leaving the green face. It's too complicated to remove with paper towel; I'll just deal with it when I get home. I pull on my comfy jeans and sweatshirt then carefully pack the black dress and accessories. Slinging my bag over my shoulder, I make my way to find my mother and help with the clean-up. I find her standing behind our snack station, studying her phone with a smirk.

"What's up?" I ask.

She looks at me. "Are you missing something?"

I frown. "I don't think so." I look behind me to make sure I didn't drop anything.

"Your phone perhaps?"

Awww, crap. I turn to her slowly. "Dane still has it."

She nods and hands her cell to me so I can read the message.

Mrs. Donohue please ask Emma to meet me in the parking lot. I have her phone. Thanks.

I pull out the best wounded puppy dog expression I can muster. "Can you go get it for me?" I beg.

She laughs. "You know that only works on your father." She plucks the phone out of my hands. "You can do it. Now go."

My face twists. "You are the worst mother ever," I say dramatically, slamming my bag down on the table.

She smiles sweetly at me and starts to pack up the cups we didn't use. I sigh and start to make my way to the front door, wishing I could just let him keep the damn thing. If I didn't have to pay to replace it and lose all my contacts and pictures...

"Emma?"

I turn. "What?"

"You might want to take that paint off your face."

Ugh! I change direction and march back toward the restroom.

"I'm not such a terrible mother now, am I?" my mom calls behind me.

I push open the bathroom door and head for the paper towel. I yank a bunch from the dispenser and run the towels under hot water. I start to wipe my face, but the green makeup is dried on and giving me a hard time. It takes several wipes in one spot just to see the skin underneath. I abandon the paper towel for a moment, squirt some soap into my hands, and rub my entire face. This turns my fingers green, too. At home I applied the makeup with a sponge, so I didn't have this irritating problem! I move to grab some fresh towels, run them under the hot water, and start wiping again. The soap helps, taking off the majority of the paint, but not all of it. By the third wipe down, my skin is starting to feel raw from the paper towel, yet my face still carries a slight green hue. *Oh well*, I think, and toss the towels in the trash. *So you're green. Get over it.* I glance at my hair, which is still pulled back from being tucked under the wig, and I remove the pins and release my ponytail. I quickly run my fingers through it. There. Maybe that will hide some of my pea green skin.

I make my way to the front doors of the community center and step outside. It's a busy place. The DJ loads his equipment into a nearby van and several people pass me, entering and exiting the building as they pack up and say good night. I walk into the parking lot and frown. Where is Dane? My eyes sweep from left to right. Did I take too long washing my face?

I cross my arms against my chest. It's cold out here. I decide to head to my right and look down a few rows of cars. Why does he have to make this difficult?

"Hey."

I spin around. Dane pushes himself off the wall of the community center to walk toward me. He's no longer dressed as the Scarecrow. His straw hair hat and patchwork costume are gone and have been replaced with a chocolate brown leather jacket and dark denim. His complexion is clear of the stitch marks that were drawn on his cheeks, and his nose is no longer a faux black triangle. As he comes closer, I can see that his jaw is set and his eyes burn. I must have pushed things too far earlier. Maybe it's a good thing I'm already green because my stomach has twisted itself into knots.

"You may have single-handedly ruined my engagement," he says.

I open my mouth to...what? Defend myself? Apologize? Does he even deserve an apology?

He stops walking when our bodies are inches apart. He stares down at me, and before I can utter a word he says, "Thank you," and lowers his lips to mine.

Chapter 14

"What are you doing?" I push him away. "Are you insane?"

"Not last I checked."

I step back and look around, half expecting Teagan to appear out of nowhere. "Just give me my phone."

"Emma..."

"I said give me my phone!"

He plants his feet and crosses his arms. "No."

I stare at him in disbelief. "What do you mean no?"

"We need to talk," he says.

I shoot him an irritated look. Since he isn't carrying my cell, it must be in one of his pockets. I step forward, reaching for his left jacket pocket, and he sidesteps me. I quickly change direction and go for his other side, but his hand swiftly catches my wrist. I instantly try to pull away, but he holds on to it firmly. I give him a stern look. "Let me go."

"Not until we talk."

"I have nothing to say to you."

One side of his mouth twitches. "I doubt that."

We stare at each other, and the longer he looks at me the more his eyes soften. I sigh and relax my arm. "I need to go back inside and help."

He tilts his head. "No, you don't."

"Yes, I do."

He looks above me for a moment, and I can see his eyes searching the parking lot. "C'mon," he says as he starts to pull me in the direction I came from.

"Could you let go of my arm?" I ask.

He glances over his shoulder. "What do you think I am? Stupid?"

I flash a sweet smile. "Do you really want me to answer that?"

He rolls his eyes and faces forward, towing me toward the entrance of the community center. I spot my mother carrying a tote a few feet into the parking lot.

"Mrs. Donohue!" Dane calls to her.

She stops and glances around to see who's shouting her name. When she sees us approaching, she sets down the heavy tote and waits for us to join her.

"Hi," Dane greets her. "I need to borrow Emma for the night, if that would be okay."

What?! That is so not okay!

My mom crosses her arms and assesses Dane from head to toe, then looks at me. I mouth the word "no" to her and barely shake my head, so he won't see. I immediately know from her expression what her answer will be, and I set my jaw.

"Sure," she says. "Our part of the cleanup is done." She bends to pick up the tote again.

"Here," Dane stops her and holds out my wrist. "I'll carry that to your car if you hold on to this for me."

She gladly wraps her hand around my forearm. "Can do."

Dane smiles and easily picks up the tote. My mom holds her keys in one hand and pushes the remote to unlock the doors of our Chevy Malibu. The headlights flash midway down a row of parked cars, and Dane takes off in that direction.

As soon as he's out of earshot, I turn on her. "What are you doing? I don't want to go anywhere with him!"

She gives me her all-knowing motherly stare. "Of course you do."

My face twists. "Why would you think...?"

"Because it's obvious. Your showdown with the fiancée proved that." She looks me in the eye. "No girl in her right mind would admit to sleeping with someone in front of her mother and his fiancée if she wasn't fighting for something."

Oh my God. My face turns crimson. "We didn't...we haven't..."

My mom shakes her head and holds out her free hand. "Stop. I don't need an explanation; you're an adult. Just as long as you're being safe."

I'm mortified.

"Believe it or not, I was your age once." She looks toward her car as Dane starts to make his way back to us. "You could do a lot worse."

Sarcasm drips from my tongue. "Maybe you should go with him."

She laughs. "If I were twenty years younger, I would."

Ew! Can the earth open up and swallow me now?

As he gets closer, I contemplate which is the lesser of the two evils: leaving with him or talking with my mom about sex. I hate to admit it, but leaving with Dane wins. And is she right? Was the motivation behind my cat fight with Teagan to stake a claim to him or simply the need to defend myself?

"You're all set," he says, giving my mom her keys.

She nods and takes them, handing me over. "Thanks." She looks at me pointedly. "Remember what I said about the safety." She leans forward to whisper in my ear. "You're still on the pill, right?"

Oh sweet zombie Jesus! I would be hard pressed to find another time I've been so embarrassed. I close my eyes. "Yes. Go home, Mom."

She laughs again. "Have a good night," she says as she walks away.

I open my eyes to find Dane holding on to my arm and staring at me, amused. "What was that about safety?"

I can't tell him my mother thinks we're sleeping together. I lift my chin arrogantly and lie. "She gave me some mace in case you try anything."

He laughs. "Right."

He maintains his grip on my arm as he leads me through the parking lot. "You don't have to hold on to me, you know. I have nowhere to run now."

He ignores me, and when we arrive at his car, he unlocks the doors of the Camaro. He ushers me into the passenger seat and then slams the door. I look around the familiar cab and stop short. Sitting in the center console is a crumpled tissue blotted with red lipstick, a bottle of nail polish, and a pair of women's sunglasses. All Teagan's, I'm sure. I pick up the sunglasses and turn them over in my hands. They're Chanel. Expensive. As Dane slides into the driver's seat, I open the arms of the glasses and push them up my nose. "How do they look?" I ask.

He turns to me and pauses. "Better on you."

Well. That action was supposed to irritate him, not melt my insides. I take off the glasses and defensively toss them back in the console. He starts the car, and I reach for my seatbelt. "Where are we going?"

He pulls the car forward slowly, looking for traffic, and then turns left out of the space. "To my place."

My response is instantaneous and adamant. "No, we're not!"

His frown is illuminated by the dashboard lights. "Why? What's wrong with that?"

What's wrong with that? The last time I was there was when we...I feel my ears get hot and push the memory away. How can I explain? Besides, if Teagan's things are in his car, what's hanging around his townhouse? Lingerie? My tone turns acerbic. "The last place I want to be is surrounded by evidence of your fiancée." I gesture toward the console. "It's hard enough with just this crap here."

He glances between the seats. When he turns out onto the road, he immediately pulls off on the shoulder. I stare at him with confusion as he grabs the tissue, nail polish, and sunglasses in one hand. He rolls down the window and throws them out.

"Why did you do that?" I ask, panicked. I look behind us he pulls away. "Do you know how much those glasses cost?"

"You didn't like them. They're gone."

I stare at him wide-eyed. "You didn't have to do that. She's going to be pissed."

He lets out a small, sarcastic laugh. "And I care why?"

I frown at him, baffled. What's he going to do when we get to his house? Go through the joint with a trash bag to make me happy? "I still don't want to go to your place."

He glances at me and sighs. "I know. I get it."

He turns his attention back to the road, and I stare out the passenger window. Neither of us utters a word as he drives. When we're just outside of town, he slows and makes a right, following the route to my parent's house. We reach the end of that street and make a left, and I'm certain that's where we're headed. My attitude must have caused him to reconsider spending time with me. As my address gets closer, my mind and my heart battle one another. Closing my eyes, I picture my emotions in a boxing ring with my voice as the MC:

"This match is scheduled for three rounds! In this corner, hailing from the dark recesses of Emma's brain and weighing in with logic and reason, our challenger, Relief! And, in this corner, hailing from Em's soul and weighing in with disappointment and guilt, our returning champion, Sadness! No punches below the belt, fellas. We want a good, clean fight." Ding! Ding! Ding!

I shake my head at my absurd reverie. I surely need some sort of therapy.

Sighing, I open my eyes, prepared to find us turning on to my street. Instead, I look out the windshield in surprise as we pass by. Where is he taking us? My question is answered when, moments later, he turns into the park entrance near my house. We follow the drive a short distance to a scenic overlook of sorts, where there are about five parking spaces for people to use at the beginning of a trailhead. He selects one, pulls in, and parks. "Will this work?" he asks.

I nod. Relief has taken out Sadness in round one and is now challenging Anxiety.

He cuts the engine, but leaves the car on accessory, so the instrument panel provides some dim light in the darkness. He takes off his seatbelt then turns to me, his hazel eyes intense. "I'm so sorry," he says. "You have to know that."

I tilt my head reflexively. "I figured."

He looks down for a moment. When he looks back at me, he sighs. "I don't know where to start other than there."

I shrug and cross my arms against the knot in my stomach. "How about with why?" I ask. "Why didn't you tell me?"

"Because I'm an idiot," he responds without hesitation.

I smirk. "You said it, not me."

He gives me a tiny smile, but it quickly fades. "When we met..." he pauses, trying to gather his thoughts. "I wasn't looking for anyone else. Or anything else. Teagan was on my mind constantly."

My face automatically twists at the mention of her name.

"Not like that," he says, noticing my reaction. "I was having second thoughts. The longer she was away, the more I started to realize that I had asked her to marry me for the wrong reasons."

I shift my weight in the seat to get more comfortable. "So why did you propose?"

"Because it was expected of me."

I shoot him a confused look. "Shouldn't you at least be in love with the person?"

"I was once," he says and leans his head against the headrest.

"And?"

He turns to me. "I'm not anymore."

Why does my heart skip a beat when he says this? I reprimand myself. Dane and I are done.

"Teagan and I were *that* couple," he says, explaining. "You know, the couple in high school brought together by friends more so than any true feelings." He looks up and stares out the moon roof of the car. "I've been with her since we were sixteen. It made sense for us to date back then. We were both popular; our parents knew each other." He looks at me again. "And she wasn't too hard to look at."

I roll my eyes. "Yes, I can see where her looks make up for what she's lacking in personality."

He laughs. "She wasn't always this nasty."

I undo my seatbelt and turn my body to face him, curling my knees up on the seat. "So what went wrong?"

"She's always been spoiled, but it soared to new levels when we went to college. I think it went to her head."

"Why didn't you break up with her if you didn't like her new attitude?"

He sighs. "It was a gradual thing. It's not like one day she woke up a complete bitch."

I laugh.

He smiles and shakes his head. "Then, after we graduated, her father offered me a job. My dream job, actually. I mean, how many grads do you know get to start their career immediately after college? Not many. Plus, it was my chance to avoid working for my dad at Bay Woods."

"Hey! It wasn't that bad."

"No," he concedes and looks me in the eye. "Not with you there."

My pulse picks up again. Does he do that on purpose? "So," I clear my throat, "you felt you had to propose because her dad gave you a job?"

He frowns and considers my question. "I guess that was part of it," he admits. "Teagan was getting anxious and bringing up marriage all the time. I understood why she was doing it; we'd been together for seven years. But, I kept putting her off. Then she was selected to be on the conservation team and was headed to God-knows-where. At the time I thought that was my sign, you know, do it now because who knows what will happen. So I did."

"I bet she was ecstatic," I say.

He rolls his eyes. "Please. The wedding talk has been non-stop. Even while she was gone her mother kept hounding me. She made me book the honeymoon a year ago because 'that's the groom's responsibility,'" he mimics Teagan's mother's voice.

I feel like I've been sucker punched. "So when's the big day?" Why does this bother me? It shouldn't bother me!

"Never," he says adamantly and leans forward. "When she left, I finally had some space to breathe, some time to myself. Time to figure out what I wanted without her in my face all the time." He pauses. "I know what I want. And I don't want her."

My mouth falls open in surprise. "Shouldn't someone inform the bride?"

He snickers. "She knows. She thinks I'll change my mind." He lets out a frustrated sigh and runs his hand through his hair. "She hasn't told anyone that we're not together. She won't stop throwing herself in my face, won't stop coming over. Won't take off the ring."

Wow. And I thought my relationship with James was messed up. Still, even with all he's told me, he hasn't answered my original question. "And you didn't tell me about her because...?"

"Because I didn't want you to think I was some jerk who runs around proposing to women and then plays around while they're out of town." He pins me with a pained expression. "I wanted to end things with her months ago, but I felt I owed it to Teagan to do it in person, not over Skype. When she came home I told her the engagement was off. As you can imagine, it didn't go over well," he grimaces. "She's been putting up a fight ever since; she let herself into my place and came across the bill for the things I sent you. If I had known she had mailed that article to you I..."

My eyes open wide. "*She* sent it?"

"When she asked me about the bill, I explained that you were Matt's friend and we had worked together. I told her we had grown close. When Matt told me how you found out about Teagan, I confronted her."

"Maybe you should get your locks changed," I joke.

"I need to," he sighs. "Just last week I found her there in my bed."

I swallow. I don't know why I even want to ask this question, but I ask it anyway. "Have you two...?"

He looks me straight in the eye. "Do you want the truth?"

No, not really. "Yes."

He leans forward and searches my face. "When she first came back, we...I...tried. You had said you didn't want me, but..." he hesitates. "But I couldn't go through with it."

"Why?" I whisper.

"Because all I could think about was you."

My heart stops. I shake my head to clear it and give him a stern look. "Stop that."

"Stop what?"

I put my feet down and lean forward. "Saying things like that! Looking at me like that!"

He tilts his head and smiles. "It's hard not to. You are an odd shade of green."

"That's not what I meant!" I push against his shoulder in frustration. My action backfires because he grabs my wrist and pulls me forward, so I'm half leaning over the console.

"I know what you meant," he says, his face inches from mine. "I'm not going to lie to you ever again. You asked for the truth, and I gave it to you."

I try to pull my arm away, but it doesn't work. "Will you stop manhandling me?"

He raises his eyebrows. "I think you want me to manhandle you."

My mouth falls open. "Arrogant much?"

Dane stares into my eyes. "When will you admit that you have feelings for me? I know that you do."

I try to remain impassive. "Even if I did I couldn't act on them."

"So you admit it then?"

Shoot! I blush and try to back track. "Nothing has changed. I still love James."

"That doesn't mean you can't love me, too."

Has he been talking to Garrett? "Dane..."

His face softens. "Em, you've told me before."

I stare at him, confused. "What are you talking about? I never said..."

"After you were attacked." He moves his free hand to cradle my face. "When I was calling for help you said I love you."

I stare at him wide-eyed as my heart begins to pound. I did say that. But I was talking to James! Dane and I remain face to face, and I'm frozen. I can't tell him I was talking to my dead boyfriend!

He leans closer, his voice dropping an octave. "I'm dying here. Would you please just kiss me?"

My pulse is racing; his lips are centimeters from mine. Am I actually considering this? "I..."

"Don't tell me you can't."

I turn my head to buy some time – and see James sitting in the back seat of the car.

"Holy shit!" I yell and scramble backwards, yanking my hand from Dane's grasp.

"What? What is it?" Dane looks panicked.

I shift my eyes to the back seat and James gives me a condescending stare. "Go ahead," he challenges me. "You know you want to."

What? He's going to choose to appear *now*? He's never done this before!

"Is everything okay?" Dane asks, worried.

I close my eyes as my mind scrambles. "I thought...maybe we should..." I open my eyes and let out a muted squeak. Meg has taken a seat next to James, her hand on top of his.

James focuses on me, clearly agitated. "So?" he asks. "Are you going to kiss him or not?"

Does he expect me to answer that?

Meg gives me a sympathetic smile and then she pats James' hand, pulling his attention away from me. James meets Meg's eyes and nods. He gives me one last look as they fade away together.

Anger builds inside my chest. How dare he!

"Emma? Seriously, you're freaking me out," Dane says.

His voice snaps me back to attention, and I focus on his face. "I'm sorry." I move my body away from the door. "I don't know what happened."

"Are you sure? You look angry."

I am angry. James knows how hard it is for me to maintain my composure when I hear him, let alone see him. He just made me look like a complete ass in front of Dane! My mind turns to Meg, and my jaw tenses. He thinks my being here with Dane is bad? Obviously he gets to hang out with whomever he wants, involve them in my personal business. Where are my choices? I look at Dane and reach for his jacket with my right hand. "Come here."

He looks confused but leans forward just the same. I grab a hold of him near his collar and pull him to me as best I can. My face hovers inches from his. "If I kiss you now it's only to prove a point."

"Prove what point?"

"That I have choices. That I am in control."

"Okay." He smiles like he knows I'm lying. "Whatever you say."

"You're that desperate to kiss me?" I ask.

"I'm always desperate to kiss you."

That does it. I catch his mouth with mine as I clutch his jacket, with both hands now, pulling him to me. His hands travel up my arms and one settles against my neck, cradling my face. His touch is hot against my skin, just like in my dream, and I allow myself to let go for once. I let him pull me closer; allow him to consume my mouth. Shivers travel up my spine as everything inside me starts to warm and soften, sending warning bells ringing in my head. It's time to stop this before it gets out of hand.

I pull away and he tries to follow me by resting his forehead against mine. "Okay," I say, trying to catch my breath. "My point's been made."

"To who?" he asks. "I didn't get it." He tries to catch my mouth with his again.

"No." I release his clothes and straighten myself in my seat. "Don't get the wrong idea. My choice. I'm in control. We can start to be friends again. That's it."

"Confused much?" he asks, mimicking my earlier comment.

I shoot him a sarcastic look. "Yes, actually." First I'm mad and now I'm kissing him? I pause. "I'm not kissing you anymore."

"Maybe not tonight." His expression is smug as he leans back. "But there's plenty more where that came from."

"Says who?"

"Says you."

I slump down in my seat. What have I started?

My inner voice, the MC, speaks up again, letting me know Anxiety won round two of my mental boxing match and is gearing up for round three. Who is the next opponent? Looks like my good friend, Doubt.

Chapter 15

The next day, I end up staying at my parents longer than I had originally planned. My brother and his girlfriend came over for dinner, which convinced me to spend a few more hours at home. It feels good to spend time with my family and away from Guardian issues. Not that James couldn't visit me anywhere at any time, but I have the feeling he's saving our next conversation for a more private location. And that's fine with me. I plan to use the long drive back to school to formulate my thoughts into coherent sentences. Every time I think about what I want to say to him, I talk myself in circles.

After hugging my mom and dad goodbye, I head out to my car balancing my keys, my backpack, and a leftover dish full of pot roast and vegetables. I sigh. I won't make it back to my apartment until after ten now. If I weren't so close to graduation, I would seriously consider transferring to a school closer to home. I toss my backpack into the passenger seat and then crawl in myself, arranging the leftover dish so it will stay in place. I pull my phone out of my pocket to connect it to the radio for the drive and start the car. I grip the steering wheel and pause, staring out the windshield at my childhood home. I really wish I could stay here.

My cell chimes and I glance down. *I didn't lose your number.*

I roll my eyes. Here we go. *Obviously.*

Where are you? Dane asks.

On my way back. I don't think it's a good idea to let him know I'm still in town.

Stop texting. Let me know when you get there.

Ok.

I said stop texting!

I laugh. Little does he know I'm parked in my parent's driveway. I remember our sarcastic banter from the summer, and I try to think of something witty to send back. I come up with nothing. I put the phone down, put the car in drive, and make it to the road. My cell sounds again.

Think about when I can visit.

I swallow. Yeah, I'm not sure if that's a good idea.

After apologizing to Garrett for waking him to get my key, I let myself into my apartment. I'm grateful to be that much closer to bed and snuggling with LB. I flip the light switch by the door and sweep the room, expecting to find her waiting for me. Instead, what I see almost causes me to drop my leftovers.

James is leaning against the arm of the couch and Meg is standing directly in front of him, too close for my liking, but apparently not for his. James meets my eyes and quickly stands as Meg takes an automatic step back. I narrow my eyes at them as anger surges through my veins. "What do you think this is? A motel?"

James gives me a condescending look as Meg takes the hint and evaporates immediately. I march into the room and throw my backpack on the floor, then turn and head to the kitchen with the leftovers. I'm afraid if I hold on to them I might throw them. I yank open the refrigerator, toss the container in, and slam the door. Since I can't physically hurt James I might as well take it out on the appliances.

When I return to face him, I stop just a few feet over the threshold from the kitchen and cross my arms. He plants his feet and does the same. We stare at each other.

Three thumps on my wall interrupt the silence. I take a few steps back, never losing eye contact with James, and hit the wall to answer Garrett's good night. When I return to my previous spot, he finally speaks.

"You two have some secret code now?" James asks bitterly.

"Yes," my voice drips with sarcasm. "That was the 'Hey-Garrett-James-is-with-Meg-again' signal."

He tilts his head. "Funny. What's the code for 'I'm-going-home-to-make-out-with-Dane-can-you-watch-my-cat'?"

I step forward. "That's not what happened."

"Isn't it?" He pauses. "It sure looked like a rendezvous to me." Using his fingers, he ticks off the details. "Parked car. Middle of the night. Secluded spot. Am I forgetting anything? Oh, yes," he looks at me accusingly, "your lips on his."

Blood starts to pound in my ears. "Are you going to let me explain? Or would you rather assume you know everything?"

His raises his eyebrows and gestures for me to go ahead.

"I didn't plan on running into Dane yesterday; I didn't know he would be at the party."

James feigns confusion. "So you ended up connected at the mouth how?"

I inhale, trying to maintain my composure. "He wanted to talk, to apologize. To explain the whole engagement fiasco."

"That still doesn't answer my question."

"Did you miss the part where I told him I was still in love with you? I wasn't going to kiss him! If you had waited to appear for, like, two seconds, you would have seen that!"

James shakes his head. "I don't believe you."

"It's the truth," I say adamantly.

"Really?" He looks me dead in the eye. "I saw what happened after Meg and I left. I heard you choose – and I saw what you did."

The mention of Meg's name irritates me to no end. "Good! That's what I wanted!"

He looks confused for a moment and then rearranges his face. I walk up to him and stop inches from his chest. "The only reason I kissed Dane was to prove to you that *I'm* in control – not him, not you, and certainly not your little girlfriend!"

His face twists. "She's not my girlfriend!"

"Is that so?" I press. "She's everywhere you are! Including in my personal space!"

He looks at me skeptically. "So I'm not allowed to have friends, is that it?"

"Am I?"

"It's not the same!" James says in frustration. He starts to pace and when he turns back to me, his eyes are hard. "I've never kissed Meg."

I look down to avoid his stare. I know how much Dane gets under James' skin. Kissing him was a childish move.

"Meg and I are working together," James says. "She understands me."

My head snaps up. "And I don't?"

"You know that's not what I meant." He walks toward me. "Meg and I, we want the same thing." He pauses and searches my face. "It's what I thought you wanted, too."

How can he doubt that I would want him to be human? "Of course I want that."

"Do you?" he asks. "Or have you changed your mind?"

My expression twists. "No!"

My phone rings from my back pocket interrupting us. I reach for it automatically as I mentally kick myself. I was supposed to call my parents when I got back.

"Gee, I wonder who that could be," James says sarcastically.

"It's my parents," I snap. I look down at the phone to answer it and find that I'm wrong. It's not my mom and dad. I stare at the phone as it continues to ring, afraid to answer it.

James crosses his arms and leans forward, taunting me. "What's wrong? Cat got your tongue?"

I open my mouth to speak and nothing comes out. What do I say? I know Dane is only calling to make sure I got back safe, but James won't believe that.

"What are you waiting for?" James asks.

I narrow my eyes at him, and the call goes to voicemail.

"Oh, I get it. It's a private conversation," he says sardonically. He takes a few steps backward. "I won't keep you."

Anger and sadness battle inside me. "Don't go. I don't want to fight."

"Really?" he asks, irritated. "You started swinging the minute you walked in the door."

"That's because I caught you and Meg in my apartment!"

"Caught us doing what, exactly?" he challenges me. "Talking?"

"She was this far from you!" I hold my thumb and forefinger an inch apart.

"And that's a crime?" he asks in disbelief.

How can he not see what a double standard this is? "If you found Dane and me like that in your place you would be just as pissed."

James eyes me. "Ah, newsflash. I already found you two together." He leans forward. "I am pissed."

My phone sounds again, this time with a text message. I resist the urge to look down at my hand and continue to stare at James. I understand that he's upset. Why can't he see that I am too?

"Unbelievable," he mutters as my cell continues to chime.

"He just wants to make sure I'm safe."

James sets his jaw. "I thought that was my job."

"Is it?" I ask, exasperated. "Because you're not acting like it!"

James opens his mouth to speak, but then stops. He blinks at me and suddenly his face goes slack. "You're right," he says without any real emotion. His head snaps to the left, clearly hearing something I cannot, and he begins to fade in front of me.

"Wait!" I reach out toward him, but he vanishes in the blink of an eye.

I stand there frozen, with my arm extended in front of me, staring at the space he just left. My mind races, and I'm taken back to the last time we fought, to the night he died. When he walked out on our argument. Just like now.

My heart aches at the memory. I wait for the familiar feeling of tears behind my eyes, but strangely, it doesn't occur.

Mechanically, I walk over to my discarded backpack, pick it up, and head to the bedroom where I find LB on my pillow, curled up and comfortable. I pet her for a few minutes and then walk through the motions of getting ready for bed in a daze. Once tucked beneath my sheets, I listen to Dane's voice mail and read his text. They're similar.

Did you make it back yet?

I send him a quick message. *Made it. Tired. Going to bed.* I call my parents next, waking them to tell them the same. After I hang up, I lie down with LB for what I'm sure is going to be a restless night. I pet her absentmindedly as James' words replay in my mind and weave through her purr. What I once felt justified in defending seems defenseless now, and my heart feels heavy.

My phone chimes on my nightstand, and I reach over to grab it. Dane is still awake.

Ok. Dream of me ;)

I give my phone a sad smile. If only it were that simple.

Chapter 16

"Okay." Garrett slams his Ethics textbook shut. "What's wrong?"

I snap back to reality. "What?"

"You haven't been yourself since you got back. What's bothering you?"

It's been four days since my fight with James. Four days. And he hasn't visited once, no matter how much I think about him or how much I'm hurting. All I can do is assume the worst and picture him frolicking in the Intermediate with Meg. I've been trying to come to grips with the fact that I pushed him away, that my kissing Dane drove him straight into her arms. I have no one to blame but myself, and it depresses me.

"Emma?"

"What?"

Garrett crosses his arms and gives me an irritated stare. "Are you going to tell me what's going on or do I have to make you?"

I frown. "You can do that?"

Garrett pauses. "No."

I stare at him and notice his bright turquoise eyes have faded to a more subdued shade of blue. He told me they will eventually turn brown, his original eye color, once his transformation is complete. He has a little less than three months to go now.

"So?" he asks.

"It's complicated," I say and go back to reviewing my notes. I don't want to get James in trouble.

"Would a certain Guardian have anything to do with this?"

I shoot him an annoyed look over my paper. "Have you forgotten that we have a midterm tomorrow?"

He reaches across the coffee table and grabs the top of my notebook, pulling it from my hands.

"Hey!"

"Listen, normally I wouldn't pry," he says. "But the only thing I can think of that would put you in this type of mood would have to be something to do with James. And seeing as how anything that happens with James is my business, I think I have a right to ask you –"

"How do you know it's James?" I snap. "What if it's something at home? What if it's something to do with my family?"

Garrett blinks. "I...I stand corrected," he says and starts to slide my notebook back to me. "I'm sorry."

I reach out and grab my notes, slamming them down in front of me. I know he's wrapped up in his own little world, but the majority of people on this planet have other issues to deal with besides Guardian ones. Let that be an important lesson in humanity.

I try to concentrate on studying, but the words start to blur as I feel Garrett staring at me. After a few moments of awkward silence, I raise my eyes to meet his. Can he tell I'm lying?

"Do you want to talk about it?" he asks quietly.

Yes, I think. This is exactly the kind of thing I need Shel for, the type of situation where you need your best girlfriend. I need a female perspective, someone who can empathize with what I'm feeling and help me sort through what's happened. But I can't talk to her. Not about this.

When I don't respond, Garrett starts to look uncomfortable. "Look, I'm just trying to help. If this is a bad time, I can come back to study." He starts to gather his things.

I let out a heavy sigh. Now I feel bad. If I don't come clean about what's going on, I'm sure karma will turn on me and something horrible will happen. "Stop," I tell him and set my hand on top of the papers that he's organizing into a pile. "You're right. It is about James."

He lets go of the papers and eyes me suspiciously. "Why the line about your family?"

"Because." I toss my notes to the side. "I don't want to get him in trouble."

Garrett raises his eyebrows. "Why would he be in trouble?"

Since I'm seated on the floor next to the coffee table, I lie back, rest my hands against my stomach, and talk to the ceiling. "We had a fight."

His face appears above mine. "About what?"

I continue to look at the ceiling. "Dane. And Meg."

"What about them?" he asks, confused. When I don't immediately answer, his tone grows frustrated and he leans closer. "Am I going to have to pull every little bit of information out of you?"

I prop myself up on my elbows, and he leans back. "I ran into Dane when I went home on Saturday."

"And?"

"James appeared unexpectedly with Meg. He challenged me to kiss Dane." I push myself to sit up straight. "So I did."

Garrett stares at me, his mouth falling open a little.

"Then, when I got back on Sunday, I found him here with Meg in my apartment."

"Doing what?" Garrett frowns.

"Who knows?" I scowl. "They were all up in each other's personal space. James said they were just talking, but seeing the two of them made me more upset. Especially after they showed up in Dane's car the way they did."

Garrett looks at me as if he's having a hard time comprehending what I've told him.

"I haven't seen him since we fought," I say and look away. I can feel tears begin to creep behind my eyes, so I reach over and open my textbook as a distraction. "That's everything," I finish as I pretend to redirect my attention.

Minutes pass. I read the same paragraph three times before I hear Garrett's voice. "James made a mistake."

I continue to look at my book. "So did I."

"I don't think you understand," Garrett says and leans forward to try and make me look at him. "Your decisions are yours to make. James is supposed to guide you in those decisions, not influence them."

My shoulders slump. "I know why he did it," I say, trying to be rational after days of entertaining every irrational thought imaginable.

"You do?" Garrett asks. "Because I sure as hell don't."

I look at him sarcastically. He should get this; it's not that hard to figure out. "I was with someone he doesn't like, someone I told him I was mad at. Someone who hurt me."

"So?" he asks, perturbed. "What's it to him as long as you're not in danger?"

My face twists in confusion.

"Were you in danger?"

"No!"

"Then James should have kept his mouth shut and stayed out of your business." Garrett sits back. "He's not allowed to be jealous."

I sigh. "I should never have gone with Dane." I rub my forehead to try and ease the dull ache that has been there all week.

"Why not?"

I look at Garrett like he's bumped his head. "Because none of this would have happened! James wouldn't have gotten jealous, I wouldn't have kissed Dane, and I wouldn't be so worried about Meg!"

He raises his eyebrows. "Are you sure about that?"

I open my mouth to speak, but then close it again. I'm starting to hate this conversation.

"Look, I'm an outsider," Garrett says and leans forward again. "Do you want to know what I see?"

This is what I would ask Shel if I could, so I nod.

"James shouldn't be jealous of anyone you're with or anything you do; his duty is to guide and protect you *in* your decisions. Period. As for Dane, I have the feeling that you would have kissed him anyway –"

I open my mouth to protest and Garrett holds up his hand to stop me.

"– if not now, then later. I know you're confused about him, and that's okay. You need to have a life. As for Meg, she's just flirtatious by nature."

My mouth falls open. "Does that give her permission to come on to my boyfriend?"

Garrett laughs. "So, if you can't have him no one can? Is that how it works nowadays?"

"He's still mine!"

He rolls his eyes. "Emma, how can you be with a Guardian? Surely you're not that delusional."

"One day he won't be a Guardian," I remind him. "Surely *you* can't be that delusional."

My comment stops him short and he stares at me, dazed. How could he have forgotten that simple fact? Talking about this would be so much easier with Shel; by nature women tend to remember even the smallest of details.

"We're going to have a human life together," I say adamantly. "Whether you think so or not."

Garrett blinks and looks away, clearing his throat. "You'll have to make up first though," he says quietly. His assured tone is gone, and his voice sounds a bit hollow. He moves to sit opposite me and starts to organize his papers spread on the table. It's clear he's uncomfortable and tension now fills the air. What does he know that I don't?

My mind races and my thoughts immediately turn to Meg. Her relationship with James must be more serious than I imagined and Garrett knows it's going to be difficult for us to move past this. If James can be human again and Meg can too...

"They're already together, aren't they?"

He looks up. "Who?"

"Don't play dumb. James and Meg."

"What? No. I mean, I've heard some rumblings that they might be starting something, but I doubt they're anywhere near marriage."

I stare at him stupidly. "From who? Shouldn't you have told me?"

"My brother," he says. "And no, because he's a little biased when it comes to Meg. It's hard to believe the accuracy in what he says when it comes to her."

"Why is that?"

"Jack and Meg have a history."

I raise an eyebrow. Jack and Meg were together? He's so gruff and she's so not. Talk about an odd couple. "I take it she gets around?"

Garrett smirks. "If you call a 25 year relationship 'getting around'."

This whole Guardian-hook up thing has my mind reeling. That is a long time to be together. "But what about their true loves? What about being released?"

"I'm pretty sure my brother never had a true love. And as for Meg, who am I to speculate on her motives? Maybe she knew her David wouldn't release her. He chose eternity after he drowned. Without her."

Okay. I have to admit that fact makes me feel a twinge of sympathy for Meg. But, I still don't like her coming on to James. He can spend unlimited time with her; there's no way I can compete. I think about my idiotic move with Dane, and my heart plummets.

"What are you thinking about?" Garrett asks.

"That I have no one to blame, but myself." I slam my book shut. "I suck at relationships."

"I could say the same thing."

James' voice startles me, and my head whips around.

Garrett pushes himself to stand and gathers his things. "I'll take this as my cue to leave," he says and tucks the items under his arm. He walks around the coffee table toward the door, making eye contact with James for a brief second. "Let me know if you want to go over anything else," he says over his shoulder.

"I will." When the door closes behind him, I study James. "Where have you been?" I ask and flinch. I think I already know the answer to that question.

He walks forward and sits on the floor in front of me, crossing his legs to match mine. He reaches for my hands, and I allow him to take them. Our eyes meet, and his expression couldn't be more serious. I think to myself that this is it. This is where he tells me that he's had enough and we're through.

"You're blowing this Meg thing way out of proportion," he says.

I study our hands. "Am I?"

"Yes," he says, his tone firm. "She's a friend. Nothing more."

"I take it you were eavesdropping on my conversation with Garrett?"

"Just the last part," he admits. His hand appears beneath my chin, and he lifts my gaze. "I'm serious. There is nothing romantic between me and Meg."

My mouth twists. "I think she wants there to be."

He shrugs. "Oh well for her."

I move his hand away from my chin and lace my fingers through his. "So, where have you been?" I ask again.

"Trying to sort out what to say to you. Trying to figure out how to apologize."

"It took you four days?"

"Em, I screwed up. Like, massively messed up. You were so angry; I didn't know if you would want to see me."

I give him an incredulous look. "How could you think that? Haven't you felt how upset I've been?"

"I know you're upset, but the emotion is all I feel. I don't know the exact cause unless I physically check on you and –" he stops.

"And what?"

His shoulders fall. "I didn't want to find you with Dane again. What if you were with him and he was upsetting you? I would have ripped his head off. Or what if you were thinking about breaking things off with me? I wanted to give you time to sort out your feelings."

"I would never break up with you! And I haven't seen Dane since last weekend. I've been putting him off, telling him he can't visit, because I'm busy with midterms."

James looks wary.

"Look, I know I started something with Dane that I shouldn't have. What I did was stupid and reactive and part of my being upset is trying to figure out how to fix that. Another part is imagining you spending time with Meg," I hesitate. "But, the main reason I'm sad is because we fought and you left. Just like the night you died."

His face fills with remorse. He lets go of my hands and quickly collects me in his arms, pulling me forward and into his lap. "I'm so sorry," he says against my hair.

"I love you," I speak against his chest. It's the only thing I can think to say. "Please don't leave me without at least saying goodbye."

He leans back, so he can see my face. "I will never leave you. Everything I've done has been for you."

"But it hasn't been easy," I say. "It's been hell. Not that I like it, but I can understand if you would want something easier, something with Meg."

He frowns. "I don't want something with Meg."

I give him a condescending look. "She's always around..."

"I have to talk to someone," James says gently. "She gives good advice; she listens when I need to vent. She helps me. She's the one who pulled me out of Dane's car before I said anything else to hurt you or before I took my anger out on him."

I study his face while I process what he's said. "I guess tell her thanks," I say insincerely, "even though I don't like her knowing my personal business."

"Do you expect me to stay mute?" he asks. "I have to deal with these feelings that I'm not supposed to feel somehow."

"What about me? I have no one to talk to about this. I would do almost anything to get Shel's opinion of how I should fix what I started with Dane. But I can't ask her because she would just tell me to go for it because she has no idea that you still exist. I can't rationally explain my feelings without mentioning you."

"What about Garrett? You seem able to talk to him."

"It's not the same. He's an ex-Guardian who can't seem to comprehend why you're having a hard time dealing with your connection to me. He seems to think you should be able to get over it and that I should move on with my life."

James frowns, but then his eyes light up. "I know. What if I asked some of the girls to come by and you could talk? Like Joss or Jenna?"

I make a face. More Guardians?

"You could ask them some questions, discuss your Guardian frustrations."

I hesitate. "I don't know."

"At least they're female," he offers.

This is true. "Joss does seem really nice," I concede.

"Do you want me to ask them?"

I shrug. "I guess. But if they can't, it's okay. I don't know how I feel about revealing my problems to strangers."

He holds me closer. "They won't be strangers for long," he assures me. "The girls are really nice."

I can't help it. "Especially Meg."

"Would you cut that out?" James squeezes me. "As I recall, we had a very similar conversation this past summer, only in the reverse."

I lift my head and look at him, scrunching up my nose.

"About Dane? That he was only being nice and wanted to be your friend?"

"You know how that turned out," I say sarcastically.

"But I believed you," he stresses. "Because I knew that's what you truly thought."

"Fine," I huff. "I believe that you're friends. But, for the record, I don't trust her."

One side of his mouth quirks up.

I sigh and then lift my face to plant an innocent kiss on his lips. "I'm glad you didn't wait any longer to come see me."

"So am I," he says and kisses me back, his kiss stronger than mine. That relaxed, calm feeling I always get when he is here takes over, and, when we part, I unexpectedly yawn.

"Am I boring you?" he laughs.

"No. Our conversation has been riveting."

"But my kiss put you to sleep?"

I smile and shake my head.

"I must not kiss as well as Dane," he teases.

My mouth falls open. "Shut up! You know why I did that!"

"Oh, I know," he smirks.

My face flushes red. "I already feel terrible. Don't make me feel worse!"

He grins then plants a kiss on my forehead. "You're forgiven, although I might have to bring it up from time to time."

I roll my eyes. "I would expect nothing less."

"What about me?" he asks. "Am I forgiven?"

I pretend to ponder his question, but of course I already know the answer. "Yes, but –"

"But what? Your forgiveness has conditions?"

I give him a stale look. "I forgive you for being jealous and disappearing on me, because those things I understand. But does Meg have to follow you wherever you go?" I look around the room cautiously. "Is she here now?"

He moves one arm beneath my knees and wraps his other arm tightly around my back and smiles. "No, she's not here now." He shifts his weight and stands with ease, holding me against him like a child.

My eyes widen in surprise as his lifts me off the floor. "This is new," I say in awe and then narrow my eyes. "Are you trying to distract me?"

"Let's just say Meg has a vested interest in what happens between us," he says as he starts to carry me toward my bedroom.

"And why's that?"

"I'm not allowed to say."

"Really?"

"Really."

We enter my room and he sets me on the bed next to LB. I swing my legs off the side and turn to face him as he leans over me, placing his hands on either side of me against the mattress. "Come on," I press. "Obviously I'm good at keeping secrets."

"She's trying to make sure I don't screw up again," he says.

I cross my arms and search his face. "I already know that. Tell me what I don't know."

His expression twists, and I look up at him innocently. "It will put my mind at ease," I say. "You would do that for your Ward, right?"

James smirks. "When did you start to play dirty? That's not fair."

I raise my eyebrows and shrug. After a moment, when he doesn't offer any information, I pout.

He rolls his eyes and stands. "Fine. How can I put this?" He looks to the ceiling in thought.

I wait impatiently. I'm about to have a concrete reason for Meg's persistent presence other than my own suspicions. These last few days have been torturous.

He finally turns to me. "Listen. This is all I can tell you, so don't ask me for anything more. Okay?"

I nod.

He steps forward. "Meg *is* helping me," he says. "But, she is also looking out for the best interest of her Ward."

Chapter 17

My conversation with James runs through my mind on an endless loop. I can't turn it off. I redirect my focus and try to concentrate on the Ethics exam in front of me. I have one more essay to finish. I need to compare the five self-interest philosophies and, if I'm not careful, I might end up writing a paragraph about why I think Meg is Dane's Guardian.

I start to write and catch Garrett out of the corner of my eye. He looks at his paper, perplexed. Guilt washes over me. We didn't study enough. My personal problems got in the way last night, even though he was the one who pressed me about them. I'll have to be sure to apologize after class. Garrett didn't sign up to be my therapist.

I finish my test as quickly as I dare, briefly mentioning each philosophy. A few missed points shouldn't hurt my grade any; I was rocking an A before this exam. I gather my things and turn my paper in to Ms. Johnson, then head out to the hallway to wait for Garrett. I place my backpack against my feet and lean against the wall as James' voice replays in my mind – *"She's looking out for best interest of her Ward."* I sigh. Meg has to be Dane's Guardian; who else would my relationship with James effect? Naturally, I tried to get James to tell me if I was correct, but he would neither confirm nor deny my assumption. Then, when he decided to stay the night, I got completely sidetracked. It's hard to ask questions when your mouth is connected to someone else's, Guardian or not.

My cell vibrates in my pocket, bringing me back from the memory. I pull it out to read the text message.

Are you finished with midterms??

Aw, hell. It's Dane. I'm going to have to think of another excuse as to why I can't see him. I stare at the phone and silently wish I could just tell him the truth.

"What's up?" Garrett asks, appearing in front of me.

I lift my head, and my shoulders slump. "Dane wants to know if I'm done with midterms."

"And that's a bad thing?"

"I can't see him."

"Why not?"

I'm at a loss for words. We're supposed to be friends, but we can't hang out. James would have a conniption fit; not to mention, I kind of kissed Dane the last time we were together. "James wouldn't like it."

Garrett's expression twists. "I told you that's none of his –"

"Yeah, yeah," I interrupt him and push myself away from the wall. I pick up my backpack with my free hand and toss it over my shoulder. "Let's go."

Garrett follows me out of the building, and we head across campus. "So, how'd you do?" I ask.

Garrett shrugs. "Okay, I guess."

"I'm sorry. We should have studied more. I'll definitely make it up to you for the final."

He smiles. "I didn't say I did terrible. I'll pass."

I nod. "Good."

We walk back to our apartments in relative silence. When we reach the street corner closest to home, Garrett asks, "So, I take it last night went well?"

"Yes."

"You're no longer fighting with James?"

I shake my head.

Garrett falls silent, and I want to ask him about Meg. Would James get in trouble for telling me as much as he did? "I have a question."

"Shoot."

"Why can't I know who a Guardian's Ward is? Say, for example, Meg's," I try to ask nonchalantly. "Why is that so secret?"

Garrett gives me a knowing smile. "You'd make a terrible interrogation officer."

I roll my eyes. "Why can't I know?"

"Let me guess," Garrett pretends to think. "James told you Meg is hanging around because it has something to do with her duty, right?"

One eyebrow lifts in question. "Are you telling me he's lying?"

He chuckles. "No. He's telling the truth."

"It's Dane, isn't it?" I stop walking. "Meg is Dane's Guardian."

Garrett stops a few steps ahead of me and turns. "Would that upset you?"

"No." I try to look unaffected and fail. "Yes. I don't know."

"And that's precisely why," he says matter-of-factly. "Guardians don't need jealousy or animosity among Wards. You're not supposed to know we even exist. It only complicates matters."

I start walking again. "How so?"

"Suppose you told your friend Shel that she has a Guardian. What would she do?"

"Probably freak out," I concede. "She'd think I was crazy."

"Exactly," Garrett says. "And if you knew who her Guardian was? Would you be tempted to tell her?"

I shrug. "Maybe."

"And if she knew? Would she be creeped out that this person felt her emotions? Was capable of watching her every move? Guided her decisions so she was kept safe from danger? Would she try to have a friendship with this person?"

"Okay! Okay! I got it." I push my phone into my pocket and reach for my keys as we approach the front door of our building. "Knowing who a Guardian's Ward is should be kept secret."

Garrett nods in agreement.

I open the door, and he follows me inside. "You know more about Guardians than any other human I've ever interacted with," he says. "You've handled it well, but I'm not so sure about the general population. You know how humans are prone to frenzy whenever they discover something they don't understand."

I laugh and throw out a couple of examples. "Crop circles? Area 51?"

Garrett smiles, then whispers, "I can vouch for the crop circles."

My eyes grow wide.

He shrugs. "Hey, a few of us got bored."

I shake my head in disbelief. "You sure know how to mess with people."

Garrett laughs as he pulls his apartment key from his pants pocket. He opens the door to his place as I turn to head toward mine. "Here's to a relaxing weekend without studying for exams," he says.

I walk backward down the hallway to my door. "That sounds absolutely perfect." I flash him a thumbs up. "I'll talk to you later."

He smiles. "Later."

I open my apartment door to find LB waiting to greet me. I toss my backpack aside and bend down to give her a good rubbing with both hands. When she's satisfied, she wanders away and I stand. Here we are with three whole days of nothing spread out before us. Again. I'm all down for relaxing, but I'd rather not be entirely alone. I pull my phone from my pocket and read Dane's message. Spending time with him is definitely out of the question. I wish I could go back in time and erase all the heavy stuff between us; so we could be friends again and just joke with each other like we used to.

Since that can't happen, I decide to call Shel. Maybe I can spend some time with her this weekend in Ann Arbor. Luckily she picks up.

"Hey there, stranger."

"Hi!"

"What are you up to?"

"I've got class in ten minutes. Why? What's up? Oh, loved your Wicked Witch costume by the way. That was hilarious!"

I smile. That party seems like it happened eons ago. "Listen, what are you doing this weekend? Are you busy? I was thinking I could come and visit."

"Aw, man," Shel groans. "I have this charity dinner thing for the hospital on Saturday night, and we're setting up all day tomorrow."

"What are you doing? Volunteering?"

"Yeah, waiting tables and stuff while the rich benefactors pay big bucks for dinner. It's a donation to the hospital."

"Sounds thrilling," I sigh and then pause. "Could you use an extra pair of hands?"

"You want to spend your weekend as a waitress?"

"Could I? Anything is better than sitting here by myself."

"Sure! I mean, I'll check with the coordinator, but I don't think it will be a problem. The more the merrier."

"Cool."

"Can you get here tomorrow night around eight or nine? We're supposed to be done with set up by then and we can hang out until we're needed the next day."

"Sounds good." I reach for a piece of scrap paper on the table. "What's the name of your new dorm again?" Shel recites her address and I jot it down. "Got it. I'm looking forward to it!"

"Me too!" Shel sounds excited. "This dinner just got a whole lot better! The time will fly by with you there."

I laugh. "I hope so! Although I don't know how good I am at waitressing."

"It'll be simple," Shel reassures me. "I think it's just clearing tables, maybe getting drinks. Stuff like that."

"I trust you." I check the clock. "Shouldn't you be heading to class?"

"On my way as we speak," I can hear Shel smile. "Talk while I walk. I heard you met up with Dane the other night."

Why doesn't this surprise me? "I'm shocked that you didn't call to grill me about it."

"Matt told me not to," she says simply. "Besides," her tone changes to imply that she's hurt, "I was hoping you'd tell me about it yourself."

"This week has been crazy busy," I say in defense. Crazy busy with exams, with worry, with guilt, with stress...

"Midterms?" she asks.

"You got it."

"Well, I'm looking forward to seeing you *and* hearing about Dane," she says as I think I hear a door opening. "'Kay, I'm at my lab. I'll let you go."

"Okay. See you tomorrow."

"Yep, bye!"

I end the call and set my phone on the table. It amazes me that my personal life remains interesting to others, but then again, your two best friends should be concerned, right?

My stomach growls, luring me to the kitchen. I move to stand in front of the refrigerator and open the door. What fabulous frozen thing can I reheat for lunch today?

So?

I rub my eyes with the heels of my hands. I blink to focus and realize I must have fallen asleep with my Communications book open in front of me. That's what I get for lying on my bed while trying to read boring material.

I glance at the message from Dane and then note the time. It's almost ten at night. I can't believe I forgot all about his earlier text. At least now I have a response, should he ask to come see me.

Sorry. Yes, midterms are over.

How did you do?

I think I did pretty well. I know I did great in three out of four anyway.

I don't miss those days.

I smile. *Are you sure you remember those days old man?* Dane is only three years older than me, but it's still fun to tease him.

Very funny. If I was there you'd pay for that comment.

How so?

It takes him a minute to respond. *That's a loaded question. Don't tempt me.*

Hmm. Maybe I should back off the humor.

What are you doing this weekend?

There it is. The question I was dreading. *Visiting Shel.*

That's not very nice.

What? *How do you mean? Shel sounded happy to have me.*

My phone rings a moment later, and I answer Dane with a bewildered, "Hello?"

"I've been asking to come see you."

I sigh. "I know."

"And the first free minute you have you run off to Shel?"

I get defensive. "She's my best friend! I haven't seen her in over a month. I saw you last week!"

I can hear Dane exhale. "It feels like you're putting me off on purpose."

Ding! Ding! Ding! You are correct, sir.

"I'm sorry," he quickly adds. "Things here are nuts. Teagan, work..."

I shudder at the sound of Teagan's name. I don't know who's worse, her or Meg. "What's going on?"

Dane's tone turns sullen. "She's involved her dad to get her way."

"Are you sure?"

"When your boss advises you to reconsider certain decisions in your life or your job is on the line I'd say that makes you 105% sure."

My mouth falls open. "That's terrible! Can he do that? I mean, legally?"

"It's a family owned business. I'm pretty sure he can do whatever he damn well pleases."

A sick feeling starts to wrap around my stomach. Why do I feel like this is all my fault? I mean, it's really not; Dane's the one who decided to break off his engagement. But, I am involved and Teagan knows it. "What did he say exactly?"

"He said he knows I'm a good kid, but he has to look out for his only daughter. He said if I can't find it within myself to follow through on my proposal, he'd understand – but I should be prepared to seek other employment."

What he says angers me. "I can't believe this. You love your job."

"Don't I know it?" He pauses then laughs sarcastically. "He did say he would write me a glowing letter of recommendation."

"This isn't right." I sit up. "There has to be something you can do."

"Yeah, there is," he says, disgusted. "Marry Teags."

"Besides that," I groan.

Seconds of silence pass then Dane clears his throat. "You know what? I'll figure something out. I have a savings. I'm employable. I can work for my dad if I have to."

I frown. I know that's the last thing that would make him happy. "I'm sorry. This whole situation sucks."

I can picture him with a wry smile. "Thanks for commiserating with me. Although a real life, in-person hug would be better."

I feel terrible for him and honestly wish I was there to hug him. "Consider this a virtual one," I say softly before I really think about it.

"Thanks," he says, somewhat sad. "So, when *will* I get to see you?"

I hesitate. If I tell him I can't see him it will only make things worse, and he doesn't need that right now. "I'll work on it," slips out before I can catch it. "Seriously, I'm not trying to be a jerk. It's just...I have a lot going on right now."

A cool arm slips around my shoulders from behind, and I immediately tense. I look out of the corner of my eye to see James take a seat next to me, his hip pressing against mine. He flashes me a smile, and I know he doesn't know who I'm talking to.

"I guess I can buy that for now," Dane concedes.

I try to relax under James' arm. "Listen, I have to go. I'll call you later, okay?"

"Why?" He sounds confused at the abrupt end to our conversation.

"I have company." I smile at James, so he won't be suspicious.

"Who?"

"I'll talk to you tomorrow. 'Bye." I end the call before he can ask any more questions and discreetly silence my ringer just in case he calls back. "Hey." I toss my phone aside and turn toward James. "I didn't expect to see you tonight."

"Surprise," he smiles at me. "Who was that?" He nods toward my discarded phone.

"Shel," I say quickly. "I'm going to visit her tomorrow and stay the weekend. I volunteered to help her with a charity dinner at the hospital."

James frowns.

"What? I told you I needed some girl time."

"I know."

"Then what is it?"

He raises his eyebrows. "Who else is going to be *volunteering* at this dinner?"

My face scrunches in confusion. "How should I know? People from the hospital, other volunteers like Shel and me."

"Volunteers like Dane?"

I lean away from him. "Seriously? I thought we were past this."

He tries to look innocent and says, "I just want to be prepared."

"No," I say adamantly. "Dane won't be there."

"You're sure?"

"I'm positive." I narrow my eyes. "You're doing that control freak thing again."

His face relaxes. "Sorry."

I close my book and push it aside. "What brings you by tonight?"

James looks around the room. "Well, there's a football game on..."

My mouth falls open dramatically. "You're using me for my television?"

"We can snuggle," he offers with a smile.

I smirk. "Anything to get your way." I push myself off the bed, extend my hand, and lead him to the living room. I hate watching football. But James is here, we're no longer fighting, and I wouldn't change that for the world.

I reach the couch before James does, and he pulls my hand back so I turn to face him. He reaches out and places his free hand around the base of my neck, under my hair, and holds my head gently as he lowers his lips to mine. My heart wants to burst.

"You didn't get enough of this last night?" I tease when he moves to kiss my forehead.

"I love you," he says against me.

"I love you, too," I say, and it's the truth. Football, control freak, Guardian, and all. I'll always love him.

Until the end of forever.

Chapter 18

"Wow."

Shel leans in to me. "When I helped set up the tables yesterday, this room looked nothing like this," she whispers.

Shel and I stand like statues, mouths agape, as we survey the ballroom for the hospital charity dinner. Dressed in black pants, white tuxedo shirts, black vests and bowties, I have to say we resemble penguins. I clutch the round serving tray in my hands and swallow. I've never been to an event this fancy.

I was mistaken in thinking that the dinner was taking place at the actual hospital. Instead, it's at an upscale hotel in the area, called The Inn at St. John's, which is just outside the city of Ann Arbor. The room is set for roughly 350 guests, all from prestigious local and international organizations. Each business has their own table or tables, distinctly marked with their company names and logos inside tall, fall-themed centerpieces that are lit from within. The tables hold more china than I thought imaginable for one dinner, and they are draped to the floor in cloths that alternate in rich autumn hues from chocolate brown to emerald green to rusty red. The chairs are covered as well, in the same deep tones, each with a precisely tied caramel colored bow. The chandeliers in the ballroom are dimly lit, which allows the centerpieces and tea lights on each table give off the feeling of a more intimate dinner. A string quartet tunes their instruments in one corner; while in another, bartenders busy themselves stocking liquor and wiping glasses.

As my eyes roam the room, I find a long buffet table that is currently being filled with every hors d'oeuvre you can think of. A tall ice sculpture bearing the University of Michigan hospital logo graces the center of the buffet, of which I can see the base being filled with jumbo shrimp and oysters on the half shell. The coordinator for the event, Dana, told us volunteers that we are to clear the empty hors d'oeuvre plates as we find them, along with any empty glasses, and return them to the kitchen. Later, after dinner, the table will be filled with desserts and we'll be on the same mission. During dinner, we are to clear empty plates and retrieve drinks from the bar when asked. She said we'd be able to eat as thanks for our service, so I'm really looking forward to trying some of this food. My mind wanders to Garrett. He would love something like this; although, he would probably choose to spend all of his time in the kitchen.

Dana claps her hands. "Okay, happy volunteers," she says. "Our guests should start arriving any minute." She divides our group down the center with a sweeping gesture. "This half works the right side of the room, this half the left." She eyes two women standing over to the side, dressed in navy pencil skirts and white blouses. "Aubrey and Sydney, you two start with coat check and handle the rush. I'll switch you out when dinner starts."

We disperse to our sides of the room and luckily, Shel and I get the side with the hors d'oeuvre table. I get an up close and personal look, taking in all of the varieties of pre-dinner snacks. There's your typical cheese and crackers, although intricately displayed in a waterfall effect, and crudité with a variety of dips. Mini quiche. Any and all kinds of fruit. The shrimp and the oysters. Caviar. Different variations of meatballs. Salmon pate. Bacon wrapped chicken bites. It's endless. I lean over to Shel. "Who can eat this much food?" I ask. "What's left for dinner?"

Shel shrugs. "Rich people? I guess when you pay $350 a plate, you get your money's worth."

"$350 a plate?" Holy crap!

As the room starts to fill with the first partygoers, the quartet begins to play. I'm surprised by their first piece. "'Is this Pumped Up Kicks?'" I ask Shel.

She tips her head toward the music then raises her eyebrows in appreciation. "Sounds like it," she says. "Not bad. Who knew Foster the People was a popular instrumental choice?"

I smile and turn my attention to the filling room. The men wear business suits, some with bright colored ties while others leave their collars open. The women are dressed in an array of different styles from cocktail dresses, to skirts, to dressy slacks, and tops. As the guests approach the food table, I can't help but notice that no one forgot their jewelry tonight. Necklaces, bracelets, rings, wristwatches and cuff links all manage to catch the dim light and reflect it. I'm beginning to think this dinner is more for show than charity.

"So," Shel asks, "have you decided?"

My forehead pinches. "About what?"

"When you're going to see Dane again."

I give her an exasperated look. We had this discussion in depth last night when I arrived, after I told her about my run in with Teagan at the Halloween party and the resulting conversation and kiss with Dane. "No. I haven't decided."

"Well," she lifts her tray, "spend this mindless night thinking about it. I'm off to collect dirty dishes."

I raise my tray as well and follow her lead, winding my way through the tables in the opposite direction. As I walk, I think about the conversation we had last night. I got no useful advice at all from Shel in regard to Dane. There's not one reason she can think of for me to end what I started with him. I hate that I am in this situation all alone. At some point I'm going to have to be the bad guy, and I wish there was one human that could understand why.

I spend the cocktail hour clearing more empty glasses than plates. Turns out, wealthy benefactors like to drink, especially vodka martinis and scotch on the rocks. As I burn another path in the carpet to the kitchen, a man in my periphery catches my attention. I slow my walk. Is he staring at me? I blink and continue on my path. No. That's impossible.

My next round through the room yields yet more glasses and a run-in with Shel. "How's it going?" I ask.

"This is a lot of work!" she says. "No wonder they're feeding us."

I agree. I fill my tray as full as I dare and make another trip to the kitchen. Not thinking, I take the same route as before and pass the same gentleman. I could swear he's watching me again. I get brave and try to meet his eyes, which he quickly shifts to another person standing in his group. Who is this guy? I've never seen him before.

After I empty my tray in the dish area, I wait around for Shel to appear. When she rounds the corner, I approach her side. "Hey."

"Hey," she says as she empties her tray.

"Look, I'm probably imagining things, but I swear there is a guy out there staring at me."

Shel's eyes light up. "Oh! Is he cute?"

"No! He's an older guy, probably my dad's age."

Shel frowns. "Creeper."

"Come out there with me and see if I'm being paranoid."

"Okay," she says. "Where is he at? What does he look like?"

We start to walk. "He's standing with a group a few feet from the kitchen entrance. He's about James' height, with black hair and a mustache."

"James' height?" Shel asks me, surprised.

"Yes, James' height. Why is that weird?"

She shrugs. "It's just...you haven't mentioned him in awhile. It's odd hearing his name."

If she only knew. "C'mon," I say and refuse to elaborate on my choice of description. "I'll walk near him and you watch."

We exit the kitchen, and I spot the guy still standing with the group. I head toward him, yet parallel, and Shel heads opposite me. I busy myself collecting plates and glasses, and I swear I can feel eyes on me. They might be Shel's though, and I may just be hyper-sensitive to the situation. I walk further into the room, looking amongst the tables, picking up an item here or there and eventually make my way back to Shel's side.

"So?" I ask.

"He is definitely staring at you."

Ick. "Why?" I ask like she will have the answer.

"How am I supposed to know? Are you sure you've never seen him before? Maybe he recognizes you from Bay Woods."

"Shel, you're a genius. That has to be it." Where else would I have run into someone with money?

The string quartet ends their latest song, and our attention is drawn to their set up as Dana speaks into the microphone. She asks everyone to find their seats as dinner will be served momentarily. Shel and I balance our trays through the crowd that converges on the center of the room, and we slowly make our way back toward the kitchen. As we pass the last group of tables, I can't help but notice the man taking his seat. My eyes jump to the company name inside the centerpiece, and my stomach drops through the floor. The business name is Legionnaire.

"It's Dane's boss!" I whisper to Shel, as we wait with the other volunteers along the back of the room while the Caesar salad is being served. "It has to be."

Shel looks wary. "Maybe, maybe not. He could just be someone who works there. Besides, how would he know who you were?"

"I told you he threatened to fire Dane if he didn't marry his daughter. Maybe Teagan showed him a picture of me or something."

Shel questions my logic. "She would go through that trouble? What, did she put an APB out on you?"

I give her a dry look. "I wouldn't put it past her. She *does not* like me."

"Still," Shel sounds unsure, "if it is him, what's he going to do? He's probably just checking out his daughter's competition."

I roll my eyes. "Great." I look down at my outfit and tray. "I can just imagine what he'll report back."

Dana approaches us and divides us down the center again. Half of us get to eat while the other half clears the room, and then we'll switch. Thankfully, Shel and I are selected for the eating group, and I can avoid Mr. Meyer for the next hour. We head to the kitchen to collect our plates and then take a seat in a small meeting room at another location in the hall. Dinner is amazing, even though I'm nervous as all heck and can only manage to eat half of what I'm given. I feel really guilty about it, too. There are people who would kill to have filet mignon and lobster tail for free.

Halfway through the meal, I hear James' voice behind my ear. "What's bothering you?"

I turn to Shel. "I need to use the restroom. I'll be right back."

When I locate the bathroom, I bend down to make sure the stalls are empty. When I turn around, James has already appeared behind me.

"You know you're in the ladies room," I tease.

He gives me a crooked smile. "What's going on?"

"I think Teagan's dad his here," I tell him. "He's been staring at me. I don't know what that means, but it makes me really uncomfortable."

"Teagan, Dane's fiancée?" James scowls.

"Ex-fiancée. Her father is Dane's boss and his company has a table at the party."

His frown deepens. "Have you met him before?"

"Never. Shel thinks the guy might not even be him, just some dude who works at the same company."

"Hmm," James contemplates. "I don't like this. I'm going to stay close."

My eyes widen. "Do you think there's going to be trouble?"

"Not necessarily. But what if this guy turns out to be some creep?"

Right. One Patrick-type in my life was enough. "Okay," I agree. "Stay close."

He steps forward and plants a kiss on the top of my head. "I'll be around," he says and evaporates.

When the time comes to go back to clearing, I really don't want to. Even though knowing James is near makes me feel better, I don't want to be forced to strategically avoid this strange man for the rest of the night. So when Dana asks our group who would be interested in helping in the coatroom, I immediately volunteer.

"Good idea," Shel nods in agreement. She knows I'm anxious. "Let's get through this so we can go home and relax."

The coatroom turns out to be incredibly boring, but easy; I spend my time straightening jackets and wraps. It's just me, seeing as how the guests will leave sporadically. Dana said she might send Aubrey or Sydney back at the end of the night to help with any rush. People start to leave in small spurts immediately after dinner, which keeps me occupied. I'm busy spacing out the remaining coats, now that there is a little more room to spread them out, when a voice interrupts my OCD.

"Excuse me? Miss?"

I turn and find myself staring directly at who I think is Mr. Meyer. Damn it.

He holds out his coat check ticket and smiles. "#1204."

I try to return his smile and take the stub from him. I locate his item, a long wool pea coat, and hand it to him over the coatroom door. "There you are, sir. Have a nice night." I have to admit that up close he's not a scary-looking guy, and he doesn't appear to be assessing me now.

He shrugs on his coat and unexpectedly extends his hand. "Luke Meyer," he introduces himself. "And you are?"

I knew it. I tentatively shake his hand. "Emma."

"Ah. I thought so," he says. He reaches into his pocket and produces a business card, which he places on the ledge of the coatroom door. "Nice to meet you," he smiles and then turns to leave.

I'm speechless as I watch him go. Apparently, I was right and he knows who I am. I don't know why I think this, but I hope this doesn't make things worse for Dane. I was perfectly polite. Maybe he'll try to use my lower social status as a case against me and for Teagan. Ugh.

My eyes fall on the white business card that he left, and I pick it up. It's full of the typical stuff – name, company logo, address, and phone number. Why did he leave this? I flip the card over and my heart skips. There, in neat handwriting, are the following words:

NO NEED TO WORRY. ALL WILL BE WELL IN TIME.

"This is the weirdest thing ever," Shel says as she holds the business card in her hand. "What does it mean?"

I give her a bewildered look. "I have no idea."

We slowly walk to her car in the parking lot. It's nearly midnight, we've cleared just about every dish, glass, and utensil imaginable, and our feet are killing us. I can't wait to get back to her dorm and crash.

"Ladies," I hear a familiar voice from my left and immediately close my eyes. This is so not happening.

"Dane!" Shel gushes from my side. "What are you doing here?"

"It took you two forever to finish in there," he says. "Matt said you'd be done around ten."

I open my eyes. Of course. Matt. He's worse than a group of gossiping women. That boy needs duct tape strategically placed over his mouth.

"There was a lot to do," Shel explains then looks at me pointedly. "Aren't you going to say hello?"

"Hey," I say and look at the ground as I internally panic. How am I going to explain this to James?

"I decided to take matters into my own hands," Dane says as he stops about a foot in front of me. "I wanted to see you." He reaches out and lifts my chin, so that I'm looking up at him. "I still need that hug."

I hear Shel let out a muted "aww" and, as if on cue, I see James materialize directly behind Dane. I try to keep my eyes focused on Dane and not over his shoulder, but it's difficult. James looks livid. Why shouldn't he be? I told him Dane wouldn't be here – no, I promised. And here he finds us, Dane touching my face and looking into my eyes, saying he needs a hug.

I react more violently than necessary, but I'm weirded out from Teagan's dad and I'm exhausted and panicky. I yank my face out of Dane's gentle grasp and take a step back. "You shouldn't have come here! I told you I would see you when I could."

Dane's face falls, hurt, and then rearranges itself. "What is with you?" he snaps.

"Why won't you listen to me?" I plead in anger. I turn to Shel. "Why won't any of you listen to me?"

Shel looks sad and confused by my question and says nothing.

I feel Dane's hand on my shoulder, and I shrug it off. "Touching me is not a good idea right now."

He holds his hands up in surrender in front of him. "Emma. Seriously. What is the problem?"

I eye James, who steps to Dane's side. He clenches his fists and looks ready to take a swing. I need to prove to him that I didn't ask Dane to be here.

"You!" I answer Dane. "You are my problem!"

Dane looks flabbergasted and beyond pissed. I'm making a fine mess of things. Guilt floods my body as I register his expression. He's never done anything to me to make me treat him this way, and my heart aches.

"Emma," Shel tries to intervene. "Maybe we should go. You guys can talk this out another time."

"No," Dane says adamantly. "Let's do this." He takes a step forward and towers over me. "Go ahead. Tell me how you really feel."

I stare up into his eyes and nearly choke on my words as I try to maintain a steady tone. "You and I can never be anything. Ever."

"Why?" His eyes narrow as he searches my face. "Give me one good reason."

My mind scrambles. "Because I'm messed up beyond words! You don't want me; you don't deserve that."

Dane scowls. "Who are you to say what I do and don't want? Isn't that my decision?"

"You think you want me, but you don't. I was just a replacement for Teagan when you were lonely, that's all."

"You know that's not true." He takes a step closer. "C'mon, you can do better than that. What's the real reason?"

The real reason is standing next to you ready to rip you limb from limb! I think. My eyes jump to James, who is standing inches from Dane, and I silently pray for him to look at me. *Look at me!* I shout in my head. *Look at me and calm down!*

"Well?" Dane presses.

I'm at a loss. I can't tell him that I'm still in love with my dead boyfriend! Or can I? "I'm in love with someone else," I say as I try to remain strong. "I'm seeing someone else." It's not a lie.

Dane takes a step back as if he's been burned, exposing Shel to my line of vision. Both of them look at me in awe. Dane sets his jaw, and his eyes harden. "Who's the lucky guy?"

"No one you know," I say as my eyes flash to James. He's finally retreated a few steps although he still looks pissed as hell.

"Why didn't you just say so?" Dane drills me.

"I didn't know how...I didn't want to hurt you."

He lets out a forced laugh and leans forward. "Let me tell you something. This wasn't the way to do it."

I feel terrible. Absolutely horrible. But what I told him was the truth; I am with someone else. I just can't be specific. I open my mouth to apologize.

He holds out his hand to stop me. "Don't," he says and starts to back toward his car. "I've heard enough for one night."

"Dane, I..."

"Don't," he cuts me off in a hard tone. "Just don't."

With that he turns his back and walks away. I try to keep my emotions in check in front of Shel and James, but it's hard. I look at James and quickly wipe away the few tears that have escaped my eyes. He nods toward me and then disappears, leaving me to wonder if he's more upset with me or with Dane. I finally turn toward Shel. Now I get to face her wrath.

Instead of words, she wraps me in a vise-like hug. It's all I can do to remain standing as my tears well over.

"Why didn't you tell me?" she says into my shoulder. "I had no idea you were seeing someone new."

I shake my head. "I'm not."

She pulls back and stares at me. "Emma! Why did you do that to Dane?"

I wipe my face. "So he'd leave me alone and move on."

She scrutinizes me. "So, you're not seeing anyone?"

My emotional state and the inability to discuss anything personal with anyone human clouds my judgment. I imagine the relief I will feel once I utter what's on my tongue. "I'm not seeing anyone new; I'm seeing someone old," I pause. "I'm still in love with James," I tell her. "I still see James.

Chapter 19

Sitting on my couch, wrapped in a blanket, I doodle in my notebook with a pencil. I've been back in my apartment since late afternoon, waiting. For James. For my head to stop pounding. For a moment of clarity. I look down and focus on my scribble. I've written Mr. Meyer's strange message repeatedly. *No need to worry. All will be well in time.*

I slam my notebook shut and toss it on the coffee table. I realize that I've left my apartment only twice since classes began, and each time I ended up in some psychotic situation. Every time I leave to help someone, I end up hurting someone else. Maybe that's the key. I should stop leaving to help people.

After I admitted that I still see James, it took most of the night to convince Shel not to call my parents to have me pulled from school and institutionalized. It was stupid of me to ever let those words leave my lips. I should have made up a story about dating Garrett instead. Of course Shel assumed I was having some sort of delusionary James visions, and I went along with her assumption to make things easier. I managed to convince her that the visions were getting better, and they were nothing I wanted to worry my family over. I told her I needed time to let myself heal from his loss and that this summer with Dane happened way too fast. I think she finally understood some of my resistance toward Dane, and she vowed to stop pushing. Finally.

I decide I need comfort food and homemade chocolate chip cookies seem more than in order. I peel myself off the couch and shuffle to the kitchen. I rummage through my cupboards and come up with every ingredient but the baking soda. I head over to the wall and bang three times. I'm sure Garrett has some. It only takes a moment for him to bang back, letting me know he's home. I leave my place and return from my baking soda mission successful, but I had to trade the soda for a promise that he could stop by in a few minutes, as soon as the first batch of cookies was done.

I set to work mixing and it calms me. When every ingredient is combined, I dole out the dough in spoonfuls on a baking sheet, place it in the oven, and then set to eating the majority of the left over batter out of the bowl with the spoon. I know it's not good to eat the raw eggs, but Nestle Tollhouse chocolate chip cookie dough is really best uncooked.

"Did you miss your mouth?" I hear James say as he appears in the kitchen.

I pause mid-lick and wipe the corner of my lip with my thumb. "Better?"

He gives me a tiny smile. "Much."

I toss the spoon back into the bowl and walk forward to wrap my arms around his waist. "Do you know how much you scared me last night? I thought you were going to punch Dane."

"I was so close," he says. "When I felt your reaction and then saw him touching you...I about went over the edge. That guy is an expert at pissing me off."

"Well, you don't have to worry about him anymore," I say quietly. "I'm pretty sure I ruined everything we ever had."

James pulls away from me slightly. "You sound sad about that."

I look up at him. "I am sad about that."

"Why?" he frowns.

"Because I hurt him," I say like it should be obvious. "He didn't deserve that. He's never done anything, but care about me."

"Whoa." James steps out of my arms. "Are you being serious right now?"

"Yes." My expression twists. "I don't get off on hurting people."

The oven timer beeps, momentarily distracting me. I grab a dishtowel off counter, use it as a hot pad, and remove the cookie sheet, tossing it noisily on the stovetop. I turn back to James. "You're mad because I feel bad about being mean?"

"I'm mad because you feel bad about being mean to *him*," he says, irritated. "Have you forgotten about the engagement? His lying to you?"

"He explained that."

James shakes his head. "And I still can't believe you bought it."

I cross my arms defensively. "What's to buy? He didn't tell me because he was ending it with her. Yes, he should have told me, I agree. But he made a mistake."

"So now he's a saint?"

"I'm not saying that!" Is this what we're going to do now? Fight every other day? I don't like it, and I'm sick of it. "Can't you just be happy? He's never going to speak to me again. Problem solved!" I march past him and into the living room. The kitchen is starting to feel claustrophobic.

James follows. "Are you walking away from me?"

"No!" I turn around. "I just need some air."

We stare at each other for a few moments. Lately, I can't keep up with his bipolar mood swings. He was never like this before he died. I miss the relaxed, fun James he used to be.

"How?" James asks.

"How what?"

"You said he cares for you. Tell me how."

I place my hands on my hips and search his face. My mind flashes back in time to my confrontation with Mrs. Davis, when Dane defended me. "This summer," I say adamantly. "Dane stood up for me when your mother called me a whore."

His expression changes from one of defiance to one of shock. We've never discussed this. "What are you talking about?"

"I ran into your mom at the grocery store while running an errand for work. She blamed me for your death and then called me a whore in front of an aisle full of strangers. Dane got me out of there; he defended me."

James' eyes cloud over. "Why didn't you tell me?"

"Because I didn't want you to think badly of your mother."

James looks down, processing what I've told him, and then his head snaps up. "Is there anything else I don't know?"

I feel the need to defend Dane and my decision to let him into my life. "He helped me take out my aggressions after you were assigned as my Guardian; he told me his mother died when he was young, and he could relate to my grief. He said, if I could ever love him, he would wait for me."

James frowns. "How is it possible that I know none of these things?"

I take a step toward him. "They happened while you were keeping your distance from me."

James studies my face for a moment. "And if I'd stayed away?" he asks. "Do you think Dane wouldn't have left you like he left Teagan?"

"Have you met Teagan? She's evil!"

James scoffs. "Not according to Meg."

I can feel my forehead pinch as I scowl. "What's Meg got to do with this?"

"Meg is Teagan's Guardian."

"James!"

Both of our heads snap toward Garrett's voice, and we find him standing just inside my doorway.

"You know that is privileged information," Garrett says as he approaches us. "What are you thinking?"

James takes a step back and sighs heavily. "Why are you here?"

"I came for cookies." Garrett looks at me. "What is going on?" he demands.

The need to tell Garrett overwhelms me. Maybe he can set James straight, help him with his behavior. He was his Guardian and mentor, after all. "James almost hit Dane last night," I confess. Under my lashes, I glance at James. If looks could kill, I would be dead. Deader than dead. James shoots daggers at me.

"Again with the jealousy?" Garrett glares at James. "Are you begging for attention? You know that is unacceptable!"

James walks toward Garrett and stops inches from him. "It's hard to control," he nearly growls. "All of my emotions are getting stronger; *nothing* is fading like you said it would!" He glances at me and then to Garrett again. "The sooner I can be human, the sooner I can be everything she needs. Then this conversation will mean nothing."

"You are everything she needs!" Garrett exclaims.

James crosses his arms. "I don't see it that way."

Garrett steps back and stares at James, shaking his head in disbelief. He looks at me and then closes his eyes, taking a deep breath. "Sit down."

When he opens his eyes, we're both still standing. "I said sit down."

I tentatively move to the couch and, begrudgingly, James joins me. Garrett follows us and takes a seat in the opposite chair. He rubs his forehead. "This is not the time I wanted to tell you this," he says, his voice tired. "But I think it might alleviate your stress." He looks us in the eyes. "Or at least allow you to move forward."

My pulse starts to accelerate.

"Emma," he turns to me, "you've become a good friend. I never expected it, but it's something I'm truly grateful for. I don't want to see you tortured any more than I want to see James struggle."

James scowls, unconvinced.

"It true," Garrett says to James. "You were my Ward. Every fiber of my being is programmed to protect you, to look out for what's best, to guide you in your decisions to a life well-lived. I still feel some of that connection to you now." He looks at his hands. "That's why, before I tell you this, I need you to know that what I did brought me physical pain. Pain I thought I no longer had the ability to feel." He looks up at James. "It was debilitating."

James narrows his eyes. "What did you do?"

Garrett sits up straight and takes a deep breath. "I assigned you to Emma, so that you could never be released and so that I could be Reborn. You can't be human again," he pauses, "unless Emma dies."

I can't catch my breath. It feels like I've fallen off a high rise and landed on the cement face first. James, on the other hand, leaps off the couch and shoves Garrett, flipping the chair over and spilling him on to the floor. "You used me!" he shouts.

"It was the best thing for all of us!" Garrett tries to stand. "You know the odds of Emma releasing you were slim!"

The sound of my name helps me to breathe again. "You don't know that!" I jump to stand.

"The fact that you two are still arguing over Dane proves it," Garrett says, regaining his balance. He looks at James. "I tied you to her for life! I knew it would be difficult, but I thought you could overcome it. I truly did."

James doesn't care. He lunges at Garrett and lands a right hook across his jaw with a sickening crunch. Garrett stumbles to side and catches himself before he hits the wall. He stands straight and shakes off the pain, taking a defensive stance.

"You let me believe I could be human again!" James swings, but Garrett's prepared and he misses.

"I had to!" Garrett circles around the couch and behind me. "We need your cooperation to stay hidden!"

"You made the wrong choice," James seethes and advances. "If I can't be human neither can you."

"You can't go to The Allegiant," Garrett says. "You'll ruin the chance for all the others."

"I don't care about them!"

"You can't take this away from Thomas! Or Joss or Jenna! Think about Meg," Garrett tries to reason. "You can't take this away from her."

When Garrett says Meg's name, James stops in his tracks. His action causes tears to burn behind my eyes. I think we all just realized how much he truly does care for her.

Garrett relaxes his stance slightly. "Please," he says to James. "If you care nothing for us and our cause, that's fine." He glances at me. "But think of Emma. If The Allegiant find out about your jealousy, you very well may lose her."

James turns and focuses on me. His expression registers both anger and pain, and tears start to make tracks down my cheeks. In a way, I've already lost him. But, I could lose him for absolute and forever if he exposes Garrett's secret. The Allegiant would know everything, and they would take his memories of us for sure. "Don't do it," I whisper.

I can see my plea register in his eyes. Suddenly, James jumps forward, taking Garrett by surprise as he grabs his shirt and throws him up against the door. "You. Owe. Me." He enunciates each word. He lets Garrett's clothes go with a rough shove and backs away from the door. He turns toward me with a vacant expression. "I need some time."

I nod in understanding. I've seen that look before; I know what it means. This is where he leaves me to try and stop loving me again. Will this cycle never end? I walk to him and wrap my arms around his waist and press my head against his chest. He hugs me back loosely, as if he's afraid to touch me. "I'll miss you," I say, muffled.

I can hear him exhale and feel him brush the top of my head with his lips. He doesn't return the sentiment or tell me he loves me. He just evaporates in my arms, leaving my chest feeling hollow and a sob stuck in my throat.

"Emma," Garrett says from across the room, "I'm sorry, but you can move forward now. You don't have to worry about a future with James."

I shoot Garrett a nasty look. "You made sure of that, didn't you?"

He starts to approach me. I can see the left side of his face is already bruised and starting to swell. "You know why I did it."

"Because you're selfish?" I spit. "It had nothing to do with what you wanted with Amelia or how it was the best thing for James and me! You're an excellent liar."

"What I said was true. I wanted to be in Amelia's life in any way possible. I would have gladly been her Guardian."

I back away from him. "You need to go. I don't trust you anymore."

"Don't say that." He looks crushed. "You can trust me."

I shake my head violently. "You need to leave. Now."

Garrett looks down and then backs toward the door. He opens it then turns to me again. "I'll be home if you want to talk."

I give him a scathing stare. "That's *so* not going to happen."

"Emma," he almost pleads.

"Leave!" I yell.

He follows my order and walks through the door, closing it quietly behind him. I sink to the floor where I stand and let the sob rip through my throat. I thought I was alone before. I had no idea I could be even more so.

Chapter 20

My body desperately wants to fall asleep, but my mind won't let it. Ever since Garrett's revelation, I've managed three, maybe four hours of sleep a night. I stopped at the store this afternoon, on my way back from class, and bought a sleep aid because I thought it would help. I glance at the clock and then roll over in frustration. It's one in the morning. I took those pills hours ago. They should have kicked in by now.

I rack my brain for things to do. I have to keep myself occupied, so my mind can't connect with my heart. I've spent the last four days attending class then working ahead in all of them, as far as I can. I've cleaned my apartment from top to bottom. I've experimented in the kitchen, making myself real meals instead of frozen ones. I've bugged LB so much that she's grown sick of me, and she hides under the bed whenever I walk into the room. Today, I even attempted an online job search and applied for three positions. I'm running out of options.

Lifting my head, I punch the pillow to fluff it, and then flip to my other side. At least I've been able to avoid Garrett. I was worried about how I would manage to ignore him in Ethics and concentrate on the lecture, but he hasn't shown up. Either he's being a coward, or he's staying away to make things easier for me. I close my eyes and grit my teeth. I refuse to believe he's doing anything for me out of kindness. The center of my chest starts to squeeze in that grievously familiar, uncomfortable way, and I try to stop thinking. Eventually, I'm going to have to come to grips with the fact that I've lost someone who pretended to be a friend.

Logical thoughts bounce around in my head. They suggest action, but my body refuses to listen and cooperate.

If you don't get enough rest, you'll get sick.

I know.

Any future with James was a long shot.

Don't remind me.

Go to sleep.

I can't.

You should take some more medicine.

Is that really wise?

Call Shel and ask.

It's after one a.m.

She'll reassure you.

That's rude.

Go over and talk to Garrett.

No.

He'll understand.

He's no longer a friend.

Call Dane and apologize.

Not an option.

It will make you feel better.

He won't believe me.

Get up and watch TV.

I need to sleep!

Well, you need to do something.

I KNOW.

I throw the covers off. This internal conversation is making my head ache. I need to feel better. Not amazing, not perfect, not happy. Just *better*. Anything other than this mechanical, numb shell of the person I used to be. I stare at the ceiling and think of home. I crave to be there. Honestly, if I could have one person here with me right now it would be my mother. I guess that should sound lame coming from a 22-year old, but it's the truth.

The thought of my family is comforting and, suddenly, I bolt upright. Why didn't I think of this before?

I throw my legs off the side of the bed and pad to the living room to find my laptop. I turn it on and, while it loads, head to the kitchen to make a mug of hot chocolate. When I return, I navigate to WMU's website and begin my search; hopefully I can find answers here. If not, tomorrow I'll be skulking around campus as I try and get some in person.

My mission is simple. I need to figure out a way to complete my last semester from home.

The next morning, I sit bleary-eyed in the Advising Office. Thankfully the advisors are still around on Fridays. My research yielded promising results; it turns out an approved internship can be used for business elective credits. I know I have four classes left to complete toward my degree, and I'm hoping that I'll be able waive a couple in lieu of an internship, while completing the other two online. I have plenty of time to hit the pavement and find someplace closer to home to intern.

"Emma?" my advisor, Mrs. Andrews, calls to me from behind the welcome desk. "Come on back."

I stand and follow the petite woman to her office. Mrs. Andrews has been my advisor since I started at Western. She assisted me when I first came to campus, after high school, and then helped me again after James' accident; I had to find out what my options were and if I could complete my courses from home. She was very understanding then. I'm hoping for the same today.

"How have you been?" she asks as she rounds her desk. "I'm glad to see you."

I take a seat opposite her and give her a small smile. "Things have been good," I lie. Well, not totally lie. My classes have been good. "I was hoping I could get some help planning my last semester."

"Sure," she smiles. "The winter course catalog went live today. Let's see what you have left to take." She turns toward her computer, asks for my student number, and then pulls up my program and transcript. "Looks like you only have nine credits left."

"Nine?" I ask, surprised. "I thought I had twelve."

She scrolls through the screens and determines that a course I took by accident my second year now counts toward my degree. This is great news. The less I have to complete, the better.

"I was wondering about an internship," I say. "I was reading online last night and saw that approved internships can count as credit."

"If you don't mind my saying so," she raises an eyebrow, "it looks like you've been spending several nights reading online. Everything okay?"

I flush with embarrassment. I must have drifted off to sleep around four or five in the morning only to wake up unrested around seven. That makes five nights with virtually no sleep resulting in some pretty impressive eye bags. "The truth is, I'm hoping to move back home for my last semester. If there's someplace I can intern close to home and take my remaining courses online that would be perfect. Being back here has been..." I pause, searching for the right words, "...a little tougher than I imagined."

She gives me a sympathetic smile. "I bet." Mrs. Andrews wasn't only my advisor; she was James' as well. We were both management majors and our last names started with D. She reviews my transcript again. "I'm impressed with your grades," she comments. "You finished last semester stronger than I would have anticipated. I assume this semester is going just as well in that department?"

I nod. "It appears so. Right now, anyway."

"Good," she says and turns around to grab a form off the credenza behind her. She consults the computer and then jots down a few items. Next, she opens a drawer, pulls out a few sheets of paper, and then pushes them toward me. "You need an economics class, and Intermediate Macroeconomics will be offered online," she explains and points to the form on the right. "Registration opens next Monday." She shifts the forms and shows me another. "This is a list of approved internship locations in the area that will count for two business electives, if you can secure at least thirty hours a week."

I glance at the list and try not to frown. All of these businesses are in the Kalamazoo area. This doesn't help me.

"Now," she continues, "you have some time. If you can find an internship at a reputable organization willing to follow these guidelines," she shows me the third sheet of paper, "as a faculty advisor I can sign off on the credit."

Now we're talking. I smile as I pick up the paper. "How long do I have to find a place?"

"Technically until the winter semester begins," she says. "But I would try to find something as soon as possible. Positions tend to fill up quickly with students looking for experience to put on resumes."

"Got it," I say and collect the other two forms. I'm beginning to feel better already.

After a moment or two of silence, Mrs. Andrews asks, "Emma, may I give you some unsolicited advice?"

I look up from the paperwork. "Sure."

"You're an excellent student," she says and folds her hands on her desk. "Your grades reflect that, but more so you don't shy away from a challenge. I know a lot of people who would have taken what happened last spring and used it as an excuse to drop out and quit. You didn't and that speaks volumes to your character."

I give her a small smile. "That's the advice?"

"The advice is to never give up," she says. "No matter what happens. Don't let adversity drain you; use it to make you stronger. You have great potential and I would hate to see that go to waste."

My eyes tingle and I focus on the ficus tree in the corner. Giving up on school was never an option. Is she telling me this because I look like I'm about to jump off the nearest bridge? "Do I really look that terrible?" I ask, trying to joke about it.

She laughs. "Actually, yes."

I shake my head and choke out a laugh, too.

"You wouldn't believe the number of students I see that can't make a move without me," she continues, sitting back in her chair. "But you're self-sufficient. You're motivated. Those are valuable skills that people either have or they don't."

I look down at the papers in my hand. "I just want to find a way to make things the best they can be for me."

"That's smart," she nods with approval. "Whatever it is that's going on in your life right now, you're using it to stay true to yourself. Use whatever it is to move you through this next semester. Before you know it, you'll be graduating."

I catch her eyes. "Thank you," I say sincerely. "I needed to hear that."

"Well, there's something else you need to hear." She leans forward. "Get some rest."

I nod and chuckle. "I think that will be easier now that I have a plan."

She smiles at me warmly. "I'm glad I could help."

As I head back to my apartment, I process Mrs. Andrews' words and hope starts to bloom inside my chest. Someone I barely know thinks I'm strong; someone recognizes my hard work and dedication. I'm not just a sorry mess dwelling on lost loves, lost friends, and loneliness. I accept challenges. I'm motivated. I have potential.

A grin breaks out across my face and I walk faster, determined. I'm not going down without a fight. I have a life to live. No James, no Dane, no Garrett, no problem.

It's time to stand up and rock my future.

"Shel?"

"Hey!"

"Listen," I shift the phone to hold it between my face and my shoulder, "I need some ideas. I have to find a business near home that will take me as an intern."

I can imagine her frown. "Why?"

"Because I'm moving back." I pick up another shirt from the laundry basket. "I found out I can intern in place of two electives next semester."

She pauses. "This is because of the James visions, isn't it? They're back, aren't they?"

She sounds concerned. I want to tell her that the James "visions" are gone indefinitely, but I opt for "No, they're not. I'm just tired of being alone."

"Well, that's easy," she says. "Bay Woods."

I groan. "Definitely not. Try again."

She laughs. "You could always try Legionnaire. Mr. Meyer seemed smitten with you."

"Ugh! Shel! I'm being serious!"

"Let me think..."

I wait in silence as I fold clothes. Where is my other gray sock?

"Duh!" Shel exclaims. "The veterinary clinic. Call Matt. His dad will take you in a heartbeat."

"Yes!" I drop my socks back into the basket. "Shel, you're a life saver."

"Well, that is the idea. I am studying to be a doctor."

After I hang up with her, I call Matt immediately. He seems just as excited as I am about the possibility of my working at the clinic. Apparently Sheila, the current office manager, is pregnant and due in January. Matt was asked to fill in for her, as he occasionally does, but he's dreading the long commitment. He, too, has some classes to finish, but he doesn't want to commute back and forth to school.

"I'll talk to my dad about this tonight," he says. "Take down his email address, so you can send him the school's guidelines."

I find a piece of scrap paper and scribble down the address as he recites it to me.

"It will be great to have you around again, Em," Matt says sincerely. Too sincerely.

"You've been talking to Shel, haven't you?" I ask suspiciously. She's probably mentioned my fake visions.

He laughs. "Only every day."

After emailing Matt and finishing laundry, I curl up on the couch and flip through the television channels. I finally settle on an episode of *Dr. G Medical Examiner*, and I imagine Shel as Dr. G. It makes me laugh. I know she prefers live bodies to dead ones, but as her investigative skills at Dane's birthday party come back to me, I think she would make a great M.E.

As the show goes on, my body relaxes. Half way through I crash hard into a deep sleep. It's so deep that I don't change positions, I don't dream, and I don't feel LB jump on or off me. I'm dead to the world, just like one of Dr. G's patients.

That's why, when I feel my body being roughly shaken, I'm startled. I lash out, kicking and hitting. My foot connects with someone, and my eyes fly open. Garrett is standing above me.

"What do you want?" I ask angrily.

"There's trouble," Garrett says in somber tone.

I force my eyes open. "What are you talking about?"

"We need to get you out of here."

He tries to grab my elbow, and I jerk it away. "No! Why?"

He looks at me with a mixed expression of anxiety and remorse. "You're in danger."

As soon as he utters those words, James immediately appears on the other side of the room. "What's going on?" he demands.

Garrett regards him with a grave expression. "The Allegiant are coming for Emma."

Chapter 21

"The hell they are," James snaps.

Garrett turns to me. "I'm serious. You need to pack, and you need to pack now. I have access to some money –"

He's cut off by James shoving him roughly against his shoulder. "She's not going anywhere!"

"Listen!" Garrett eyes the both of us. "The Allegiant know." He kneels in front of the couch to meet my eyes. "They will use James to get to me and use you to get to James."

A thousand questions blaze through my brain. I know I should be scared, but all I feel is anger. "Then why don't you disappear?"

"I will," he says, and then looks at James over his shoulder. "We all need to."

"What happened?" James presses, stepping forward. "Emma has done nothing wrong; she's got nothing to do with being Reborn."

Garrett stands to face to him. "Meg and Jenna were overheard."

James squints in confusion. "So? Whatever was heard could easily be written off as gossip."

"Not this time." Garrett shakes his head solemnly. "Meg was Touched."

My stomach starts to knot in an uncomfortable way. I have no idea what that means, but judging from James' dazed expression, I know it can't be good. His eyes gloss over, and he looks as if the breath has been knocked from his lungs. After a moment his eyes dart to mine, and he moves to stand in front of me protectively, crossing his arms. He's all business as his eyes lock on Garrett. "Tell me what we have to do."

"Wait." I jump off the couch. "What does that mean? She was Touched?"

James turns his face toward me. "The Allegiant can render you immobile and force you to speak the truth."

I start to nod in understanding, but then stop as I process what that means. I give James a wary look. Meg knows about Garrett, obviously, but she also knows about James. She knows about us, about his inability to let go. My voice sounds small. "Do you think –?"

James assumes my question and interrupts. "Absolutely." He sets his mouth in a grim line.

"We need to get moving," Garrett redirects our attention. He looks anxious as he addresses me. "You have a suitcase, right? Or a bag?"

My mind scrambles. He wants me to pack? For where? My eyes catch the paper on the coffee table that holds Dr. Randall's email address, and this afternoon floods my memory. I remember how confident and happy I felt about my plans. I was going home. "No," I say to myself and then raise my head adamantly. "No. I'm not going anywhere."

"Emma." Garrett gives me an exasperated look.

I eye both him and James. "In case you haven't noticed, I have a life to live. I have obligations. I can't just pick up and leave! What about school? What about my parents?"

Garrett reaches for my elbow. "We'll work on that while we drive."

I yank my arm away. "Drive where exactly?"

Garrett's eyes flash to James. "We need to work that out."

I laugh sarcastically. "So, there's no plan? We leave and drive aimlessly? I kick you out of the car in one town and then hole up in another? Alone?" I shake my head. "I don't think so."

James wraps his cool hand around my arm in a reassuring way. "You don't have a choice."

I shoot him a scathing look then stalk away from him, pulling my arm through his grasp. I set my hands on my hips and face them. "I always have a choice."

Both of them regard me with a mixture of frustration and concern. I know The Allegiant finding out is bad news, but there has to be another way to work through this. Running and hiding sounds cowardly and childish.

"Em," James says, pleading. "You don't understand."

"You're right," I scowl. "If The Allegiant show up, what can they do? If you two leave, I won't know where you are. I'll have nothing to tell them."

"You're wrong," Garrett says. "You'll have your thoughts and memories to share." He walks toward me. "Do you want James taken from you? Your past together erased?"

My face twists as James picks up on Garrett's pause. "They'll hurt you, Em." He looks nauseous. "They'll put you in danger, so that I'll have no choice but to come to you. They'll use our bond against us."

His tortured expression puts a dent in my defenses. I have to admit that being in pain is not something I enjoy, nor do I want him gone from my life. My eyes lock on James. "I would never want that."

He approaches me slowly. "I know. We'll work things out, I promise. Your classes, your parents..." He stops in front of me. "But I have to keep you safe. It's my only priority."

Internally, I struggle trying to strategize. I know the connection James has to me is a problem, but it's not his fault. None of this is our fault. Forget Garrett and his quest to be human. "What if we stayed?" I ask.

He frowns. "What do you mean?"

"Wait for The Allegiant with me; we can explain that we're pawns." My eyes flit accusingly at Garrett. "You didn't ask to be my Guardian."

James searches my face as he considers my proposition. From what I know, our situation is unique. The Allegiant may be open to an honest discussion; they may have mercy on us. In my book, Garrett is the real offender.

"Emma," Garrett interrupts, appearing by my side. "That won't work."

"Why not?"

"The Allegiant are not forgiving," he says and eyes James. "They won't accept explanations, especially now."

I'm not letting this go. I want to stay in familiar surroundings with James in my life; I want to follow through on my plans for graduation. I know I just came up with them today, but it hurts my heart to think otherwise. "How do you know?" I point at Garrett's chest. "How do you know they'll refuse to listen?"

He crosses his arms impatiently. "Because I do."

His arrogance bothers me, and I narrow my eyes. "You need a better explanation." I defiantly look at James. "If he doesn't have a better answer, I'm staying. I mean it."

James assesses me for a moment then turns to Garrett. "She's not kidding. We'll have to make her leave."

I step away from them. "You wouldn't dare!"

Out of nowhere, an unfamiliar phone rings. I look at the two of them in confusion as Garrett reaches into his back pocket and reluctantly produces a cell phone. He walks away to take the call, and James and I look at each other, puzzled. Since when does Garrett have a phone?

It's a short conversation. After his initial greeting of "Yes?" the only other word James and I hear him utter is "no" before hanging up. He stands with his back to us, head down, revealing nothing. James and I give each other a wary look, and I wrap my arms around my waist.

It seems like minutes before Garrett turns around, but I'm sure only silent seconds have passed. He regards us with a sober expression as his face registers our questions. He slides the phone back into his pocket. "That was Lucas."

"Lucas who?" James asks.

"Lucas was my Guardian," he says and closes the distance between us. "And he's now one of The Allegiant."

My jaw hits the floor. I look at James, and he's equally as shocked. As he regains his composure, I can see tension take over his face and radiate down his neck to his shoulders. "Start talking," he seethes.

Garrett nods toward me. "I'll start talking when she starts packing."

James abruptly grabs my wrist and pulls me toward the bedroom. I willingly follow, not that I could resist him. He's gotten stronger, and I'm sure he would have picked me up and carried me if he had to. As we enter the room, he flips the light switch and tows me toward my closet. He throws open the door and looks pointedly from my suitcase to me. I nod and he releases my wrist, stepping around me to face Garrett. I grab my suitcase and toss it on the bed.

"Don't you have anything bigger?" Garrett asks.

I shoot him a sarcastic look and then head to my dresser, yanking open the top drawer. Behind me I hear James snap, "You've been working with The Allegiant all along?"

"Just Lucas," Garrett says. "He was the only one who knew."

"Why?"

"Becoming Reborn was his idea; he knew I missed humanity."

I grab a handful of socks and underwear and turn back toward the bed to put them in my bag.

James frowns. "I thought being Reborn was a secret The Allegiant didn't allow."

"You're right," Garrett says. "Lucas' views vary from his brothers; they follow an ancient doctrine. He's trying to prove a point, and he needs me to be successful."

"What's he trying to prove?" I ask, pausing over my suitcase.

Garrett shakes his head. "He hasn't revealed that to me, in case I'm caught by the others. All he said was that it would benefit humanity."

"And you believe him?" James asks skeptically.

"Of course I do," Garrett looks offended. "He was my Guardian."

James looks doubtful. "Do the other Guardians know?"

Garrett opens his mouth to answer then pauses. He eyes my nearly empty suitcase and then meets my gaze. I get the hint. No more information if I don't start moving. I turn back toward my dresser.

"Just Jack," Garrett continues. "Lucas was his Guardian too, since we're twins. He brought being Reborn to both of us."

I pull out a few sweaters from my dresser then move down a drawer to grab some jeans.

"Why didn't you tell us?" James asks in frustration. "It would have been easier knowing we had an ally."

"If you knew and you were caught, Lucas would be exposed," Garrett says. "The only reason he was able to warn me about Meg and Jenna was because they were kept in the dark."

"What will happen to them?" I ask quietly, my arms full of clothes.

Garrett gives me a grim look. "Right now, they're being held for information while The Allegiant try to locate the rest of us. Thankfully, Jack was visiting me when I got the call and he's disappeared."

My stomach drops as I think of Jack running. He came across so tough. I start to feel even more ill at the thought of Thomas and Joss being captured; they're so kind and Thomas would do anything for Joss, including put himself at risk.

Garrett continues. "Lucas called to ask about our progress. He's been pretending to be outraged while stalling at the same time. That's why we have to move; we have to scatter."

I drop my clothes into the suitcase as James says, "So let's go."

"None of us can know where the others end up," Garrett strategizes with James. "You need to stay out of the Intermediate and away from Emma."

The thought of being alone in some strange place doesn't sit well with my heart, and suddenly I have a hard time catching my breath. My mental state already took a hit this week; I don't know how much more I can handle. Top that off with trying to figure out how to finish school and avoid my parents, and I'm about ready to hyperventilate.

James immediately senses my anxiety. "What's wrong?" He steps away from Garrett and walks toward me, taking my hand and leading me to sit on the bed. He looks into my eyes with a mixed expression of fear, concern, and utter helplessness.

It's in that moment that I resolve to get through this. I concentrate and work on steadying my breathing to a natural rhythm. I can't have him worrying about me and torturing himself to stay away. "It's okay," I say and stand back up. "I just panicked for a second. I'll be all right." I reach for my suitcase and busy myself organizing things so they will fit.

James' attention is pulled away from me by Garrett. "I'll go with Emma. We'll take her car and head out; it's the fastest way to get me out of town. She'll drop me somewhere, but I won't stay. Then she can head someplace else."

My head snaps up. "Can I go home?" I ask hopefully. Surely I can give my parents a good excuse as to why I've moved back.

Sadly, Garrett shakes his head. "I'm sorry. If James is found by The Allegiant, they would know to look for you there."

"But if they have James, why would they need me?" Not that I want James caught.

"To use you against me," James says quietly.

"And to try and locate me," Garrett adds. "They'll assume you know more than you do."

Damn it. I go back to shoving my clothes into my suitcase. The realization hits that I'm really going through with this, and I'll need more than clothes. I head out of the room, to the bathroom, to start collecting my toiletries. The boys follow me and resume their discussion in the living area, and I'm glad. I need a few minutes to concentrate on what I need to bring rather than all the what-if's. If I allow myself to think about this too much, I'll probably freak out again.

I collect my things from the bathroom cabinet and move to the bedroom, catching snippets of their conversation.

"...once things are safe I'll contact Emma. You'll feel it through your bond."

"How long do you think that will be?"

"At least until I'm human, I'm sure."

I shudder when I hear that answer and try to tune them out. I squish my bathroom bag into the front pocket of my suitcase and realize I forgot my shower stuff. I head back to the bathroom.

"...wish we had more time to plan."

"Don't I know it."

"I'm not comfortable with her being alone."

"Neither am I."

I peruse the bathroom to make sure I have everything and head back to the bedroom again.

"...are you sure?"

"...Evelyn said..."

I manage to fit my shower items into a side pocket and zip it up tight. I stand and look around my room. I'll need my textbooks, my laptop, LB of course, her stuff... I walk to my closet and fish out her carrier.

"Do you need any help?"

I peer around the closet door to find Garrett standing in my room. "Yes," I sigh and hold out the carrier. "Can you get LB into this? She hates it."

He nods and walks forward to take the carrier from my hands. He sets it on the floor, opens the door, and then leaves the room to round up LB. When he returns with her a moment later, I watch in amazement as he gently places her in the carrier without any trouble and shuts the door tight. She doesn't make a peep.

"How did you do that?" I ask wide-eyed.

"Reiki, remember?" He gives me a crooked smile.

I sigh and give him a defeated smirk in return. Who knew I would miss the reiki days?

I move to pick my backpack off the floor and start to stuff my textbooks and notes inside. Garrett collects a book and hands it to me. "I'm really sorry about this," he says sincerely. "I wish we didn't have to go."

I take the book from him. "We don't have a choice, remember?"

He nods and picks up my Ethics folder, turning it over in his hands as I continue to pack. When I finally take the folder from him, he sets his hand tentatively on my shoulder. "I hate that you're mad at me."

Well, I hate it too. I pretend to organize my bag.

"Will you look at me?" he asks.

I try to remain impassive and turn my head.

"If there was any other way to be Reborn, I would have chosen it," he says. "I want you to know that I didn't do this to purposefully hurt you or James."

I stare at him in silence. I'm not ready to forgive him just yet.

He looks sad and awkwardly removes his hand from my shoulder. "I just...I hope one day we can be friends again."

I look away from him and nod in agreement. "Maybe one day." I pretend to look for more items to pack. I realize my computer is in the living room and turn to go get it. "I need my laptop." I walk past him and out of the room without any reconciliation between us. I don't know when I'll be able to move past what he did.

I find my computer on the coffee table, where I left it, and gather it with a few other papers. As I head back to the bedroom I realize James is gone. I sidestep and glance around the kitchen, although why he'd be in there I don't know. I return to the bedroom, frowning. "Where's James?"

Garrett faces me. "He wanted to investigate some options."

"Options?"

"He doesn't like the idea of you being alone in an unknown place, especially since he can't check on you."

I feel my face contort. "I thought time was of the essence. Shouldn't we get going? When will he be back?" I would like to see him once more before I leave for Nowheresville.

"I gave him an hour," Garrett says. "If we don't hear from him by then we're out of here."

What's with the hurry up and wait? I don't need time for second thoughts! I roughly push my laptop into my backpack and walk over to yank the charger from the wall.

Garrett and I spend our time in relative silence, working to gather as much as is necessary. He empties LB's litter box so I can take it with me, and I scour the kitchen bagging her food, dry snacks for me, and bottles of water in a grocery bag. Who knows how long I'll be driving? Once that stuff is collected, we carry everything to my car and fill the trunk. On the way, we stop at Garrett's apartment where he grabs a full duffle bag.

"When did you have time to pack?" I ask.

"Jack did it for me before he left," he says. "So that I could warn you."

Once the car is loaded, we head back to my place to wait for James with LB. Garrett pulls his phone from his pocket and takes a seat next to me on the couch. "What's your number?" he asks.

"Since when have you had a phone?"

"Since always." He navigates to his contact list. "Your number?"

I recite it to him and watch as he enters it, saving it without a name assigned. I notice he has only two contacts.

"I won't call you until things are safe," he says and studies my face. "Or unless Lucas calls with another warning to move."

"Because they can trace me through James?"

"Yes, and they can trace James through me. I still carry some of his bond. I'm not fully human yet." He looks remorseful. "That reminds me," he says and opens a notes app on his phone. "I need your bank information."

"What for?"

"Lucas transferred an obscene amount of money into my account to facilitate this move and any others that might come up; he's been the one supporting me. He requested that I get your information, so that he may do the same for you."

"Really?" That's kind of nice, I guess.

"Believe it or not, he feels bad. He doesn't enjoy hurting others."

I shrug. What the hell? It's not like I'm rich and this Lucas is apparently loaded. I don't think he's going to drain my account. I give Garrett my bank name and checking account number.

I glance at the time and James' hour is nearly up. There's been no word from him. Garrett paces as I mindlessly flip through the television channels for a distraction. I guess I should start thinking about which direction to drive. Should I head north and stay in Michigan or drive out of the state? I've never been further west than Chicago, when we went there for a weekend school trip. Maybe I should pick a big city; it would be easier to get "lost."

Garrett's cell phone rings, scattering my thoughts and making me jump.

"Hello?" he answers. I watch him look at me and nod. "We're leaving now." He hangs up.

"Who was that?" I ask, my nerves rattled.

"James," he says. "It's time to go."

"Where?"

"Kalamazoo International Airport."

It takes only fifteen minutes to get there. I lug my overstuffed backpack and LB inside; Garrett carries my suitcase. We find a long bench opposite the ticket counter, and Garrett takes a seat.

"Now what?" I ask. "Where are we going?"

"Only you're going," he says and looks around. His eyes land back on me. "But I don't know where."

I roll my eyes. Fabulous. More unanswered questions. I plop down next to him on the bench. The stress and anxiety of the last couple hours is taking its toll. It's late and I'm exhausted; my interrupted nap did nothing to compensate for my lack of sleep over the last five nights. I yawn as I ask, "So, what do we do? Wait for James?"

He nods.

Well, he should be here any minute, diligent Guardian that he is. I try to people watch as I comb through the possibilities. Where would James want me to go by plane? He must want me to get as far away as possible. Alaska? I shiver at the idea. I hate the cold. Garrett said James didn't want me to be alone. I have no family out of state except a few cousins in Colorado that I never see. That must be it. James has never met them, and I've never visited there. But, wait, no. They would be sure to call my parents and let them know I unexpectedly traveled across the country to visit unannounced. My mind continues to spin and then starts to fade as my eyes grow heavy. I find myself falling asleep and then jerking awake as soon as my chin hits my chest. Garrett notices.

"You can lean on me if you want."

The offer is enticing. What I wouldn't give to lie down right now. He nods toward his shoulder and I lean over, setting my head against it. He wraps his arm around my back and side to keep me upright. I feel myself fading into sleep again as I wonder what is taking James so long. Let's do this already.

As I'm intermittently awakened by flight announcements, I lose track of time. I fade in and out of consciousness, and gladly too. My body and my mind need to rest. I do think about LB though, and if she needs to use the litter box. Poor thing. I hope Garrett's reiki calmed those urges, too; I have no idea where I could take her. As time passes, a deeper sleep finds me and I welcome it.

"Emma? Emma, wake up."

I hear James' voice and feel my shoulder being nudged.

"Wake up, Em. It's almost time to go."

I force my eyes open to a squint, and James' face is fuzzy. "You're here," I croak, my throat thick with sleep.

His face is level before me, and he gives me a sad smile. "I am," he says. "You need to start waking up. Your flight will be boarding soon."

I try to widen my eyes and focus. "What took you so long?" It feels like I've been passed out for hours.

"I brought someone to go with you," he says. "So you won't be alone."

My face twists. Is he kidding? That can't be possible. I blink and things go fuzzy and then clear again. I must be dreaming. I rub my eyes to make sure. No, I'm awake.

James stands and steps to the side, so he's no longer blocking my line of view. Who he reveals makes me second-guess my sanity. Maybe I am still asleep. That or I've stepped into an alternate universe.

My travel companion steps forward. "Hey, Grace."

Chapter 22

I'm speechless.

I look from Dane, to James, and then to Garrett in disbelief. "Did you know about this?"

He nods.

"Why didn't you tell me?"

"I asked him not to," James says, redirecting my attention. He glances at Dane. "I wasn't sure if he would play along."

I stare at James wide-eyed and then look at Dane. He gives me a small shrug and shifts his weight uncomfortably. Never in a million years did I think anything like this would ever happen.

"Come on." James reaches for my hand. "We have to get you two through security."

He helps me stand and my legs feel stiff and disjointed after sitting for so long. "What about LB?" I ask. "Did you make arrangements for her, too?"

"Shit." James drops my hand and looks at Dane. "We forgot about the cat."

"I've got it," Garrett says and stands, looking at me. "You need to get going. I'll take her with me," he hesitates. "That is, if it's okay with you."

I look down at LB. I know I'll miss her if I send her away. I lift the carrier off the floor, placing it on the bench, so I can peer inside. The movement wakes her, and she hisses at me. Apparently she won't miss me as much. "Love you, too," I tell her and give her a sad smile. I stand and turn to Garrett. "I think she likes you better anyway. Thank you."

"I'll take good care of her," he promises.

My eyes jump to Dane, and I see he has my suitcase in one hand and his in the other. I turn around to grab my backpack and throw it on my shoulder, then pause. "Here." I reach into my purse and fish out my car keys, handing them to Garrett. "You'll need LB's things, so you might as well take my car. It doesn't look like I'll need it."

He pulls the keys from my hand. "I'll take good care of that, too," he says quietly.

Dane clears his throat. "We should probably get these bags checked in," he says. "Our flight leaves in less than an hour."

My eyes lock on James. He nods his approval, and I follow Dane as he tows our luggage to the ticket counter. The woman working the desk gives us a friendly smile and asks Dane's last name.

"Walker," he says.

"Party of two?" she confirms.

"Yes."

"Checking any bags this evening?"

He eyes my backpack. "Do you want to carry that or check it?"

It's heavy and bulky. "Check it, please."

"Three."

The woman asks to see our ID and then presses a few keys. "I'll have your boarding passes in a moment," she says and steps away.

"Wait," I say in surprise. "When did you buy the tickets?"

He gives me half a smile. "About three hours ago."

The woman returns with the passes, tears them apart, and hands them to Dane. She then grabs the luggage tags and loops them through each suitcase handle. I hand her my backpack. When everything is tagged, she says, "You're all set. Enjoy the Caribbean."

What?

"Thank you," Dane smiles and turns away from the counter.

"The Caribbean?" I ask under my breath as we make our way back to James. "Isn't that a little extravagant?"

"We'll talk about it later," he whispers.

When we reach James and Garrett, Dane gives them a nod and leaves me alone with them, walking several feet away to lean against a post. My throat goes dry and my heart begins to pound.

"Stay safe," Garrett says. "Remember, I'll only contact you if it's necessary."

I inhale like I'm confident. "Got it." I gesture toward LB. "Don't let her take advantage of you."

He gives me a timid smile. "I'll try not to." He looks between James and I. "I'll let you two have a few minutes. I need to get going myself." He turns and collects LB, then looks at me sincerely. "Have a safe trip."

I nod and my throat constricts. When will I see them again? *Will* I see them again?

Garrett pauses next to James. "You too. Be careful."

James and I watch as Garrett carries LB toward the exit. When he reaches the sliding doors, he gives us one last look and a small wave, which makes the blood drain from my face.

"Hey," James steps to my side. "Everything will be all right."

I give him a wary look.

"Listen." He stands directly in front of me, placing his hands on either side of my face, cradling it. "I'm not going to let anything happen to you. Got it? Believe in that."

I close my eyes and whisper, "It's not just me I'm worried about."

His cold lips graze my forehead. "I'll be fine."

I open my eyes. "You promise?"

He nods and steps back, his hands sliding down my arms. I catch a glimpse of Dane over his shoulder and ask, "You're sure you want me to do this?"

He gives me a questioning look.

"Run away with Dane?"

"No. I want to be the one you run away with." He glances over his shoulder. "But since I can't be," he turns back around, "he's the next best choice."

My mouth falls open.

"The most important thing is your protection," James says earnestly. "I remember what he did for you last summer. He did something I couldn't, and he's here to do it again."

"But..." I protest.

"Regardless of how I feel, this isn't about me. It's about what's best for you. Dane and I had a long talk about it on the way here," he says and looks into my eyes. "Let him take care of you, Emma."

I can't believe I'm hearing this.

"Um, guys?" Dane asks, hushed, from behind James. "People are staring."

I glance around and catch a young couple avert their gaze.

"It looks like you're talking to yourself," Dane says.

I quickly adjust my features and focus on Dane's face. "Thanks."

James looks from Dane to me. "You should go. You don't want to miss your flight to where ever," he says, trying to be lighthearted.

My pulse accelerates. "I don't want to say goodbye."

"Then don't," he says in all seriousness. "I'll see you soon. Before you know it."

I remain motionless as he steps forward and kisses me softly on the lips. Every part of me wants to wrap my arms around him, but I don't. I don't want to draw attention to myself again.

"I love you," he says.

"Love you, too," I barely whisper.

And just like that, he vanishes.

I blink away the few tears that pop into my eyes. When they're clear, I raise my head to find Dane standing with his back to me, blocking me from the view of the ticket counter and the people that wait there.

"He's gone," I say and step around him.

Dane looks at me with a mixed expression. I can't tell if he feels bad for me or if he is irritated. He starts to walk in the direction of the escalators, and I follow.

It doesn't take us long to get through the security line; Kalamazoo International is a relatively small airport. Dane waits for me to retie my tennis shoes and slip my jacket on before heading to the gate. We round a corner and end up at gate four, destination Miami, Florida.

"Miami?" I ask as we find two empty seats.

"We have a small layover." He leans forward to rest his elbows on his knees and gives me a wry smile. "It's the best I could do on short notice. Then it's on to St. Thomas."

My eyebrows shoot up. "As in the Virgin Islands?"

"The same."

Of all the places in the world, how did he come up with the Virgin Islands? Not that I'm complaining. If anything, it's not Alaska. I can do tropical.

"So..." Dane drifts off and looks uncomfortable.

He looks lost for words, as am I. I twist my fingers in my lap. He must have a million questions.

"James never left you," he says matter-of-factly.

I shake my head, sheepish. "No."

"It explains a lot," he says and looks at his feet. "It explains a whole lot."

"I'm sorry." I lean forward and try to catch his eyes. "You know why I couldn't tell you, right? I tried to deal with things as best I could, but I was terrible at it. I'm so s –"

"Stop," he interrupts and looks at me. "It's not your fault."

I frown. "Of course it's my fault! The last time I saw you, I handled it completely wrong, and I hurt you, and –"

He sets his hand on my knee. "I said stop."

I shut my mouth.

"There's only one person I blame for your actions and it's not you," he says as he searches my face. "So stop apologizing."

Who does he blame? Himself? That's not fair. "You can't blame yourself," I say, appalled. "You had no idea what was going on."

He snorts. "I don't blame myself."

A voice comes over the PA. "Good evening, passengers. We will now start boarding flight 513 with non-stop service to Miami. At this time, we'd like to start with our first class passengers and any guests that require special assistance. Again, that's flight 513 with service to Miami. Welcome aboard."

Dane stands. "That's us."

A line of elderly people begins to form near the jet way. I see a man in a wheelchair and a woman using a walker. I look up at Dane and smirk. "Do I require special assistance?"

He rolls his eyes. "No, doofus. First class. Let's go."

I stand, impressed. "Do you treat all the girls you save from the supernatural this way?"

He grins. "Only you, baby. Only you."

Our seats are in the second row of the plane. Dane graciously allows me to take the window seat, and I fiddle with the seatbelt as he gets comfortable. I look around and play with the window shade, and then pluck the safety card out of the seat pocket in front of me. As the other passengers file in, I open the card and study the pictures of the emergency exits and use of the oxygen masks.

"What's so interesting?" Dane leans over my shoulder.

"Have you ever heard of the oxygen masks actually being used?"

"No. Why?"

"Just curious."

I continue to study the card, twisting around to locate another exit. First class is blocked by a partition, and I can't see more than two rows behind me.

Dane frowns. "What are you looking for?"

"The exits," I say seriously. "I've never flown before."

"You're kidding." He looks shocked. "You've never been in a plane?"

I shake my head.

"Ever?"

I roll my eyes. "That's what no means."

He looks amused. "Are you scared?"

I give him a stale look. "No, I'm not. I'm just trying to be prepared."

He tries not to smile. "FYI, your seat cushion can be used as a flotation device."

"That's very helpful," I say sarcastically, "seeing as how we'll be flying over land the entire time."

He laughs.

Eventually, the plane is full and the flight attendants give us their spiel as we taxi. When it comes to the actual takeoff, I have to admit that it's kind of a rush, and I like it. Dane gives me a few sideways glances; I think to make sure I'm not nervous, or ready to puke, or anything. As we climb higher in the sky and the plane levels itself, I stare out the window into the darkness as a realization settles over me. I've just left behind everything comfortable and familiar in my life. I've left behind everyone I love for something I can never explain, and they don't even know it. I feel my throat constrict.

Dane nudges my arm. "Would you like something?"

I rip my eyes from the window and see one of the flight attendants hovering over him. "Like what?"

"We have water, coffee, juice, soda, wine, and liquor. Would you like a cocktail?" she asks, too perky for this time of night.

"Um, water. Please."

She hands me a bottle from her cart. "And for you, sir?"

Dane looks at me. "I think I could use something stronger than water." He turns back to Ms. Perky. "What have you got for mixed drinks?"

I focus my attention back on the night sky, blocking them out and ignoring what he orders. He deserves to have whatever he wants; shoot, give him the whole damn bottle of whatever. Tonight, he left his life behind, too.

All because of me.

I close my eyes as the thought weighs heavily on my conscience. How will I ever repay him?

"Here." He nudges my arm again and hands me a small plastic bag. Ear buds. "They're complimentary."

"Thanks," I say quietly and slowly take them from his hand.

His hazel eyes register concern. "What's wrong?"

I immediately force a weak smile. "Nothing. Just tired."

He frowns. I know he doesn't believe me. I busy myself by tearing open the bag and locating the connection in the armrest, just like I saw the woman across the aisle do. I pop the buds in my ears and find the first tolerable music station, then close my eyes and lean back in my seat to lose myself. I can't have a heart to heart talk with him right now. You think a crying baby on an airplane is bad? Nobody wants to have their flight ruined by a sobbing mess of a grown woman.

Our layover in Miami is only thirty minutes, which allows us just enough time to get from one gate to the next. The plane we're taking to St. Thomas is nothing like the jet we took from Kalamazoo; it's tiny, with propellers on the wings, and we have to walk out onto the tarmac to board. When we're seated, the plane holds only six passengers, including us. Two of them are clearly a couple; they're all over each other kissing and giggling.

"Geez," I mutter under my breath. "Get a room already."

Dane snickers.

The flight is a short hop to the island, and I'm so grateful to be nearing the end of this journey. The Cyril E. King airport in St. Thomas is even smaller than K Zoo International, and it takes us no time to collect our three bags. I follow Dane to the car rental counter.

"Why don't you sit down?" he suggests, concerned. "You look like you're ready to keel over."

I eye a nearby bank of chairs and shuffle my way to one of them. I take this opportunity to remove my jacket. It's hot here, even in the dead of night. If I'd known where I was headed I wouldn't have chosen my jeans and tennis shoe ensemble. My feet are starting to sweat in my socks. I can't wait to lie down in a bed, with blankets and sheets and a pillow. A random thought hits me. Where are we staying? Was there enough time to find a place or will we have to search for an open room somewhere? Will we end up camping on a beach? The thought of more uncertain travel makes me scowl.

"Is there a problem?" Dane asks as he approaches me, his hand full of papers.

"Please tell me you know where we're going," I nearly whimper.

"I know where we're going," he says confidently.

"Thank God," I sigh and pull my body off the chair. I adjust my backpack on my shoulder and gesture ahead of us. "Lead the way."

Outside in the airport rental lot, Dane consults the papers in his hand to locate the parking space that holds our car. When he stops in front of a red Aveo, I burst into a fit of giggles, wrapping my arms around my sides. "You're not serious?" I laugh. This car is the size of a roller skate; Dane will never be able to drive it.

"Hey," he gives me a crooked smile. "Beggars can't be choosers. It's late and we didn't have a reservation. This is what we get." He unlocks the car and lifts the hatch. Only one of our bags and my backpack will fit in the trunk; the other bag has to go in the backseat.

I climb into the passenger side and Dane wedges himself in to the driver's seat, sliding it back as far as possible to accommodate his legs. Even with the seat adjusted his knees still hit the steering wheel.

"Do you want me to drive?" I ask, suppressing more laughter.

"Have you ever driven on the left side of the road?"

I shake my head. "No, but it's late. There's probably little traffic."

He buckles his seatbelt. "I'm driving." He sets his phone in a cup holder on the dash and pulls up an address. "Here we go," he says and starts the car.

"I take it you've been here before?"

He looks over his shoulder to back out of the parking space. "To vacation, yes." He faces forward and puts the car in drive. "But not at this same place."

We leave the airport and pull out onto a deserted two lane highway. As Dane follows the GPS instructions, I stare out the window, following the coastline as we drive. I roll the window down and a blast of salty sea air hits me. The headlights bounce off the palm trees that line the road, and I allow myself a small smile. Under different circumstances, this could be my type of place.

The GPS tells us to turn left ahead, then right, then left again. Around twenty minutes later, we end up in a residential area, where huge homes are sporadically spaced. Some of them have gated drives, some don't. Most have impressive landscaping that is lit up in the night; I even catch a few water features here and there. We're clearly passing through a wealthy part of the island; there's no way we're staying anywhere around here. There aren't any hotels as far as I can see.

As usual, my assumption is wrong as the GPS tells us our destination is approaching on our right. Dane slows the car and then turns onto a short paved drive which is lined with palm trees. We roll to a stop in front of a large three car garage where he cuts the engine and turns to me with relief. "We made it."

I shoot him a look of disbelief. "Here?" I glance to the garage and back to him again. "We're staying here?"

One side of his mouth quirks up. "Yes. Well, in the house attached to the garage, yes, we're staying here." He smiles. "Let's go." He opens the car door and pulls himself out of the small space, standing and stretching.

I push my door open and exit the roller skate, slamming it behind me. I walk around to the back of the car to join Dane, who already has my backpack and suitcase unloaded.

"Here." He reaches into his back pocket and opens his wallet. He hands me a piece of paper. "This is the security code to unlock the front door. Go ahead; I'll be right behind you."

I take the paper from him and pull my backpack on to my shoulder. He grabs my suitcase and carries it around the side of the car as he retrieves his. I turn and walk slowly up the well-lit cobbled path that leads to the front door, admiring what I can make out of the intricate landscaping. This place must be gorgeous in the daylight. When I pry my eyes away from the yard, the front porch appears before me and I walk up two steps to the door. The outside of the house is covered in an aggregate of large stones, each a different shape and color. I search for a keypad and find it off to the right, under a folded note taped to the stone. The paper has Dane's name scribbled across it, and I remove it to punch in the code. I hit enter, hear the definite click of the door unlock, and let myself inside.

Holy crap. This place looks like I just stepped into an episode of HGTV. My wide eyes roam the surroundings, and I take a few tentative steps forward. The entryway spills into a tiled great room, the ceiling made up of exposed weathered beams. The walls are covered in a rich wood paneling, and the entire wall opposite me is constructed of floor to ceiling windows that are covered in ivory drapes that billow and puddle on the floor. The living area is full of plump furniture in a sage green trimmed in honey oak with end tables to match. A large flat screen adorns the wall across from the couches, and a dining table sits back by the windows, carved from the same honey oak, and surrounded with chairs to seat six. Fresh flowers adorn every flat surface, and I can see that the room extends to my left, rounding a corner. My mind races. Whose house is this? I glance down at the note in my hands and unfold it.

Mr. Dane & Mrs. Teagan Walker,
Congratulations on your recent nuptials! We are so happy we were able to accommodate the change in your rental date. We hope that you find everything to your satisfaction. Should you require anything or have other concerns, please contact us directly at 340 691 6143. Our staff is on call 24 hours a day, seven days a week.
Thank you for choosing Luxury Retreats International! We appreciate your business!
Sincerely,
Loretta Young
LRI, Inc.

A sarcastic snort of laughter escapes as I let my backpack fall from my shoulder. There's no way this day could get any more bizarre; my exhaustion level must be through the roof. I could swear I just read that Dane and Teagan are married. I reread the letter. No, that's what it says.

I hear the door open behind me and the sound of suitcases being set on the floor. "So," Dane appears by my side, "what do you think?"

I look up from the note and into his eyes, my expression wracked with confusion.

"What's the matter?" he asks, searching my face.

I swallow. "You brought me on your honeymoon?"

Chapter 23

Dane looks guilty and trips on his words. "No! Well, yes...kind of." He steps toward me as I step back.

I curse without thinking twice. "Teagan is going to flip her shit! She already despises me!"

"She has no idea we're here."

I shake my head in disbelief. Have I stepped into some sort of Twilight Zone?

He puts his hands on his hips. "Remember when I told you her mom wouldn't let up on the wedding plans? That she made me book a honeymoon?"

I nod as I remember the conversation we had in his car after the Halloween party.

"Well, this is it," he says. "It was supposed to be a surprise; Teagan never knew this was the destination. And since it's non-refundable and I'm not getting married..." he trails off and sighs. "I think it turned out to be quite convenient if you ask me."

My face falls as I attempt to process everything that's happened in the last 24 hours. Super excited about future – check. Forced to run away from home and abandon said future – check. Tucked away on a tropical island on someone else's honeymoon – check. I glance down at the letter in my hand and slowly hold it out to Dane. "There's an emergency number listed in case you need it."

He takes the paper. "What? Are you upset now? Mad? Talk to me."

I blink in slow motion. "I'm not sure what I am." I bend to pick up my backpack and then stand, frowning. "I'm overwhelmed. Everything's happened so fast..."

His eyes search mine. "Tell me about it."

We stand there regarding each other for silent seconds. A realization hits his features and he backs away, pulling his phone from his pocket. "I forgot; I need to send some messages."

He opens his email and runs his finger up the screen, scrolling. "One to my dad," he says, staring at the phone, "telling him I've been called out of town for work." He selects the message and hits send. "And one to my boss," he continues and scrolls some more, "with my resignation."

"Wait!" I blurt out. "Don't send that! When did you decide to resign?"

"On the plane while you slept." He gives me a knowing look. I wasn't really sleeping.

"You can't resign from your job! Especially over me!"

"Emma, I was going to be fired anyway," he says. "This just gives me an excuse to quit early." He deliberately holds out the phone, so I can see him press send.

I look away and fight the angry tears behind my eyes. Is there any part of this man's life that I haven't ruined? I work to pull myself together as I gather my suitcase. "I need a shower and some sleep," I mumble as I walk past him and into the great room. "This way?" I gesture to my left.

He shrugs in ignorance and grabs his suitcase to follow me.

We walk through the living area and around the corner. A modern kitchen greets us, complete with an island and breakfast bar. Fresh fruit, crackers, cheese, and a bottle of wine sit in a basket on the island next to a white card that reads *Congratulations!* I choose to ignore it and keep walking. At the end of the hallway is a large set of double doors. I press down on the handles and push the doors open, revealing a spacious master suite.

I step inside as my eyes roam the room in awe. The dresser, armoire, and bedside tables are all made of a rich, dark wood. Large sliding glass doors make up most of the wall to my right and through them I can see a spot lit patio. The same tile and exposed beams found in main part of the home cover the floor and the ceiling, but these walls are painted in a pale sage. More fresh flowers and plants adorn the surfaces in the room, and there is even enough space for an additional wicker couch and chair. And the bed – is there a bigger size than a king? This bed is huge, made of the same dark wood, and covered in plush beige comforter with a leaf design. I abandon my luggage to walk forward and run my hand across it. I want to dive into this bed and never get out.

Dane breaks my bed-swimming fantasy by walking into my line of vision. He heads for an open door and flips a light switch. "I found the bathroom," he says, clearly not as impressed as I am in regard to the room's decor. I look at the bed of dreams and sigh, wondering if the guest room contains the same thing. Obviously this will be Dane's room; he paid for the place. I turn and walk back toward the double doors.

"Where are you going?" he asks.

"To find the guest room," I say, tired. I grab my things and head down the short hallway, passing the kitchen. I walk through the living area and head for the opposite side of the house. There's a closed door off the entryway and when I get to it, I pull the handle with gusto and blink into the darkness of a hollow space. I fumble for a light switch and end up hitting a button. I jump as a bright light pops on and one of the garage doors starts to loudly rise. The garage? I found the freaking garage?! Where's the guest room? A house this size surely has more than one bedroom. I sigh and press the button to lower the door. After closing the interior door behind me, I cross my arms and survey my options.

"There's supposed to be another suite in the pavilion off the patio," Dane says, appearing around the corner.

I frown at him. "Why didn't you say so?"

"You walked away before I could."

I make my way to the glass wall and find one of the sliding door handles. I unlock it and step out into the tropical night with Dane behind me. A warm breeze blows, rustling the palm trees that dot the patio. I spy the pavilion on the opposite side of the swimming pool and walk around the blue water to reach it. The pavilion door is another sliding one, and I locate the handle in the dim light and pull. It's locked.

"You have got to be kidding me," I groan and rest my head against the glass.

"Let me try," Dane volunteers and gives the handle a tug. "Yeah, that's locked," he says and steps back.

"Maybe there's another keypad?" I ask and start searching the stone wall for buttons.

Dane cups his hands around his eyes and peers into the pavilion against the glass. "It wouldn't matter," he says and moves down a few steps to look again. "There's nothing in there but patio furniture."

"What?" I copy his stance, pressing my hands against the glass and looking inside. Tables and chairs in various shapes and sizes are crammed together and stacked haphazardly on top of one another. I back away from the building. "I think this qualifies as not finding everything to our satisfaction."

"They probably figured we wouldn't need two bedrooms," he says in defense of the retreat company. "Besides, I only gave them – what? – eight hours notice? We're lucky the place was even available."

I scowl. "I thought you said you prepaid?"

"I did," he sighs, exasperated. "But I never gave them a time frame. We still hadn't picked a wedding date."

I stare at the ground. All I want to do is shower and go to sleep. That's it. That's all.

"C'mon." Dane reaches out and takes my hand. He turns me around and tows me toward the main house.

"Where are we going?"

"To bed."

I stop walking and try to pull my hand away. "I'm sorry?"

"Don't be dramatic," he says over his shoulder and tugs my arm, forcing me to follow. "We're tired, it's late, and we're sharing a room. Get over it."

We step over the threshold into the main house and he slides the door closed behind us, never letting me go. My mind flashes back to the night of the Halloween party, where he led me around by my wrist. We walk over to my suitcase and backpack, which I abandoned by the garage, and he picks them up in one hand. He leads me down the hallway and back in to the bedroom, tossing my bags on the bed.

"There," he says and lets go of my hand. He regards my expression and rolls his eyes. "Please. It's not like we haven't slept together before." He walks around to the opposite side of the bed, unzips his suitcase, and starts to unload his clothes.

I reach for my bag to follow suit as my mind races with sarcastic thoughts. Sure, why shouldn't we share a room, let alone the same bed? There's absolutely *no way* this will be awkward, none at all. I forcefully unzip my bag and start to rummage through it for clean underwear and pajamas. What is he thinking? Isn't he the least bit uncomfortable with this? He knows the truth now; he knows James is still in my life.

I catch a glimpse of him under my lashes as he locates what he was looking for. He tucks a pair of dark blue sleep pants under his arm, picks up his toothbrush and toothpaste, and looks at me. "I'll just be a minute. Then you can shower or whatever."

I nod as he turns to head into the bathroom, closing the door behind him. I sigh and return to digging through my clothes. I've found the underwear, but I can't find my pajamas. And what am I going to do with all of these jeans and sweaters? I can't wear this stuff here. I'm going to have to pick up some new clothes. Either that or roast to death.

Minutes later, when Dane emerges from the bathroom, I'm still searching.

"What exploded?" he asks, eyeing my strewn clothes and empty suitcase.

I throw my hands up. "Apparently I forgot to pack pajamas." I look up from the bed and stop in my tracks. He's standing in the doorway shirtless, wearing only the pants. My eyes slide over his hard chest and I blush, remembering the last time we were in a bedroom alone together.

He smirks upon seeing my reaction and tries to contain it, stepping forward to snag a t-shirt off his clothes pile. He walks around the bed toward me, pulling it over his head. "Are you sure?"

I roll my eyes. "Um, yeah. I'm sure."

He peruses my garment mountain and a slow smile spreads across his face. He reaches out and plucks a pair of underwear off the bed; unfortunately, they're the pale pink granny kind. "Yet you remembered these?" he asks, grinning.

"Give me those!" I grab them from his hand. "You're not helping!"

He laughs and then reaches across to his pile. "Here." He tosses me one of his t-shirts. "Wear this."

I unfold the black shirt to find it's a concert tee from a Kings of Leon show.

"That should be big enough to cover everything," he says, chuckling. "Even if you're wearing a pair of those." He nods toward the underwear in my hand.

I narrow my eyes and hold the shirt to my chest. I pick up my toiletry bag and shower supplies, and then skirt around him toward the bathroom. "Not everyone can afford to shop at Victoria's Secret you know."

I hear his voice from behind. "Well, maybe we can change that."

My face flushes and I turn around. "I wouldn't bet on it," I snap and shut the door with my foot. The nerve!

The bathroom is just an impressive as the rest of the house. There's a sunken tub with spa jets surrounded by candles and a separate shower, along with two sinks, and mirrors that travel from the counter to the ceiling. It's not difficult to catch a glimpse of yourself in such a large piece of glass, and I cringe at my reflection. I look like absolute hell. Anyone who looks like this should be wearing granny panties.

I set my things on the counter and then take my shampoo, conditioner, and razor to the shower and place them inside. I turn the faucet and hold my hand under the water, waiting for it to warm up. Once it's toasty, I step out of my clothes and under the water, letting it beat on my back. I turn around and realize the showerhead is adjustable and play with the settings. I find one pattern that's particularly nice and stand beneath the pounding water with my eyes closed. I have died and gone to shower heaven.

After I use all of the hot water, I get out and dry off with what has to be the softest towel on the planet. What is this made out of? Kittens? I get dressed, pulling Dane's shirt over my head, and turning around to check my reflection in the mirror to make sure it's long enough. It hangs shapelessly off my body and, thankfully, falls to the middle of my thigh. I cannot believe I forgot to pack pajamas. I brush my teeth, comb through my wet hair, gather my clothes, and take a deep breath. I'm sure Dane has found more things to ridicule me about, especially since I left my stuff lying all over the place.

To my surprise, I open the door to a darkened room. Once my eyes focus, I can see that our clothes and suitcases have disappeared and Dane has crawled beneath the covers to sleep on the side nearest the bathroom. I tiptoe around the foot of the bed, dropping my dirty clothes on the floor. I carefully pull back the blankets, so as not to wake him, and my body tenses as I slowly lower myself to the mattress.

"It's not made of glass you know."

"AHH!" I jump and pull my knees to my chest. "You scared me!"

He laughs.

"I thought you were asleep!" I hiss and scoot down, being sure to jostle the bed as much as possible to get comfortable.

"I should be. How long were you in there? An hour?"

"At least," I say, my voice dripping with sarcasm. "What? Is there a time limit?"

"No." I can feel him roll over. "I thought you had drowned."

"In the shower?"

"Given what's happened today, anything's possible."

I can't help but smile. "Well, just for the record, I take really long showers."

"Noted," he says and adjusts his weight again.

We fall silent, and I close my eyes. I stare into the blackness behind my lids and work on relaxing my body, trying to erase all thought from my mind. It's not easy. Just as I find that precious precipice of sleep, Dane's voice pulls me back.

"Seriously?"

I groan. "Whaaat?"

"You're balancing yourself on the edge of the bed like I have the plague. This thing is big enough to hold twenty people; move over for Christ sake! You're making me nervous."

It didn't register until now, but I am teetering precariously near the edge. A subconscious move, I'm sure. "Its fine," I huff and plump my pillow. "I'm perfectly comfortable."

"And when you fall asleep and roll off the side?"

"I'll wake up and you'll laugh," I say, closing my eyes again.

He lets out an exasperated sigh and moves; I'm sure turning away from me. I decide that my location is kind of silly and slide back, conceding an inch or two. At least I'm able to pull my knee up to the side now.

"That's so much better," he grumbles.

I decide to ignore him and pretend he doesn't exist. There's no other way I'll get to sleep if I don't. It takes longer than necessary, but eventually I drift off, welcoming sleep's mindless embrace.

Sunlight blasts my face, making me squint, even though my eyes are still closed. I move and stretch, reaching my arms above my head and pushing my legs in the opposite direction. When I peel my eyelids open, I find that I'm alone in the middle of the bed with a pillow under my head and one at each side. Yikes. Did I take over the place during the night?

I sit up and blink at the sunlight streaming in through the glass doors. I glance at the bedside table and see that it's nearly noon. Noon! Throwing the blankets aside, I push myself off the bed and pull my "pajamas" down to cover my behind. I walk to the bathroom and quickly brush my teeth and hair, then head out of the room in search of Dane.

I find him outside by the pool, lying in a lounge chair, and eating an apple. He looks at me over his sunglasses. "Ah. She lives."

I take a seat by his feet at the end of the chaise. "It's late. Why didn't you wake me?"

"Tried," he smirks. "You were snoring."

My mouth falls open. "I don't snore!"

He takes a bite of his apple and grins. "You so snore."

I cross my arms and defend myself. "I haven't gotten much sleep over the last few days."

He tilts his head. "Why is that?"

I relax my arms and my shoulders sag. "How much did James tell you?"

He pretends to think about it. "You mean after he appeared and scared the hell out of me or during our car trip across the state?"

I give him a sympathetic look. I fainted the first time I saw James as a Guardian, by all accounts he's handling this really well.

Dane sets his elbow on the armrest and pushes himself higher on the lounge. "He introduced himself and said a few choice words to make me believe him. Then he said that you needed me."

I feel my forehead pinch. "Didn't you ask any questions?"

"He said there was trouble; that you had to disappear and he could no longer be near you. He didn't want you to be alone and thought I might be up for the job." He raises an eyebrow. "Care to enlighten me as to how he got that impression?" He takes another bite.

I give him a dry look as he chews. "You already know."

He pauses and regards me for a moment. "Do I?"

I sigh. "We fight about you a lot."

He looks impressed. "Really?"

"All the time."

"Huh," he says and looks toward the pool. He smiles, clearly enjoying this, and turns back to me. "What do you fight about exactly?"

I shoot him an exasperated look and he shrugs.

I know what he's trying to do; he's trying to get me to admit that I have feelings for him. It's the same discussion we have every time we're alone together. How did we go from my lack of sleep to this? "He's around a lot, okay? He's seen just about everything between us."

"He said he was there the night you were attacked."

I nod.

"Did he see our last talk? After the dinner?"

"He was there."

"Did he see our first kiss?"

"Yes."

"Did he see our last kiss?"

I roll my eyes. "He was in your backseat."

Pausing to think, he sets the apple core on the ground and moves forward on the chair, turning his body, so he's sitting next to me. "So, let me get this straight. Because of this trouble, he can't watch you or visit you or anything?"

I wrap my arms around myself and look away from him, out toward the pavilion that should have been my room. "Yeah."

I can feel his stare before I feel his touch. He tucks a piece of hair behind my ear, and I turn to face him, noticing he's taken off his sunglasses. "Sorry. My hair is crazy." I automatically reach back and smooth it, pulling it over my shoulder.

His hazel eyes lock on mine and I freeze, knowing what's going to happen next. If I'm at all honest with myself, I should have seen this coming. It was only a matter of time.

He leans forward and places a gentle kiss on my lips. When I allow this to happen, he sets his hand against the side of my neck and kisses me harder. Warmth travels from head to my toes as I wrap my hand around his wrist and kiss him back. His voice replays in my mind – *"He can't watch you or visit you or anything?"* – and my eyes fly open. I feel bad about taking advantage of the situation and pull away from him, meeting his questioning expression with a defeated one of my own. "James is my Guardian," I say quietly.

"So?"

He has no idea the depth of the situation. "Do you even know what a Guardian is?"

He leans forward and looks directly into my eyes. "Emma, I've known about Guardians since I was fourteen years old."

Chapter 24

I'm dumbfounded. "Say again?"

"I've known about Guardians since I was fourteen," he repeats himself. "Since my mom died."

I stare into his eyes as my heart pounds. "She's a Guardian?"

"Not anymore. She was released this summer."

I look down as I try to collect my thoughts. To think that I've been craving to speak with someone about James and that someone turns out to be Dane? For so long I've wanted to be able to talk about what's going on and how to cope with it. My eyes flash back to him. "I wish I had known this sooner."

He gives me an empathetic smile.

"No wonder you didn't have a problem believing James."

"He knew I wouldn't," he says and sets his elbows on his knees. "He knew my mother. Using her name was all it took to convince me that I wasn't going crazy."

The knowledge that he has been in my shoes peaks my curiosity. "What was her name?"

"Evelyn," he smiles.

"When did she start visiting you?"

"About a year after she died. At first I thought my mind was playing tricks on me. I was just a kid, after all. I tried to talk to my dad about it, but..." his voice fades and his jaw tenses.

"It didn't go well?"

He scoffs. "That's an understatement. He put me directly into therapy and let them dope me up on some stupid

261

medication." He grimaces. "I learned pretty quickly to shut up about things."

My face twists. "That's awful."

"Yeah, well, let's just say our relationship went downhill from there."

I feel terrible for him. He was so young; I can't imagine how hard that must have been to deal with.

Dane notices my concern. "Hey," he gives me a small smile, "it's all good. My mom helped me work through things and to understand. She didn't want to be away from her only child, so she chose to be a Guardian. She fulfilled her duties and checked on me from time to time. I still had her in my life. I wouldn't change that for anything."

"I wish I could have met her. Were you sad when she was released?"

He shakes his head and smiles. "A little, but she had to go sometime. She was released by her true love. What could be better than that?"

My smile fades into confusion. "Wait. How was she released if your dad is still alive?"

"John let her go," he says. "He passed away this August. He and my mom were having an affair before she died."

My mouth falls open. "How did you know?"

"We found out shortly before she was diagnosed. She was going to leave my father. Then, the cancer hit, and everything happened pretty fast. That's a big part of why she stayed," he says. "She felt bad about how things were left between us."

I give him a sympathetic look, then rest my head on his shoulder. "That's why James stayed, too. The night he died, we fought. He didn't want to leave things that way. He didn't want to leave me."

Dane reaches for my hand and weaves his fingers through mine.

"I wish our story could have a happy ending like yours and your mom's."

"Why can't it?" he asks softly. "If you two can't be together, at least he's still in your life, right?"

I raise my head. "You sound like Garrett. It's not that simple."

He gives me a wary look. "Garrett? The guy at the airport?"

I nod.

"The guy who is almost human? The one you said wasn't hot?"

I smile as I remember my mistaken text messages. "That's the one."

He gives me an irritated look. "You lied."

"About what?"

"His looks."

I roll my eyes. "Please. Garrett is not hot."

"Says who?"

"Says me!"

He frowns. "I didn't like finding you curled up against him on that bench. First James shows up and then this Garrett guy is all over you –"

"Whoa." I pull my hand from his and sit back. "He wasn't all over me! I was tired and he offered a shoulder, that's all. Besides, we're barely speaking after what he did."

"You mean the whole assigning you to James to become human thing?"

I look at Dane, impressed. "James told you a lot."

He smirks. "It was a long drive."

"Then you know," I say, exasperated. "Things between James and I aren't simple! Every time we see each other we're reminded of what we can't have. Not just in this life, but in the next. I'm his Ward; I can't release him. He's stuck in the Intermediate until I die, and then..." I hesitate. "And then maybe he'll have a chance at being human again. Without me."

Dane searches my face, thinking about what I've said and how to respond. He can't dispute the truth. My heart is broken; there's no quick fix.

"Listen," he finally says, his eyes locking on mine. "I know what you and James had was real. Part of your heart will always belong to him. But, I'm a firm believer in fate. What happened was meant to happen. You have to believe that, for whatever reason, it was meant to be. You can't change it, but you can learn to live with it. Trust me, over time, things *will* get easier."

I look down as he reaches over and winds his hand around mine again. All I want to do is feel like myself, like I did before James had his accident and everything went to hell. "I just want to feel better," I say as I fixate on our locked fingers. "Is that really too much to ask for?"

He runs his thumb across the back of my hand. "Not at all. I've had eleven years to wrap my mind around the Intermediate, and I still don't get it. You've had what? Six months?"

I look up and give him a tiny smile. "Seven."

"Oh, well then, that makes a difference." He smiles back.

We sit in silence for a few moments. I look around the patio, taking in the stonework, the palm trees, and the potted hibiscus. How is it that I ended up in paradise under these circumstances? Life sure is a funny thing, and I don't mean funny ha-ha.

"Here's what I propose," Dane says, pulling my attention back to him. "Let's make a pact to live the most normal lives anyone has ever lived."

"How?"

"By keeping each other focused on the future and not the past. You need to finish your classes, and I need to find a new job."

"I still can't believe you quit!" I admonish him. "What were you thinking?"

"I had to cut all ties," he says. "Teagan should get the hint now that I've voluntarily resigned. She has nothing left to hold over me."

I tilt my head. "She still won't let you go?"

He grins. "Can you blame her?"

I roll my eyes and pull my hand away from his. "So, where do you think I should start? I have to lie to my instructors, lie to my parents. I should probably throw a couple of lies to Shel and Matt..."

"I say we start with getting you dressed," he says. "We can begin our normal lives with a normal trip to the grocery store. I'm starving."

I nod and stand. "About that, I'm going to need to stop somewhere and get some clothes. Everything I brought is way too warm." I eye his khaki cargo shorts and shoot him an annoyed look. "You, on the other hand, are completely prepared."

"Hey, I can't help it I saved the day with a prepaid vacation," he says and swings his feet back up to lounge on the chair. "But I agree. You do need some different clothes and pajamas."

"What?" I look over my makeshift pj's. "You don't like me wearing your shirt?"

"Just the opposite," he says and slides his sunglasses on. "I like it too much."

In the bathroom, I stare at myself as I try to contain my unruly hair. The humidity is making it curl, which is unusual for me; I've never been in such a warm climate before to know it would do this. I mean, occasionally I'd get a curl here or there in the summer at home, but this is full on waves. I sigh as I pull it back into a ponytail for the third time, trying to convince myself that no one cares how I look but me.

When I leave the bedroom, I find Dane leaning impatiently against the couch with his arms crossed. He gives me a once over. "Where'd you get the shorts?"

I hold up my hand to reveal the scissors I found in the kitchen. "Old pair of jeans," I explain and walk around the breakfast bar to put the scissors back. "I thought you were relaxing outside."

"I was until I realized you were taking forever and my stomach started to eat itself. Are you ready?"

"Yeah." I pick my purse up off the counter and grab a pear out of the *Congratulations!* fruit basket. "Let's go."

Dane tells me he's taking us to Charlotte Amalie, where there are plenty of places to shop. I roll the window down and nibble on my pear as he drives. The fruit is kind of mushy and unappetizing, making me want something more substantial. "Can we stop for lunch?" I ask.

"That will be the first thing we do," he says and pats his stomach.

The farther we drive, I realize that he knows exactly where he's going without any help. "When were you here last?"

"About three years ago."

"On vacation?"

He nods. "We took a cruise from Miami and docked here for two days. We were supposed to see the whole Caribbean, but we liked St. Thomas so much we ended up staying," he says. "We caught the next ship that came into port a week later."

"We?" I raise my eyebrows.

He glances at me out of the corner of his eye. "Teagan and me."

Of course he would be vacationing with his ex-fiancée. My face automatically wants to express how I feel about her, but I manage to remain impassive. "Sounds like you had a good time." I take another bite of my mushy pear.

He ignores me and concentrates on the road.

When we pull into the city it's busy with tourists, but Dane has no problem finding a parking spot for the roller skate. As we walk along the street, I can see that the town backs up to the coast, where sailboats dot the water and two large cruise ships sit in port. We pass several small shops and boutiques housed in historic looking buildings until Dane turns down an alleyway. I follow him until we end up at a restaurant called Gladys' Café, where he holds the door for me. Inside, I find a cozy place with a mahogany bar and native stone walls. Appetizing smells waft through the room, and Sinatra plays in the background.

266

"The food here is amazing," he says as we're led to a small table near the front window. "You should try something local."

I pick up the menu and eventually settle on the crab and avocado salad; I'm not sure I'm brave enough to try the curried goat. Dane chooses a Grouper sandwich then we sit and wait. I sip my water as my stomach growls. I can't remember the last time I had an actual meal.

"So, where do you want to start?" Dane asks.

I set my glass down. "With what?"

"Shopping. We can hit some of the stores here and then head outside of town to Kmart –"

"St. Thomas has a Kmart?" That sounds so odd to me.

He nods. "We can get groceries there or this other place like Costco. I forget the name."

I think about all the cute shops that we passed. Normally I'm not a fan of shopping, but I'd like to see what they have. "Let's start here," I say, "and support the local economy."

He smiles.

Mentioning money reminds me. How much do I have to spend? My checking account had around $200 in it when I left yesterday. I need to transfer some cash. I pull out my phone.

"Who are you calling?"

"My bank," I say and dial the automated line. "I'm going to need some money."

He frowns. "Don't worry about it."

I give him a condescending stare as I listen to the robotic voice. "Thank you for calling State Bank. Enter your account number." I press the buttons. "Thank you. Press one for balance information. Press two..." I press one. "Please wait." I tap my fingers on the table. I have $5,000 in my savings. I should probably transfer at least a thousand to get me through today and the next few weeks of groceries and gas... The bank voice interrupts my thoughts. "Your current balance is $30,198.52. Thank you for calling State Bank. If you would like to repeat this information, press three. If you would like to transfer..." I slowly press three. "Your current balance is $30,198.52. Thank you for calling State Bank. If you…"

I stare at the phone like it's foreign. Garrett said Lucas wanted to give me some money. But thirty grand? That's insane! I can't believe there is that much money in my account.

"What's wrong?" Dane asks. "I said not to worry about it. If you need –"

"No." I shake my head and end the call. "I have enough money."

"You look confused."

"I am," I say and slide my phone back into my purse. I grab my water glass again. "Lunch is on me."

Lunch turns out to be the best salad I think I've ever eaten. Dane knows better than to harass me about paying after the incident at Mario's last summer, and when we finish our food and leave Gladys', we have happy stomachs and much more energy. We head back out in the throng of tourists, and I find a small boutique that looks interesting. "Let's stop here."

Inside we find racks of sundresses and swimsuits, t-shirts, hats and bags, scarves, and sunglasses. I immediately head to the swimsuits. I didn't bring one and there is no way I'm not getting in that pool.

I thumb through the rack as Dane heads to the opposite side. Everything looks so tiny. I wander down the aisle, looking for something with more material.

"You should get this." Dane smiles as he holds up what I think is a bikini. All I know is that it's red and has three triangles.

"Definitely not," I say sarcastically. I continue to look through the suits until I stumble upon the men's wear. I laugh as I pluck a fluorescent yellow Speedo off the rack and hold it up. "I'll buy that if you get this."

He makes a disgusted face. "No man looks good in a Speedo."

Actually, I agree, but this could be fun. He wants me to wear skimpy clothes? "Oh, I don't know," I say and look at the suit.

"Some men might." I pretend to think. "Channing Tatum, for example. He would probably look good in this."

"Ugh! Not you too." He gives me a dry look. "What is it with that guy? Is every woman in love with him?"

I shrug. "Possibly."

"Why?"

I shoot him a look like it should be obvious and tick the reasons off on my free hand. "Let's see. His face, his abs, his laugh, his acting, he can dance – that's a big one –"

"Okay, okay, enough," he stops me. "You're running out of fingers."

I laugh and put the Speedo back. As I continue to peruse the suits, Dane asks, "Women really like guys who can dance?"

I stare at him over the rack, completely serious. "Absolutely. Dancing is hot."

Eventually, I do find a suit, a navy blue two-piece with a top that ties around the neck and stops just below my rib cage. I also buy some flip flops and sunglasses before heading to the next store. It quickly becomes apparent that these small shops hold primarily touristy-type items, and I'm not going to find anything utilitarian, like pajamas. I manage to find two sundresses that are cute, and then call it quits. We head to the Kmart for groceries, and, I hope, shorts and pj's.

Luckily, the Kmart on the island is huge and has every department, including its own restaurant. I send Dane for groceries while I head to the clothing section. I quickly find shorts, collecting several pair, and t-shirts that don't say *St. Thomas Virgin Islands* on them. I also grab two sets of pajamas, tank tops with sleep shorts. As I pass the lingerie department, my mind actually considers purchasing new underwear. My conscience immediately chastises itself, and I continue walking. There is no reason that I need new underwear. Absolutely none.

I run into Dane as I head to the market section of the store, and I'm pleased to find that he has a cart full of actual food, not just Twinkies and Kraft Mac and Cheese. I see eggs, bacon, vegetables, milk, orange juice, lunch meat, bread, cereal, chicken, pork chops, and even steak. I silently hope he knows how to cook that because I don't.

By the time we arrive back at the rental house and get everything unloaded, it's nearly eight o'clock. I put off the unavoidable task of lying to my friends and family by meticulously cutting off the tags of my purchases and trying things on. Everything fits, but really, I knew that. Eventually I shower, change into my new pajamas, and pick up my laptop and phone. I grab some grapes to snack on and head outside for two reasons: One is to enjoy the last rays of the day's sun, and the other is to complete the inevitable task of contacting home, alone.

Dane looks away from the TV as I open the sliding door. "What are you doing?"

"Heading out to lie to my instructors and my family," I say and nod toward my laptop. "Wish me luck."

I make my way to one of the lounge chairs by the pool and sit down. I turn on my computer, set it in front of me, and cross my legs to wait while it loads. Once it's ready, I open my email and read through what's there, saving what's important and deleting the rest. I sigh when I'm finished and begrudgingly compose new messages, one to each of my instructors. I blatantly lie, telling them an unexpected family emergency occurred which has called me out of town for the rest of the semester. I ask for their permission to submit my remaining assignments online and attach those that I have already completed as proof of my good intentions. I finish by asking them to send me any remaining exams via email, with the full understanding that they do not have to go out of their way for me. If I can't take the tests, hopefully my homework and existing grades will allow me to at least pass each class.

Once the emails have been sent, I turn the computer off and pick up the phone. The family emergency excuse won't work with Shel and my parents. I stare at my cell as my mind spins. What can I tell them? What would suddenly pull me out of town, especially through the holidays? My mom is going to flip out when she learns I won't be home for Thanksgiving or Christmas.

I lie back in the chaise and hold my phone to my chest. Think, think, think. Where else could I be? What might they believe?

A thought jumps into my brain. I dial Shel's number first.

The phone rings and rings. No answer. It's Saturday night; she's probably out with Matt. When I get her voice mail, I try out my excuse for the first time and attempt to sound excited, not fake. "Shel, it's Em. Guess what? Western chose me for a study abroad trip! I'm leaving tomorrow for..." I hesitate. Where in the heck am I going? I pick the first place that pops into my head. "Ireland! I'll be in Ireland for the rest of the semester, maybe longer." I decide to create more lies. "They told us cell reception is spotty over there, but call me when you get this. My email works, though, so you can email me too. Actually, email is probably better." I pause to think. "I'll give you the details when we talk. I have to get off the phone and start packing. This happened so fast! Take care of Matt and let him know too, please. I'll miss you guys and I'll talk to you soon. Bye."

I hang up and breathe. I don't know how good of a job I just did. I hate lying. I'm awful at it. Lying to my parents is going to be worse. I let my pounding heart calm a little before I dial home. Maybe my parents are out too, and I'll get the answering machine.

No such luck.

"Hello?" It's my mom.

"Hey, Mom." My voice wavers and she can hear it.

"What's wrong?" she immediately asks. There's no fooling her.

I try to sound upbeat. "Nothing's wrong! Actually, I have some pretty exciting news."

"You're pregnant," she says in a dry tone.

"What? No! Mom! Come on!"

"Well?" I can hear the smile in her voice. "Something's up. I'm your mother, I know these things."

I take a deep breath. "I've been selected by the school for a study abroad trip."

"That's great!" my mom exclaims. "How'd that happen?"

Oh boy. More lies. "Um, a student that was supposed to go couldn't, so my advisor nominated me."

"Where are you headed?"

"Ireland."

"Really?" She sounds impressed. I hear movement against the phone. "Dale, guess what? Your daughter has been selected to study abroad in Ireland!"

I can hear him say something in the background. It sounds like "Wow. When?"

My mom comes back to me. "Yeah, when? Next semester?"

"No, mom, actually..." my voice fades. "I leave tomorrow."

I can picture her frown. "Tomorrow?"

"Well, the trip's been planned for awhile and I was just added. I'll be gone for the rest of the year." At least.

Her tone turns suspicious. "Why would the school plan a trip in the middle of the semester?"

"I don't know." I shake my head against the phone. "I'm just taking advantage of the opportunity."

My mother pauses for a moment then throws out my entire name. "Emma. Lynn. Donohue."

Shit.

"You mean to tell me that you are leaving the country tomorrow without any notice? You have to have time to plan; you need a passport!"

"I have a passport," I lie.

"Since when?"

"Since last year."

"So your father and I won't get to see you before you go? You'll be gone for Christmas?"

I can barely find my voice. "Yes."

"Emma, I don't like this," my mom says, irritated. "We hardly get to see you as it is, and now you'll be gone for the holidays?"

"I don't like the timing either." I try to defend my false story. "But this is a once in a lifetime chance. The school's paying for everything; how would it look if I said no? I was nominated."

She sighs loudly then silence is heavy over the phone. When she breaks it, what she says crushes my heart. "I feel like you're lying to me."

That's because I am, my mind responds. How can I put her at ease? "Would you like to talk to the advisor?" I ask. Dane will do an impersonation for me. "I can have him call you tomorrow when we leave. Will that help?"

She doesn't immediately respond, and I don't know what else to say. She doesn't deserve to be fed this silly story, but the truth is unbelievable and out of the question.

"Can we call you while you're gone?" she finally asks.

"Of course. And you can email, too."

"What time do you leave tomorrow?"

"Early. Six a.m."

"From Kalamazoo?"

"Yes."

"I still can't believe you waited until now to tell us," she says. "When *did* you find out?"

"Yesterday," I whisper.

"Yesterday?!" She sounds upset. "Emma, what in the world is going on?"

"Mom, please," I almost beg. "Support me in this. I promise you it's the best decision for me to make right now. I need to get out of here." It's time to play the James card, even though I didn't know I had a James card to play. "This campus, the memories, what was supposed to be...I'm suffocating. I need to finish school, and I will get credit for this trip. I need to graduate and get the hell out of here." Normally, I don't swear around my parents, but maybe my curse will relay the seriousness of what I say. All of this is true.

"I knew you shouldn't have gone back there so soon," she says with regret. "Honey, why didn't you talk to me about this sooner?

We could have made arrangements; you could have taken a semester off. It's not like your dad and I were kicking you out of the house."

"I know," I say, holding back tears. "Listen, I really have to go. I need to pack."

"What about the cat?" she asks. "Who's watching LB?"

"My neighbor Garrett's taking her."

She sighs again. "I'm worried about you. You know that right? I want you to call and email me every chance you get."

"I will," I promise.

"Starting with tomorrow. I want a phone call when you land, got it?"

"Yes, ma'am." I almost smile. "I'm going to miss you."

"I'm going to miss you, too. I already do," she says. "I love you."

"I love you, too."

"Do you want to talk to your father?"

I don't think I can handle anymore right now. "No, Mom, I'm already emotional. Tell him I love him and I'll miss him – and I'll drink some authentic Irish ale for him. Tell Mike, too."

She manages a small laugh. "I will." She pauses for a moment. "Take care of yourself, Em. I'm serious. If that means you come home early, you come home early. I'll fly over there and get you if I have to."

"I know you would," I say as a tear travels down my cheek. I wipe it away and clear my throat. "I have to go. I love you. I'll talk to you soon."

"Tomorrow," she reminds me.

"Yes, tomorrow."

"Okay. Have a safe flight."

"I will, Mom. Bye." I hang up before she can keep me any longer. I drop the phone onto the chair and stare out past the patio toward the ocean. The tears I was holding back trail silently down my face. I want to be home for Christmas; I want to be home for Thanksgiving. I want to be home now.

"Hey."

I look over my shoulder and find Dane standing a few feet behind me. I wipe my cheeks. "How long have you been there?"

"A minute," he says with a sad expression. He walks over to where I'm sitting and kneels beside me. He reaches out and wipes a tear from my chin. "I hate it when you cry."

I shrug, defeated.

"Move over," he says and picks up my laptop and phone to set them on the ground. I slide over against the armrest of the lounge, and he takes a seat next to me, stretching out in the chair. It's a tight fit. He wraps his arms around me and pulls me over him, against his chest. I tuck my head under his chin and weave one leg through his, so we have enough room. As my tears continue to wind their way down my face, he rubs my back.

"I don't want you to be miserable," he says quietly. "Tell me what I can do. I'll be whatever you need."

"You can't," I mumble against him.

"Try me."

"Can you be my home?" I ask into his chest. It's a silly request and one that doesn't quite make sense.

He squeezes me tightly and doesn't even question it. "Absolutely."

Chapter 25

Inevitably, time passes. One week later, I sit at the dining table swirling the remains of my cereal around in my bowl. I need to get motivated; I have two tests to take today.

Thankfully, all of my instructors responded to my email in a positive way, save one. Mr. Carlos will allow me to submit my assignments online, but not take the tests. He says it wouldn't be fair, since I have access to my materials, but don't have access to a "secure testing location." Whatever. My other teachers are working with me, and three out of four ain't bad. I should have no problem passing this semester with at least a B average.

The door to the garage opens and closes behind me. "Morning."

I look over my shoulder. "Good morning." I unfold my legs from under me and slide off the chair. "Do you want breakfast?"

Dane walks toward me, pulling off his sweaty shirt. "What are you making?"

"Frosted Flakes," I say and hold up my bowl. "It's a very complicated procedure."

He pouts. "Aww. I was hoping for real food like an omelet."

I roll my eyes as I walk into the kitchen. "You're on your own." I reach the sink and turn on the faucet to rinse my bowl. "How was your run?" Dane was big into cross country in high school and he's decided to take it up again, now that he has nothing better to do.

"Great," he says as he stands opposite me across the breakfast bar. "You should join me. It's cathartic."

I'm the biggest wuss when it comes to any kind of endurance sport. "I told you before; I won't even make it half way. You'd have to carry me back."

He places his hands against the countertop and leans forward. "And that would be bad why?"

"Shut up." I shake my head and place my bowl in the dish drainer. The day wouldn't be complete without some sort of smart comment coming out of his mouth.

I leave the water running and decide to wash the few dishes that remain in the sink. There's not many, just a few glasses and the bowl that held the popcorn. Last night was movie night. *21 Jump Street* was on TV. I blush as I remember the constant ribbing Dane gave me over watching Channing Tatum.

He walks around the breakfast bar and opens the refrigerator, pulling out the orange juice. He sets it on the counter beside me and then places his hands on my hips from behind, making me jump. "What are you doing?"

He leans around me to grab one of the glasses I just washed out of the dish rack. "Getting a glass."

"There's a whole cupboard of clean glasses behind you."

"I know," he grins.

I shoot him a condescending look. "Do we need to have a conversation about good touch, bad touch?"

He places an innocent kiss on my cheek. "Touching you could never be bad." He picks up a glass and steps to the side, removing his other hand from my hip. As he pours the juice my face flushes. He's upped the ante on the innuendo today.

I finish washing the popcorn bowl and turn off the faucet. "Are you headed to the shower or do I have a few minutes? I want to get dressed before I take my tests."

He swallows. "You know, the beauty of online classes is that you can take your tests in whatever you have on."

"I feel more prepared when I'm presentable." Actually, I just want to get out of my pajamas. I'm feeling particularly vulnerable all of a sudden.

He tilts his head. "Yes, right now you are a complete mess. In fact you are so unpresentable, I think you need a shower." He sets down his glass. "I'll join you."

My mouth falls open. "What has gotten into you?"

He laughs. "I just had a good run, that's all."

I give him a wary look. "I'm going to get dressed."

He picks up his glass again. "Okay. I'm going to make bacon."

I turn toward the bedroom and then stop when I see his wet t-shirt lying on the counter. "Pick that up," I say and make a face. "It's gross."

He leans across the counter and grabs his shirt. Satisfied, I head to the bedroom.

WHACK! His sweaty shirt hits me squarely in the back, and I stop in my tracks. I turn around and catch him trying to hide his grin behind his glass like nothing happened. Apparently, today, we've stepped back in time to kindergarten. I bend down slowly, pick his shirt off the floor with two fingers, and raise an eyebrow. "That's how you want to play?"

He shrugs.

I can't launch the shirt at him because it will only make it half the distance. I don't have many options standing here in the hallway, so I decide to bide my time. "You have no idea what you just started," I threaten and narrow my eyes. "Watch your back, Walker."

"Is that a promise?"

I give him an adamant nod and then carry his shirt into the bedroom. As I close the door behind me, I can hear him laugh.

Later that afternoon, after I've read a few chapters and taken my tests, I lounge on the couch, surfing the internet. I'm sleepy today. I don't know why; I've slept like a rock the past few nights. Maybe I toss in my sleep more than I realize. Dane hasn't said anything though; you'd think he would if I'd accidentally kicked him or something. My thoughts turn to payback for earlier today, and I'm just about to Google pranks when he comes through the sliding door.

"Are you finished yet?"

"Yep." I sit up. "Do you need the computer?"

He nods. "I want to work on fixing those pictures for your mom."

My mother has requested that I send her photos of Ireland. Since I can't do that for real, Dane, master graphic designer that he is, bought Photoshop and has been working with the program and some images we pulled off the internet. He has four pictures finished where he's imposed me from photos I had on my phone to stock photos of popular sites in Ireland. He wants to do a few more, so I can send her a couple at a time.

Sitting down next to me, he takes over my laptop and sets it on the coffee table. "Where's the mouse?" he asks.

I reach into my computer bag on the floor and pull out my little pink wireless mouse; it's funny to watch him use it.

"Did you call your mom today?" he asks while he connects the mouse USB.

"Nope. I emailed her. And Shel." He never lets me forget to contact them every couple of days.

"Matt called," he says absentmindedly while he opens Photoshop. "He wanted to know if I wanted to go to the bar. I guess Shel's busy tonight."

"What'd you tell him?"

"That I was still out of town," he says and clicks the file he wants. He looks at me. "He mentioned that you were in Ireland. I guess he thought I'd want to know."

I smile. "Ireland is unseasonably warm and sunny for this time of year. You should join me there."

He smirks. "Already done." He looks back at the screen and sets to work magnifying and dragging and clicking. I have no idea how any of this program works.

I lean forward to watch him and set my chin on my hand. "You know, you could go home. You don't have to stay here."

He frowns at the screen. "Do you want me to leave?"

"No," I say abruptly and shake my head. "But, maybe you should make an appearance and then come back. How long can you use the 'out of town for work' excuse? Especially since you no longer have a job."

He says nothing.

The idea of not having him around makes me sad, but I have to consider what's best for him and our ruse. "Besides, your family will want you around for the holidays. I can stay here and hold down the fort. You could go home and celebrate and then come back to me."

"Leaving you is out of the question," he says. "My family and I aren't close. It's not a big deal if I miss Christmas."

I find this incredibly sad and my face shows it. When he looks at me he notices and sighs. "Listen, this is how it works in my family. My dad and my stepmother will have a huge dinner Christmas Eve. They will invite everyone involved with Bay Woods; that's about a hundred people. They'll spend the night hobnobbing with business associates and employees who really don't want to be there but feel obligated to attend because my dad is their boss. I will hang in the background, as I usually do, with a fake smile plastered on my face and answer the same question a thousand times."

"Let me guess," I say. "Why aren't you working at the golf course?"

"Exactly. Then, after the catered spread is gone and the liquor starts to dry up, the guests will leave to spend time with their own families. My dad will ceremoniously hand me a check, his gift to me every year, and I'll wake up Christmas morning like it's any other day. The End."

"I don't like that," I say.

"Me either."

We stare at each other for a few moments and then he turns back to my laptop. I immediately regret bringing up the subject. Maybe we could start a new tradition this Christmas. Decorate a palm tree or something.

"So, will we be here in December?" I ask.

"We can be. I rented the place for a month, but the agreement can be extended." He looks at me again. "Or we could move on to somewhere new. This may be your chance to travel the world." He smiles.

"Sounds tempting."

"Well, we have three weeks to decide," he says and goes back to clicking.

I try to watch him work, but it's boring and I keep yawning. "I'm going to go lay down. I'm tired for some reason."

He nods, concentrating on the screen, and I stand to walk around him. I pass the sliding doors and eye the hammock strung between two palm trees on the patio. I have yet to use that. I change direction and head outside to crawl into it for my late afternoon siesta. It takes me three tries, but I finally find myself in the middle of it without feeling like I'm going to fall out. The hammock is made from a solid sheet of fabric, not rope, and it wraps around my body slightly.

The sun warms my skin and the gentle breeze rocks me as I close my eyes and settle in. My mind turns to thoughts of James and Garrett and where they may be and what they may be doing. I think of LB and hope she's not giving Garrett too much grief, although he deserves it. My thoughts wander and I try to imagine where I'll be in a month or two. There's no place else I'd rather be, except for home. I wouldn't mind staying here. It's practically perfect.

When I open my eyes, I know time has passed because the sun has shifted in the sky. I must have dozed off for an hour, maybe two. I'm hot from lying in the sun so long, and I feel sticky. I look to my right and notice Dane lying on his stomach, floating on a raft in the pool. I try to get out of the hammock gracefully, but my muscles are stiff from being cradled in the same position for so long. I half step-half tumble out and catch my balance by grabbing on to the material. I roll my eyes as I wait for his teasing to begin, but it doesn't come. I walk over to the side of the pool and stare at him. When he doesn't so much as twitch after several minutes, I realize he's asleep under his sunglasses. My mind flashes to this morning and it's hard to suppress my grin. This is too easy.

I move around the pool to where I'm closest to him. My plan is to jump in and scare him, so he'll flip off his raft. I crouch down and sit on the balls of my feet, waiting for him to float just a bit closer. But as I watch him, I hesitate. I'm not sure if it's from all the comments he's been throwing around today or what, but I take this private moment to look at him. I mean really study him. It's hard to find the right words to describe his appearance. Handsome? Beautiful? Good-looking? Hot? He's all of those things. My eyes roam over the tanned length of his body, and I wonder what in the hell is he doing here with me. No wonder Teagan is upset at losing him, vain woman that she is. He is arm candy. But, he's also so much more than that. He has one of the kindest hearts I've ever known.

"I can see you," he says out of nowhere.

Damn! Rather than show my embarrassment, I tip my head and say, "Oh, really? Can you see this?"

And with that, I stand and launch myself into the pool, pulling my knees up and landing just to the side of his raft. The splash feels enormous, and I'm confident I've completed my mission.

When I pop up from beneath the water I see any empty raft floating in front of me. I know I'm in trouble, so I swim as fast as I can toward the stairs of the pool. I feel a hand graze my ankle and let out a yelp as I try to swim faster. Darn clothes! They're holding me back! By some miracle I manage to get to the steps and out of the pool before he catches me. I turn around to face him, dripping. He's standing waist deep in the pool with his arms crossed, his sunglasses lost, and a smirk on his face.

"I told you to watch your back," I laugh and reach up to wring my hair.

"Looks like you were the one watching."

Whatever. I will not allow him to rattle me and take away my victory. "This makes us even." I point at him. "That will teach you to throw around your stinky clothes!"

"You talk a good game," he says and walks toward me. "Come here and show me you mean it."

I don't think so. He's not luring me back into the water. All he has to do is get ahold of me the right way and it's over; before I know it, we'll be making out in the pool. I shake my head and look at myself. "I need to change." I back toward the sliding door. "We're tied; there's nothing to prove." When I reach the door, I turn around. "I'm hungry," I shout to him. "You want anything?"

He gives me an exasperated stare, and I realize I just asked a loaded question. I open the door and step inside before he can answer.

"Hello?"

Dane answers his cell without looking at it. We've just returned from a grocery run and my arms are full of bags. It's nearly the end of second week together and we were just about out of everything. I'm glad we made it back in time too; the sky looks like it's about to open up any minute and dump buckets of rain.

"What?" he scowls into the phone.

I set the bags on the counter then turn around to help him by taking the ones he is carrying. He doesn't look happy.

"That's none of your business," he snaps.

I walk around the breakfast bar, setting the remaining bags on the island. I start to unload what we bought and pull out the deli meat to put in the refrigerator. I hear Dane sigh loudly, and when I look at him, he has his head down with his hand on his hip.

"He's right; I did quit."

He must be speaking with his father. This could get ugly.

"No!"

I avert my eyes and busy myself with the groceries.

"There's nothing to discuss...no, I'm not telling you when I'm coming back...because it doesn't matter! Whatever. I told you before I don't want it. I don't know! Keep it, sell it, I don't care."

I open the pantry to find a home for the chips.

"Who cares what they think? Tell them the truth...fine, then, lie! We all know you need to protect your precious reputation!"

I sneak a glance at him. He's upset.

"Really?" He laughs sarcastically. "You need to take a long look in the mirror before you can say that to me...What? You've forgotten all about Brock?"

Who's Brock?

"That's right. You keep living in your delusionary world." He eyes flash to me, and I look away.

He lets out a frustrated breath. "Then go get it, who's stopping you? I want everything out by the time I get back."

He remains silent for a moment and allows the caller to rant. I can tell by the way he shakes his head that what they're saying is ridiculous to him. Finally, he cuts the person off in a harsh tone. "I'm done with this. Get your stuff and get out," he snaps and hangs up. He looks at his phone and then at me, his mouth set. "I'm sorry you had to hear that."

"It wasn't too bad."

He comes around the counter to help me unpack. We work in silence until he stops, paper towel in hand. "Can you believe her? She told my dad I quit."

"Her?"

"Teagan."

Ah. That's not good. "I'm sorry."

"Anything to meddle in my life," he mutters.

"Who's Brock?" I ask.

He snorts. "The guy she was sleeping with in South America."

My eyes grow wide. "What?"

He gives me a sarcastic smile. "It gets lonely in the jungle."

"Oh." I feel bad for him, and I can sort of relate. "At least James can't sleep with Meg."

"Who's Meg?"

I roll my eyes. "James' Brock."

Dane stops in his tracks and looks at me, surprised. "James has a Guardian girlfriend?"

"Possibly." I shrug and take the paper towel from his hands. I bend down to put it under the sink. "He says they're just friends, but I'm pretty sure she wants more. He denies it, though." When I stand Dane is frozen, staring at me. "What?"

"James is messing around with another girl?"

"No; well, he says he's not. I mean, I know he cares about her, but she's been captured, so..." I can see the wheels turning in his head. What is he thinking?

Lightning flashes, drawing my attention to the windows. "Looks like the storm is here."

Dane turns to look, too. Thunder cracks, effectively ending our conversation, and we finish putting the food away.

Within the next half hour, the wind starts to pick up and rain pounds against the house. Thunder that sounded distant at first creeps closer with every rumble. It's kind of scary being surrounded by this much glass, and I watch the palm trees on the patio bend and sway. I wonder if we should have at least stacked the patio furniture to prevent it from being tossed in the wind.

"Well, that's that," Dane says from behind me.

"What's what?"

"The satellite went out." He tosses the remote on the couch. "Now what?"

I shrug. "Guess you'll have to pick up a book and read."

He makes a face.

"Wait." I walk down the hallway toward the bedroom and open the small linen closet there. I remember seeing some board games when I was looking for towels the other day. "Do you want to play Clue?" I shout, my head buried in the closet. I loved this game as a kid. He doesn't answer me, but I grab the game anyway. I bring it out to the living room, smiling. "I said do you want to play Clue?"

He notices my excitement and grins back. "I take it you do?"

I nod and set the box on the coffee table, open the lid and start setting up the game. I hope all the pieces are here. I was fascinated by all the rooms and little weapons when I was younger. Apparently, I still am. "Who do you want to be?" I ask.

"Give me the Colonel." He holds out his hand.

I give him the yellow pawn for Colonel Mustard. "I'll be Miss Scarlet," I say and place my red piece on the correct space.

"Miss Scarlet?" Dane smirks. "I thought you'd choose someone more pure, like Mrs. White."

"The maid?" I scowl. "I can be a maid in real life. I want to be the sexy vixen."

His eyes shoot up, and he suppresses a grin.

I give him a tally sheet then divide the game cards into piles: one for the rooms, one for the weapons, and one for the suspects. I take a card from each pile and place them in the secret envelope then shuffle the rest. I give them to Dane to divide evenly between us.

Once we're ready, I roll the dice and move four spaces. Dane rolls and moves ten, landing in the lounge. "Okay," he says. "I think it was Professor Plum in the lounge with the..." He peruses the board. "Knife." He moves both Plum and the knife into the lounge.

I sift through my cards and show him the knife. He marks it down.

I roll again and move, ending up in the hall. "I think it was you," I move his piece, "in the hall with the candlestick."

He flips through his cards and shows me the hall. I mark it on my paper.

"Do you ever wonder why Mr. Boddy was murdered?" Dane asks, referring to the fictitious victim in the game of Clue.

"Because he was rich?"

He shakes his head. "I don't think it was the money. I have another theory." He rolls the dice.

"What's that?"

"I think," he moves seven spaces, "that Mr. Boddy was having an affair with Miss Scarlet, but he thought she was also having an affair with the Colonel."

I smirk. "You think he committed suicide because she was cheating on him?"

"Nope," he says and folds his hands. "Mrs. Peacock was the Colonel's ex and was unhappy that he had moved on with that hussy Scarlet."

"So Mrs. Peacock did it to frame Mustard?"

"She wanted to, but she didn't have it in her. She contracted Mr. Green, who used to be Boddy's business partner, but was recently let go under suspicious circumstances. She hired him to do it."

I pretend to be shocked and bring my hand to my chest. "Mr. Green killed Mr. Boddy to frame Mustard and avenge Peacock, just because she was upset with the Colonel for banging Scarlet?"

He smiles. "Yes. But unfortunately, neither Peacock or Green nor Boddy knew that, in reality, Mustard and Scarlet hadn't done anything. They were just friends."

I pretend to pout. "Poor Mr. Boddy."

"Yeah," Dane fakes sympathy. "The least Scarlet and Mustard could have done was actually sleep together. Then Boddy's death wouldn't have been in vain."

I see the parallels he's drawing here. I roll my eyes and hold out my hand. "You have a very active imagination. Give me the dice."

He grins.

After a few turns, I've narrowed the weapons down to the poison. I'm still stuck with two suspects though, the Colonel and Mr. Green, and four rooms. I'm feeling really competitive; maybe it's the sound of the raging storm outside that fuels my desire to win. Or maybe it's Dane. Every time I compete against him – mini golf, Go Karts – I can't bear the thought of losing.

Suddenly, a brilliant flash of lightning illuminates the patio and thunder rips through the sky. It sounds like it's directly over the house, and I jump. The lights flicker, and we lose power. I stare across the table at Dane in the dark. "Crap."

He laughs. "I think there's a flashlight under the sink."

We both get up and head toward the kitchen, using the sporadic flashes of light to guide the way. I make it around the dining table and to the counter. "We're going to need more than a flashlight," I say. "We can use those candles from around the bathtub."

"Got it," he says and heads off toward the bedroom.

I get to the sink and open the cupboard, but I can't see a damn thing. I reach around blindly, knocking over the paper towel and, I think, a bottle of soap. I feel something cylindrical and grab it. When I pull it close to my eyes, I find that it's a small fire extinguisher. I put it back and feel around some more. Ah ha! Bingo. Flashlight.

I turn it on and the beam is dim, but it works. I start opening drawers to find matches or a lighter. There's a grill on the patio, surely there's a lighter here somewhere.

With no luck in the drawers, I turn to the cupboards. Way back in the corner of one, I think I see what might be a box of matches. I set the flashlight down and heave myself on to the counter, kneeling, to reach it.

I feel hands around my waist.

"AH!" I fall to the side on my hip and whip around. "Don't sneak up on me!"

Dane laughs. "I don't want you to fall."

"I won't fall!"

289

He leaves his hands around my waist. "Why are you up there?"

"I'm looking for matches to light the candles. It's going to be hard to play Clue in the dark."

"I know something else we can play in the dark."

What?

He turns me by my waist and pulls me forward, causing my legs to fall off the counter and land on either side of him. It feels like he might pick me up, so I brace myself against his shoulders. He doesn't lift me though; he just pulls me as close to him as possible. As I sit on the counter facing him, he closes the short distance between us in seconds, finding my mouth. This isn't like the kiss we shared the first morning we were here; this kiss is reminiscent of last summer when things got out of hand. Instinctively I lean back, but he follows me and there's really nowhere to go. His hands leave my waist, traveling over my hips and down my thighs to rest on my knees. He pulls them both to his body and holds them there, pinning himself between my legs. My heart races and my insides start to knot.

His mouth leaves mine, tracing a hot trail along my jaw. My mind flashes to his earlier scenario. "I'm not Scarlet," I protest.

His lips leave my skin. "And I'm not a Colonel." His mouth finds mine again and as I kiss him back, I'm one person divided: half of me shouts, "This is wrong!" while the other half screams, "This is so right!"

His hands leave my knees and move up to my hips again. He grasps them as he pulls his mouth away for a moment and rests his forehead against mine.

"Then what game is this?" I whisper.

His lips move back to my neck. "Naked Twister."

Chapter 26

"Wow!" I lean to the side. "Just come out and say it, why don't you?"

He moves his face in front of mine. "Subtlety wasn't working."

My eyebrows shoot up. "You've been subtle? I got every message you've sent."

I can see him frown in the darkness. "Then what's taking us so long?"

"So long? We've been here two weeks!"

He takes a step back from me. "Are you serious? We've known each other for months."

"Yes, but..."

"But what?"

I hesitate. How do I explain feelings that I don't understand?

"Emma," he says. "What's holding you back? You have to talk to me."

A low rumble of thunder passes overhead, and I wrap my arms around my waist. "I don't know where to start."

He steps forward and sets his hands on either side of me, against the countertop. He leans close and looks directly into my eyes. "Now is the time to be honest. Can you do that?"

He knows everything now; I would never lie to him. "Of course."

"Do you have feelings for me?"

I can't deny that I do. I have since last summer. I hold his gaze and nod.

"And what do you think will happen if you give in to those feelings?"

I lower my eyes. "A lot."

"Name one thing."

I give him a defeated look. If he can see it in the darkness, I can't tell. "I've only ever been with James...this is really new for me."

"So you're nervous?" he guesses.

I shrug.

He gives me a crooked smile. "Well, you're not alone. I've been with Teagan since I was sixteen; I think this is something we can work on together."

I roll my eyes. "That makes it worse."

"Why?"

"Have you seen her?" I ask incredulously. "She's gorgeous. Like straight out of a magazine super model material." I unfold my arms just as lightning lights up the sky and look down at myself. "This is not that."

He stands up straight and takes my wrists in his hands. "There's no comparison."

My heart flips when he says this, but I still give him a dry look. "Come on."

"You think you're worried about competing with Teags?" he says and lets me go. "I have James to live up to. You've put him on a pedestal, and he's tied to you for life. Competing with a Guardian isn't easy."

My expression twists. Dane has never come across as anything but confident; I took it for granted that he truly was. "I've never compared the two of you, I swear. You're different people."

He places his hands on my knees. "Then you see my point."

I stare at him, mute, accepting his logic. The only sound is the rain that continues to pound against the house.

"It appears we stand on even ground when it comes to the exes," he says. "What else are you worried about?"

"James isn't an ex," I say automatically.

He gives me a confused look. "But you can't be together. Or did I misunderstand something about the whole assignment thing?"

"No; you're right." I shake my head. "It's just that we'll never be apart. He'll know you and I are together; I'll feel like I'm cheating on him."

He frowns. "And he's not cheating on you with this Meg? Or how about that other girl, the one from the bonfire? What was that?"

I stare at him speechless. I can't believe he brought that up.

He sighs. "I'm not trying to make you feel bad. It's just...from the outside, it appears someone has a wandering eye."

Stubbornly, I cross my arms. "I trust James. He said nothing was going on with Meg."

"But, you're still suspicious. Yes?"

I give him an exasperated look, and he leans in close. "In my experience, where there's smoke there's fire. That's all I'm saying."

I scowl. "It sounds like you're trying to make him look bad for your own benefit."

He pauses, shaking his head. "Believe that if you want. What I'm trying to do is ease your conscience."

Memories flood my mind. I think about what happened with Rebecca, James' consolation of her, and their kiss. I think about how much their interaction meant to her. I recall his defense of Meg, when he didn't deny she might have feelings for him. I remember the way he looked when he found out she could still become human, and again, when he learned she'd been Touched. My shoulders sag. "You might be right," I concede quietly.

Dane reaches for my hands, and I unfold my arms. Our silence allows me to listen to the wind; it's let up and the rain doesn't fall as hard against the house. He squeezes my fingers. "I never want you to feel guilty about us. Everything that has happened, and anything else that does, will never be meaningless."

"I would never think it was." My heart knows that what happens between us will only make us stronger, and that's a little scary. Am I ready to take that step?

He leans forward and places a gentle kiss on my lips, then pulls on my hands. "I don't think the power will be on any time soon. Let's finish this conversation in a more comfortable place."

I ease myself off the counter and set my feet on the floor. He releases one of my hands and leads me to the bedroom where he lets go and moves around his side of the bed to change. I do the same. It takes me a minute to find my pajamas in the dark, but once I do, I feel my way to the bathroom to put them on and brush my teeth. When I'm finished, Dane trades places with me.

I crawl onto my side of the bed and try to get comfortable, hugging a pillow to my chest. I think about what we've discussed and feel some weight lifted from my shoulders. It's comforting to know he's not as confident as I assumed; this is all new for him, too. He knows about my guilt surrounding James, and I don't have to make up excuses as to why I feel conflicted. As for the idea of James cheating on me, well, that's going to take a minute to process. But, what Dane says is true. As much as it hurts, James and I can't be together, and he's going to move on. His duty leaves him no choice. Would it be so horrible if I did the same?

The bed moves when Dane gets under the covers, and, a moment later, I feel him directly behind me. He speaks over my shoulder. "I'd prefer if you'd hug me instead of the pillow."

Honestly, I'd prefer that too. I glance behind me as he slides his arms around my waist, pulls me back against his chest, and moves us both to the center of the bed. I reach up and arrange the pillow under my head, as he gets settled, then tuck myself into him as closely as possible.

"I take it this is okay?" he asks.

I nod against him and weave my fingers through his.

He rests his chin in the crook of my neck. "Is there anything else you want to talk about?"

"I don't think so. I feel better."

"I'm glad. I'm sorry I brought up the cheating thing."

I shrug. "The truth hurts sometimes. It's not like you haven't been there to know."

He holds me tighter.

The warm feeling of him surrounding me makes me sleepy. I close my eyes and give in to the comfort of his presence.

"Can I ask you a question?"

I turn my face toward him as much as I can. "Sure."

"It's a big one."

Yikes. I shift my body to lie next to him on my back, so I can see his face. "That worries me."

He props himself on his elbow and looks down. "If you can't give me an answer, I'll understand. Just be honest with me, okay?"

Now I'm really concerned. "Okay," I say, uncertain.

He takes a deep breath. "What else can I do to prove that I'm in love with you?"

My heart stops. Did he just say...?

He leans over me. "Name it. I'm serious."

I swallow and meet his eyes. Even in the dark I can see how much feeling is there, how much he means what he says. What did I ever do to deserve him? Absolutely nothing.

He gives me an anxious smile. "So? I'm waiting."

I push myself up on my elbows and hold my face inches from his. "You've already given me so much. There's nothing else I need." Once that statement is out of my mouth, I realize that there is something that he needs. I can at least give him that, right? After everything he's done for me?

He reaches up and runs his fingers from my temple to my chin. "Are you sure?"

I know what he's asking. Too many emotions race through my heart. When I decide to give myself to him, I want it to be the only thing on my mind. "Patience," I say. I know it's a lot to ask.

"Done." He wraps his arms around me again and pulls me against him. We lay down as we were before.

"I'm sorry I'm being difficult."

"What's new?"

I can hear the smile in his voice, and I elbow his side. He laughs and then sighs. He squeezes me again and plants a kiss by my ear. "I could get used to this."

"What?"

"Holding you like this."

I smile. "Well, get used to it." If I can't give him everything right now, I can at least give him some things. "I'm feeling mighty comfortable right here. It may be the only way I can sleep from now on."

"You promise?" he asks.

I nod.

He gives me another innocent kiss, where he gave me the first, then I feel his head hit the pillow. "Good night," he says.

I push myself back against him, eliminating any space between us. "'Night."

As I float on my back in the pool, I think about the last few days and smile; so far, it's been the best time I've had here. Our discussion the night of the storm ushered the elephant out of the room. Now, Dane and I are more relaxed around each other.

Okay, I take that back.

He's the same he's always been except he now knows I'm not going to freak out if he touches me. I'm the one who feels liberated. If he makes a suggestive comment, I smile. If he wraps his arms around me I lean into him, instead of away. If he kisses me, I don't think twice about kissing him back. To say that it's nice would be an understatement. Who knew things could be this easy? The twinges of guilt that still pop up from time to time are nothing near what I used to feel. Don't get me wrong; I'm completely dreading the moment when I have to explain myself to James. But, he has to feel that I am happy and that should count for something. I hope.

I turn over and swim to the stairs, sufficiently chlorinated for ten in the morning. Stepping out of the pool, I make my way over to my towel and dry off. As I wrap it around myself, a pair of arms circles me from behind.

"Morning swim?" Dane asks over my shoulder.

"Yep," I smile. Under his arms I pull the towel tight around me. "You're back early."

"I got a brilliant idea," he says and turns me around. "Tomorrow is Thanksgiving."

"Yeah, I know." I will miss my mother's cooking and the smell of pumpkin pie.

"Do you want to do the whole traditional turkey and stuffing thing?"

My nose scrunches. "I don't think eating a turkey prepared by me is such a good idea."

He smiles and his eyes light up. "I thought you might say something like that." He kisses me softly then releases me, turning toward the house. "I'm going to get cleaned up then I have some plans to make. I shouldn't be long."

"Where are you going?"

He grins. "None of your business."

I eye him suspiciously. "Just tell me."

He opens the sliding door and sets one foot inside. "Let's just say what I'm planning for tomorrow will keep your mind off of home."

I don't know why, but an image of bungee jumping immediately springs to mind. "Don't plan anything crazy," I warn him. I don't want him to be disappointed if he gets me all the way to wherever and I refuse to cooperate.

"Don't worry," he smiles. "I'll be back in a few."

I watch him shut the door and disappear. I look up at the blue sky and decide sunbathing is in order. It's technically Thanksgiving break, right? I head over to the lounge and spread my towel on the chair, then lie on my stomach to tan. As the sun warms me, I relax. I should only lie here a few minutes; I need to get dressed and start my day. For what reason, I don't know. My class work is beyond caught up and I've made the requisite emails for the week. I should call my parents tomorrow, though, for the holiday. I think about what I would be doing if I were at home and frown. I definitely wouldn't be doing this; it's probably freezing and snowy. My frown turns upside down. This is better.

Unfortunately, hours later, I'm feeling the polar opposite of better. At noon, I started to get antsy. At two, antsy turned into worried. At three, worried morphed into anger. And now, at five, the anger has subsided into something worse. Panic.

Dane hasn't come back.

I hang up my cell in frustration as I get his voicemail for the third time. I would call more but I don't want to come across as needy, even though I'm about ready to hyperventilate. He's never left me alone this long before. As I pace the floor, I try to stop my mind from weaving a tapestry of unpleasant scenarios. He must be hurt if he's not answering his phone. What if he got into an accident? The hospital wouldn't know to contact me.

And then another equally unpleasant thought enters my psyche. What if we've been found? I knew things were too good to be true. What if The Allegiant have taken Dane and are planning on using him against me? It's not out of the question. What if James slipped up because of my happiness and got caught? The thought of losing either of them to The Allegiant twists my heart. And if the reason isn't supernatural, I don't think my soul could bear losing Dane the way I lost James. I imagine him on the side of the road, bleeding, and my body starts to shake. I can't lose him. I can't.

I sit on the couch, clutching my phone, and wrap my arms around my waist. I need to hold my insides together. I don't know what to do. We never discussed this; we don't have a plan if something happens to one of us. I know this isn't the inner city, but we should have known things couldn't be left to chance. The fact that we're in the situation we're in should've given us a clue. I stare at the floor as the tears that dance behind my eyes take center stage. How long do I wait before I head on foot to search for him?

Mercifully, minutes later, the door to the garage opens. I whip around and stand as Dane finally makes an appearance. He sees my expression and his face immediately softens.

"I'm so sorry," he says.

I stare at him for a moment to make sure he's really there. I wipe my face then walk around the couch. He holds out his phone.

"My battery died," he glares at the phone, "and I lost track of time."

I want to be stern, but my voice wavers. "How dare you? You've been gone for seven hours!"

He gives me a look of genuine remorse. "I got talking and then Charlie offered me a beer. Time got away from me..."

I close the distance between us and throw my arms around his neck. "Don't you ever do that to me again."

He wraps his arms around me. "I'm sorry; I won't." He kisses the top of my head then tries to look at me, but I remain wrapped around him. "You were really that worried?"

I raise my head. "Have you forgotten my last boyfriend left me and never came back alive? I thought you'd been in an accident! Or captured. Do you remember we're in hiding?"

He looks at me and a slow smile spreads across his face. It annoys me, and I push against his chest. "This isn't funny! I nearly had a heart attack!"

He rearranges his features. "You're right. It's not funny."

I cross my arms. "Then what's up with the grin? Knock it off."

"Do you realize what you just called me?"

I give him a sour look. "Inconsiderate? Irritating?"

He shakes his head. "You called me your boyfriend."

I narrow my eyes. "I did not."

"You did so," he smiles again. "You said 'my last boyfriend left me.' Which would mean I'm your current one."

I open my mouth to dispute him, but nothing comes out. He steps forward and wraps his arms around my waist.

"I really am sorry," he says and dips his head to kiss me.

I move out of the way and set my jaw. "It's going to take more than that."

He looks to the ceiling in thought. "Dinner," he says and refocuses on my face. "Let me take you to dinner. To make up for my inability to tell time."

I eye him suspiciously even though my heart is overjoyed at seeing him safe and alive. "That's a start," I concede.

He wipes my cheek with his thumb. "How long until you're ready?"

"Give me ten minutes," I say and back away from him. There's no way I'm letting him out of my sight for anything longer than that.

We end up at a restaurant just east of Charlotte Amalie called the Fat Turtle. Even though it's early evening, I can tell this place turns into party central at night, especially the day before a holiday. The restaurant is located on the waterfront where large yachts, too many to count, have set anchor. There's an open air bar, along with inside seating, and an area for dancing. Dane requests a table outside, and I get the feeling that he has been here before. Teagan's image materializes before my eyes and I imagine them here together, sipping cocktails and dancing close. The thought leaves a sour taste in my mouth.

Once we're seated, we order and our food comes fairly quick. It's good, but not as good as Gladys' in my opinion, and I pick at the chicken on my plate. When we finish our meal, Dane pays the bill and then moves us to one of the bistro tables closer to the bar.

"We're staying?" I ask.

He nods. "It's nice to get out, don't you think?"

I look around. The place is filling up. It will be nice to stare at something besides the flat screen for a night.

"So, what do you want?" he asks, standing to get a drink.

"I don't know. Something fruity?"

"Something fruity," he repeats and smiles. "You're fruity."

"Okay, then. Scotch on the rocks." Like I would ever drink that.

He frowns. "Never mind. Something fruity it is."

Apparently he doesn't want to scrape me off the floor later. He heads to the bar, and I watch him go. When he reaches it, he squeezes in between a blonde and another guy about our age. The blonde is wearing the tightest mini dress I've ever seen. She has the body to pull it off, but wow. What exactly is she advertising? Dane orders and the blonde notices, turning to him and tossing her hair. She beams at him, introducing herself, and Dane smiles politely. The bartender eventually retrieves our drinks, and Dane makes his way back to me. He holds a bottle in one hand and a glass that contains liquid as blue as pool water in the other.

"Here you go." He hands it to me.

"What is it?"

"It's called Turtle Soup," he smiles. "Don't worry. No turtles were harmed in the making of it."

I roll my eyes and take a drink. It's really good; it's frozen and tastes like melon. I'm going to have to pace myself. Alcoholic drinks that taste like Kool-Aid are dangerous.

"So," he leans over the table, "am I closer to being forgiven yet?"

"Marginally," I say and play with my straw.

"You can't be that mad," he says. "I've seen you mad and this isn't it."

I look him in the eye. "I was more worried than anything. You'd be just as concerned if I went missing for hours."

He smirks. "Would I?"

I kick him under the table; he grimaces as I connect with his shin. "You'd better be."

He laughs, but then his face falls with concern. "You know I'd be sick with worry."

I take another drink. "Well, then, welcome to my world."

As the place gets crowded, Dane and I spend the time people watching. I'm sure my karma is ruined with the comments I've been making, especially toward little Miss Mini Dress. But, it's fun to laugh and forget this afternoon. As evening falls, a DJ starts to play and the dance floor fills. Dane heads back to the bar. "You want another?"

This would be my third. "I don't think that's wise." I feel pretty good, but then again I'm seated. I don't want to risk it.

Dane makes a face at me and leaves. I guess I'll be driving home. I watch him weave his way across the dance floor and disappear through the bodies. When he reappears, bottle in hand, the blonde from earlier swoops in from his right, setting her hands against his chest. Her invitation is clear. She wants to dance.

At first it looks like he's going to refuse, but then he glances at me. We make eye contact and a knowing smirk spreads across his face. My mouth falls open as I watch his bold move. He decides to dance with her. What is he trying to do? Piss me off?

Little Miss Mini Dress smiles broadly and runs a hand through her hair as she moves. I watch them and a stunned expression takes over my features. Dane can dance. Like really dance. My face flushes as I remember my comments from the other day, when I told him I thought guys who could dance were hot. I adjust my face and my posture, crossing my arms and trying to look impassive. The blonde puts her hands on him, he shoots me a look, and I raise an eyebrow. I know why he's doing this, but it still doesn't stop the jealousy that seers through my veins.

"Who's your friend?"

I look to my right and find a guy standing beside me. He's blonde too, with perfectly styled hair and tanned skin. He rests one hand on the table, and I can tell just from his arm that he's built. I follow his line of vision and see that he's staring at my floorshow.

I shake my head. "She's not my friend."

He smiles. "Not her. Him."

"His name is Dane." I uncross my arms and turn my body to face him. "And you are?"

He holds out his hand. "Aiden."

I take it. "Emma."

He reveals his perfect smile again. "So, Emma, is your friend, Dane, available?"

What? I look at Dane and then back at Aiden. "Um, no. He's not."

He sighs. "Figures." I must look really lost because he elaborates. "He doesn't look that into her and he's not dancing with you, so I thought maybe..."

The light dawns, and I suppress a giggle. "I'm sorry; I'm afraid you're not his type."

He nods like he knew that was coming then steps back. "So, I take it he's with you?"

I shrug. "We're working on it."

"Well, you're not getting anywhere sitting here," he says and extends his hand again. "Would you like to dance?"

Would I? I grin. "Yes, thank you." I take Aiden's hand and hop off my seat. He leads us into the crowd and I shoot a look over his shoulder at Dane, which is hard because he's quite tall. Dane gives me a nod with both eyebrows raised. Game on.

Aiden turns out to be a pretty good dancer and it's not long before I'm lost in the fun of this. It's only when I glance at Dane and Brittany Wannabe that I come crashing down. He's not touching her, but she's all over him. The longer they're together the more irritated I get. I can't blame the alcohol; I only had two drinks and I feel fine. As the songs morph into one another, one thought becomes crystal clear – he's mine, damn it, and you can't have him.

Aiden notices my distraction and places his hands around my waist, turning me, so my back is to Dane and Brittany. He leans in to my ear and speaks over the music, "I'm going to move you his way then you cut in, okay?"

I nod and follow his lead. When we get close, Aiden reaches out and practically turns me between them, cutting off Miss Mini Dress and distracting her. I land in front of Dane and he grabs me, pulling me close. He smiles as he finds my ear. "It's about time you came to save me."

I smirk. "You're the one who decided to dance with her."

"You know who I'd rather dance with."

I lean back. "Speaking of, you've been holding out on me."

He grins. "I can't reveal all my secrets. I have to play them when the time is right. I wouldn't want you to fall in love with me too fast or anything."

I shoot him a sarcastic look; although, the way we're moving is making my heart race.

He looks over my head. "Who's your new pal?"

I glance over my shoulder and find Aiden a few feet away. He's doing an excellent job of leading on the blonde. I smile, and he winks at me. I turn back to Dane. "That's Aiden. Actually, he wanted to be your friend not mine; if you get what I mean."

He suppresses a smile. "I take it you told him otherwise?"

"He delivered me to you didn't he?"

Dane leans closer. "Remind me to thank him later."

We stop talking as we continue to dance. More people must have joined the party because Dane and I end up pressed together to make room for more moving bodies. He takes the opportunity to catch my mouth with his and kisses me in a way that should be illegal. Blood pounds behind my ears as I clutch his arm to steady myself. Desperate thoughts of earlier today race through my mind and mix with the jealous emotions from moments ago. I thought I'd lost him. Other women *and* men want him. What's wrong with me? The decision hits me like lightning.

When he releases my mouth, I stand on my toes and find his ear. "Take me home."

He leans back and gives me a confused smile. "I thought I was your home."

I shake my head and find his ear again. "You don't understand. Take. Me. Home."

When our eyes meet the realization hits. I don't have to ask him a third time.

Chapter 27

A numb feeling radiates down the left side of my body, waking me. My eyes flutter open to find both my arm and leg trapped beneath Dane, asleep and useless. The morning sun bleeds through the windows and I lift my head to peer down the length of the couch, my eyes catching on his shirt that hangs off the back. My gaze moves from the shirt to the floor, where I find small piles of the rest of our clothes. Memories of last night slam into my brain and my face immediately flushes.

Yeah. We didn't even make it past the living room.

I lower my head to his shoulder, and he instinctively pulls me closer. One of his arms is beneath me, and I'm sure it's just as asleep as my limbs are. I dread the prickling sensation of the blood returning to my arm and leg once we move, so I close my eyes, hoping to ignore the feeling and remain where I am. It's no use. As much I as want to stay cradled in his arms, I need to sit up.

His eyes pop open as I try to disentangle myself. "Hey –"

"Go back to sleep," I whisper.

"What are you doing?"

"My arm's numb," I say, shaking it as I sit. The throw blanket, that used to hang over the back of the couch, crookedly covers us; I reach out with my good hand to bring it up to my chest.

He smirks and props himself on his elbow. "You're going to be modest now?"

I give him a stale look. "I'm not going to start parading around here naked, if that's what you're asking."

He raises an eyebrow. "I've already seen everything. What's the point?"

"The point," I fake arrogance, "is that I'm a lady. Not an exhibitionist."

He snickers. "A lady, huh?"

"Yes."

"Since when do ladies blatantly ask to be taken home and, ah...what's a good word?"

My mouth falls open. "Would you rather I hadn't?"

He smiles. "Most definitely not." He places his hand on the side of my neck, cradling my face, and pulls my mouth to his. He gently kisses me then leans back, his expression serious. "Not in a million years."

I smile, biting my lip. As I look into his eyes, my pulse starts to race. Images from last night flash in my memory. I have no complaints.

"I would have broken out the dance moves sooner if I'd known," he says and lies back, crossing his arms beneath his head.

"Known what?"

"The effect they would have on you."

I scoot down, propping myself on my side. I rest my head on my tingling hand. "It wasn't the dancing."

"No?" He smiles.

"Okay, maybe a little," I concede.

"I knew it."

I laugh, but then my smile fades. "Do you want the truth?"

He looks at me concerned and then mirrors my pose. "Always."

Carefully, I select my words. "It was the overwhelming fact that I could lose you. The panic I felt when I thought you were hurt...or worse. Then, that woman was all over you. And Aiden! Even guys want you." I look down. "You've done so much for me, and I've done nothing for you. I've pushed you away a million times, and you keep coming back." I meet his eyes. "It was time to give you something to come back for."

He searches my face. As silent seconds pass, I start to feel self-conscious. "Well, say something."

"You're so wrong."

My expression twists. "About what?"

"Everything." He leans closer. "I will always be there for you. You've changed my life."

Disbelief clouds my features. "That's not true."

"It is. Do you want to know what my life was like before we met? Every day was the same. Go to work, try to contact Teagan, and fight with my dad. Then, I'd wake up the next day and do the exact same thing. Go to work, Skype, and fight," he pauses. "Until I met you. You turned my world upside down."

My skeptical expression melts a little.

"The more time we spent together the more I realized what I did and didn't want. You forced me to take a good look at myself and make some tough decisions."

"That doesn't sound good. I never meant to –"

"I know; that's the beauty of it." He tucks a wayward piece of hair behind my ear. "You challenged me in ways I've never been before. You gave me something to look forward to each day, and I craved your attention. You know why?"

I give him a crooked smile and get sarcastic, "Because there's nothing like picking up the pieces of a stubborn girl's broken heart?" I still don't know why he's put up with me.

"You do have the damsel in distress thing going on." He smiles and wraps his arms around my waist, pulling me close. "Honestly, though, it was because your attention was never a sure thing. When most people find out I'm Charles Walker's son they get all clingy and twitchy, but not you. Your attitude toward me never changed. I had to work hard to impress you; it made me question who I really was."

I look down.

"Remember the day we ran into James' mother at the store?"

I nod. How could I forget?

"That was the moment I realized what I had."

My eyes meet his. "And what was that?"

"Someone to fight for; someone who needed me. No one has needed me in a really long time."

With wide eyes, I reassure him, "You are so needed. I don't know what I would do without you."

His expression softens in response to my admission, and he stares at me intently. Slowly, he traces the side of my face from my temple to my chin, as if committing the curve to memory. "You give me a reason to get up in the morning. Don't ever say you've done nothing for me, because it's not true. You've done more than I can ever explain."

His touch lingers on my chin, and he gently nudges my mouth toward his. I oblige him and he plants a soft kiss on my lips.

"I think your sacrifices outweigh mine," I whisper. "What I've done wasn't even on purpose."

He gives me a knowing look. "Last night was on purpose."

I immediately blush. "Last night didn't change your life."

"Yeah, it did."

"Please," I laugh. "I'm so glad I could help."

He leans forward. "Would you care to help again?"

"Right now?"

"No, next Tuesday. Yes, right now." I catch his sly smile before his lips find my neck.

"Don't we have somewhere to be today?" I ask as I wind my fingers through his hair.

His voice is muffled under my chin. "Right here works for me."

I giggle and move to the side. "No; what's my surprise for Thanksgiving?"

He picks up his head and glances at the clock near the television. "We have two hours until we have to be at the dock."

"For?"

"Fishing," he says. "I've chartered a boat. Have you ever been deep sea fishing?"

"I've never left the continental United States. So, no."

"I think you'll love it." His mouth finds mine and he speaks between kisses, "You won't miss being home at all."

"I think you're right," I say as my head swims. "Although, there's one thing I do miss."

"What's that?"

"The feeling in my leg." It's pinned beneath him again. "Is it possible to move to a different location?"

He raises an eyebrow. "You want to move to a different spot?"

"Yes, please."

"Right now?"

"No, next Tuesday."

He grins and shifts his weight. "Will you allow me to sweep you off your feet?"

I can't help but smile. "I think you've already done that, but sure."

He moves his legs beneath mine and wraps one arm around my waist. He slides his other arm under my knees and stands, lifting me and holding my body against him. I curl one hand behind his neck and set the other against his pounding heart. He kisses me again as he carries me away from the couch and into the bedroom.

"Are you ready?"

I tighten my ponytail as I walk toward the foyer. "Yep. Ready to catch me a shark."

"It's more like a marlin or a tuna," Dane says. He opens the front door. "Did you grab the sunscreen?"

I hold out my hand. "Got it."

He makes sure the door is locked from the inside. "This is your last chance to back out."

"You wish," I say and push against his arm to get him moving. Last night's decision has created a monster; he's been trying to get me to forego the fishing trip and stay in. "Like I said before, you shouldn't have told me what you had planned. I want to go; I've never been."

He smiles and shakes his head. "Stubborn."

"Who's being stubborn?" I push him harder. "Move!"

He laughs as he steps outside. I follow behind him, grabbing the door handle as I go. Suddenly, he stops short, and I nearly bounce off his back.

"What are you doing here?" Dane snaps.

"Well, it's a pleasure to see you, too," I hear a male voice chuckle.

I can't immediately place the person behind the voice, but I know I've heard it before. Tension radiates off Dane as I remain behind him, unseen. I decide to stay put.

"May I come in?"

"I was just leaving. I have an appointment."

I hear footsteps. "It took me awhile to find you," the gentleman says. "You could at least afford me a few minutes of your time."

Dane lets out a heavy breath. "Did she send you?"

"Of course she did. Do you think I run around looking for errant employees for the fun of it?"

The light dawns and my stomach twists. Mr. Meyer is standing on our doorstep.

"Listen, I'm sorry about the way I left."

"Your lack of professionalism was a bit shocking," Mr. Meyer says. "You gave me no notice and quit over email? I would never have expected that from you. I had quite a mess to clean up with the Harris account."

I take a step back. Should I run and hide or stay and defend Dane? Defending him sounds like the better choice. Besides, I owe him.

Dane scoffs. "Harris will be fine; you have everything I was working on. Designers are a dime a dozen; go find yourself a fresh college grad. Besides you should be thanking me. You can get away with paying the newbie a lot less."

Mr. Meyer sighs. "This isn't about money or the company. This is about my daughter."

"We've had this conversation," Dane argues. "I can't believe you flew all the way down here! Teagan and I...I don't love her. She doesn't love me. It's done."

I hear another step. "My daughter is distraught. I poured over at least a hundred flight manifests to find you. Can I at least be allowed inside to sit down while we discuss what may or may not be?"

I know Dane doesn't want to let him in for a number of reasons, namely me. I decide to take one burden off his back and step around him, exposing myself to Teagan's father. "Come on in."

When Mr. Meyer's eyes meet mine the look on his face is indescribable. Obviously, he recognizes me from the charity dinner, and he's surprised to find me here. Has the realization finally hit that Dane is no longer in love with his daughter?

"What are you doing?" Dane turns and asks, blocking me.

"The man asked to come inside. You're being rude." I widen my eyes to subliminally send him a message. *It's okay.*

Dane sets his jaw and shakes his head infinitesimally. His expression screams that it's not.

"Emma."

Mr. Meyer's voice pulls our eyes away from each other, and Dane looks confused. "How do you know her?"

Teagan's father looks at me pointedly. "Who else knows you're here?"

His tone sends a chill down my spine, and I don't think twice about answering. "No one."

He looks between Dane and me, clearly agitated. "It's imperative that I speak with both of you."

I step back to allow him through the door, and Dane begrudgingly does the same. It's clear he's unhappy, but what if we can put this whole Teagan mess behind us? If we can convince her father that it's over maybe he can, in turn, convince her too.

When Dane closes the door, Mr. Meyer turns to me. "We've never been properly introduced." He extends his hand. "My name is Luke Meyer."

I take it and nod. "I'm familiar. Emma Donohue."

He grips my hand. It's not painful, but it's not an ordinary handshake either. I meet his eyes with a questioning look.

"Your friends call me Lucas."

At first his comment doesn't register, and I maintain my puzzled expression.

"I assume you received the money I sent."

Fear consumes me. I try to yank my hand away, but he maintains his firm grasp. Dane immediately steps to my side.

"I'm not here to hurt you," he says sincerely. A familiar, calm feeling radiates up my arm and then travels down my body. Reiki.

"I had no idea you were here," he says. "I came only on my daughter's behalf." His eyes flash to Dane. "I was clueless that James' Emma and yours were one in the same."

Dane looks blindsided, yet he sets his hands protectively on my shoulders. "Let her go."

Lucas obliges, allowing me to step back against Dane. "I thought...at the dinner..."

"I was there to pacify Jack," Lucas says. "I normally don't attend frivolous work functions. But, he asked that I check on you to make sure you could be trusted." He smiles at me in a genuine way. "I told him his worries were unfounded."

"Who is Jack?" Dane demands.

"Jack is a Garrett's twin, a Guardian," I say. "He doesn't like me."

"Ah," Lucas disagrees, "he likes you just fine. You can trust that his intentions are pure. He only wants what's best for his brother."

Dane steps to my side and takes my hand in his. He looks at Lucas with disdain. "And just who exactly are you?"

Lucas regards him. "First and foremost, I am a husband and a father."

"And?"

"And I am also one of The Allegiant."

My knees feel weak at hearing him admit this. I didn't realize how much fear of The Allegiant I held in my heart. James and Garrett did an excellent job of placing it there.

"Speaking of," Lucas says as if he has read my mind, "they're safe. You don't need to worry about them."

"On the contrary."

Dane and I spin around at the sound of a new voice behind us. A man materializes with broad shoulders, sandy blonde hair, and blue eyes. Dane clutches my hand and my heart completely stops as two more men appear beside the first, one on his left and one on his right. All three of them are intimidating figures, tall and muscular. One has dark hair while the other's is so gray it's nearly white.

"Excellent job," the sandy blonde says over our heads to Lucas. "You've practically led us to them."

Blood pounds behind my ears. I look at Lucas, and he appears defeated, but not fearful.

"You've been spying on me?" he asks, offended.

The dark one scoffs. "You didn't think we'd catch on? You're not above us!"

"It was just a matter of time until you tripped up," the blonde one says. "Thankfully, patience is one of our many virtues."

Lucas remains confident as he defends himself. "Before you do anything rash..."

It's too late. I barely see the blonde nod and in the blink of an eye the other two men spring into action, grabbing Dane and me and wrenching our hands painfully apart. They hold us by our shoulders, across the room from one another, while the third man renders Lucas immobile by light that emanates from the palm of his hand. I can see Dane's eyes fill with panic as he struggles against his captor, but it has no effect on the Guardian. I don't even bother to move against mine; if Dane can't break free surely I don't stand a chance. Terror and utter sadness threaten to crush my chest.

My captor speaks and his voice rumbles over me. "Kellan," he says, pulling the sandy blonde's eyes our way. "Shall I do it now?" His grip around me tightens and fear cuts through my body.

"You're right to be afraid," Kellan says, giving me a tiny, malicious smile. "This is going to be incredibly painful."

Chapter 28

Inky darkness surrounds me as if the very sun has been extinguished. I am blind, my eyes slowly beginning to burn. It's as if a match has been lit inside my skull, and the flame is crawling along my optic nerves, incinerating them. Blinking does nothing to soothe the intense ache behind my eyes, so I close them tight, praying for tears to put out the fire. None appear.

An image is placed behind my sightless, burning eye sockets; I know this because I physically feel it. It's like my mind is a View Master loaded with a picture reel, and what I see defines the meaning behind Kellan's threat of pain. I realize this torture will be infinitely more mental, more emotional than the initial threat could allow me to comprehend. The flames in my head change direction to consume my heart as I'm forced to memorize things I've never seen before. My chest constricts as I try to scream, but I am rendered incapable as bile rises in my throat. My legs give out as the images change:

James lying in his casket, so swollen and caked in make-up that he's barely recognizable.

James naked in the morgue on a silver table, his face sliced, his chest badly beaten and bruised.

Paramedics holding his limp body drenched in blood, his legs twisted in an unnatural way.

His open, lifeless eyes as he stares into nothing, slumped in the front seat of his truck.

"Enough!" I hear a voice, and my vision immediately returns; I'm on my hands and knees in front of the dark haired Guardian that held me. I concentrate on breathing as the burning pain inside me fizzles.

"I'm here! You can stop!"

The pain leaves my body.

Lifting my head, I find James in the middle of the room, his eyes trained on me with a look of desolation. Relief washes over me at seeing him whole again, and I push myself to stand despite my shaking legs. I want him to know I'm okay, and I can handle this. The Guardian behind me collects my shoulders to restrain me a second time, but not as strongly.

"That was quick," Kellan says to James, impressed, as he continues to hold Lucas immobile. "Now if you would just lead us to your former mentor, we could end this little game."

"I'm willing," James says. "But I don't know how."

"Abraham," Kellan calls to the Guardian that holds Dane then looks in my direction, "Ethan."

Both men release us, and when they do, Dane is in front of me in an instant, frantically gathering my face in his hands. "Are you all right? Are you hurt?"

"I'm fine," I say, although the images seared into my brain will haunt me forever.

A sharp intake of breath redirects my attention, and I look around Dane to see The Allegiant standing on either side of James, one of their hands on each of his shoulders. They must be doing to him what they did to me and he closes his eyes, clenching and unclenching his fists. My gaze jumps to Lucas, still frozen by Kellan, then back to James. I'm helpless to stop any of this.

"I feel the bond," Abraham finally says. Ethan nods in agreement.

"Well, what are you waiting for?" Kellan snaps. "Fetch him."

The Guardians disappear, and James slowly opens his eyes. He blinks to focus his vision and then turns toward Dane and I. Crestfallen, his clear blue eyes lock on mine. "I hope you two will be happy together," he says, his voice heavy and stuck with emotion.

It's in that moment that I know, without a doubt, what he was shown. What else would cause him pain to reveal Garrett's bond? Both Abraham and Ethan touched Dane and I; they read our minds, they saw what happened between us. James just received a first row seat to last night's show. The urge to throw up overcomes me and I swallow, breaking out in a cold sweat. It's one thing to hear what happened. It's quite another to witness it firsthand.

"Aw," Kellan interrupts, mocking us. "Do I sense a love triangle?"

Both James and Dane shoot him an irritated look. Kellan gives me a once over and then leers. "She's pretty; I'll give you that."

His comment makes my skin crawl.

His tone changes as his eyes leave mine and harshly turn to James. "Might I remind you that your feelings for her are forbidden? You're aware of this, yet you continue to feel the way you do? Act the way you do? And now you've taken part in this scheme? Enabling renegades? You should be banished!"

James lowers his eyes. He can't defend himself; Kellan will know he's lying. He clenches his hands into fists again, as if preparing for what's coming. He always said he would be punished if The Allegiant discovered his actions, and my heart races in anticipation of the worst. Is Kellan going to hurt him right here, right now?

Impulsively, I take a step around Dane. "It's not his fault!"

Dane tries to stop me, by grabbing my arm, but I look at him and mouth the word "no." My argument for staying at school, instead of running away, comes back to me. "He's been used; we've both been used."

Kellan looks at me, his mood shifting again as he offers me a maliciously arrogant retort, "A fact we've taken in consideration, I can assure you." He gives me a sly smile. "I said he should be banished not that he would be." He winks. "Your decisions are about to get a lot harder, sweetheart."

Before I can ask what that means, Ethan and Abraham reappear with Garrett in tow. My mind reels trying to figure out how that's possible. Dane steps protectively to my side, wrapping his arm around my shoulders.

"Well," Kellan says. "Look at what the cat dragged in."

Abraham and Ethan push Garrett to his knees. His eyes grow wide as he sees Lucas trapped in Kellan's hold. He looks to his left, spotting James, and then to his right, finding Dane and me. A defeated look crosses his features, but he regains his composure and faces Kellan.

"What? You still feel justified?" Kellan asks. He nods toward Lucas. "You still believe in his cause? You don't even know what he was fighting for!"

"And you do?" Garrett asks.

Kellan scoffs. "I know a hell of a lot more than you." He looks at Ethan who lashes out with his fist, connecting with Garrett's temple. I cringe against Dane's side.

"You went against everything you've been taught, everything we stand for," Kellan growls. "To hurt our Wards goes against the essence of our very being, yet you wounded yours beyond repair for your own selfish gain!"

Abraham gives Garrett a sickening kick to his lower back, which causes him to fall against the floor. As much as I despise what Garrett did to James and me, I can't bear this. Garrett was a friend.

Kellan turns and unexpectedly releases Lucas from his hold, his body crumpling to the floor in a heap. He walks over to him and kneels by his side. "Your muscles have been severed, but your senses have been spared," he says in an eerie tone. "How does it feel?" He pretends to listen for an answer that doesn't come and smiles. "That's what I thought."

He rises, grabbing one of Lucas' hands in the process, and drags him across the floor toward Garrett. "You wanted to be human?" he spits. "You sacrificed the Choice for a human life?"

Garrett clenches his jaw as he pushes himself back to his knees. He defiantly stares at Kellan.

"What you desire will not be yours," Kellan says. "Your mentor should have known better. Now he will watch as you are destroyed, and he will know the cost of his mistake." He looks to the others, and they step around Garrett to stand beside him. The four of them make up a line, Lucas included, although he is lying defenseless on the ground. They leer over Garrett, each of them touching one another at their feet, with the exception of Kellan, whose foot is set against Lucas's head.

Tears spring behind my eyes, and I lean into Dane, grabbing his shirt and twisting it in my fist. He clutches my shoulder and reaches up to shield my face against his chest. Neither of us thought we'd be witnessing a murder today.

Even though my eyes are closed, I still see the blinding light behind my lids. I can feel it, too. Instantly, the temperature in the room increases by multiple degrees. After several seconds, it returns to normal with a cool rush of air, leading me to believe they have incinerated Garrett. Tears course down my cheeks.

"Emma look," Dane whispers.

I open my eyes expecting to see a pile of ashes where Garrett knelt, but instead find him still there in one piece. My face twists in confusion until my eyes land on James. He's holding his hands out in front of him, examining them, with a look of complete awe.

Kellan leans down, leveling his face with Garrett's. "Your Ward now has what you so desperately wanted," he says with a smug expression. "What you thought you'd taken from him, we've given back." He presses the palm of his hand against Garrett's forehead. "While you rot for eternity as one of the Banished, keep this one thought close," he sneers. "He's human and you will never be."

321

With those words, the patio door shatters with a deafening crash. Dane pulls me to the ground and covers my body with his as shards of glass fly across the room and rain over us, hitting the floor and bouncing off the wood around me. I lift my head to see a man charging through the broken glass, arm raised, a crude weapon flashing from his hand. He's headed straight for Kellan.

Suddenly, the protective weight of Dane's body is pulled from covering mine. I look above me to see him wrestle out of a woman's grasp. "I'm not going to hurt you!" she says, her emerald eyes wild and anxious. She looks at the action in the center of the room and back to Dane. "Pick her up!"

Dane does as she requests and heaves me off the floor by my arm. The woman moves us back from the chaos, shielding us from the battle that's now taking place. Dane stands with his back against the wall, his arms around me, as I'm sandwiched in between him and the stranger.

Under her outstretched arm I can see the man who came crashing through the door as he attacks The Allegiant. They dance around one another, and I notice he appears to be larger than the others. His brown hair is parted down the middle of his head, falling to his chin and catching the stubble on his jaw as he dodges a blow from Kellan. The man still holds an unrecognizable weapon – is it a knife or a dagger? – and I notice his outfit as reminiscent of another time. Suddenly, a woman with a long gray braid appears from nowhere, ripping my attention away from the man. I watch as she starts to assist him in the fight. They work together, as if they've rehearsed this routine, and my eyes jump to where Garrett and James once were. I find them defensively standing together near the kitchen. My heart threatens to beat through my ribs. What is going on? Who are these people?

"My name is Madeline," the woman in front of us answers, as if she read my mind. She looks over her shoulder. "That's Ash and Claire. You don't have to be afraid of us."

I take a moment to look at her and she's gorgeous. Her eyes are wide, a shocking shade of green; her black hair is braided like the other woman's and it falls past her lower back. Her clothes look almost medieval, and I notice a stunning bracelet on her wrist. It's made of thin, knotted leather and a shiny silver amulet sits in the center.

I hear a guttural growl and pull my attention away from her. I catch a glimpse of Abraham as Claire pulls her weapon from his side. He stands frozen for a moment then bursts into dust, literally disintegrating before my eyes. Kellan and Ethan look at each other frantically as Kellan maneuvers his way toward Lucas.

The battle is more evenly matched now, even though Claire is looking winded. One of the end tables and a lamp goes flying across the room, and Madeline lowers her arms from her protective embrace around us. She looks as if she's contemplating joining the fight.

"Go on," Dane tells her. "We're okay."

She looks at us then charges forward, pulling an identical weapon from her belt. Claire sees her coming and looks relieved. Madeline heads straight for Ethan. Beyond them, I notice both James and Garrett inching their way toward us. Dane and I look at each other and silently decide to meet them half way. We take only two steps when suddenly Claire's body comes hurtling toward us. Both Dane and I try to catch her, but the force of her body being thrown through the air sends us sailing backward. My head cracks against the wall, next to Dane's shoulder, as James and Garrett give up being stealthy and rush to our side.

Garrett rolls Claire over as I right myself, and James grabs hold of my upper arms as he looks me up and down. "Are you okay?" he asks, panicked. I feel Dane appear at my shoulder.

"I'm fine," I say and turn to make sure Dane is all right as well. He nods as my eyes are drawn to the woman on the floor. She's the one who needs help. She's bleeding heavily from her abdomen, so I immediately crouch beside her. There's got to be a way to stop the blood with my hands.

Garrett moves beneath her and holds her head in his lap. "Claire! What can I do?"

My confused gaze snaps to Garrett. Does he know her?

She looks up at him and shakes her head, giving him a small smile despite her pain.

"No!" he shouts. "You can't die!"

She glances around the faces that surround her until she finds mine. She stares into my eyes and gives me a genuine smile, then grimaces.

"ARGH!" I hear another loud groan and all of us turn to see what's happened. Madeline has wrestled a dagger from Ethan because she now holds one in each hand. He must have taken Claire's weapon and struck her with it.

Fingers wrap around mine, and I turn to find Claire grasping my hand. She raises her head and pulls me forward, her strength impressing me for a dying woman.

"She wants you to come closer," Garrett says.

I oblige her and hold my face inches from hers. Her kind expression shatters my heart. How can she look so peaceful while bleeding to death?

Garrett cradles her head and helps her bring her mouth to my ear. "Respira," she whispers, almost inaudibly. "Respira."

I have no idea what that means. I lean back and look at her, giving her a tiny smile like I understand. I don't want to disappoint her even though we've only just met.

The fray continues behind us, and I hear something crash to the floor. My instincts tell me it's the flat screen. I try to look, but Claire pulls on my hand. She wants my attention on her. Releasing my hand, she removes a bracelet, identical to Madeline's, from her wrist and places it in my palm, folding my fingers over it. "Safe," she says and her eyes grow wide. She nods, asking if I understand.

"Yes," I promise her. "I will keep this safe."

"No." She shakes her head and rasps, "Keep you safe."

Before I can ask how, Garrett moves out from under Claire and gently hands her off to Dane. I give him puzzled look, and Dane's eyes flit to the sparring combatants. I follow his gaze and it appears Ethan has the upper hand with Madeline, and he's backing her into a corner. James and Garrett take one look at each other and decide to enter the fight. I watch in horror as the two of them attack Ethan from behind in an effort to give Madeline the advantage.

Suddenly, the pressure around my hand releases, and I turn to watch Claire fade before my eyes. In one blink she's there and the next she's gone. My hand that clutches her bracelet is smeared with her blood, and I watch in amazement as the fresh bloodstain fades from my sight as well. It's like she never existed. My chest feels hollow as I unfold my fingers and stare at her gift.

"I think that's important," Dane says as he kneels in front of me, his face pale after what we've just witnessed. "You should put it on."

I agree. As I start to slide my fingers through the knotted leather band, an unnatural howl bellows from behind us. My head snaps around to find Kellan emitting the sound, his eyes locking on mine, his face contorted.

Distracted by his outburst, Ethan turns and is immediately dispatched by Madeline, falling into a cloud of dust as she twists both knives into his back. Kellan's gaze is pulled from mine; he knows he's outnumbered. He moves quickly opposite Ash and holds him with a beam of light similar to the one he used on Lucas. He kneels and collects Lucas under his free arm as Madeline, James, and Garrett advance. I feel the bracelet slammed on my wrist and turn to see Dane's hand around it. My eyes flash back to Kellan who's staring maliciously at Dane and me. My pulse accelerates sending a clear warning that resonates to my core.

Somehow, some way, I know Dane is the next target of Kellan's beam of light. He cannot be hurt; I won't allow it.

Without thinking, I launch myself at Dane, wrapping my arms around his neck and pressing my body against his. "I love you," I gasp and block him just as Kellan aims directly at us. I catch Kellan's beam in the center of my back, absorbing the blow. It feels like a million knives are cutting my skin as waves of electricity course through my body. Mercifully my senses shut down, unable to manage the pain, and I melt to the floor. My world turns black, my body goes numb, and my ears ring.

I have no idea how long I lie there until a peaceful feeling finds me. It creeps in and slowly weaves itself around my body and into my mind. It envelops my world, and I welcome it with open arms. It erases my wounds. It eases my pain. It soothes me, and I let it lure me into a deeper darkness.

Chapter 29

"She moved."

I hear a voice that I do not recognize.

"Are you sure?" another unfamiliar voice asks.

"Yes, her arm twitched."

Someone grasps my hand, and I feel my arm bend at the elbow. "Emma? Can you open your eyes?"

They know me? I try to lift my lids, but they feel like they weigh a ton.

"If you can't, can you squeeze my hand?"

That I can manage. I tighten my fingers around the hand that holds mine. In response, I hear a surprised gasp.

"Did she do it?" a third person asks.

The first voice floods with relief. "Yes!"

How many people are here? I could have sworn I was alone when I went to sleep. Should I be afraid? I concentrate and pry one eye open and follow with the other. My vision is blurry, and I blink the haze away. Three faces hover over me, none of which are familiar, and my adrenaline spikes. Who are these people and what do they want? I try to lift my head, try to sit up, but my body feels stiff and won't cooperate. From what I can tell, I'm lying in a bed that is foreign to me. Where am I?

"Emma? Are you okay? Talk to me."

I meet the worried gaze of the guy who holds my hand. He's handsome, despite his disheveled dark hair and five o'clock shadow. His complexion is slightly pale and his hazel eyes look worn and tired, as if he's recently been sick.

"How do you know my name?" I rasp. My throat feels drier than the desert at high noon. He looks at me with utter confusion. "Who are you?" I ask.

"Let me try," a voice on my left says.

I turn my head to see another male, about my age I'd guess, with light brown hair that falls over his forehead and the bluest eyes I've ever seen. He, too, looks distraught and attempts a nervous smile as he takes my other hand in his. "Do you know who I am?" he tentatively asks.

I have no memory of this person. I shake my head against the pillow. "I don't. Should I?"

His face falls at my response.

I hear a heavy sigh from the end of the bed, so I lift my head, successfully this time, to find the third person in the room. He focuses his eyes on me; they're an interesting shade of blue mixed with brown. "Let's try something." He moves from the bed to stand closer to me. "Do you want to sit up?"

I nod and both of the men who hold my hands help me. One props a pillow behind my back while the other reaches for a glass of water sitting on the bedside table. He hands it to me and I gladly take it, swallowing half the water in one gulp. I regard the three of them over the rim of my glass as logic tells me I should be scared to be surrounded by strangers. Oddly, I'm not.

"Do you remember my name?" the one with the interesting blue-brown eyes asks me.

I search my brain as the three of them look at me expectantly. I want to remember for them, but I can't. I frown and shake my head no.

He leans forward, placing both hands against the bed, as he asks, "What's the last memory you have?"

I think back. My mind is foggy in some areas and crystal clear in others. "Falling asleep in my apartment."

The three of them regard each other, sending silent messages between them that I don't understand. I look down and notice a unique bracelet on my wrist. I don't typically wear jewelry. "What is this?" I ask and hold out my hand.

Interesting-eyes asks another question. "Do you know what a Guardian is?"

I give him a blank look as I questioningly state the obvious. "Someone who guards things?"

Everyone around me looks dumbfounded and let down. I wish I could cooperate more, but who are these people? An uneasy feeling starts to build in my chest the more I come to and take in my surroundings. Last night, I was in my apartment at school; now, I'm in a tropically decorated bedroom surrounded by strange men. Someone needs to start giving me answers.

"What happened?" I ask.

All three sets of eyes dart to one another as if debating whether to share knowledge that I don't have. It makes me angry. "Tell me!"

The one who's been asking questions looks defeated. "Erasure," he says.

His answer makes no sense and it frustrates me. "What is that?"

He draws a heavy breath. "Your memory has been erased."

About the Author

Sara Mack is a Michigan native who grew up with her nose in books. She is a wife and a hockey mom on top of being trapped in an office – which now has a window! – forty hours a week. Her spare time is spent one-clicking on Amazon and devouring books on her Kindle, cleaning up after her kids and two elderly cats, attempting to keep her flower garden alive, and, of course, writing. She has an unnatural affinity for dark chocolate, iced tea, and bacon.

Connect with Sara and The Guardian Trilogy:

On Facebook:
www.facebook.com
Search Sara Mack

On Twitter:
www.twitter.com/smackwrites

Blog and Email:
www.smackwrites.blogspot.com
smackwrites@gmail.com

Check out Spotify for the Allegiant playlist:
www.spotify.com
Search smackwrites

and Café Press for Guardian & Allegiant merch!
www.cafepress.com/IndieFriends

Excerpt from Reborn

Book 3 of The Guardian Trilogy

Prologue

Do you dream in color or black and white?

The last few nights have brought me brilliant, prismatic dreams. I've never dreamt like this before. My hope is that the odd images will continue and reveal the missing pieces of my past. I need to know what I've been told is true by seeing it for myself with my mind's eye. It will be easier for me to accept my new reality through my memories because right now things are just...

Unbelievable.

Garrett says the blast from The Allegiant's hand should have killed me. He owes my survival to the charm I wear around my wrist; a bracelet given to me by someone I don't remember. I play with it now, turning it around and around, as the airplane descends. After three days of living with complete strangers in a foreign place, I'm almost home. The familiarity of it beckons me. I keep telling myself I'll be able to think clearly – remember more – surrounded by what I know.

As the wheels of the plane touch down, relief courses through my body. I'm here; I made it. I can pick up where my life left off and things will make sense again.

I hope.

✶✶✶✶✶

My phone chimes. *Welcome back! Check your email.*

I read the cryptic text from Matt as Dane lounges on my couch flipping channels. He hasn't said much since our neighbor's arrival, and I can tell he's trying to relax but failing miserably. I feel bad for him and want to make it better. Why does his being upset bother me? He's practically a stranger.

"Who's on the phone?"

Dane's question breaks my train of thought. "Um, Matt," I say quickly as I redirect my attention and open my email. "He sent me a message."

His note is the first in my inbox.

Em –

Glad to hear you're back! Attached to this are the forms required for the internship you asked about. My dad signed off on everything. I would have sent them sooner, but I didn't know when you would be back in the States. I hope you're still thinking about working for us – I don't make a great receptionist and Sheila is about to explode! Let me know your decision when you get a chance.

We'll have to get together soon!

Matt

My memory reels back to my last day at Western. I recall the overwhelming need to move back home, but don't remember what set it off. I re-live the conversation with my advisor, Mrs. Andrews. I remember talking to Matt about interning at his dad's veterinary clinic in lieu of classes; I remember falling asleep content with my plans for the future. And then I remember waking up with my world turned upside down.

I read over Matt's email again and a calm feeling settles over me. I still like this idea a lot. Moving back home sounds amazing.

I hear a knock on the door then see it crack open. "Are you busy?" It's Garrett.

334

Dane sighs and turns off of the television. "Do we have a choice?"

Garrett and James enter my apartment, and I push Matt's message to the side for now. I readjust myself in the living room chair as Garrett takes a seat opposite Dane. James chooses to stand, leaning against the wall. It's times like this that I really need a dining table.

"Do you want to sit?" I ask James and start to unfold my legs.

He shakes his head. "Standing doesn't bother me." He gives me a small smile. "I'm still getting used to being human."

Oh. Right.

"Now that things have calmed down, we need to have a serious discussion," Garrett says.

Dane frowns. "About what?"

"For one, the likelihood of Kellan's return. He's not going to easily forgive what happened."

Dane scowls as I recall who Kellan is. He's the one who nearly killed me, but somehow took my memories instead.

Garrett takes a heavy breath. "Obviously, we've lost all ties to the Intermediate. We have no idea what's taking place. We can only assume Kellan returned with Lucas after he blasted Emma given that humanity isn't in chaos. Kellan needs Lucas to maintain order; two of the four Allegiant are dead. He's probably forcing Lucas to carry on as usual and biding his time until he can devise his revenge."

"We haven't heard from Thomas or Meg or any of the others either," James says. "It's probable that they're still captive."

Who are Meg and Thomas again?

"If only I could get a hold of Jack," Garrett mutters. "It would really help."

"Jack is?" I ask.

"My brother," Garrett answers. "My twin."

Yes. I'd forgotten.

Dane leans forward. "So you're worried about Kellan coming back? I understand he's pissed that your friends killed his buddies, but shouldn't he take it out on them?"

335

"I'm afraid he will, but he still has a score to settle with me," Garrett says. "He didn't get to exact his punishment and now that you and Emma are involved...we're all at risk."

James turns to Dane. "You know Kellan was gunning for you."

Dane sighs. "Yes, you've made that clear."

"Why?" I ask. "What did Dane do that was so wrong?"

Garrett nods toward the bracelet on my wrist. "He placed that on you."

"So?"

Garrett shares a knowing look with James that raises my suspicions. "That's another thing we need to talk about," he says. "Do you remember me telling you about Madeline and Ash? The people that showed up to help us?"

I nod.

"James and I stopped to speak with them briefly before coming here. We asked if they could help us understand what happened, why the bracelet protected you in some ways but not in others. They told us it was because you are Lost."

My face pinches. "I'm what?"

James moves closer. "All humans are supposed to have a Guardian. I was yours."

"Yes, you told me."

"When The Allegiant restored my humanity my duty vanished. You no longer have a Guardian." He pauses and eyes Garrett. "Emma," he says seriously, "there's no one in the Intermediate to assign you. You are unprotected. You're what we call Lost."

I give him a wary look. "And that's a bad thing?"

"For an ordinary human it's a very bad thing," Garrett says. "But you're better off. Until we know how much protection the bracelet offers you, one of us will need to be near you at all times."

I hesitate trying to process the information. "So, you're saying I need a babysitter."

Garrett shifts his weight to the edge of his seat. "It'll be more like having a bodyguard. We'll need to know your schedule, where you plan to be, and with who."

This is really awkward and my expression twists. Will I ever have privacy? "I do have some common sense; you can't spend all your time hovering over me."

Garrett nods. "You're right. We'll need to take shifts and the more help we have the better. That's why we –" He pauses. "I mean that's why *I* would like Dane to help as well." He turns to look at him. "Will you consider it?"

Dane doesn't even think twice. "I'm in."

What? These three can't just integrate themselves into my life! "Hold on a minute," I protest. "You can't monitor my every move!"

James tries to reassure me. "It won't be that weird. Garrett and I will be right next door."

Matt's email flashes through my mind and I snort. "Not for long. I'm moving after the semester ends."

James face falls. "Where? Why?"

My eyes dart to Garrett and Dane and they are equally surprised. "I got permission to take an internship during the winter semester. I'll be working for Matt's dad and living with my parents."

I can't help but notice the smile Dane tries to hide. Clearly he's pleased, but why?

James moves to crouch in front of me. "Emma, I can't follow you there. Your hometown is mine too; I can't be seen by people who knew me. You have to stay here."

Ah. That's why.

"I'm sorry, but this is *my* life," I say adamantly. "My decision. I'm moving."

James opens his mouth to dispute me, but Garrett interrupts. "It's okay," he says and directs his attention to James. "We can make this work; we can move. Lucas gave me money, and I believe he gave Emma some too."

I have money?

"That's if you're willing to share," Garrett quickly amends and gives me an apologetic smile. "We can live outside of town and James can escort you when it's safe for him to do so."

I narrow my eyes. Damn it! I need some time to myself!

"Actually, this might work better," Garrett muses and turns to Dane. "You have to return home eventually. It will be more convenient with Emma closer to you."

I tap my fingers impatiently against my knee. They're all so great at planning my life. "How long is this going to last? You can't possibly take me everywhere. What if I need to go to the gynecologist?"

All three of them blanch and I smirk. "See?"

I can visualize the wheels turning in Garrett's head. "We'll have to take each situation as it comes and stay behind the scenes if necessary." He looks to James and Dane. "The main point is that we are near Emma should she need us."

They all nod and I roll my eyes. Am I even here? Does my opinion matter? I get it; I'm at risk without a Guardian and Kellan seeks to hurt me. But wait...why is he mad at me again? So Dane put a bracelet on my wrist and I'm somewhat protected. Big deal.

"Can someone explain why Kellan hates me?" I ask. "Because I don't get it."

Garrett and James exchange another knowing glance. I'm starting to hate those.

"Madeleine and Ash will be here in a few days to explain," Garrett says. "My knowledge of the Larvatus is limited. I'd rather you hear it from them."

"The who?"

"The Larvatus. Translated it means Charmed."

"Madeline and Ash are charmed?"

"Yes," Garrett says. He pauses and looks at his hands then back at me. "And from what little I understand, now you may be Charmed, too."

Look for the third book in The Guardian Trilogy:

Reborn

Coming early 2014!

28253971R00182

Made in the USA
Lexington, KY
11 December 2013